PATHS OF GLORY

The major's golden smile showed. "The name Chandos mean anything to you, my lad?"

"Sir John Chandos," said Audley.

"That's the man. Chandos, Manny, Holland, Burghersh, Audley, Mowbray, Beauchamp, Neville, Percy—aye, and the Black lad himself . . . all names to conjure with, David. As fine a band of cutthroats as ever left home to make their fortunes at someone else's expense! But Chandos first and last—and best."

Audley glanced at Butler sympathetically. "Hundred Years' War and all that, Corporal—the Black Prince and the battle of Crécy, 1346—" he blinked and cut short the recital of facts as though they irritated him.

"He was the greatest captain of the age—the complete fighting man, you might say." Suddenly the major grinned disarmingly, displaying the full range of gold in his mouth. "Welcome to Chandos Force, David"—he took in Butler with the grin—"and you, Corporal."

THE '44 VINTAGE

THE '44 VINTAGE

BY ANTHONY PRICE

THE MYSTERIOUS PRESS

New York • London • Tokyo

MYSTERIOUS PRESS EDITION

Copyright © 1978 by Anthony Price
All rights reserved.

This Mysterious Press Edition is published by arrangement
with the author.

Cover design by Stanislaw Fernandes

Mysterious Press books are published in association with
Warner Books, Inc.
666 Fifth Avenue
New York, N.Y. 10103
A Warner Communications Company

Printed in the United States of America

First Mysterious Press Printing: November, 1988

10 9 8 7 6 5 4 3 2 1

For Norma and Howard Austin

For who is he whose chin is but enriched
With one appearing hair that will not follow
These culled and choice-drawn cavaliers to France?
                                                    —*Henry V*

He is trampling out the vintage where the grapes
of wrath are stored.
                        —*Battle Hymn of the American Republic*

CONTENTS

1. How Corporal Butler was saved by his boots

The toes on Corporal Butler's left foot were bright purple.

He remembered, as he almost unfailingly did when he peeled his sock off, that purple was the chosen colour of kings and emperors in the olden days: he had read in a history book somewhere that "to assume the purple" was for them the very act of putting on their power and glory.

The trouble was that whatever it had meant in those old palaces and courts it told a very different tale in the Mill Street elementary school and in King Edward's Grammar School: there it was a mark of shame indelibly painted on dirty boys who had dirty diseases.

Dirty boys from dirty families, publicly disgraced by the disfiguring patches of colour on their faces and on the shaven areas of their heads and condemned to sit by themselves in a leper-group at the back of the class. For it was common knowledge that where purple was to be seen there were also probably fleas and nits and bedbugs lurking unseen, eager to crawl across the intervening desk spaces onto clean boys from respectable families.

Onto clean boys like Jack Butler.

From dirty boys like Sammy Murch.

Corporal Butler sighed at the memory. Sammy Murch had been a good friend of his until the morning Sammy had arrived at school with the purple patches, when Butler had shunned him like all the other clean boys. And that had been the end of friendship.

And maybe more than the end. Because it had been next year that he'd won his scholarship, and the year after that Sammy had been up for breaking into Mr. Burns's sweetshop on the corner; which hadn't surprised him one bit, because theft seemed a natural progression from *impetigo contagiosa*. In fact he'd been much more surprised when his dad had gone to court to speak for Sammy—though of course he hadn't done that so much for Sammy as for his father, who had been with him in the trenches and come back with a lungful of phosgene, and his two uncles, who hadn't come back at all.

He stared at his toes with disgust, deciding as he did so that Sammy Murch had been nicely avenged even though it wasn't impetigo—and even though vengeance had come too late for Sammy to enjoy since the Germans had caught the *Spartan* off Anzio.

He lowered his foot into the stream. Fresh water probably wouldn't do it much good—sea water, the book said, but against all expectation and hope he'd come ashore dry-shod and there'd been no time for paddling after that. But it was cooling and cleansing, and that was better than nothing ("Look after your feet and they'll look after you," his dad had said that last time, old-soldierly).

He reached down and unbuckled the gaiter on his right ankle. For some obscure reason his right foot had resisted the infection of *Epidermophyton inguinale,* but it was better to be safe than sorry.

Gaiter, boot, grey woollen sock: he stacked them carefully on the bank above the ledge where the rest of his equipment was piled, then bent over the foot to search for the faintest telltale signs between the fourth and fifth toes.

EPIDERMOPHYTOSIS or Athlete's foot is a condition of ringworm of the skin between the toes, usually between the fourth and fifth (He knew the hated details in Pearce's *Medical and Nursing Dictionary* by heart now)—

It is due to a fungus—

The thought of a fungus attacking him, a loathsome fifth column in his boot, was frightening and disgusting.

He wrinkled his nose as he gently parted the toes, as the

breeze reminded him that there was something else disgusting not far away from where he was sitting, upwind from him.

Something not alive, like the fungus, but disgustingly dead.

It had come to him a few minutes before, on the first breath of the breeze, as he lay in the tall grass of the roadside verge a dozen yards away, half dozing and half watching a formation of high-flying Mustangs. He had just finished reasoning out their presence as cover for an earlier flight of rocket-bearing Typhoons when the smell had blotted out the sound, telling him that there was dead flesh at ground level nearby that was as high as the Mustangs.

It was, he had nearly convinced himself, a poor dead cow, probably lying bloated and stiff-legged in the field beyond. He had already seen and smelt such cows, and this was close enough to the smell of recent memory. What was certain was that it was a very bad smell, although if his father was to be believed horses would smell worse than this and mules were in a class of their own.

With a conscious, deliberate effort he breathed in the corrupted air. What was even more certain was that there would be many more bad smells, and a good soldier simply took them for granted.

More than anything else in the world Butler wanted to be a good soldier.

So—the cow was dead and he was alive, which was better than the other way round; and he would worry no more about rotting cows than live cows would worry about dead and rotting soldiers.

Also he could see that his right foot was still clear of infection under its purple dye, which was a positive cause for rejoicing. Because despite Sister Pearce's claim that *this condition is easily treated* the raw cracks between the toes on the other foot had so far obstinately refused to heal; though to be fair to the Sister he lacked the permanganate of soda and the chlorinated soda and boric acid which she prescribed; and even if he had possessed them he would never have been able to find a way of soaking his feet in her weak solution of those chemicals. He just had his handy bottle of gentian violet.

He reached over to his left-hand ammunition pouch and carefully extracted the precious bottle from its nest of cotton waste between the Sten magazines. The luxury of privacy was another thing to be thankful for. This time at least he would be free from the humiliation of painting his feet while others were watching.

He set the bottle on the ledge beside the boot, noting as he did so that it was still nearly half full. With a little luck it could still outlast the fungus if used sparingly, with no need to report sick . . .

He stared down with concentrated hatred at his left foot through the distorting glass of the cool water, wishing irrationally that it was acid which might burn and cauterize both the infection and the treacherous toes. The colour was a filthy, degrading colour, and the toes were his enemies—he, who had always been the smartest and the cleanest man in the platoon. And *they,* the toes—his own flesh, *they* were the source of his waking and sleeping nightmare of being unfit for duty when at last there was real duty to be done.

He could hear his father's voice in his inner ear:
Look after your feet and they'll look after you.
And—
Trench feet? The bad battalions had it, but not the good ones.

He didn't even know what trench feet were. But they had to be something like this.

Something had moved in the corner of his eye. Or maybe it was a slight sound, or a shadow, or the warning of a fifth sense that told him he was no longer alone.

He reached for the bottle of gentian violet, to hide it away in his ammunition pouch.

"*Hände hoch, Tommy!*"

Butler froze, unable to believe his ears, his hand halfway towards the little bottle.

"*Hände hoch.*"

The impossible words came from behind him, quite close. But where they had been almost conversational the first time, more a suggestion than an order, now they were a harsh command which made his back a yard wide.

Butler raised his hands.

"Gut. Steh jetzt auf."

The words banged against each other in his brain like goods wagons in a shunting yard, their meaning clanging out loudly.

He stood up in the stream, feeling the water crawl up his legs to soak his trousers below the knee.

The meaning expanded. First, it wasn't possible: this was ten miles, more than ten miles, behind the front line of a retreating enemy.

And then, because it was happening, it was no longer impossible, only cruelly unfair.

It must be an escaped prisoner...or maybe a bailed-out Luftwaffe pilot?

No, hardly an airman. Because he hadn't even heard a German plane, never mind seen one, in the last twenty-four hours. But if an escaped soldier...that was a frightening thought, because the shambling prisoners he had seen had seemed relieved to be out of their defeat alive. Anyone determined to fight on would have to be a hard man, most likely a dyed-in-the-wool Nazi from the SS units.

"Dreh dich um...langsam."

Langsam? Butler scrabbled desperately in his German vocabulary, fear sharpening his memory to a razor-edge.

Slowly.

He turned round slowly.

To his surprise there was no one to be seen. The strip of rough pasture between the stream and the hedgerow was empty, and the open gateway to the road through which he had entered the field over the tank-crushed remains of the gate was empty too.

"Gut...zuwelchem Truppenteil gehörst du, Tommy?"

The voice seemed to come out of the thin air of the gateway, for choice from the left of it where the vegetation was thickest.

Butler licked his lips nervously, sorting out the words for their meaning and trying at the same time to divine the intention behind that meaning. The German obviously wanted to know his prisoner's unit as a prelude to asking if he was alone. But why should an ex-prisoner want a prisoner of his own when he ought to be avoiding all contact with his enemies?

The answer came back frighteningly quick: the uniform he was wearing was what the German wanted. A nice clean British uniform, without holes or bloodstains—which was why he was using words and not bullets.

"*Zuwelchem—Truppenteil—gehörst-du . . . ?*" The German spaced the words patiently, as though he had all the time in the world.

Butler was suddenly and shamefully aware that he was sweating profusely. Fear wasn't cold, like the books said, but hot—and he was bathed in sweaty fear. It was running off him and down him like water.

He was going to die.

In ten minutes' time the major would arrive to find him naked and dead beside the stream.

With purple feet.

No, his brain screamed at him.

"*Tommy—*"

"*Nein,*" said Butler.

His own voice surprised him—it didn't sound like his voice: it was someone else's voice in someone else's language. But it also roused him to fight for his life with the only weapon he had. His eye fell on the Sten gun lying on the ledge in the bank, beside his boots and equipment. But that wasn't his weapon—yet.

His weapon was time.

"*Du hast*"—he fumbled for the right word—"*du hast überhaupt keine Chance.*" It was the first German sentence he had ever spoken to a German—it was like firing the first shot in anger. "*Du hast überhaupt keine Chance—meine Kameraden werden bald zurückkommen.*"

"Eh?"

That had given the bugger something to think about, thought Butler—the confident assertion that he had no chance because the place would soon be crawling with British troops.

"*Deine Kameraden?*" The German seemed surprised.

"*Ja.*" Butler nodded vigorously. But then the thought hit him sickeningly that he had maybe given his captor a bloody good reason for pulling the trigger straight away and then getting clear as fast as he could.

He had said exactly the wrong thing, bugger it.

"*Deine Kameraden?*" the German repeated.

Think. Say something. Say *anything*.

"*Ja . . .*" The words dried up in Butler's throat. He must give the man a reason not to fire.

If he fired they would hear it.

"*Ja. Wenn du mich tötest—*" To his horror Butler discovered that he couldn't remember the German word for *hear*. All he could think of as an alternative was to make a direct threat: if the German killed him then his mates would extract vengeance. "*Wenn du mich tötest, werden sie dich sicher töten.*"

The hedge was silent, and as the seconds ticked away a small flame of hope kindled inside Butler. Every second was a small victory advancing him towards the rendezvous hour.

Always supposing this Major O'Conor was a punctual man—

God, please make Major O'Conor a punctual man!

The German chuckled nastily—it was the dry, contemptuous chuckle of the confident man who held all the cards in his hand and didn't care who knew it.

"*Kummere dich nicht um mich, Tommy. Komm heraus and argumentiere nicht.*"

The flame was gone as though it had never been. Instead there was only another wave of dead cow to remind him that in the moment he stepped out of the stream, away from the Sten, he was as dead as the cow.

Dead with his purple feet for the German to laugh at.

Dead without his boots on.

His boots.

From his hiding place in the hedge all the German could see of his equipment was a pair of boots—the rest was out of sight on the ledge. And what he couldn't see he couldn't know about.

What was the German for "boots"?

Stiefel.

That one word carried Butler from despair to resolution.

"*Meine Stiefel . . .*" He tried to sound abject. "*Aber lass mich meine Stiefel aufnehmen.*"

"*Deine Stiefel?*" Another chuckle. "*Ja, ja! Also—nimm deine Stiefel auf.*"

The contempt in the man's voice was the final spur Butler needed. He took a step sideways, settling his feet firmly on the bed of the stream, and bent over slowly as though to pick up his boots. Then, in the very instant that his right hand seemed about to close on them he doubled up below the lip of the bank.

The fruits of a hundred weapon drills were harvested in seconds: cocking handle slammed back to "safety"—magazine from the open pouch snapped firmly home—stud on "automatic"—cocking handle off "safety"—

Now it's not meine Stiefel, you bugger—it's meine Sten!

Viewed from where he knelt in the water the stream was a wide, shallow trench meandering across the open field roughly parallel to the hedge and the road beyond. To his right the bank was open, but six yards to his left there was an enticing clump of willows. That was the obvious place to head for—but that was also the way the German would expect him to go—

And if the German had a grenade—

A grenade?

Butler's nerve snapped and his instincts took over: before he could stop himself he had straightened up and loosed half the magazine into the hedge. Dust and fragments of wood splattered around the foot of the gatepost in the opening.

"All right, Corporal Butler—cease fire!"

Butler was turned to stone.

"Put it on 'safety,' Corporal—d'you hear?" The voice came from the hedge where the German had been. "Put it on 'safety' and then I'll come out . . . and if you shoot me I'll *never* forgive you—d'you hear?"

Butler stared at the hedge uncomprehendingly.

"This is Major O'Conor speaking, Corporal. I'm ordering you to put that Sten on 'safety'—d'you understand?" the voice barked, with exactly the same shift in tone from the conversational to the peremptory which had characterised the original German order to surrender.

The same tone—and the same voice.

There was another sound too now, of a rapidly approaching vehicle. As Butler struggled to make sense of events a cloud of white dust rose from behind the bocage and a jeep skidded to a halt in the gateway.

The dust cloud swirled around the vehicle, enveloping its khaki-clad driver momentarily. Until it settled he sat like a statue, still grasping the steering wheel with both hands as though he was holding an animal in check.

"All right, Sergeant-major." The voice from the hedge was almost back to conversational level. "No damage, no casualties."

"Sir!" The sergeant-major killed the engine, twisted towards Butler—and stiffened. *"You—"* he shrieked, stabbing his finger after the word, *"don't point that machine carbine at me! What d'you think you're playing at?"*

The familiar formula broke Butler's trance. He lowered the Sten shamefacedly, automatically pulling back the cocking handle into the safety slot as he did so.

"That's better!"

Butler was suddenly aware that he was no longer hot—he was deathly cold. There was a jungle of other feelings churning around inside him, some of which could not safely be expressed aloud in the presence of an officer—a field officer —never mind a sergeant-major. He was conscious that he had been cruelly and unfairly treated; that he had been the subject of some sort of joke which had been no joke at all, and which could have ended in tragedy. But chiefly he was conscious of feeling cold—the top half of him cold and clammy, the bottom half cold and soaking wet.

And he had also made a perfect fool of himself.

He set the Sten down on the bank beside his boots and reached for one of the magazines which had fallen into the muddy edge of the stream. As he did so he noticed the bottle of gentian violet still standing on its ledge, safe and sound. . . . Well, that at least was a mercy. There was no question of continuing the treatment here and now, but there would be other opportunities. He would beat that fungus if it was the last thing he did—

"Well now, Corporal Butler—"

Butler straightened himself into attention as best he could
—it wasn't easy to smarten up while standing up to one's
knees in muddy water and trying to conceal the telltale bottle
at the same time—and steeled himself to look Major O'Conor
straight in the eye.

In fact he found himself looking directly at Major
O'Conor's fly, two buttons of which were undone. It occurred
to him irrelevantly that the major hadn't appeared as soon as
the sergeant-major had arrived because he had been pissing in
the hedge—and that might be why the sergeant-major had sat
rigidly to attention in the dust cloud.

He raised his gaze to an angle of forty-five degrees.

Major O'Conor's eyes were a pale, washed-out blue,
slightly bloodshot. Or at least one of them was—the kindlier
of the two; the other was cold and fishlike in its intensity.

And the major was tall and thin and leathery and grey-
grizzled . . . though the greyness might simply be due to the
fine coating of dust that covered him.

And the major was also bleeding from a cut on his cheekbone; as Butler watched a small bright ruby of blood rolled
down the major's cheek, slowing down as it gathered dust
until it was caught in the grey stubble on his jaw.

"Hah!" The thin lips, dirt-rimmed where the dust and spittle
had mixed, opened to reveal a glittering array of gold teeth.
"Nearly got my bloody head blown off—that's what the sergeant-major's thinking, isn't it, Sergeant-major?"

The sergeant-major came into Butler's range of vision beside the major, half a head shorter and a half a body wider.

"Sir!" said the sergeant-major neutrally.

Eyes slitted under bushy eyebrows and a Guards moustache
under a squashed-in red nose was all Butler had time to assim-
ilate before the major spoke again—except that the sergeant-
major exuded disapproval like body odour. It was going to
take more than one lifetime to live down that improperly
pointed Sten.

"And quite right too." The major nodded at Butler. "Nearly
did get my bloody head blown off—and serve me jolly well
right—the sergeant-major's also thinking that—eh, Sergeant-
major?"

"Sir!" The sergeant-major had obviously perfected that neutral tone over long years of unanswerable questions.

"But . . ." The major's left eye blinked while the fishlike right one continued to stare through Butler. "But we do know he really can speak German—we know that now, don't we, Sergeant-major? And we also know that he can lie in it when he has to, by God!"

This time the sergeant-major let the echo of his previous answer do the work. The major nodded again, but more appraisingly.

"Wouldn't pass for a German, though—not unless they have Germans in Lancashire."

Butler's cheeks burned. He had worked for two years to eliminate that accent, and to have it betray him in a foreign language was galling.

"Lancashire—yes," repeated Major O'Conor contentedly. "But he wasn't taught by a Lancashireman—or by a German either, come to that." He paused, pursing his lips for a moment. "By a Pole, I'd say . . . Remember that fellow in Mersa —the big chap with the fair hair . . . can't recall his name—couldn't pronounce it if I did—but I never forget a voice."

"Sir." There was a fractional variation in the sergeant-major's own voice.

"I knew you'd remember him. First-rate interrogator. Exactly the same German accent—minus the Lancashire, of course." The major turned away from Butler at last, towards his sergeant-major. "Stand at ease, Corporal."

Butler twitched unhappily, unsure of himself. The major had stared at him and spoken to the sergeant-major. Now he was looking at the sergeant-major, but not talking to him.

"Are you *hard of hearing,* Corporal?" snapped the sergeant-major.

Butler stood at ease so quickly that he almost lost his balance in the mud.

"How old are you, Corporal?" As he spoke the major swung towards him again, his left eye blinking disconcertingly. In anyone else that might have been a wink, but it just wasn't possible that—

A glass eye—he had a glass eye!

"Are you *dumb* as well as half deaf?" The sergeant-major paused for a half second. "Answer the officer!"

"Nineteen, sir." Butler's voice cracked. "And a half."

"And a half?" Major O'Conor smiled. "And have you ever fired a shot in anger . . . other than just now?"

Butler clenched his teeth. "No, sir."

"How long have you been in Normandy, Corporal?"

"Th-three days, sir."

"Three days . . ." Major O'Conor nodded. "Well, there's nothing wrong with his reflexes, Sergeant-major. He ducked down like a jack rabbit—and came up like a jack-in-the-box. And nothing wrong with his guts, either."

Butler warmed to the major, all his hatred transferring itself in that instant to the sergeant-major. The major was eccentric, but some officers were eccentric, it was a fact of life. And the major was also old—that grey stubble on his bloodstained cheek was grey with age, not dust—but he was also wise and as sharp as a razor, the insight into his German accent proved that.

His eye was caught by the faded double strip of colour on the major's left breast: and the major was also brave. The blue-red-blue and white-blue-white which led other ribbons he had no time to distinguish were the badges of courage he coveted and dreamed of and honoured—

He had seen them before, on another uniform . . .

The major had seen service, had fired shots in anger—had *led* men in battle.

The thing Butler desired above all things stood before him, the thing Butler wanted to be with all his heart.

And to be led by such a man was the next best thing to that, because by observing him he could learn how the thing was done. Learning was no problem—learning was the easiest thing in the world; and learning by example, as he had expanded his German by listening to the Polish sergeant in the NAAFI night after night, was the easiest way of all.

"Except that if I had been a German he'd be dead, of course," said the major. "Because he popped up in exactly the same spot as he went down, and Jerry would have been waiting for that. But next time he'll move first, Sergeant-major—he won't forget that next time, I'm willing to bet, eh?"

"No, sir," said Butler.

"'Willing to learn by his mistakes'—mark that up, Sergeant-major. . . . And taught himself German." Major O'Conor wagged a thin finger at the sergeant-major. "He'll do. He'll do."

At that moment whatever it was the major wanted him to do—whatever it was he had been taken from his friends and his battalion to do, even if it had involved charging a regiment singlehanded—Butler would cheerfully have done.

"Let's have you out of there, Corporal," said the major, leaning forward to offer Butler a hand.

In the instant that Butler reached for the hand with his own free left hand—the bottle of gentian violet was still palmed in the right one—he remembered his purple feet. But there was no possible way of rejecting the bony fingers which fastened on his wrist in the very next instant; all he could do was to try and hold that one good eye with his own, and let himself be heaved up the bank.

Even that was a failure: the major released his hand and looked him up and down—down to his feet.

And then up again—

"All right, then. Get yourself cleaned up, and we'll be on our way again." The major nodded and turned away as though there had been nothing to see, leaving Butler with his mouth open.

The sergeant-major leaned forward. "Get that carbine of yours unloaded, Corporal," he hissed. "And don't you ever point it at me again—unless you intend to shoot me with it. . . . Is that clear?"

"Yes, Sergeant-major." Butler fixed his eyes on an imaginary block of concrete three inches above the sergeant-major's head.

"I hope so—for your sake, Corporal." The sergeant-major's gaze moved inexorably downwards, his nose wrinkling. It could be the cow to begin with—the poor rotting beast seemed to have ripened measurably in the last quarter of an hour. But at the end it would be the feet, thought Butler despairingly.

"And get those feet of yours cleaned up . . . *on the double!*" concluded the sergeant-major.

Butler looked down at his feet in surprise.
They were encased in thick brown mud.

2. How the corporal missed the battle of Normandy

There hadn't been much room in the back of the jeep even
before Butler had added himself and his belongings to its
cargo, but that didn't worry him; in exchange for the privilege
of not having to march he was prepared to adjust himself to
almost any discomfort. What shocked him now was not the
amount of the cargo but its nature: it looked most suspiciously
like plunder.

Then shock became instant embarrassment as the major
swiveled in his seat to catch the expression naked on his face.

"Not for us, Corporal, I'm sorry to say. Not for us." The
major shook his head and grinned at him, the gold of his smile
matching exactly the gold of the serried ranks of bottle tops.
"Besides . . . it wouldn't taste very good in this heat, you
know. Chilled is the only way to drink it."

Butler stared fascinated at the bottle tops. Champagne, it
must be, and that was one drink he'd never had the opportunity of trying. Or, to be honest, one of the many drinks; he'd
not even had the chance of any of the cider for which this bit
of France was supposed to be famous, like Somerset back in
England—

He felt the major's eyes on him. "Yes, sir." He found himself automatically copying the sergeant-major's impassivity.
"No, sir."

"No—" The jeep jerked forward sharply and without warning under the sergeant-major's hands, cutting off the major's
sentence and nearly dislocating Butler's neck with the whip-
lash. As with men, so with machines, he thought critically:
both were there to be driven hard. But with the major it would
be different.

"No, indeed." The major had the trick of riding the sergeant-major's driving, rolling easily with each jar and bump.
"You see, Corporal, this is a trading mission we're on now.

And these"—he patted the champagne bottles—"these are the trade goods for our next port of call."

The sergeant-major grunted—it was the most eloquent sound he had made yet—and swung the jeep regardlessly off the track onto the main road in a cloud of dust, tyres squealing, missing by a full yard the burnt-out hulk of a Sherman which had been shunted into a gateway almost opposite the junction. In the very nick of time Butler tensed himself and leaned into the swerve, pressing against the side of the jeep to counteract the force which threatened to hurl him at the Sherman. He had just been getting the hang of the major's easy riding technique—

Trading mission?

The major took in his bafflement. "He wants to know what we're trading in, Sergeant-major," he murmured. "The old merchandise, that's what—the old merchandise . . . not sandalwood and cedarwood, or emeralds and amethysts . . . or cheap tin trays either . . . just the old merchandise, the perishable goods, that's what."

He flicked another quick glance backwards, and then shrugged away a second before Butler could find his wits and give him some sign of recognition.

> *With a cargo of ivory,*
> *And apes and peacocks,*
> *Sandalwood, cedarwood, and sweet white wine—*

He flushed with annoyance at his slowness in meeting the challenge, even though it wasn't fair expecting him—expecting anyone—to pick up poetry straight off in this place, at this time—

> *Quinquireme of Nineveh from distant Ophir—*

The verses, hard-learned under the eagle eye of the Third Form English master at King Edward's, came back now to mock him as he stared at a German Mark IV stranded in the cornfield just ahead on his left, its long gun drooping submissively. That corn had been harvested after the tank had been knocked out, he could see that from the thin screen of standing stems along its side: the farmers had come back after the battle and—

It wasn't fair. And it was doubly unfair because he wasn't used to being talked to like this by anyone, least of all by an officer—and a field officer too, a major.

But that was this officer's way of going about things, he told himself grimly, to test men with the unexpected to gauge their capabilities. Where the sergeant-major was looking for the exact performance of a man's duties, the major was looking for something more.

Looking—and not bloody well finding this time, he thought bitterly.

He had been tested once, in oral German, and he had passed by the skin of his teeth. But he had failed the cultural test and the major would have him tagged as a German-speaking clod with quick reflexes. And it was far too late now—and he was far too shy anyway—to tap the officer on the shoulder and say "John Masefield, sir, that was, sir." All he could do was to learn his lesson and be ready for—

Ready for what?

Detached for Special Duties.

The words had made him gawp at the RSM for a moment like a recruit who didn't know his left foot from his right. And then, in sinking through to the first layer of his understanding, they had made him do something which two moments before he would never have dreamed of doing in his wildest fantasy: he had questioned the RSM's order.

"What duties, sir?"

He heard the question after he had spoken it, it had hung in the air between him and the RSM, surprising both of them.

The RSM had looked at him, and he had the feeling that he was really being looked at by the RSM for the first time as a person, not as 944 Butler J., Corporal, "B" Company.

The RSM sighed. "Corporal . . . ask me no questions, son, and I'll tell you no lies." And then he had paused, and had looked down at the papers on the table as though to recall himself to the matter in hand.

"Ten minutes—you have ten minutes to get your kit together and report back here on the double—ten minutes. And

then regimental transport will take you to a point one mile
south of—of"—he looked down again uncertainly—"Meznil
—lez-Bockage . . . that's   it—Meznil-lez-Bockage . . . where
you will rendezvous with a Major O'Conor at precisely eigh-
teen hundred hours." He had looked up at Butler, eyes
opaque. "Is that clear, Corporal?"

It had been all too clear then; it had been appallingly clear;
it had been *Detached for Special Duties*.

"But, sir—"

"Ten minutes. By which time the relevant documentation
will have been completed."

The finality of the RSM's voice had broken through the
final layer. The words on that piece of paper were chiselled in
stone.

"Away from the battalion?" It hadn't really been a question,
and it certainly hadn't been addressed to the RSM; Butler had
simply been talking to himself.

But it had been spoken aloud.

"Away—?" The RSM had started to speak sharply; but
then, as the cry from the soul had registered, his expression
had changed. Loyalty to the battalion was something he took
for granted, but it was still not a quality to be spurned. It was
something which merited an answer.

"Now then, son . . ." The RSM had struggled briefly with
the problem. "You do speak German—you are proficient in
that language, aren't you?"

Butler swallowed, unable to deny what he was so proud of.
"Not . . . I wouldn't quite say that, sir."

"Proficient." The RSM held on to the word. "That is what
the record says . . . and there is a requirement for a German-
speaking non-commissioned officer."

Butler's heart had beaten faster then. The requirement was
not for him—not for 12048944 Butler J., Corporal, 2nd/4th
Royal North-East Lancashire Rifles. Nor was it for a red-
haired soldier suffering in secret from *Epidermophyton inguinale,* who had been born in Jubilee Street, Blackburn,
nineteen and a half years before. It was just for an NCO who
could speak in German. And that could be—anyone.

"With respect, sir—I'd like to stay with the battalion, sir."

The RSM had frowned at that. "What you'd like—and what you don't like—don't come into it, Corporal."

The frown had frightened Butler. But the prospect of what was proposed for him had terrified him beyond fear: his instinct made him fight before his reason had time to instruct him otherwise.

"I've been with the battalion for two years, sir."

The frown had deepened. Two years or ten minutes—two years *and* ten minutes—it was all the same to the RSM. He needed a better reason than that.

"The battalion's just about to go into action, sir," he had said.

Slowly the frown had cleared, until the face was expressionless again.

"My . . . my father was with the regiment in 1916, sir."

Now there was an expression, but he couldn't identify it.

"Aye, I know, son." The RSM had nodded slowly. "And he was RSM, 1st Battalion, at Ypres in '18."

It had been Butler's turn to frown then. Because that knowledge had been just too exact, too precise. It had been all very well for "the record," whatever it was, wherever it was, to note that he could speak German. He had never concealed that—he had been proud of it. But how could the RSM—?

The question answered itself before he had finished formulating it in his mind. Somewhere, wherever that record was, probably far away back in the regimental depot, there was a sheet of that thick white writing paper which General Sir Henry Chesney always used . . . he could almost see the beautiful copperplate writing on it. There was a sheet of the same paper, with the same copperplate, in his pocket now—

Dear Jack,
By the time you receive this letter I expect you will be in the thick of it—

It would be like the general to do his best for him, unasked, with just such a letter of recommendation. And it was—what was the word, "irony" was it?—an irony if that recommendation was now taking him away from the battalion.

Unless—the thought had come out of nowhere and he had

clutched it desperately—unless they were now giving him a chance to distinguish himself, perhaps?

In that instant he had stopped fighting and had started to think about a Major O'Conor who required a German-speaking NCO for Special Duties.

His eyes met the RSM's.

"I'll get my kit, sir," he had said then.

Ready for what?

They were driving steadily southwards; or perhaps, from the position of the early evening sun, south inclined a few degrees eastwards. But then the road had twisted and turned so many times that they could just as easily have drifted westwards first . . . the three-tonner which had carried him away from battalion headquarters had certainly left Caen—or the rubble that had once been Caen—on a more or less southwesterly route.

Butler's head swam with the effort of trying to work out where he was and where he was heading. He had studied a map of Normandy carefully back in England only a week before, but that seemed a very long time ago, and it hadn't been this part that he'd concentrated on—at least, so it seemed to him now, because the names on the signposts were all strange and new to him.

And the places themselves, they were all the same, most of them fearfully knocked about, some of them no better than Caen itself; blank empty windows and smashed-up churches with holes punched methodically into their towers where the snipers had been.

And the civilians . . . he had half expected, even more than half expected, that there would be cheers and flowers for liberation, or at least that some pretty girl would wave at him. But he hadn't heard a cheer or seen an arm raised, never mind a pretty girl. Half the time they didn't even look at him, any of them, and he didn't blame them a bit now for that, with their homes in ruins.

But, one thing, the country was different here. Not flat and open, but closed into small fields with high earth banks out of which the trees and hedges sprouted, and rolling up and down into deep little valleys full of trees.

And the fighting, although it had passed now—away almost due east, so far as he could judge the sound—it had been bad here. In one place they passed three British tanks, Cromwells all of them, blackened and burnt and shunted into a twenty-yard stretch of ditch; and he caught a glimpse of others, one with its turret lying beside it, through a gap in the earth bank on his left.

"Getting warm," said Major O'Conor. "Take the left fork at the next junction, Sergeant-major. If there's a sign it'll be for St. Pierre-sur-Orne, most likely."

Butler blinked and stared at the weatherbeaten back of the major's neck. The Orne flowed northwards into the sea from Caen, but before that . . . where did it come from?

And now the sound of the distant guns seemed to be coming more from the southeast than the east . . .

Butler shivered. Whatever it was doing, it wasn't getting warm at all, it was almost chilly. Or maybe the sight of those burnt-out Cromwells had chilled him.

The major twisted in his seat. "Been admiring the scenery, Corporal?"

"Yes, sir," said Butler.

"Quite right, too. Lovely countryside, and we're just getting into the best of it. And you know what they call it?"

Butler thought of the Cromwells again, and then with a start realised that he was about to be told where he was.

"No, sir."

"La Suisse Normande, Corporal—'the Norman Switzerland.' Actually, it's nothing like Switzerland, but it's the nearest thing they've got, and the food's a lot better." The major looked around proprietorially. "Not a place to fight in, of course . . . if you've got to do the attacking, that is . . . but fortunately, Jerry has pressing business elsewhere and other things in mind, so we don't have to worry about that."

So the Germans really were retreating, thought Butler. All the rumours were true after all.

"Sir?" he inquired hopefully.

The major smiled. "Another five or ten minutes, and you'll be able to stretch your legs. And then after that I fancy you'll be able to travel more comfortably too."

He turned away, leaving Butler not very much the wiser. La Suisse Normande might be anywhere; it certainly wasn't a name he'd seen on any map. But the Germans had retreated through it, and the major obviously wasn't contemplating attacking them.

Yet in the last second before he turned away, the major's medal ribbons had again caught his eye. Blue-red-blue, white-blue-white, and then faded red-white-blue—he knew them all, and they did leave him wiser, and not a little confused.

The major was a proven soldier, they told him that, the first two of them—a fighting soldier for sure with that white-blue-white to prove it. But the faded red-white-blue, faded and fading off into each other, that also made him an *old* soldier, older even than he looked. For though Butler was no judge of age, and the older the more inaccurate, he knew a 1914–18 Victory Medal when he saw one. Both his father and the general had that one in their collections.

It was strange how he could never think of either of them now without the other intruding almost immediately.

No, "intruding" was the wrong word, he decided. They had become inseparable antagonists inside his head, just as they were in real life, but he could never make them act out of character there.

Sometimes he had tried hard to imagine them arguing over him, about what he was resolved to do with his life. He had done—or tried to do—this not because he wanted it to happen (the very thought of it doing so was painful to him), but because it seemed to him that if he could eavesdrop into such a fantasy he might be able to understand better why he felt the way he did.

But not even in his imagination could he make them say anything more to one another than he had heard them do in reality.

The general would always speak first: "Good morning, Mr. Butler," he would say politely, with just a touch of briskness, raising his bowler hat as he did so.

"Good morning, sir," his father would reply, just as politely, touching his cap in a gesture of recognition to the raised bowler.

Other people would say "Sir Henry," or occasionally "General," but his father would never say more than "sir" and the general would never say less than "Mr." which he rarely did for anyone else.

For a long time this exchange of greetings had baffled young Butler. When the owner of Chesney and Rawle's met the secretary of the Graphical Association union branch (and father of the Union Chapel at C & R) there should have been a certain wariness; when the president of the local Conservative Association met the chairman of the local Labour Party there ought to have been a clear antagonism; and when the man whose influence and organising ability had helped to break the General Strike in the town met the man who had been one of the strike's leaders, there could only be bitterness. Butler himself had been not two years old then, and this December he would be twenty; but there were still men who wouldn't talk to those they felt had betrayed them then, or at the most not a word more than was needed to get the job done.

Yet when the general and his father met there was neither wariness, nor antagonism, and not a hint of bitterness.

It had been in Coronation Year—the year after he had won the scholarship—that he had caught a glimpse of the explanation.

The year he had gone to work for the general.

He had known without a word being said that his father expected him to take the paper round which had become vacant and which was his for the asking. And he had also known that although this was required of him as his proper contribution to the family income, they had in fact managed perfectly well since his mother's death and its real purpose was "to keep his feet on the ground" (as Uncle Fred put it) now that he was a scholarship boy at the Grammar.

But he had also known, above all, that he had not the slightest intention of taking the paper round. He didn't like papers (or printing, for that matter), and he would sooner go kitting milk than delivering them. So when Mr. Harris the maths master had let slip that the general's head gardener was in the market for a part-time boy, the nod was as good as a wink and he was off like a hare after the last lesson to the big house in Lynwood Road.

It never occurred to him that he might not get the job.

Rather, he regarded his successful application as already assured. For the general and he had already met, and the general would certainly remember the boy to whom he had last year awarded the Scholarship prize (E. Wilmot Buxton's *The Story of the Crusades,* a splendid, gold-embossed book which Butler treasured) in the final term at North Mill Street Elementary.

It had simply not dawned on him that it would not be the general, but the head gardener, who didn't know him from E. Wilmot Buxton, who would be conducting the interviews for the part-time boy; nor had it occurred to him that others might have learnt of the vacancy, and that one in particular, a large boy with a BSA bicycle, would easily outdistance him to Lynwood Road.

All this became apparent in quick succession, first the bike propped outside the back entrance, then the large boy with a smug look on his face, and finally the head gardener himself, who obviously could not know of his special relationship with the general.

He had been in front of the head gardener, out of breath and near to weeping for this lost certainty, when there had come a shadow and a sound behind him in the doorway of the greenhouse. The head gardener had looked over his shoulder and stood up deferentially, and Butler had known instantly who was there and had heard the tap of the general's stick sound as sweet inside his head as the distant trumpets of the relieving force to the last survivor of a beleaguered outpost.

But at first the general didn't seem to recognise him in the cool green light of the potting shed; he had looked questioningly at the head gardener.

"The part-time boy, General," the head gardener had reminded him.

"Ah, yes." The general had nodded and had turned to consider Butler properly.

But then, to Butler's surprise, he had not said, "Of course —you are the Scholarship boy from North Mill Elementary to whom I presented E. Wilmot Buxton's *The Story of the Crusades* last year."

"You are Mr. Butler's son," the general had said.

"Yes—" Butler had floundered for a moment, unable to decide how to address the general. The head gardener had said

"General," but outside St. Michael's Church on Sundays and in front of the War Memorial on November 11 his father had never used that rank. "Yes—sir."

"You remember RSM Butler, Sands," said the general to the head gardener. "At Messines with the 1st/4th—and he was also with me at Beaumont Hamel the year before... before you joined the battalion... he was one of my platoon sergeants then." He pointed at Butler's head. "The same red hair, man—and the same look in the eye, too, by God!"

The head gardener stared at Butler. "Aye, you're right, General," he agreed finally, in a voice which suggested that maybe not all his dealings with RSM Butler had been happy.

The general had chuckled. "D'you know anything about gardening, boy?"

Butler thought of his father's allotment, but the easy lie choked in his throat. "No, sir."

"What about your father's allotment?" The general seemed to have a way of reading his thoughts. "Don't you help him with that?"

Butler felt committed to the whole truth now. With that sharp eye on him nothing else would be of any use anyway, he suspected. "He likes to do it himself, sir."

"I see. And of course you've been busy studying, eh?"

"Yes, sir."

"And how are you going to continue studying and work for me at the same time now?"

"I can make the time, sir."

Nod. "See that you do, boy." The general's eyes lifted away from him to the head gardener. He knew that he'd got the job, but there was no longer any particular triumph in the knowledge now that he was aware his father had more to do with his success than E. Wilmot Buxton.

He thought irrelevantly how very blue the general's eyes were for such an old man. Snow-white hair—and bushy white moustache in the middle of a brick-red face. But bright blue eyes. Except that red, white, and blue were proper colours for a general.

And that red, white, and blue ribbon.

"Here we are," said Major O'Conor.

3. How Colonel Sykes lost his rugby team

The major was right: this Norman Switzerland wasn't at all like the real thing, or not like the full-page colour photographs of it in the Q to Z volume of his father's Illustrated Encyclopaedia of World Geography; if anything, it reminded Butler of the foothills of the Lake District at home, where he had camped with the school scout troop in the last year before the war.

There were cliffs, certainly—he could see them rising out of the thick woods across the valley into which they were descending. But there were no snow-capped peaks and the trees weren't Swiss firs. The Orne (presumably it was the Orne, anyway) rippled over its rocky bed just below him now, with a group of Frenchmen fishing in it, quite unconcerned by the jeep's noisy approach. There were even a couple further down watering their horses in the shallows, in the shadow of a high-arched stone bridge which joined the tree-lined road embankment—

A high-arched stone bridge—

The incongruity of the scene suddenly hit Butler. The trees shouldn't have been nodding gently in the breeze, they should have been lying in a tangle across the road ahead, blocking the approach to the gaping ruins of that bridge, the demolished stonework of which should be choking the river twenty feet below; or, at best, the shattered trees should have been bulldozed over the embankment to make way for the Bailey bridge across the ruins.

Instead it was all as peaceful as a picture postcard—as peaceful as Switzerland or the Lake District—with the picturesque bridge, and the fishermen—there were more of them fishing happily from the bridge itself—and the horsemen watering their horses. For a moment the war was a million miles away and it was hard to imagine that this same river flowed through the stinking ruins of Caen to the invasion beaches.

There was a tank under the trees just across the river. And another just beyond it. And another—

The jeep squealed to a halt in the middle of the bridge, beside the first fisherman.

"Second South Wessex Dragoons?" barked the sergeant-major.

The fisherman turned, took in the front-seat occupants of the jeep, and straightened up, one hand still grasping his home-made rod. He wasn't likely to catch anything from the bridge, thought Butler—and certainly not with that apology for a fishing rod.

"That's right, sir," said the fisherman.

"Colonel Sykes, we're looking for," said the major.

"Sir." The fisherman turned away to scan the riverbank below him. Suddenly he pointed. "Down there, sir—just getting off his horse, sir—besides Major Dobson and Mr. Pickles."

His *horse*? Butler craned his neck to follow the pointing finger. The two horsemen who had been watering their horses had been joined by a third, who was in the act of dismounting. All three were wearing riding breeches, booted and spurred. Butler goggled at them.

"I see—thank you," said the major politely. Then he smiled. "The regiment's getting horsed again, then."

The fisherman regarded him stolidly. "Be an improvement if it was, sir," he observed, unsmiling.

Butler frowned and looked away, back down the river. Beyond the horsemen and the anglers on the bank there was a group of naked soldiers skylarking in the water with a make-shift ball. The Wessex Dragoons evidently weren't taking their war very seriously, so far as he could see.

"Ah—it would that, sir," murmured one of the other anglers.

"And where did you acquire the—ah—the remounts?" inquired the major.

"German army, sir."

The major nodded approvingly. "Jolly good. Drive on, Sergeant-major. We'll park down the road there, just after the end of the parapet."

The sergeant-major crashed the gears brutally, but managed to coax the jeep another twenty yards without mishap.

"Fine . . . Now if you'd guard our other possessions,

Sergeant-major . . . and the corporal would help me . . ." The major trailed off.

Butler looked at the sergeant-major, bewildered.

"Get those cases out of the vehicle, man," snapped the sergeant-major. "And don't you dare drop them."

His eyes dropped from Butler to the boxes with the champagne, and then lifted back to Butler. All was at last revealed in that look, and Butler's faith in both men was restored: *trade goods* and a *trading mission*, the major had said, *not for us*. So if the bottles were plunder they were at least not to be used improperly, but in the line of duty to obtain some necessary item from the dragoons in exchange; and it did look as though they were the right sort of trade goods for such a unit—the major and the sergeant-major might disapprove, but they knew what they were about.

What *the old merchandise, the perishable goods* were, was not yet clear, but would no doubt be revealed soon enough. What was obvious was that protocol would not permit the sergeant-major to carry the trade goods when there was a junior NCO present to do that work, which meant that the sergeant-major must stay and protect the jeep from the thieving hands of soldiery and civilians, who would strip anything left unattended.

He balanced the cases carefully on top of one another and set out after the major, peering round them as best he could to see where he was going. It was going to be tricky though, getting down the embankment to the water-meadow below.

The major came to his rescue, thoughtful as ever.

"Here, Corporal . . . there's a bit of a path just here . . . mind how you go . . . left a bit—that's right . . . steady, steady . . . you can rest up against that tree if you like."

Butler was sweating. "I'm all right, sir."

"Just this last bit, then . . . well done!"

At last the ground was flat again under his boots, though they were still under the canopy of the trees which grew thickly all the way down the embankment. Butler stopped to get his breath.

Suddenly there was a thud—or a cross between a thud and a thump—away to his left somewhere. To Butler's ears it sounded suspiciously and horribly like a two-inch mortar going off, and a moment later he was aware of something descending through the leaves and branches above him to confirm his horrible suspicion.

Time slowed almost to a standstill as he stood, rooted to the spot, clasping the major's case of champagne to his chest.

"Sir!" He appealed helplessly, trying to catch the major's attention.

But the major's attention was already caught: he was staring upwards into the branches as though to judge the line of the mortar bomb's descent—indeed, judging by the movement of his hands, almost as though he intended to catch it.

Butler closed his eyes in the very instant that something crashed through the branches almost directly above them. There was another thump—

This time more a slapping thump than a thudding one—and then a second or two of silence finally broken by the distant whinnying of a horse.

He opened his eyes again.

The major was now holding a rugby football in his hands.

"Hmm . . ." he said, raising the eyebrow over his good eye at Butler. "In my young days it was hunting, fishing, and shooting they played at. Now it seems to be hunting, fishing, and rugger. I suppose they've had a bellyful of shooting for the time being, poor devils. . . . Come on, Corporal."

As they came out of the shadow of the trees a hulking young soldier, naked to the waist, appeared out of a gap in the bushes just ahead of them. If this was the rugger player, his side had been the losing one, thought Butler critically; he spotted a great purple-black bruise on his left cheekbone, and another on his shoulder to match. There was a rather bedraggled field dressing on his right forearm.

He stopped abruptly as he saw the major, blinked in surprise, and opened and shut his mouth as though the first words he had thought of were not the ones he now wanted to say.

"Speak, thou apparition," said the major.

The young soldier blinked again, and then produced a nervous half-smile. Under the tousled thatch of light brown hair his face was dead white, except for dark rings under his eyes, the angry bruise of his cheekbone, and an acne rash on his chin.

"C-can we have our b-ball b-back, sir?" he stuttered in an exaggerated public-school drawl.

Butler's normally dormant class prejudices stirred. The apparition was an officer, for all its appearance, which was not improved by a suggestion of pale stubble on its chin—though to be fair that might be due to the acne.

And, to be fair also (when the prejudices stirred Butler instinctively leaned over backwards to silence them), he wasn't a chinless wonder of the Guards variety; the stubbly chin was square and hard, and the pale blue eyes were hard too. It was a rugger player's face, and the physique below it was built to match.

It was the dead-giveaway voice, the arrogant stutter, which nettled him, reminding him that cavalry regiments notoriously recruited just this type of subaltern, at least in the old days. In the Royal Lancs the officers were, with exceptions, gentlemen, and none the worse for that (and one day Butler himself intended to be one of them, and no exception). But in at least one of the county's yeomanry regiments the commissions before the war went exclusively to the gentry, to men with land under their belts (as his father put it), or to their sons and brothers. Even the general had counselled him against volunteering for that regiment, though he had produced other reasons for his counsel.

"By all means," said the major suavely, tossing the ball to the apparition. "Come on, Corporal."

As he strode past the young officer, the crowns on his shoulder seemed to register for the first time, and the boy stiffened. "Thanks most awf'ly, sir," he called after the major's back. "I'm afraid I sliced the k-k-kick rather b-b-b"— he paused to concentrate on the word, looking blankly at Butler—"rather *badly*," he concluded with unnatural emphasis.

A very strange character, thought Butler as he stumbled past, aware that his arms were beginning to ache painfully under their burden. But then it seemed a rather strange unit, so no doubt the strangeness of its officers passed unremarked.

Something squashed under his right boot, and the rich smell of horse manure rose to his nose, reminding him sharply for a second of General Chesney's rose garden, onto which he had forked tons of the stuff. Then just as sharply, he was aware that the major had stopped just ahead of him, and that they had reached the horsemen.

He peered cautiously round the cases, wondering as he did so whether it would be safe to put them down. Better not, he decided; his arms were now locked in position, at the limit of their sockets. If he did put them down he might not have the strength to pick them up again.

"Willy, my dear fellow!" The third horseman—the one who had dismounted and who therefore must be Colonel Sykes, appeared from between the horses. "So you found us all right."

Colonel Sykes shook the major's hand warmly.

"No problem at all." The major cocked his head on one side. "The trail was . . . unmistakable."

"Hah!" Colonel Sykes shook his head. "Yes . . . I suppose it must be, at that."

"It looked as though you've been having a rough time, Chris."

"Perfectly bloody, not to put too fine a point on it. All the way from just south of Caumont—perfectly bloody, Willy. If it wasn't Tigers it was damned self-propelled guns, and this bocage country is no place to fight either of them, especially with these wretched Cromwells. So . . . we've been swapping at about the rate of six to one half the time."

The colonel stroked his horse abstractedly, and the two men shook their heads at each other. Butler forgot about his arms and thought instead of the anglers on the bridge, and also of the burnt-out tanks they'd passed along the way. There had been rather a lot of them, he remembered now.

"And here am I, come to deplete your strength further," said the major apologetically. "I'm sorry about that, Chris."

"My dear fellow!" Colonel Sykes raised his hand to cut off the apology. "Think nother of it. Fact is, it's all the same to me now—we're being disbanded, you see."

"Good Lord! I'm sorry to hear that. That's damn bad luck." The major managed to make the banal phrases sound sincere, Butler thought. But if the two were old friends, maybe he really meant them.

"No good crying about spilt milk. The same thing's hap-

pening to the 2nd Northants, they've caught a packet too...
once you go beyond a certain point it's the best thing to do,
really." Colonel Sykes shrugged. "So I'm off to 21 Army
Group and the rest are mostly going to the 7th Armoured—
they've got Cromwells too, poor devils... No, as a matter of
fact, Willy, you're doing me a good turn if what I hear is
true."

The major half-turned, and for the first time since the conversation had started, Butler could see his face. But then he
saw it was still only the blind side, which never seemed able
to betray any emotion.

"What do you hear?" The major's question was as devoid
of curiosity as the blind side was of expression. "What's that,
then?"

"Well, Brigade made it sound like a holiday jaunt—a sort
of tourist excursion to some desirable resort, with no Tigers or
such things in attendance," said the colonel airily. "Didn't say
what it actually was—that was all hush-hush as usual. But
they made it sound like just what the doctor ordered for my
lad, certainly."

"What the doctor—?" The major sounded wary now.
"Come on, Chris—you're not giving me walking wounded,
are you?"

"I don't mean *literally* what the doctor ordered." Colonel
Sykes swung on his heel, taking in the whole scene: the anglers, the bathers, the horsemen who had mounted up and
were cantering away over the meadow. "They're all a bit battered, but there's nothing wrong with any of them. Tanks—
third-rate; morale—first-rate, you might say. Could give you
any one of them, and you'd have a bargain. Fact is, I'm giving you one of the best... absolutely bulging with brains,
almost too much for his own good."

"I want one bulging with French, Chris. Not brains, just
French."

The colonel waved his hand. "Fluent, even though he's a
history scholar—French, Latin, Greek—Russian too, for all I
know. Even a bit of German."

"Just French."

Butler was beginning to think faster. There had been a requirement for a German-speaking NCO; presumably there was also a requirement for a French-speaking one too.

On a holiday jaunt, a tourist excursion.

"Speaks it like a native, Willy. I've heard him myself—he was apologising to an old Frenchwoman who came out of her front door with a bottle of calvados and a Union Jack thirty seconds after we'd put a burst of machine-gun fire through her bedroom window." Colonel Sykes stared past Butler across the field. "I sent young Pickles to rout him out, so he should be appearing any minute now—" He broke off, staring this time directly at Butler.

The major followed the stare and started guiltily as he set eyes on Butler. "Good God, Corporal—put those cases down at once! They must be killing you!"

Butler lowered the cases to the ground. He hoped devoutly that no sort of introduction requiring a salute would now take place, or at least not until he had the use of his right arm again.

But the major merely gestured towards the cases. "Present for your mess, Chris—in exchange for one guaranteed French-speaker. Top case is champagne, courtesy of the German Army. The rest is scotch, which is said to have fallen off the back of an American half-track . . . I heard tell you were living on cider and army rum."

"My dear fellow—too kind! We have been rather short just recently—ah, here he comes now—"

Butler was standing at ease, with his hands clasped behind his back, which was about the most comfortable position his arms had been able to find. But as the major stared fixedly over his shoulder—the good eye appeared as fixed suddenly as the false one, so that for a moment he couldn't make out which was which—he couldn't resist turning himself to get a look at his comrade in good or bad fortune, the French-speaking NCO.

He understood instantly why the major was staring. Of course, no one had actually said the French-speaker was to be a two-striper like himself, but he had simply assumed it to be so. And he had assumed wrong.

Even in immaculate Canadian battle dress, trouser creases knife-edged from the iron, pistol at his hip, there was no mistaking the apparition. If anything, the smart black beret, its prancing horses badge catching the red of the setting sun, emphasised the black and white of the face.

"Ah, David . . . good of you to join us"—Colonel Sykes acknowledged the OCTU-fresh salute—"David, this is Major Willy O'Conor, to whom you are being sent for the time being, as I explained to you this morning . . . Willy, this is David Audley, my best French-speaker—and the best-educated officer in the regiment, come to that, I shouldn't wonder, so take good care of him."

Audley saluted again, and then accepted the major's hand.

"We have met, actually," said the major. "But we didn't get round to introductions."

Colonel Sykes looked at his subaltern inquiringly.

Audley's blackened left cheek could betray nothing, but there was a suggestion of colour in the undamaged right one. "I'm afraid I nearly b-b-brained the m-major with m-my"— Audley paused as he had done before, as though he could see the words ahead like tests in an obstacle course and was gathering his strength to meet them—"my—my rugby *ball*."

"I see." Colonel Sykes smiled. "David has a mighty right foot, Willy. He never missed a penalty and the regiment carried all before it back in England—didn't it, David?"

Audley's good cheek twitched. "I'm a bit. . . . a b-bit out of practice now." He eyed the major searchingly. 'D'you want me to t-travel light, sir?"

Presumably people with their own twenty-seven-ton transport travelled with more worldly goods than the poor bloody infantry, thought Butler enviously. Then the memory of the blackened Cromwells reasserted itself, and the envy evaporated.

"As light as you reasonably can, David," said the major. "Ten days, we're reckoning on. Possibly less. But we'll be travelling by jeep all the way."

All the way. Butler packed the words away with the other information he had in store. But all the way *where*?

"Five minutes, and I'll be ready, sir," said Audley.

"Right. We'll meet you on the road, at the end of the bridge, then." The major nodded.

For a few seconds they watched the apparition stride away,

then the major turned to the colonel. "I'm afraid I'm weakening your all-conquering rugby team too," he said, the regiment's disbandment apparently forgotten.

The colonel was still watching the departing figure. "No, not weakening it, Willy—finishing it off," he said softly. "Young David is the sole survivor, as it happens."

"Hmm . . . he looks a bit shaky to me."

The colonel turned towards the major. "He's all right."

"For a holiday jaunt, you mean?"

"I mean . . . all right for duty." Colonel Sykes's voice had hardened. "I told you I'd given you a good one, and I have. But he's been unhorsed three times in a fortnight, and the last time he was blown clean out of his tank by a Tiger."

"He's lucky then." The major's voice was harder too.

"Luckier than the rest of his crew—yes." The colonel paused. "But if he reckons he's on borrowed time it isn't surprising. So what I'm relying on you for, Willy, is to borrow him another fortnight with this special operation of yours while I pull a string or two to get him where he can do the job he's best fitted for, with his brains."

"Uh-huh? Which is some form of intelligence, I take it?" Suddenly the major's voice was soft as silk. "In which cushy billet he can survive the war to help build a land fit for heroes?"

The silken covering didn't conceal the bitterness from Butler's ear. It might have been his father talking, in a different accent about a different war, but with the same meaning.

"Better him than superannuated cannon fodder like us, Willy."

The major gave a short laugh. "Speak for yourself, my dear chap."

"Very well! Superannuated cannon fodder like me—and a bloodthirsty old bandit like you. We've been on borrowed time since '40. That's what I mean."

"Hah! And I fully intend to stay on it—that's what *I* mean—" The major checked himself. "But don't worry, Chris. I'll try to include your protégé in my survival plans. In fact, if all goes well with our little jaunt, I shall be giving him the chance of winning his spurs in the field of intelligence, I shouldn't wonder."

Butler closed his eyes for a moment and soared away on the wings of his own ambition. They had spoken, had argued and fenced with each other, as though he hadn't existed; as though he hadn't been standing there, three yards away from them, as patient as the ex–German army horse. And in the end he had almost forgotten that he existed himself.

Now he could feel the reality again. The field of intelligence had no particular attraction for him, the only field for a soldier was the battlefield and the only part worth playing on it was the infantryman's—that lesson from the general he had learnt, and that was the lesson in which he believed totally.

But if there were spurs a French-speaking second lieutenant could win in this operation there ought also to be spurs which a German-speaking corporal could win.

And if there were, then Jack Butler was going to win them.

4.   How Major O'Conor set a history test

Butler knew exactly what was going to happen.

Or, since Major O'Conor was obviously not a conventional officer of the line, he didn't know *exactly* what was going to happen, but he had a bloody shrewd idea.

One way or another young Mr. Second Lieutenant Audley was going to be put to the test, as Corporal Butler had been.

There was a part of him which was already protective of the subaltern, and sorry that he had had no opportunity to warn him of what was to come. Because that was what a good NCO should do—and because one day he hoped there'd be a good NCO to do it for him, the Second Lieutenant Butler of the future, God willing.

But there was another (and larger) part of him which awaited events with more than professional curiosity. Knowing one's officer was almost as important as knowing one's sergeant, and he had another bloody shrewd idea that there wouldn't be much time to get the measure of Mr. Audley before life-and-death matters were put to the test. Because that casual banter between Colonel Sykes and the major about a "holiday jaunt" had had a distinct whiff of sulphur about it:

they had been reassuring each other and lying to each other in the same breath, and both had known it—like a couple of RAF types he had once heard talking in a pub about a raid which was going to be "a piece of cake," when the scraped white look on each of their faces had belied what they were saying.

He took a quick surreptitious look at Mr. Audley, whose black and white countenance had that same air-crew pallor.

Second Lieutenant Audley would bear watching. About the major he had not the very slightest doubt: he had seen it all and survived it all, and that talk of surviving at any cost had been just talk. But not all Mr. Audley's injuries—the bandaged arm and the bruises—were on the outside, for a guess. And they might be the result of being blown out of his tank, which to be fair sounded like an uncommonly unpleasant experience—especially when he remembered all those knocked-out Cromwells along the way to the bridge. Yet they might also be the symptoms of that dreadful incurable disease the general had once spoken of which was stamped on the records of failed officers.

Lack of moral fibre.

If Second Lieutenant Audley suffered from LMF, then it was better to discover it now, at the major's hands, than later, at the Germans'.

One thing was for sure: Mr. Audley might be bulging with brains and scholarships, but he was bloody slow adjusting to the sergeant-major's driving. Every time the jeep juddered over a pothole or skidded to the left (which was every time they came to a pothole, because the sergeant-major drove in a straight line), and every time they came to a corner, because he drove too fast, he rolled heavily against Butler.

Each time they collided Butler was enveloped in a mixed smell of carbolic soap and sweat, and had his hipbone gouged by the subaltern's pistol butt.

Each time they collided Mr. Audley winced with pain and apologised.

And each time Butler couldn't quite summon up enough courage to suggest that if Mr. Audley would just hold on to his side of the jeep the collisions would not be necessary.

The jeep lurched again, and Audley lurched with it.

Carbolic soap, sweat, and *ouch!*

"Sorry," said Audley for the twentieth time.

"Sir," said Butler for the twentieth time.

The major turned in his seat and fixed his good eye on Audley. He hadn't said a word since they'd set off, so it might be that he was coming to the same conclusions about his fluent French-speaking dragoon subaltern, thought Butler.

"Where did you pick up your French, David?" The major spoke conversationally. "School?"

"And F-France, sir," said Audley, rubbing his shoulder.

"On holiday, you mean?"

"F-f-friends of the f-family, sir. I was b-billeted on them every summer holiday up to '38, to learn the language. W-wouldn't say a w-word of English to me—bloody awful."

"But you learnt the language, eh?"

Audley grimaced, which with his bruised face was easy. "It w-was that or starve to death, sir. W-wouldn't even let the doctor speak English to me when I w-was sick—even though he spoke it better than I did." He grinned suddenly. "Matter of fact, I've g-got a rotten accent—no ear for it. But I know the right words."

"Well, that's all we shall be needing." Major O'Conor nodded at Butler. "Corporal Butler here wouldn't pass for an *Obergefreiter*—not unless the Germans have been recruiting in Lancashire anyway. But he knows the words, I'll say that for him."

Butler's cheeks burned as Audley turned to him. "Good show, Corporal," said Audley.

Butler searched the white face for the patronising expression which ought to go with the words, but found only a polite innocence worn like a mask. Whatever Audley thought about his situation was locked up inside his head.

"You've got some German too, I gather?" said the major.

"S-school Certificate German. I can maybe read it a bit, but not much more as yet," said Audley self-dismissively.

Butler bit his lip. Not so long ago the acquisition of School Certificate German had been the limit of his ambition, looming larger than anything else except the Army itself. But here was Audley shrugging it off as a thing of little importance.

"You have a history scholarship?" The major's tone was casual. "Am I right there?"

Hände hoch! thought Butler. The complete unimportance of Mr. Audley's education could only conceal a hidden ambush to come—and there was nothing he could do to warn the subaltern.

"Yes, sir." Audley relaxed.

"Oxford, I presume?"

"Cambridge actually. The climate in Oxford . . . it's terribly muggy. I didn't fancy it at all. I think Cambridge is much *healthier*."

Butler was impressed. The subaltern might be exaggerating, but he had spoken as though he'd had a choice between the two ancient and exclusive seats of learning, and not even the great Dr. Fredericks of King Edward's had ever boasted of that so far as he could recall.

"Besides, there was this fellow at Balliol who was mad keen for me to read Greats, and the truth is I've never been absolutely sold on the classics since—"

Butler had just worked out that "Greats" must be Latin and Greek when the jeep hammered violently over a pothole again, catching him unprepared and throwing him sideways against Audley before he could swing against the lurch. He felt the subaltern shrink away from him, and then tense up with pain as their shoulders met.

"Sorry," said Audley for the twenty-first time, automatically.

Butler looked away, embarrassed. Ahead of them the road now arrowed towards a far skyline that was just beginning to blur with the haze of evening. They had left the Norman Switzerland behind them and were heading into a countryside untouched by war. But for the evenly spaced trees along the road and the hedgeless fields beyond them, it might almost have been the anonymous landscape of southern England he had glimpsed on the battalion's journey southwards a month before. It hardly seemed possible that only a few days back this might-have-been England had been German territory.

Audley lapsed into silence, leaving the sentence unfinished, as though the pain had reminded him where he was. He had managed all those words, from "Cambridge" onwards, without a trace of a stutter, Butler realised.

"So you decided to study history?" The major seemed determined to drive the young officer from cover. "A more useful subject—eh?"

Audley gave the question some thought before answering. "I wouldn't go so f-far as to say useful. I certainly d-didn't find my knowledge of . . . W-William the Conqueror's f-feudal administration in Normandy awfully useful in the *b-bo-cage*." He made a ghastly attempt at a smile. "M-medieval history doesn't help against eighty-eights, I found."

"Medieval history?" The major's good eye widened. "Now there you might just be wrong, young David, you know."

"I b-beg your pardon, sir?" Audley looked at the major with a mixture of surprise and unconcealed curiosity.

"I said you may be wrong—eh, Sergeant-major?" The major sought confirmation from what Butler regarded as a most unlikely source.

The sergeant-major grunted knowingly.

"Sir?" Audley's interest fluttered like a bird in a cage.

The major's golden smile showed. "The name Chandos mean anything to you, my lad?"

"Chandos?" Audley repeated the name, frowning.

"That's right. And there was an Audley too in his time, I rather think—does he ring a bell with you?"

"Sir James Audley," said Audley.

"An ancestor perhaps? That would be highly appropriate." The eye closed for an instant. "The O'Conors themselves were kings of Connaught in those days, would you believe it! But Chandos now—"

"Sir John Chandos," said Audley.

"That's the man. Chandos, Manny, Holland, Burghersh, Audley, Mowbray, Beauchamp, Neville, Percy—aye, and the Black lad himself . . . all names to conjure with, David. As fine a band of cutthroats as ever left home to make their fortunes at someone else's expense! But Chandos first and last—and best."

Butler looked questioningly from one to the other, completely at sea, and the major caught the look. "Never heard of

Sir John Chandos, Corporal? What *did* they teach you at school?"

Butler flushed with shame at his latest display of ignorance. The full extent of his medieval history lay between the covers of E. Wilmot Buxton, but there had been none of those names in those pages; and the rest of his historical knowledge coincided exactly with the School Certificate syllabus, which had acknowledged nothing before 1815.

His tongue was like a piece of balsa wood in his mouth.

"Tell the man, David," said the major.

Audley glanced at Butler sympathetically. "Hundred Years' War and all that, Corporal—the Black Prince and the battle of Crécy, 1346—" He blinked and cut short the recital of facts as though they irritated him.

"Go on," the major urged him. "Sir John Chandos?"

Audley turned towards him. "What's Sir John Chandos got to do with us . . . sir?"

"I said *go on*, Mr. Audley," said the major. "And I dislike repeating instructions."

Audley's chin lifted. "I didn't know it was an order, sir. Chandos was a fourteenth-century soldier, one of Edward III's field commanders and a comrade of the Black Prince's. That's all I know about him—except that he was famous for his courtesy and good manners."

Butler held his breath as the major's good eye became as fishlike for an instant as the glass one. Then the corner of his mouth twitched upwards.

"Not just for his good manners, David," he said coolly. "He was the greatest captain of the age—the complete fighting man, you might say. Crécy, Poitiers, and Najera, and a hundred skirmishes."

Audley met the stare. "Yes, sir?"

He hadn't actually said "So what?" but he hadn't left it quite unsaid, Butler realised. It had never occurred to him that officers as well as other ranks should have mastered the art of dumb insolence—or it might be better described as dumb arrogance in young Mr. Audley's case; and somehow he didn't think that it was a newly acquired skill.

But at least the set of the subaltern's jaw and the obstinate expression in his eyes settled one question: whatever there was wrong with Second Lieutenant Audley, it wasn't LMF.

Suddenly the major grinned disarmingly, displaying the full range of gold in his mouth.

"Welcome to Chandos Force, David"—he took in Butler with the grin—"and you, Corporal."

Butler kicked himself for a fool. He had quite forgotten that any test set by the major would be as foxy as the major himself.

Chandos Force?

"I—" Audley's jaw dropped. "Sir?"

"Chandos Force. Which I have the honour to command, and in which you have the honour to serve now—both of you."

The jeep was slowing down. As Butler was grappling with the significance of what had gone before he was also aware that the sergeant-major was searching the line of trees on the left of the road.

The major looked ahead briefly. "Another two hundred yards, Sergeant-major—you'll see the broken signpost on the opposite side." He swivelled back to them. "And what is Chandos Force going to do, eh?"

"Yes, sir." Audley sounded a little chastened.

"Naturally. Well, that one will discover in due course. But one is entitled to add two and two if one wishes—as I have . . . that is, if one is good at history as well as arithmetic."

The test wasn't over.

The jeep was crawling now, almost down to walking pace. But that didn't matter.

"I thought code names weren't meant to mean anything," said Audley slowly. "But this one does—is that it?"

"So I am authoritatively informed." The major nodded. "It was apparently coined by a historian like yourself—with an historical sense of humour, so I'm told."

The major was no historian obviously, thought Butler. But the major was the sort of man who would do his homework if he got half a chance, that was for sure.

"Then I presume we're going to follow in Chandos's footsteps, sir," said Audley. "I seem to remember . . . he covered a lot of country in his time."

The jeep turned off the road, though mercifully it was moving so slowly that there was no danger of a twenty-second collision in the back. Ahead of them Butler saw a track leading across open fields towards a low huddle of farm buildings from which several slender columns of smoke rose vertically in the still air, pale blue in the evening light.

Cooking fires, decided Butler hopefully.

"Very good, David! All you need now is the right word," said Major O'Conor.

The right word? There were vehicles under camouflaged netting among the trees ahead—the right word?

"Chevauchée," said the major. "We're going on a *chevauchée,* my boy."

"A *chevauchée*?" The incredulity in Audley's voice helped Butler to concentrate on his ears rather than his eyes. They would reach the buildings soon enough.

"One of Chandos's specialities. You know what it means?"

"Well . . . in modern French it's . . . 'a ride,' I suppose," said Audley pedantically. "But in medieval French . . . it was a raid—and more than a raid."

Audley had known more about the Hundred Years' War than he had admitted, but the major let that pass.

"Yes, David?"

Audley drew a deep breath. "It was the classic English tactic for taking what they wanted—take and capture, or rape, burn, pillage, and plunder on the march. That is, unless the people agreed to s-s-submit to their rightful lord, King Edward. But our chaps usually forgot to ask first."

There was a bearded man in a check shirt just ahead. He had a machine-pistol slung round his neck and a cigarette in his mouth.

"Yes . . . well I can't promise you all of that, though we'll do our best of course," said the major. "But we are going to take something, certainly."

The check-shirted man gave them a cheery wave without removing the cigarette. He wore khaki battle-dress trousers and army gaiters, Butler noticed with sudden surprise.

The farm buildings loomed up ahead.

"What are we going to take?" asked Audley.

Major O'Conor chuckled. "Why—a castle of course, just

as Chandos would have done. Except we're going to take it from the Germans, naturally."

5. How Second Lieutenant Audley chanced his arm

The men of Chandos Force shuffled into the barn in ones and twos for their final briefing.

From his chosen spot in the darkness just beyond the dim circle of light cast by the hurricane lamp Butler watched them with a sour mixture of contempt and disapproval.

The mixture embarrassed him, and also confused him because he couldn't square it with his impression of either Major O'Conor or Sergeant-major Swayne, who belonged to the world of soldiering which he understood. But these men—the major's men, the sergeant-major's men, and also (Jesus Christ!) his new comrades—came from another world altogether, and one which he did not understand at all.

He knew he was green and raw and wet behind the ears, and that the memory of the only shots he'd ever fired in anger —at the major himself—made his cheeks burn at the very thought of it.

And he knew that first impressions could be false impressions—

Must be false impressions.

It had looked more like a bandit encampment than a unit of the British Army about to go into action.

Not so much the weird assortment of non-uniforms—of knitted cap-comforters instead of berets or steel helmets, of flak jackets and camouflage smocks instead of battle dress, of bandoleers and belts of ammunition instead of standard webbing pouches. . . .

Not so much even the weirder assortment of weapons— machine pistols and automatic rifles, and LMGs which looked suspiciously German but just might be American; the anti-tank rocket launchers stacked by the farm gateway were certainly American; but there was not a Bren or a Sten to be seen, never mind an honest-to-God Lee Enfield rifle. . . .

No, not the dress and not the weapons . . . but the savoury cooking smells and the card games and the dice; and the casual greetings—no salutes—and the laughter in the background, all of which he had smelt or heard or glimpsed during the last half hour. All it had needed was a girl or two—say Dolores del Rio in a low-cut dress, with gipsy earrings—to complete the picture.

Chandos Force.
The Chandos Gang—

Must be false impressions.

Butler struggled with the evidence of his senses and his limited experience, as the sudden glow of the half-smoked dog-end in the mouth of the next man to enter the barn caught his eye. As the man stepped briefly into the lamplight Butler saw that he sported an Uncle Joe Stalin moustache.

In the Lancashire Rifles no rifleman or junior NCO dared to grow a moustache. In the Lancashire Rifles men stood close to their razors every morning without fail.

And when the ACIs were pinned on the notice boards appealing for volunteers for the paratroops or any other strange and wonderful units like this one, Lancashire Riflemen did *not* volunteer—the senior NCOs saw to that, their official reasoning being that anyone wishing to quit the best battalion in the finest regiment in the whole British Army must be bloody mad, and it wouldn't be right and proper to saddle other units with such madmen, particularly units which must already have more than their share of thugs, misfits, and criminals.

Over two happy years of mastering the basics of the only trade he had ever wanted to learn, Butler had become convinced of the inner truth of that simple logic. Everything he was told and everything he learnt fitted in with everything he had ever read and with those things which General Chesney had told him: that the highest moment in war was the ordinary line infantryman setting his face and his best foot towards the enemy in battle. All the rest—all the tanks and artillery and planes and staffs and generals—were but the means and the auxiliaries to that end.

He had tried to prepare himself for the ugly facts of pain and discomfort and dirt and smells which he knew would mask this truth. But he discovered now that he had relied far more on the shelter of the battalion itself: he had not prepared himself for this kind of war in this kind of unit.

He *wasn't* afraid, he told himself. Because this wasn't the feeling he had had by the side of the stream, when the major had shouted at him in German.

But he was alone, and he was unutterably and desolately *lonely*.

A sudden stir among the bandits, and then a spreading hush of their muttered conversations, roused him out of self-misery.

The sergeant-major strode into the lamplight and glowered around him into the darkness. He was still wearing his leather jerkin, but had forsaken his beret for a knitted cap-comforter.

"Purvis!" he barked into the gloom.

"S'arnt-major!" one of the bandits barked back.

"Everybody here?"

"S'arnt-major." Purvis paused. "One extra."

The sergeant-major frowned for a moment. "Corporal Butler!"

"Segeant-major!" Butler attempted to bark, but his voice cracked with the effort.

"Right." The sergeant-major swung round towards the doorway, his hand coming up to a quivering salute. "All present and correct, sir!" he roared into the darkness.

Second Lieutenant Audley stepped cautiously through the doorway into the circle of light, stooping to avoid the lintel.

The bandit in front of Butler inclined his head towards his neighbour. "Cor, bleedin' 'ell," he said in a deliberate stage whisper.

It was true that Audley looked absurdly young, despite his size. Indeed, his size seemed to emphasise his youth as he blinked nervously around him, with the squatter but menacing figures of Purvis and the sergeant-major on the edge of the light on either side of him, like wolves bracketing a newly born bull calf.

"'E wants 's mummy," stage-whispered the other bandit.

Bastards—Butler thought of the burnt-out Cromwells—
bastards.

The sergeant-major swung sharply towards the direction of
the whisper, his chest expanding. But Audley forestalled him.

"All right, Sergeant-major Swayne," he said softly. "Let
it . . . be."

He stared around him slowly, no longer blinking, as though
his eyes had become accustomed to the darkness and he could
see every last cobweb in the barn. The bruise on his cheek
seemed larger and blacker, brutalising one side of his face.

Maybe not a bull calf after all, thought Butler, but some
other animal. Or at least not a newly born bull calf, but a
young bull not so easily to be taken for granted.

Then the spell was broken as the other officers of Chandos
Force came out of the darkness behind him, two of them almost indistinguishable from the rank-and-file bandits, but the
third contrasting strangely with them because of his conventional smartness—

Three pips for a captain—Butler craned his neck and
strained his eyes—by God! not three pips, but a crown and
two pips—a full colonel, and with ribbons to match too! So
Major O'Conor wasn't in command of Chandos Force after
all. . . .

But it was the major who came in last, and it was the major
who took the centre of the lamplight, with all four officers
joining his audience.

The glass eye glinted unnaturally in its fixed stare as the
good eye ranged among them fiercely for a moment or two.

"All right, then"—the eye stopped for an instant, then
darted again left—right—left—"what I shall say now I shall
say once and once only, as is my custom . . . which all of you
know—and some of you know to your cost."

No one laughed. So that wasn't a joke, thought Butler; so
perhaps the bandits knew more about discipline than he had
thought on first sight.

"All except two." The major paused. "Mr. Audley you
have just seen. He comes to us from the South Wessex Dragoons and he speaks fluent French." He paused again, and
Butler tensed himself just in time. "Corporal Butler—come
here!"

Butler shouldered his way to the light, managing in the process to tread heavily and satisfactorily on the foot of the bandit who had whispered about Audley's mother.

"You see now Corporal Butler." Butler glared into the darkness—it was surprising how this one dim light could be so blinding. "The corporal comes to us from the Lancashire Rifles and he speaks fluent German—right, Corporal."

Butler made his way back to his original position. This time the bandit was ready for him, but this time he trod on the other bandit's foot.

"Mr. Audley and Corporal Butler are replacements for Mr. Wilson and Sergeant Scott. As such they have no formal duties at present—"

Butler frowned in the darkness, wondering what had happened to Sergeant Scott. Possibly his German hadn't been fluent enough for Major O'Conor's purposes?

"—with me—right." The all-seeing eye settled on Butler, as though the major knew that his attention was straying from the words which were only going to be said once. With an effort he shook himself free from Sergeant Scott.

The eye left him. "Now I am fully aware that there's only one damn question you want answered—namely, why we should have been transported across the length of Europe from our own private war into someone else's fight . . . particularly when our war was taking such a . . . promising turn.

"I am also fully aware that you are now confidently expecting the usual pack of lies which is the stable diet served to us by the Gadarene swine at GHQ."

Butler stole a glance at the bandit beside him. Somewhat to his surprise he saw in the dim light that the bandit was grinning; evidently the major was running true to form.

"However . . . in this instance the answers I have been able to elicit may actually bear some resemblance to the truth . . . indeed, even more incredibly, they show some faint glimmering of rational thought and old-fashioned common sense—to our advantage."

There was a slight ripple of movement among the bandits —either it was the word "advantage" or they knew that the preamble was over. What was certain, though, was that the major and his men understood each other perfectly.

"I say 'answers' because there are two of them.

"And the first one is that greater events swallow up smaller ones." The major smiled. "By which I mean that while we have been busy bringing aid and comfort to an ungrateful collection of Communist cutthroats, the Allies have been winning the war."

Butler frowned into the darkness. There had never been any doubt in his mind about that, not even in the blackest days of 1940 when he had known no better. Even when the *Hood* had been sunk his schoolboy confidence had only been shaken momentarily. It seemed more than unnecessary to restate the obvious now, deep in France in 1944—it almost seemed bad form.

The major rocked on his heels. "Ah . . . now I think you may be in danger of mistaking me . . . I cannot see all your expressions, but judging by the look on Sergeant Purvis's face—am I boring you, Purvis?"

All Butler could see of the moustachioed sergeant was his back, which was now rigid beneath its enveloping smock.

"Sir?" Purvis temporised. "No, sir."

"Perhaps you think I am making a patriotic address—do you think that, Purvis?"

"No, sir." This time there was no hesitation.

"I should damn well think not!" The major paused. "However, I can imagine that some of you may find it difficult to grasp literal truth when it is plainly stated. . . . Mr. Audley there, for example—his regiment has been mixing it with Panzer Group West and the German Seventh Army, who have no doubt been giving as good as they got."

Audley's chin lifted. "R-rather b-b-better than they g-got, actually," he said defiantly.

"Indeed?" The major's eye lingered momentarily on Audley. "Well then—I have good news for you, Mr. Audley"—the eye lifted—"and for all of you. Within the next forty-eight hours Panzer Group West and the Seventh Army will have ceased to exist—what's left of them will be in the bag just south of Falaise, caught between our army and the Americans. And it'll be the biggest bag since Stalingrad."

He paused more deliberately this time, to let *Stalingrad* sink in.

"But that isn't the point. The point is that there is no German army betwen Falaise and the Seine. And there is no German army behind the Seine . . . in fact, gentlemen, there is no German army between this barn and the river Rhine."

The place names bounced off Butler's understanding. The Seine was remote enough. But the Rhine—that was a river on another planet.

"What it amounts to, quite simply, is that the German front in France has collapsed," went on the major in a flat, matter-of-fact voice. "Last night a special light reconnaissance unit of the American army crossed the Seine west of Paris, and they crossed unopposed. Their armoured columns are already beyond Chartres and Orléans—they delayed at Chartres to spare the cathedral, but elsewhere they're meeting virtually no opposition. Some of their tanks are making sixty miles a day —their main problem is petrol, not Germans. According to the Air Force, there isn't a single major enemy unit moving west. What there is that's moving . . . is heading east, towards the Fatherland, as fast as it can go."

The Rhine—

No German army between this barn and the Rhine—

Sixty miles a day—

The Rhine.

The sense of what the major was saying finally penetrated into Butler's brain and exploded there.

The literal truth: *the German front in France had collapsed*.

"It's 1940 all over again," said the major. "Only this time they are on the receiving end, and they've no Air Force left and no Channel to hide behind. And there are ten million Russians breaking down their back door."

The literal truth: *the Allies have won the war*.

The full extent of the catastrophe overwhelmed Butler. The war was ending too soon for him—it was ending and he would have no part in it. While the Rifles were advancing to victory, he would be pissing around interrogating prisoners for Major O'Conor, far in the rear. He would wear a Victory Medal, and all it would mean was that he had passed School Certificate in German.

Peace loomed ahead of him like a desert.

"Very well, then!" The major's tone became brisker. "The

first answer leads to the second. To the north of us our armies
and the Americans are tidying up. To the west they are taking
the ports of Brittany. To the east they are in open country. To
the south they have stopped along the line of the river Loire
from the sea to Orléans."

He was playing with them, thought Butler bitterly.

"We are going south, across the river."

Butler's heart sank. If there was any real fighting left it
would be to the north and the east. The south could only be a
backwater.

There was a slight stir in the darkness to his right, and the
sound of a throat being cleared.

Major O'Conor picked up the signal. "Yes?" he challenged.

The throat was cleared again. "I was just wondering,
sir..." The sing-song Welsh voice trailed off hesitantly, but
Butler guessed instantly the question which must be uppermost in the Welshman's mind: there must still be a lot of
unbeaten Germans south of the Loire who might not yet have
heard that the war was over.

"Yes, Corporal Jones—you were just wondering?"

"Yes, sir—I was just wondering, see ... would that be
where the wine comes from, in the south like?"

"The wine?" The major was as unprepared for the question
as Butler was.

"Yes, sir. Lovely stuff it is, the French make—much better
than the Eyeties even. But they don't make it round here—no
grapes, see—and I was thinking ... not warm enough here.
But down south, that would be where they would be making
it." Corporal Jones sounded well pleased with his reasoning.
"And a lot of it, they make, too," he added. "So I believe."

"Then we must hope the Germans haven't drunk it all,"
said the major dryly.

"Oh ... now I hadn't thought of that, sir." The corporal
took the hint obediently. "Would there be enough of them to
do that then, sir?"

Butler watched the major intently. Every good unit had its
self-appointed funny man, and although he himself was fre-
quently unable to see the humour in the jokes they revelled in
he had learnt from his platoon sergeant that they performed a
useful function in relieving tension. The Welshman was a cut

above most of them too: he had let the major call him back to the serious matter in hand without conceding that large numbers of Germans were more important than large quantities of alcohol. Now it would be interesting to see how the major handled his question, because clever officers never attempted to beat such men at their own game.

"Yes . . ." The major pretended to give the question serious consideration. "Well now, perhaps Colonel Clinton could answer that one for us?" He turned slowly towards the little group of officers.

Good, thought Butler. The best way of all was to play humour straight, as though it was perfectly serious.

The full colonel stepped into the light and swung on his heel towards the audience. In catching his badges of rank Butler had missed his face; now he saw that he was youngish for that extra pip and that he didn't have the look of a regimental officer. The first of his three ribbons was a DSO certainly, but that could be won from a chair by brains or cunning. Only he also didn't have the sleek authority of the staff officer . . . more a hungry, almost suspicious look which Butler hadn't encountered before.

"Yes . . . well, it isn't easy to say with any certainty what the present strength of the German First and Nineteenth armies is." Colonel Clinton's voice wasn't regimental either; it was educated, but classless and quite different from both the drawl of Audley's colonel and Audley's own public-school stutter.

"Ten weeks ago they fielded thirteen infantry divisions, including five training divisions, plus three Panzer divisions and one Panzer grenadier division. But they've been bled white since then. Today . . . maybe eight infantry divisions, all well under strength and including Russian and Polish ex-POWs. Plus one first-class Panzer division—the 11th." Colonel Clinton gazed into space for a moment, as though mentally adding long field-grey columns of figures. "With a substantial noncombatant military element . . . say a quarter of a million uniformed personnel."

The figure of a quarter of a million hung in the darkness and silence of the barn. Butler hadn't thought to count Chandos Force, but he knew it couldn't be much over thirty.

"Thank you, sir," said Corporal Jones. "Thank you very much, sir."

Military intelligence, thought Butler. Only military intelligence would have figures like that, down to divisional numbers, at its fingertips.

"Quarter of a million men"—as though by tacit agreement Major O'Conor took over again—"who are not of the slightest interest to us."

It occurred to Butler that it was the Germans' likely interest in Chandos Force, not Chandos Force's lack of interest in the Germans, which was of more pressing concern; but nobody—not even Corporal Jones—seemed disposed to raise that point.

"Nor will we be of the slightest interest to them—certainly not since oh-eight hundred hours this morning"—the major paused very deliberately—"when the American Seventh Army and the French Second Corps landed in the South of France."

There was a stirring of excitement in the barn, and Butler closed his eyes. He had already accepted the bitter truth—*the Allies have won the war*—but the acceptance was still raw enough to render each piece of confirmation painful.

"So as of this morning what fighting strength they have will be drawn southwest, to delay the Americans and the French while the rest of the ragbag heads for home.

"We're not going to hinder them—we're not going to lift a finger against them—and provided we can reach our objective without getting in their way, there's no reason why they should want to lift a finger against us. All they want is a clear road to Germany, and we're not going to knock down any signposts—is that clear?"

For a moment there was silence. Then Audley made a curious hissing noise.

"Ssss . . ." The young subaltern fought the stutter briefly, shaking his head against it. "S-supposing we do run into them?"

The major smiled. "That's a fair question from a newcomer. And the answer is that we're here now because we're experts in not running into Germans behind their own lines. We've been doing it for six months in Jugoslavia in rather more difficult circumstances, and the powers-that-be reckon we can do it in France too. Does that answer your question, Mr. Audley?"

Butler found he could guess very well why Audley of all people would have found that fear uppermost in his mind: his whole brief military experience in the bocage country consisted of running headlong into Germans, with unpleasant results.

"Yes, sir," said Audley manfully.

"Good. Now—are there any other questions?"

Sergeant Purvis's back straightened again. "Sir!"

"Yes, Sergeant?"

"The objective, sir."

Major O'Conor's last remark in the jeep flashed into Butler's memory: *We're going to take a castle from the Germans.* But that didn't quite square with not lifting a finger against them, somehow.

The major looked towards Colonel Clinton. "Sir?"

The colonel nodded. "The exact nature and location of the objective is still a classified secret, Sergeant. All I can tell you is that . . . we are going south of the Loire to repossess certain items of property belonging to His Majesty's Government . . . extremely valuable property. You will be told the location when we are closer to it, but I'm afraid that I am not at liberty to reveal what the property is."

Not a castle, but *property*, thought Butler quickly.

Or . . . property *in* a castle.

Repossess. That was a black word in his vocabulary: it was what the bailiffs did at home when someone fell too far behind with the rent.

The thought of home reminded Butler again that he was in the midst of strangers. And yet when he thought about his homesickness he realised that he wasn't homesick for home, but for the comradeship and comfortable certainties of the battalion, where briefings were clear and concise, and objectives unclouded by mysterious secrets.

He was aware at the same time that he was desperately thirsty and lightheaded with hunger, and that the infection between the toes of his foot was itching abominably again. In the scale of his present unhappiness the first two weren't at all serious: he had water in his water bottle and plenty of his favourite oatmeal blocks, which were the unexpected delicacy of the twenty-four-hour ration packs. But that treacherous foot presented a real problem now, after he had missed out on the last treatment and might not have any privacy for some time to come. Opportunities for foot and sock washing, not to mention the application of the gentian violet, would probably be few and far between once Major O'Conor's *chevauchée* had begun.

"From whom, sir?" said Audley.

Butler couldn't make sense of the question, and from the look on his face neither could Colonel Clinton.

"From whom, Mr. Audley?" he repeated patiently. "What d'you mean—from whom?"

Butler felt sorry for the young officer. Whatever he was after, that patient tone made him look a fool. The odds were that even if he did get an answer now it would be a humiliating one.

"Y-yes, sir." Audley swallowed, swayed nervously—but stuck to his guns. "You said . . . r-repossess His Majesty's . . . property," he said, fighting the words with obstinate deliberation.

"So I did—yes, Mr. Audley," the colonel admitted.

"Will the . . . French Resistance . . . forces be co-operating with us in the . . . operation, sir?"

That was an unexpected question, but only because it didn't seem to follow from the previous one. It was also a disappointingly unimportant line of inquiry; maybe Audley wasn't so full of brains after all, but merely liked the sound of his own voice in spite of his stutter.

"No, Mr. Audley, they will not be." The colonel's tone was sharper now. "This is a strictly British military operation. We shall be travelling across the American Third Army zone— the Americans will assist us as necessary and will pass us through their southern flank into enemy territory. After that we will be on our own. We will thereafter use any local intelligence the French may be able to give us, but nothing more than that. Our only allies are speed and surprise. We're going in quickly and we're coming out quickly."

He raised his eyes from Audley to include everyone in the

barn. "I was coming to this part of the operation later, but I may as well deal with it now. I don't need to spell out what will happen if you get caught—the rules are the same here as they were where you've come from. It's up to you whether you want to be brave or not, but if you decide to talk . . . when you talk your cover story is that you are reinforcing an SAS party in the Morvan Mountains between Nevers and Dijon, but you've been airdropped prematurely because of engine failure. Your code name is Bullsblood, which they will have reason to believe because we've already planted it, and your rendezvous is at the old viaduct five kilometres south of Sauleuf. Your mission is to interdict the main road to the west— they'll believe that too, for the sufficient reason that the SAS is already at work there."

Butler wondered what the rules were that the colonel didn't need to spell out. But he could ask about them later, even though he had the feeling that he wouldn't like the answer.

"The difference this time is that your cover story goes for everyone you meet across the river, not just for the enemy. If you get separated and the Resistance or anyone else picks you up you are still Bullsblood, bound for Sauleuf. As far as you're concerned Chandos doesn't exist—you've never heard of it and you don't want to join it." The colonel's gaze returned to Audley. "Does that answer your question, Mr. Audley?"

For a bet it had answered it more fully than Audley had expected, Butler thought grimly.

For a moment Audley said nothing. Then he nodded his head. "Not exactly, sir. . . . B-but I can add t-two and two."

There was an undisguised note of arrogance in the subaltern's voice that turned the words into a challenge. Butler had never heard a second lieutenant speak to a really senior officer like that—he had never heard *anyone* speak to a superior like that. Either Audley was unbelievably innocent or after having had three tanks blown from under him he just no longer gave a damn for anyone.

The colonel looked at Audley curiously. Possibly he wasn't sure he'd heard the challenge—that his ears had deceived him. But the silence in the barn must surely confirm his suspicion, thought Butler: no one wanted to breathe for fear of missing his reaction.

"Two and two"—the colonel's curiosity got the better of him—"Mr. Audley?"

"Yes, sir. We're not going to fight the Germans—and we're not going to tell the . . . French. So . . . neither of them . . . knows about it—the property, I mean." Audley paused. "Not yet, anyway. So we're just going to nip in and p-p-p-pinch it from under their noses."

Bulging with brains, decided Butler.

And arrogance.

And innocence.

He stared at Colonel Clinton quickly—

The colonel was smiling. Or at least half smiling.

"Well . . . I hope you're right." The colonel shook his head. "Because if you aren't, then Chandos Force is going to have to fight an awful lot of Germans and Frenchmen during the next week."

6.   How Corporal Butler tasted the wine of Touraine

Sergeant Purvis shouldered his way through the crowd towards Butler.

"Harry Purvis," he announced, thrusting out a large hand.

The voice and the hand were friendly, which was a double relief when the two bandits on whose feet Butler had trodden had been watching him with what could only be hostile intentions.

"Jack Butler, Sergeant." He released his equipment for a moment in order to accept the hand.

"Harry," the sergeant corrected him. "Glad to meet you, Jack. Here—give us that"—he reached down and lifted the tangle of webbing pouches and pack before Butler could stop him—"and come along with me. Have you had anything to eat yet?"

Butler began to feel better. Irregular units like Chandos Force were bound to be informal, and no doubt Sergeant

Purvis had been told to look after him. But this easy comrade-ship was morale-raising.

"Not since this morning," he admitted.

"Christ! You must be bloody starving. We'll soon put that right," Harry Purvis nodded encouragingly. "And thirsty too, eh? Well, Taffy will fix that double quick."

Better and better, Butler congratulated himself as he strode through the bandit encampment beside the sergeant. Obviously he had let appearances deceive him; he should have known better that a man like Major O'Conor wouldn't run a sloppy show. Misfits they might be (his Rifleman's lessons couldn't be unlearnt in an hour), but the excellence of their commanding officer was bound to rub off on them as it did in any unit.

"That young sprig of yours—with the stutter—he's a bloody caution," confided Purvis, steering Butler round the corner of the barn towards the back of the house. "Does he always chance his arm like that?"

"I don't know," said Butler. "I only met him for the first time this evening. He's supposed to be very clever."

"Too clever by half, if you ask me. Lucky for him he was cheeking that colonel they just sent us, and not our Willy—he'll take a joke with the best of 'em, Willy will"—Purvis pointed to a doorway—"but he can't abide clever buggers. . . . In here, Jack."

Butler pushed open the door and stepped into a large lamp-lit room. The farmhouse kitchen it must be, he thought, as the warmth he always associated with kitchens engulfed him. The scrape of his iron-shod boots on the stone floor and the glint of lamplight on pots and pans hanging on the wall confirmed the thought.

There was a group of bandits clustered round something at the far end of the room to his right—clustered almost guiltily, like schoolboys, so it seemed to him as they turned towards him.

Harry Purvis came from behind him, and the schoolboys relaxed.

"What the hell are you lot up to?"

"Trying to get a cork out of a bottle without a corkscrew, boyo," said Corporal Jones.

"What have you done with the corkscrew?"

"Our Willy's taken it, that's what," said Jones with feeling. "And a couple of bottles to go with it, too."

Judging by the number of bottles at Jones's feet generosity was not one of his virtues.

"Well, push the bloody cork in then—haven't you got any sense?" snapped the sergeant. "Jack here's got a terrible thirst on him."

"Push the cork in? Man, you can't do that! This here is good wine—Grand Vin de Touraine, it says. You can't treat it like it was London beer, that would be a crime. Besides, it doesn't pour properly if you do that."

Butler felt in his pocket for his clasp knife. "I've got a corkscrew," he said. "It's not a very good one, but . . ."

"No such thing as a not-very-good corkscrew." Jones advanced towards him. "Jack is it? Well, I can see you're a man to know, Jack boyo. A man to keep in with . . . so you shall have the first drink from this bottle, by God!"

There was nothing Butler wanted less than alcohol on an empty stomach; what he had been thinking of longingly was a huge mug of hot, sweet tea. But it would clearly be a bad mistake to reject the Welsh corporal's offer in the circumstances, when he had made such a good beginning.

"There now!" Jones drew the cork and poured a generous measure of wine into a tumbler. "Grand Vin de Touraine—which is where we're going to, so nothing could be more fitting for the occasion. Like a taste of things to come, you could say, eh Jack?"

He offered the glass to Butler.

Which is where we're going?

Harry Purvis was off the mark a second later. "What d'you mean, Taf—where we're going?"

"What I say, that's what I mean, Harry boyo." Jones drove the corkscrew into another cork.

"You know something I don't, then."

"I shouldn't wonder at all." Jones drew the next cork, put the bottle on the table beside him and seized another bottle. "I know a lot of things you don't, and that's just one of them."

Butler put his glass to his lips and sipped cautiously. The wine shone pale yellow-gold in the lamplight, and it tasted

pale yellow-gold too, light and dry and infinitely refreshing. It
was the heavy red wines that must be dangerous, he decided
—this was little more than a fruit juice. He drained the glass
thirstily.

"That's the spirit!" Jones filled his glass again, nodding his
head approvingly. "This Touraine is going to be a bit of all
right, I'm thinking." He lifted a glass of his own.

"Who told you it was Touraine?" asked Harry Purvis.

"Who told me? Who told me?" Jones drank, winking at
Butler as he did so. "Why, man, our Willy told me, that's
who. Who d'you think I get my information from, eh?"

"When?"

"Just now he did—just before you came in, when he took
our corkscrew." Jones snapped the clasp knife shut and returned it to Butler. "Nothing wrong with that, Jack, so you
look after it carefully. I had a little knife like that once—sto-
len by an Albanian it was. He didn't call it stealing though,
'redistribution of property' he called it, and he was a terrible
redistributor of other people's property until the Eyeties
caught him at it. Then they redistributed him. So I got myself
a bigger knife from one of his friends, but it doesn't have a
corkscrew, I'm sorry to say."

Harry Purvis sighed. "What did our Willy say?"

"I was just telling you. Came in looking for a corkscrew, he
did. And then he spotted these here bottles, and he said 'I'll
have a couple of those, then,' bold as brass." Jones shook his
head. "Of course, I didn't say anything, but he saw the look
in my eye and he says 'Is there anything the matter, Corporal?' as though he doesn't know perfectly well that I had a
whole case of red wine sent to the officers' mess. And so I
said, 'I thought you liked the red better than the white, sir'—
which is nothing less than the truth, although it wasn't what
I'd had in mind when he laid hold of our bottles, I can tell
you.

"And he said 'Aye, so I do. But this that you've kept for
yourself, Corporal, comes from where we're going, and I've a
mind to try it'—now, isn't that what he said, lads?" Jones
appealed to the other NCOs.

There was a chorus of agreement.

"Not that I disagree with him, mind you." Jones splashed

some more wine into his glass and then into the empty glasses which were stretched out towards him. "Knocks spots off what we've been used to, and that's a fact—here, Jack, you're missing out, and there's plenty more where this came from."

Butler's glass had emptied itself again somehow. Two pints of beer was his self-imposed limit, but this wasn't in the same class as beer. And besides, he hadn't had half a pint of it yet, so far as he could judge, so he could take no very great harm from another cup or two.

Jones nodded encouragingly as he filled the glass. "There now . . . so it's Touraine for us then, wherever that is. But if there's plenty of this"—he raised the bottle—

"And no bloody Germans," said someone.

"Ah, now *there*"—Jones pointed the bottle at the speaker —"now there you have put your finger on a matter of greater interest to us, I'm thinking."

"But they're all buggering off home, Taf. Our Willy said so."

"So he did, boyo, so he did. And maybe it's true, and maybe it isn't."

"Oh, come on, Taf! If the Yanks are over the Seine—"

"And we've landed in the South of France, Taf—"

Jones raised the bottle to silence them. "All right! If it's the Gospel truth, then it's in a mean, nasty, and disinheriting mood they'll be in, I'm thinking—remember those Waffen SS troops that chased us that time? The ones out of Sarajevo? Nasty, they were . . . and I can't see them going home without a fight, either, no matter what."

"But they're in Jugland, Taf."

"Those ones are. But what about the ones that are here, eh?" Jones shook his head mournfully, reducing the company to silence in contemplation of unpleasant possibilities. Butler was reminded suddenly of Colonel Clinton's reference to the rules which didn't need to be spelt out.

For once his curiosity was stronger than his shyness. "What happens if we get captured?" he inquired. "I mean . . . I know what the officer said, but . . ." He trailed off helplessly.

"Get captured?" Taffy Jones seemed highly amused. "Name, rank, and number—and just leave the rest to them."

He put the bottle down on the table and drew his finger across his throat, grinning horribly.

"Put a sock in it, Taf," said Sergeant Purvis sharply. "We don't get captured, Jack—that's the short answer."

"Ah—but he wants the long answer, Harry," said Jones, unabashed. "And the long answer is . . . make sure that you're taken by the proper German army, boyo. Not bad fellows they are—just like you and me . . . shoot you, they will, most like—just like we'd do in the same place—unless you're a *very* good liar, that is . . ."

Butler stared at him.

"But that's all they'll do," continued Jones. "But now . . . if it's the Abwehr or the Feldgendarmerie—what are like our Redcaps, the Feldgendarmerie—if you're lucky then they'll shoot you too. But you've got to be lucky, mind."

He picked up the bottle and filled Butler's glass.

"It's the SS you've got to steer clear of. Because they don't take name, rank, and number for an answer, they don't. They like a lot more than that, and they aren't fussy about how they get it, either. So with them it's like Harry says: you don't get captured." He smiled. "It's like at the pictures, with the cowboys and the Indians—you save the last bullet for yourself, see?"

Butler was appalled.

Sergeant Purvis shook his head in exasperation. "I didn't mean that at all, and you know it full well, you stupid Welsh git." He turned towards Butler. "With the major running things we just don't get caught, that's what I mean, Jack. It was that bloody colonel—what's-'is-name—who started that bloody hare, because he doesn't know any better. Our Willy's always one bloody jump ahead of everyone—the bloody SS included, you take it from me, Jack. Otherwise we wouldn't be bloody here, and that's a fact."

The chorus erupted again—

"Aye—"

"You're dead right there, Harry—"

"You silly sod, Taf—"

—reassuringly. Butler smiled foolishly, ashamed of his momentary cowardice. Every unit had its Taffy Jones. What he must remember was that every unit did not have its Major O'Conor.

"All right, all right, *all right*." Taffy Jones acknowledged defeat. "In any case, that's not what's really important—not what's really *interesting*."

He was changing the subject now the joke had gone sour on him, thought Butler. One beneficial effect of a glass or two of wine was that it sharpened the wits: he could see clear through the little Welshman—and out the other side.

"What's so interesting?" he asked magnanimously.

"Ah—I can see you know, Jack," said Jones, first pointing the empty bottle at Butler, then sweeping it round to include the other NCOs. "But they don't—they haven't thought of it even!"

"And what's that then, Taf?" Someone caught the Welsh intonation, saving Butler from having to reveal that he was as much at sea as the rest of them.

"Why, man—His Majesty's *extremely* valuable property, of course." Jones looked round triumphantly. "What is it that we're going to . . . *repossess*? That's what I'd like to know, eh."

His Majesty's extremely valuable property . . . the Welshman was right at that—it was interesting. Butler found himself exchanging a glance in silence with Sergeant Purvis, and for a moment it was like gazing into a mirror revealing his own mystification.

Jones's eyes settled on him. "Now you, Jack . . . you've been with our Willy all the afternoon. So it's wondering I am whether he maybe let slip a little something, eh?"

Butler scratched his head. "Well, Corporal—"

"Taffy's the name, Jack boyo."

"Taffy . . . well, all he said was we were going to take a castle from the Germans—" he began doubtfully.

"Ah—from the Germans. So we *are* going to fight them!"

"Not necessarily," said Sergeant Purvis. "Could be that they're going to move out and then we're going to move in—before the bloody frogs do, like."

Jones gestured with the bottle. "Now, you could be right there, Harry—that fits in with it nicely, that does. If we're not going to have anything to do with the Frenchies, that could

mean we're more worried about them than about the Germans
—and that also explains why we've to nip in quick-like, before they can do the same." He nodded at the sergeant.
"Ye-ess, Harry boyo—that would account for it."

Butler frowned. "Does that mean we may have to fight
them?"

"Won't be the first time if we do, Jack." Jones looked at
him seriously. "Terrible funny lot, the Frenchies are—proud,
like."

"But . . . we're on the same side."

"Oh yes—we're on the same side. But they're not on our
side, see. They're only on their side."

"Like Wales, Taf," said one of the NCOs. "You're not
fighting for the ruddy English, are you?"

"I am not," Jones said with a flash of anger. Then he
smiled. "Except that somehow you've got the whole bloody
world fighting for you. . . . But I'm right about the frogs. They
don't love us, and that's the truth. Not since we sank those
ships of theirs after Dunkirk—in North Africa somewhere."
He nodded, turned the nod into a shrug, and then turned
quickly towards Butler. "And that was all he said, our Willy,
Jack?"

"Aye." Butler concentrated on the valuable property problem. "Couldn't be a secret weapon of some sort, could it?"

The sergeant pursed his lips for a moment, but finally
shook his head. "No, I shouldn't think it's that. Bit late in the
day for secret weapons now . . . and . . . 'certain items of property' was what the man said. That doesn't sound like a
weapon to me."

" 'Valuable,' he said too," said Jones. "Extremely valuable."

"Sounds like money to me," said the man who had ribbed
Jones.

"Or gold and jewels," said a tall, hatchet-faced man. "Like
the crown jewels, maybe. Or old pictures, like they have in
the museums—and that sort of stuff. Some of it's worth a
fortune—it must be, because they have burglar alarms and
people watching over it all the time."

"Now *that's* what I call good thinking, Vic." Taffy Jones
produced another uncorked bottle from somewhere and filled

everyone's glass. "Because that's the way I was thinking. See, there was something in the way the colonel spoke made me think this stuff's been there a tidy old time—in Jack's castle —maybe ever since 1940, say. And what I was thinking was that it 'ud make sense if they couldn't get it out of France then to hide it away somewhere safe-like, just so the Germans didn't get it, whatever it is. But now maybe the Frenchies have got wind of it, see."

"But if it's British property—the property of our government—" Butler protested.

"British property? British property?" Taffy Jones repeated the words, his voice rising incredulously. "Boyo, you know what we are?" He tapped his chest with the new bottle.

"We—are?" Butler blinked. "Well...we're Chandos Force."

Jones tutted sarcastically. "No, no—we're the British Liberation Army, that's what we are. And the French, they are the French Liberation Forces. And *this*"—he put down his glass and his bottle carefully on the table beside him and pulled back his cuff—"what do you think this is?"

"It's a watch," said Butler.

"It's a gold watch—a *liberated* gold watch. I know, because I liberated it myself. And I hope to liberate a lot more before I'm finished"—Jones picked up the glass and the bottle again—"like liberating this Grand Vin de Touraine."

Butler couldn't help smiling back at the grinning Welshman. The doctrine was familiar—everything that wasn't screwed down was fair game, and there were plenty of men like Taffy who also carried screwdrivers; even the general had praised the Aussies as being the finest thieves in the 1918 army as well as the best assault troops. But this was still accepting robbery on a grander scale than was right and proper.

Sergeant Purvis clapped him on the back, laughing. "You stick close to Taf, Jack—he's born to be hanged....But the little bugger's right: the bloody Germans had been stealing the bloody frogs blind, so you can't blame them for trying to do the same to us. Ony I still want to know where this Touraine place is, that's what I want to know."

"Now there you have me," said Taffy Jones. "If it was

Koritsar, or Monastir, or Gostivar . . . but Touraine—" He
looked at Butler questioningly. "You have the sound of an
educated man, Jack. Or maybe you have a map of France in
your pocket like you have a corkscrew, eh?"

Butler grinned back a little foolishly. He was far from the
bit of western Normandy he'd studied back in England, and
School Certificate geography had left him no memory of the
different parts of France. But Touraine sounded as though it
was connected with Tours, which so far as he could recall was
a city right in the middle of the country—a city on the river
Loire, which they were about to cross.

"I think it's just across the river—the river Loire," he said
hesitantly.

"Go on! Maybe we're not going to have to travel so far,
then!" said Jones enthusiastically. "I don't really like all this
driving down roads like we owned the place—it's all very
well for our Willy, he travels in the middle, like. But I always
seem to be in that front jeep, clinging onto a bloody great
machine gun—I think the Swine's got it in for me, you
know." He wagged his head at Butler. "That's our good friend
Company Sergeant-major Swayne, in case you haven't met
him, Jack."

"I have met him," said Butler. For once his shyness had
deserted him, he felt. But then it was impossible to be shy in
this friendly company. "I pointed a Sten at him, and he didn't
like it."

"What happened? Did it jam?" said someone.

"Of course it jammed," said Jones. "Here now—we'll give
you something better than a Sten, you don't want that cheap
mass-produced rubbish." He reached under the table and produced a stubby submachine gun with a wooden stock, quite
unlike anything Butler had ever seen. "Beretta .38—best little
gun ever made, you take it from me, Jack. None of your
Thompsons or Schmeissers, so-called. That's real high-quality
steel, that is, machined the hard way. You wouldn't get better
stuff out of Ebbw Vale than that—that's made to last, that is."

The Welshman stroked the gun with the same reverence he
had earlier bestowed on the wine bottle. His enthusiasm was
clearly split fifty-fifty.

"Did you really point a Sten at the sergeant-major?" asked someone.

"Well—not deliberately—" began Butler.

"Swayne by name and swine by nature," said Jones to no one in particular. "But a good soldier, I'll give him that."

"Wonder what he'll do now we've won the war."

"They'll send him to fight the Japs."

"Buggered if I'm going to fight the Japs. He's welcome to them."

"The Americans'll fight the Japs."

"What about the 14th Army in Burma—they're fighting the Japs. I've got a brother in the RAF there. He says they call it 'the Forgotten Army.' "

"Ah—well that must be why I'd forgotten about them, then."

Everyone laughed, and Butler found that he was laughing with them. It was a good joke, that one: the forgotten Forgotten Army.

Taffy Jones tugged at his sleeve. "Have you that corkscrew of yours handy?" He upended the bottle he was holding in order to illustrate his need.

Butler fumbled in his pockets, eventually found the knife and promptly split his thumbnail prizing open the corkscrew.

"All in a good cause," said Taffy, spearing the cork. "And what are you going to do after the war then, Jack? Smart lad like you will have a cushy billet lined up, I'll be bound."

It seemed unreal, talking about the war's end. Everything he had planned had been based on the war giving him the training and the professional polish he needed. Now that it was ending prematurely he could no longer see his way clearly.

He held out his glass. Taffy Jones filled it carefully and then stared at him across it. "Don't look so miserable, boyo. With just a bit of luck we're not going to have to do any more fighting. Our Willy'll see to that, and he's a man you can rely on."

"That's just it," confided Butler miserably. "I was relying on taking part in the fighting."

"Now—there you surprise me." Taffy looked around for his glass and finding nothing in reach drank from the bottle.

"It's a nasty rough business, fighting is. Fighting"—he tapped Butler on the chest—"fighting should be left to soldiers."

Butler frowned at him, remembering his recent testimonial for the little Italian submachine gun. "But we are soldiers," he said stupidly.

"No, we're not." The finger which had tapped Butler's chest now waved in front of his eyes negatively. "We're civvies in uniform. I was a tool-maker before the war—a trained tool-maker. You were—whatever you were." The Welshman took another swig from the bottle. "And after the war we'll go back to civvy street, and they'll expect me to be a tool-maker again . . . and you'll be—whatever you were before."

"No," said Butler, thinking of his school blazer, which had been too small for him during the whole of his last year. "No."

"Yes. When I say 'soldiers' I mean professional soldiers."

"But that's what I want to be—a professional soldier," said Butler.

Taffy Jones stared at him incredulously. "Go on? You want to march up and down in a red coat, all bullshit and saluting? Never!" He blinked. "How long have you wanted to do that?"

"Ever since I was a little lad. Ever since I saw our county regiment march through the city with fixed bayonets and drums beating—it was the most beautiful thing I've ever seen—" Butler stopped abruptly, shocked by his own words. He had never told anyone that, not even the general. He'd never even put the thought into words before.

Taffy scratched his head. "And what do your da and your ma say to that? If I'd have told my da I was going for a soldier he'd 'uv tanned my arse for me."

"My mum's dead. And my dad doesn't know." It was easier to speak now; it was almost a relief. "He'll be wild when he does find out. He thinks the Army is there to hold down the workers—like in the General Strike."

"Dead right he is too." Taffy nodded vigorously. "That's what they did in Wales, by God—Winston Churchill sent them down to do it, and he'll send them down again without a second thought, I shouldn't wonder . . . and then will you fix your bayonet on your own da, Jack?"

Butler tried to thrust the image out of his mind. "It won't

happen like that again—things have changed since then." He reached for something to obliterate the image, since it wouldn't go away. Anything would do. "I'm going to be an officer, too. My company commander says he'll sign my WOSB application. It's a good career, the Army is. You know where you are in the Army."

"Jesus Christ!" Taffy Jones's face seemed to float away. "D'you hear that, Harry?"

Butler was flustered by Sergeant Purvis's presence at his shoulder. He had the feeling that he'd been talking too quickly and too loudly—and saying too much. It didn't seem to matter that the Welshman had heard him, somehow; but the thought that anyone else had overheard him was embarrassing.

"Not going to put the bayonet into his da, he isn't—he's only going to give the order for it," said Taffy. "Jack boyo, I'm disappointed in you, I am."

"Well, I'm not," said Sergeant Purvis. "It's the right place to be—giving the orders. And the right place to be giving them is in the Army, too. You're the bloody fool, Taffy—not Jack. He's the smart one."

"What d'you mean?"

"I mean, you bloody Welshman, that it isn't going to be all beer and skirts in civvy street after this little lot. It's going to be hard work and ration cards if you're lucky, and the dole queue and a small packet of Woodbines if you aren't." Purvis looked at Butler. "Unless you've got a nice fat nest egg tucked away somewhere, which none of us have—and I don't mean the demob gratuity they've promised either, because no one's going to get fat on that."

Butler frowned at him.

"The best place to be is in the Army of Occupation *and* an officer, like Jack says," Purvis continued. "That way you'll get the best of everything—the best food and the best drink and the best women."

Butler was disappointed in Sergeant Purvis. He was also aware for the first time that he was a little lightheaded, so that he couldn't think of the right word with which to express his feelings. The trouble was that he had clean forgotten to eat anything—that was the trouble.

"The thing you've got to worry about, Jack," said Purvis, "is whether you really can get that commission of yours, because as of now they're not going to be so easy to pick up, once they start cutting the Army down. The bastards are going to be able to pick and choose from now on—and they'll pick bloody hah-hah jobs like your Mr. What's-'is-name with the stutter."

Taffy nodded his agreement. "You're dead right there, Harry. It'll be like before the war—not what you are, but who you are. And not what you know, but who you know."

Butler looked from one to the other. They were good blokes, he decided—the best, in fact. But they were absolutely wrong.

The only problem was that he couldn't remember why they were wrong any more.

"Influence in high places, that's what you want," said Taffy Jones wisely. "Influence in high places—and that's what you and me haven't got, boyo."

Influence—

Suddenly it all came back to Butler with a rush, why it wouldn't be the same as last time.

Because this time there were the Russian Communists— millions and millions of them, all armed to the teeth. That was why there'd be a big Army still, and a place for him in it.

The arguments were all there now, at his fingertips. But they were jumbled up like the pieces of a jigsaw. It hadn't been his father who had said that about the Russians, for all that he loathed the Communists and was always scheming to keep them out of the union's affairs. They weren't to be trusted—the general said the same thing, and when his father and the general agreed on something then it had to be true, he felt that in his bones.

The general!

He pointed triumphantly at Jones. "But that's just it, Taffy: I *have* got influence in high places—I've got the general-in-chief of the regiment, who is a colonel . . ." That didn't sound right. ". . . I mean, the colonel-in-chief of the regiment, who is a general—he's a very good friend of mine. A friend of the family. My father was his sergeant-major."

He found to his surprise that he was looking at the end of

his finger, which was waving in the front of the blur of Taffy Jones's face. He noticed that he'd broken the nail on something.

Someone took his arm—it was Sergeant Purvis.

"What you need, mate, is something solid in your stomach," said Purvis distantly. "Taffy—there's some cold stew in the pot. Get it heated up."

Butler had just been thinking happily that the irritation between his toes had entirely disappeared—he couldn't feel a thing even when he stamped his foot. But now there was something very strange and unpleasant going on in his stomach—something the mention of cold stew was causing to rise—

"No—" he began thickly, as the room started to tip up under him.

7.   How Corporal Jones answered a civil question

The darkness was thick and warm, and it revolved around Butler not in a circle but in a great swirling ellipse.

He steadied in it and was sick.

Then he was on his knees, the sweat clammy on his face, and he was being sick again.

And again.

Now there was a hand on his shoulder.

"That's right, boyo—get it off your chest—that's right . . . Now, put your finger down your throat—go on . . ."

Butler leaned forward until he lost his balance. His head struck something hard and rough, preventing him tipping over altogether. It was a stone wall, and he felt grateful to it for being there.

Then he was sick again, and this time his stomach hurt with the spasm of it. He'd made a terrible fool of himself, but the sickness mattered more than the foolishness.

*   *   *

Then he felt a little better.

"Jack?" A hand touched his shoulder.

Feeling better made the foolishness matter more than the sickness. He pretended not to hear the voice.

"He still out?" Another voice, harsher and further away.

"Doesn't know whether it's Monday or Christmas. Proper waste of good wine."

Taffy Jones.

"But you got what we wanted?"

Harsher voice.

"Oh yes . . . spilled the beans he did, before he spilled his guts. Like taking chocolate from a baby." Taffy Jones's voice grew fainter. "I tell you—"

A wave of nausea cut off the fading words. There wasn't anything left inside him to throw up, but his stomach was still behaving as though there was. More than that though, he was angry that he was missing what was being said about him. Beans and chocolate weren't things he wanted to think about, but there was something there which he must try to remember, and already he was beginning to forget it.

The stone wall was hurting his head, so he put his hands flat on it and took the strain.

That was better. And he wasn't feeling so bad now either— he was just feeling awful.

Also . . . there was something he had been meaning to ask Sergeant Purvis, and he had forgotten to ask it, and now he couldn't remember what it was. Or he'd meant to ask somebody, and Sergeant Purvis would be more likely to give him a straight answer than Taffy Jones.

Because like the Communist Party, Taffy Jones wasn't to be trusted.

The voices were coming back.

". . . get him put together. He can't travel like that."

The harsh voice again—he couldn't place it.

Taffy Jones said something he couldn't quite catch. Then—

". . . we can put him in the truck to sleep it off."

Grunt. "So long as he don't vomit over the equipment."

Butler closed his eyes in the darkness. That grunt had been expressive of complete contempt. If there was anything worse than getting what one didn't deserve, it was getting in full what one did deserve, he reflected miserably.

A flashlight threw his shadow against the wall.

He heard noises, voices.

"Come on, then," said Taffy Jones. "Let's be having you."

Butler sat back on his heels.

"Drink this."

He was about to protest that he didn't want to drink anything when he felt the heat of the mug which was thrust into his hands.

"Drink it up."

Not tea but coffee. Scalding-hot unsweetened coffee, black in the light of the torch. It burnt his mouth.

"It's too hot."

"Shut up—and drink up. We're moving out, man."

"W-what?"

"Drink."

Butler drank, feeling the fierce heat course down into him, cauterizing as it spread.

"Get up."

He was past arguing. The cup was taken from his hands. His equipment was draped over his shoulders. First the webbing belt was clipped together, then his shoulder flaps were unbuttoned to receive the cross-straps and then buttoned over them. He was being put together again. Finally his Sten was hung round his neck and something was pulled down roughly on his head—whatever it was, it wasn't his steel helmet.

"Come on, then." A hand propelled him.

"Where are we going?" he asked hoarsely.

"To the Promised Land. And you're going to travel there in style, boyo. So make the most of it."

The torch flashed ahead of him and he saw men moving in its beam. Men loaded with equipment. Engines started up all around him. The light picked out a truck directly in front, a small three-quarter-ton weapons carrier. The tailboard was down and the canvas flaps thrown back to reveal its load of miscellaneous equipment and jerrycans.

"In you go, then," said Jones briskly, directing the torch beam into a small space between the jerrycans.

The night air and the walk and the coffee were working inside Butler to restore him to the human race. He could even feel a stirring of anger now; chiefly it was directed against himself for the sort of behaviour he had hitherto observed with contempt in others. It was true that he hadn't set out to drink too much, as they so often did on a Saturday night with such mindless enthusiasm. But it was also true that he didn't even like alcohol very much—and more, that he had been warned against it by both his father and the general, each in his different way. It was the general's more oblique warning which hurt him more now, because in cautioning him to watch out for the untrustworthiness of men who drank too much the old man had taken for granted that he would never be such a man.

"Go on," urged Jones, more impatiently, taking his arm.

Butler shook the hand away. A little piece of that anger tarred his father and the general for not warning him more strongly when to beware the demon, but a much larger one blackened Taffy Jones, who had filled him up with wine and then betrayed him.

But there was nothing he could do about that now, when he was in the wrong himself. That accounting would have to wait.

He reached forward and took hold of the side of the truck. As he lifted his leg to lever himself aboard his knee struck the butt frame of the Sten, driving the gun upwards. Somehow the sling had twisted during the walk in the darkness and the movement of the gun tightened it round his neck, half choking him and throwing him off his balance.

"Oh, for Christ's sake!" exclaimed Jones.

Butler untangled the Sten with clumsy fingers in the light of the torch, grasped the side of the truck once more, and attempted to hoist himself up. But this time, just as his foot was settling on the floor, he felt Jones pushing him from behind. His boot skidded along the metal, bounced off a jerrycan, and lost its foothold altogether.

Meine Stiefel, he thought irrelevantly. Meine bloody Stiefel.

Jones gave an exasperated growl. "For fuck's sake," he hissed at Butler, "get into the bloody truck, man!"

Butler started to move again, and then stopped.

Meine Stiefel!

He turned towards Jones. "What happened to Sergeant Scott?" He stared blindly into the torch's beam. "And Mr.—Mr. Wilson—the men we're replacing?"

There was noise and movement all round him, he could sense it in the darkness. But he could also sense the silence behind the beam of light which blinded him.

Then the light left his face. "None of your business, boyo," said Jones, reaching forward to push him towards the truck again. "None of your business."

Butler's anger erupted. Before he could stop himself he had swept Jones's arm out of the way and had grabbed the little Welshman by the throat with one hand while the other spun him round against the tailboard. The man's cry of surprise, half stifled by the choking hand at his neck, turned to one of pain as he was bent backwards into the jerrycans.

"I said—what happened to Sergeant Scott?" Butler brought his knee up into Jones's crotch menacingly as he felt a hand clawing at him. The hand went limp

"Arrgh-arrgh-arrgh," mouthed Jones.

Butler slackened his throat-grip, at the same time grasping the free hand which had tried to claw him and slamming it hard against the truck.

"You f— *ahhh!*" Whatever Jones had planned to say was cut off by renewed pressure. "You're breaking my—breaking my back."

"What happened to Sergeant Scott?" Butler repeated, wishing he could see the Welshman's face.

Jones whispered something, but Butler resisted the temptation to lean forward to catch the words. The strength of his grip depended on his straight arm; once he bent his elbow he would also bring his face into range of a head-butt, which was the oldest last resort of all.

"Speak up, you little bugger," he snarled.

Jones relaxed. "Accident," he said hoarsely. "Had—an—accident."

"What sort of accident?"

Jones lay very still. "Shot himself."

"How?" Butler frowned in the darkness. He hadn't expected this answer, but when he thought about such an acci-

dent it wasn't so very surprising, particularly with the out-
landish selection of weapons favoured by Chandos Force.

"Cleaning his rifle," said Jones.

Butler was disappointed. "And Mr. Wilson?"

This time Jones seemed unwilling to remember. Butler
lifted his knee a little to jog his memory.

"Accident," said Jones quickly.

"Cleaning his revolver?" Butler kept the knee in position.

"No. Stepped on a mine." Jones's voice rose plaintively.

"Corporal Jones!" The sergeant-major's shout was unmistakable.

Jones struggled convulsively.

"CORPORAL JONES!" The shout was louder and nearer.

Butler held him down. "Next time I ask a civil question,
you give a civil answer—remember that," he said, quickly
letting go of the Welshman and stepping smartly to the side
out of his reach as he did so.

The sergeant-major loomed up in the darkness just as Jones
had managed to straighten himself. "Are you *deaf*, Corporal
Jones?"

"Sergeant-major!" Jones's voice cracked.

"Well—get that man into the truck double-quick and then
report to Sergeant Purvis *on the double, Corporal!*"

Butler didn't wait to be helped. Pushing Jones out of the
way, he hauled himself up among the jerrycans.

"Tailboard!" roared the sergeant-major.

Jones slammed the tailboard up and groped in the darkness
for the locking pin. He had lost his torch, thought Butler with
malicious satisfaction. Serve the little bugger right!

"Remember?" Jones hissed at him. "I'll remember, boyo—
you can bet on that."

"You do," said Butler.

"Don't you worry"—the little man was clumsy with rage;
Butler could hear the pin scraping as he searched for the
hole—"don't you worry about that."

"I won't," said Butler.

"No. You worry about having another accident—you worry
about *that*, boyo . . . just you worry about *that*."

*   *   *

The truck rocked as its crew came aboard. Away to the right a motorcycle was kicked into life. The shaded headlights of first one jeep, then another, then others, were switched on.

Chandos Force was going to war.

"You all right back there?"

Butler grunted and settled himself as best he could among the jerrycans. He wasn't at all sure that he was all right. He wasn't even sure why he had lost his temper with Jones like that; it had been as though there was someone else inside him. That was what drink did to a man, of course: he had remembered that simple question, the one he'd wanted to ask about Sergeant Scott, and——

The truck jerked forward, bumping over uneven ground and then tilting steeply up an incline before turning sharply onto a smoother surface. He watched the jeeps' headlights buck and tilt as they crossed the same ground, then flicker on and off as the trees of the farm track obscured them. They were heading for the main road——

He stared at the lights, hypnotised by the return of his memory. The simple question had not received a simple answer: Taffy Jones had been by turns unwilling to speak, and then frightened, and finally threatening. Yet even before that, when he had been throwing up the contents of his stomach against that stone wall——

Spilling the beans?

"Did you get what we wanted?"

That harsher voice questioning Jones—the voice he couldn't place at the time, but which now seemed oddly familiar.

"Yes . . . spilled the beans he did . . ."

What beans?

What did "we" want?

Who were "we"?

Too many accidents——

The truck swung sharply to the left, then slowed as the driver crashed the gears. They had reached the main road.

"Keep it moving, buddy!" shouted a rich American voice.

Chandos Force was going to war.

But there was something very wrong with Chandos Force.

8. How Corporal Butler heard of his death

Butler munched an oatmeal block and tried to analyse why he felt much better than he had any right to feel.

It was true that he still felt thirsty, even after having drunk at least a quarter of the precious contents of his water bottle, so that he had decided to forgo the extra pleasure of a couple of boiled sweets from his twenty-four-hour pack, since they were notorious thirst-increasers.

It was also true that he had slept most of the night away in spite of his cramped position, with only the haziest impression of numerous stops and starts, several rumbling Bailey bridge crossings, and shouted American exhortations at intervals to keep closed up and to keep moving.

But the fact remained that when he shook his head vigorously—he shook it again just to recheck the evidence—there was no headache, and the oatmeal block was expanding comfortably inside him. Indeed, if anything he was feeling rather better than he usually did before he had had the chance of a wash and a shave.

Maybe it was because he didn't feel as awful as he deserved that he was feeling better. But it was more likely, he decided dispassionately, that he had been lucky enough to be very sick before all the alcohol in that deceptively innocent wine could infiltrate his bloodstream. In fact he could recall now (and too late) that according to the hardest drinker in the platoon at the Depot the secret of heavy drinking lay in the proper defensive preparation of the lining of the stomach. Once the alcohol had advanced through that lining into the bloodstream then resistance was in vain, according to Rifleman Callaghan, who was accustomed to fortifying himself in advance with a huge, greasy fry-up of sausages and chips before drinking all comers under the table—a sovereign recipe he claimed to have had from a quartermaster who had devoted a lifetime to the study of the subject.

That problem resolved to his satisfaciton, Butler felt ready to tackle two more pressing ones.

Viewed from the vantage point of a clear head after several hours' sleep, the previous evening had the unreal shape of a nightmare. What was certain was that he owed an abject apology to Corporal Jones, who had encouraged him to be sick and whom he had rewarded with weird suspicions and physical assault, the very memory of which now made his flesh creep with embarrassment.

He swallowed the last of the oatcake and decided not to eat another. Instead he took an extra swig of water.

So the first thing to do was to apologise to the Welshman.

The second thing was to find a private place and treat his left foot with gentian violet. He could already feel the sharp irritation between the toes—after missing the treatment for a full twenty-four hours it was noticeably worse, not very far from being actually painful; which was hardly surprising since regular application was the key to the treatment.

He leaned forward and parted the canvas flap. The pitch blackness of the hour before dawn had passed, and he could feel the coming of daylight even though he couldn't yet see the division between land and sky. He sniffed at the air, but there was no strange smell other than exhaust fumes and warm rubber, which were familiar now. Yet there was still something disquieting to his senses.

Suddenly he knew what it was. Beyond the sound of the engines of the truck and the jeeps there was *no* sound. No distant gunfire, no drone of aircraft—nothing.

No flashes either—he stood up and twisted his neck to get a look ahead—and no flashes in that direction. He had had the distinct impression during the moments of half-consciousness on the journey that they had been travelling at breakneck speed, far too fast for safety, as though the Americans were determined to deliver them on time for some impossible pre-arranged zero hour. But it looked as though they hadn't come nearly as far south towards the river as he had estimated—that they were still in the middle of nowhere in the newly conquered territory of the Third Army.

Which was disappointing. They'd never manage a dawn

crossing of the Loire now, which was the obvious moment to slip across the river and through the German lines.

Someone was coming, he could hear the sharp tap of metal heel-plates on the tarmac.

"Five minutes... five minutes..." The voice that went with the metallic taps was Sergeant Purvis's. "Five minutes..."

Butler ducked down inside the back of the truck. Sergeant Purvis was one man he was ashamed to meet after his performance of the previous night.

"Five minutes"—the flap was jerked aside—"are you awake in there, Corporal Butler?"

"Yes, Sergeant," said Butler quickly.

A torch shone into his face. "How d'you feel, lad?" asked the sergeant, not unkindly.

"Okay, Sergeant."

"Then you must have a head like a bloody rhinoceros," said the sergeant. "We'll be stopping here for five minutes, anyway. So if you want a quick shit, now's your chance."

Butler thought of the water he'd just drunk. "Right, Sergeant."

Purvis watched him as he climbed out of the truck, which reminded him of the trouble he'd had getting into it. If Jones had told the sergeant about it, then this might be the occasion when the sergeant would choose to dress him down for his behaviour. Or he might be just checking to see that he was in a fit state for duty.

He stamped his feet and pulled his equipment straight. His knees ached a bit, but the ground had a good firm feeling to it. He reached back inside the truck and lifted out his Sten.

The sergeant was still watching him.

"Anything the matter, Sergeant?"

"Here, lad—" Sergeant Purvis handed something to him— it was smooth and cold. It was a bottle. "The hair of the dog... if you're feeling as rough as I think you are that'll set you up again."

Before Butler could reply the sergeant had turned on his heel and continued down the road.

"Five minutes... you've got five minutes—"

He hefted the bottle in his hand. It was about half full, he judged, and there was nothing in the world he felt less like than drinking. But in this darkness that at least was no problem. He made his way cautiously off the road onto a grass verge beside which a big motorcycle was parked. He had the vague impression that there was a field of low bushes, maybe waist-high, beyond it, but as he was about to cast the bottle into the bushes there was a movement among them. A moment later a string of curses in an exasperated American voice issued out of the darkness and a match flared among the bushes.

For a bet, that must be the owner of the motorbike, decided Butler. And for another bet, the owner of the motorbike would know where the convoy was heading.

The flame kindled again—it was a cigarette lighter, not a match—and there came a satisfied grunt with it: the Yank had found whatever it was he was looking for. Butler waited patiently beside the motorbike, listening to his precious minutes tick away, until a darker nucleus loomed up out of the field.

"Who's that?" said the Yank.

"A friend—British," said Butler. "Would you like a drink, Yank?"

The figure approached him. "What you got?"

Butler remembered that Americans were devoted to whisky. "Only wine, I'm afraid," he answered apologetically.

"Hell, mac, that's better than nothing. I've swallowed enough dust, my mouth's like the bottom of a birdcage."

"Help yourself then." Butler thrust the bottle into the American's hands. "I'll be back in a minute."

"Okay. But watch yourself down there . . . and don't eat any of those goddamn grapes—they'll give you the runs."

Grapes! So the low bushes were vines, Butler realised—and so they had indeed come far south of Normandy. He strained his eyes into the darkness as he unbuttoned his fly. He could just see—or now imagined he could see—a faint difference between the blackness of the sky and that of the land. But it was impossible to estimate how big the vineyard was—if it was a big one then the Loire couldn't be too far away.

He made his way back to the road.

"Thanks, mac," said the Yank.

"Keep the bottle, Yank," said Butler. "Where I'm going I'm told there's more of it."

"Uh-huh?" The American chuckled. "Smoke?"

It was on the tip of Butler's tongue to admit he didn't smoke, but then he remembered what he was about. "Thanks."

"Keep the pack. One thing we've got plenty of—and you won't find more of them where you're going, that's for sure."

"Thanks." Butler extracted a cigarette from the packet and leant forward towards the flame extended to him. He must remember not to inhale the smoke, which would make him cough if he did—

Christ! The broad white stripe and the white letters "MP" on the American's helmet were momentarily illuminated in the light of the flame: he had cheerfully offered illicit alcohol to a Military Policeman in a forward combat area!

The smoke found its way into his lungs and set him coughing. If anything, American cigarettes tasted even fouler than British ones.

But the American MP seemed as friendly as ever, the red tip of his cigarette glowing bright as he drew on it. "Ranger outfit, are you, mac?" he said amiably.

Butler managed to find his breath. Maybe American MPs were less bloody-minded than British ones; or maybe they took a more lenient view of foreign allies. "Ranger?" he repeated stupidly.

"Aw, hell—what d'you British call 'em—Commandos, that's it."

Butler thought of the brigands he had seen the previous night, and wasn't sure whether he was flattered or not. "Well —sort of, yes," he admitted.

"Uh-huh." The red tip flared. "Well, you should be okay getting across down there. There's a bunch of kraut infantry about five miles up river, where the bridge was—there was a couple of days back, anyway. But we haven't seen anything on this stretch so far. Real nice and quiet, it is."

Butler stiffened. The way the American talked, the Loire was not far away, but right there in front of them in the fast dissolving darkness.

"We're near the river, then?" he asked, casually.

The cigarette glowed. "Uh-huh."

"How far?"

In the distance Sergeant Purvis's voice started up again: *"Mount up . . . mount up."*

"How far, Yank?" Butler repeated the question.

"Mount up."

"Four-five miles, maybe." The cigarette glowed and then out into the vineyard. "Couple of miles from here, we drop down into the flood plain. Another two, there's a levee— that's where the 921st is, the bottom land there this side of it."

"Mount up."

"What's the river like?"

The American glugged the last of the wine and then heaved the bottle carelessly among the vines. "Nothing special. Wide, sandy bottom, lots of little islands covered in brush— not much water coming down now, so most of the channels are dry . . . pretty much like rivers back home, I guess: mean in the spring, but kind of lazy in the summer, 'cept where the current is." He grunted reassuringly. "No sweat crossing, that's for sure. I heard tell the 921st got a patrol on the other side a couple of days ago—no trouble. So you should get over real easy."

The Americans hadn't let the grass grow under their feet, thought Butler approvingly. But that had been what the general back home had said about them out of his experience in the great battles of 1918, when he had had a regiment of them attached to his division: what they lacked in experience they made up for in enterprise.

"How far did your patrol go?"

"Aw, not more than maybe five-six miles." The American paused. "Where you heading for, mac? You going far?"

It was annoying not to be able to answer that question. If this was the Loire just ahead and Touraine started on the riverbanks, then they could be quite close to their objective. But if Touraine was the size of Lancashire or Yorkshire . . . ? "I wish I knew," he began apologetically. "But I think—"

"Corporal Butler!" Sergeant Purvis's voice came sharply from just behind him.

Butler snapped to attention. "Sergeant!"

"Are you all right, Corporal?"

"Yes, Sergeant."

"Right. Fourth jeep in the rear, you'll find Mr. Audley. You'll be his driver from here on—understood?"

"Yes, Sergeant," answered Butler automatically. Then a hideous thought struck him. "But, Sergeant—"

"Don't bloody argue, man—*move!*" Sergeant Purvis banged the side of the truck with his fist. "Mount up!"

"But, Sergeant—" Butler trailed off as he realised he was no longer talking to anyone. Even the American had turned away towards his motorbike. He was alone with his problem.

Leaden-footed—and the treacherous left one was reminding him again of its troubles, he realised bitterly—he made his way down the line of vehicles. As he passed each one he could feel the eyes of the occupants on him in the fast-dissolving darkness.

That's Corporal Butler—the one that was pissed out of his wits last night, the silly bugger . . .

He came to the fourth jeep, which had only one occupant.

"Corporal B-Butler?"

"Sir." Butler gripped his Sten with one hand and saluted with the other. "Sergeant Purvis sent me down . . . to be your driver, sir."

"Righty-ho. Climb aboard, then, Corporal."

Butler stood his ground, at a loss to know how to say what had to be said.

"What's the m-matter, Corporal?" Audley sounded worried.

"Sir"—Butler despised himself—"I can't drive, sir."

Audley sat back. "Oh, is that all? Well, that's no problem —I'll drive. You come round this side and I'll move over."

When they had rearranged themselves they sat in silence, Audley lounging comfortably, Butler sitting stiffly. He felt he ought somehow to apologise for his incapacity, except that apologies usually made things worse. Also it was possible that Audley already knew about his disgraceful performance of the previous night—from the tone of that first worried question and the relief implicit in his reaction to the answer that seemed more than likely.

The thought made him squirm inside with shame. Then his resolve hardened: if Audley didn't know it would be better to tell him—and if he did know there was nothing to be lost in the telling.

"Sir—"

"Yes, Corporal?"

"I got drunk last night, sir. On wine, sir."

Audley was silent for a moment. "Tricky stuff, wine."

"Yes, sir." Relief suffused Butler.

Audley was silent again. Then——"But you haven't drunk anything since last night?" he inquired casually.

"Sir?" Butler was puzzled by the question.

The young officer turned towards him. "Have you had anything to drink this morning, Corporal?" he asked.

"No, sir." Butler heard his own voice rise. "Except water from my water bottle."

"No wine?"

"Sir?" Butler frowned in the half-light. "No, sir—of course not. I—I couldn't stand the sight of it." Puzzlement gave way to a quick, cold suspicion. "Has someone——" He broke off, appalled and confused at the same time by the suspicion.

Audley looked away. "No, I didn't somehow think you had been." Then he turned again towards Butler. "And . . . yes, Corporal Butler, someone has."

They stared at each other in silence. Away somewhere, far to the north, there came a distant drone of aircraft engines.

"In fact, for the last hour I have been regaled with a c-catalogue of your . . . vices, Corporal," continued Audley. "Including a . . . warning that you were probably on the b-bottle again by now."

Butler was outraged. It was Corporal Jones, for sure it was Corporal Jones.

"That's a lie, sir," he spluttered. "A rotten lie!"

And it must have been Jones who had given Sergeant Purvis the bottle, too; which was a filthy trick, though perhaps understandable as revenge for what he'd done the night before. But what wasn't understandable—what was unforgiveable——was that Jones should then have betrayed him to an officer.

"Yes, I rather think it was," said Audley.

The drone of the engines was louder now. And there was activity along the shadowy line of vehicles. One of the men in the jeep just ahead of them had lifted a small, square box from the back of the vehicle. He bent over it and for an instant his face was illuminated with a ghastly green light.

"Now that's interesting," said Audley. "Marker lamps." He swivelled in his seat to stare up into the lightening sky. "I think we have friends up above."

The drone had turned into a steady beat. It seemed to come slightly from the right now, but as the green lamps went on it appeared to turn towards them.

In a flash Butler understood. "The river's just ahead of us, sir," he said. "They're going to cover the sound of our engines with the plane, I think, sir."

Someone in the distance shouted "Start up!" and the call was taken up ahead of them.

"I think you're right, Corporal," said Audley. "Full marks. And it is rather comforting to know that somebody's got himself properly organised."

"That'll be Major O'Conor, sir," said Butler.

"Yes, I think you're right again. The major did strike me as being"—Audley started the jeep—"a downy bird."

" 'Downy,' sir?"

"Downy—yes." Audley launched the jeep with a jerk that reminded Butler of the sergeant-major. "You must forgive my bad driving. I completed the carrier and light tank course at Sandhurst with a Grade Three pass, which is the lowest one available—I never got round to telling them that I'd never actually learnt to drive ... I presume Sergeant What's-'is-name didn't get round to asking you whether you could drive either, Corporal?"

"No, sir." Butler warmed to the young officer.

"Well, that's the Army for you. Round pegs and square pegs, and square holes and round holes. And the Army just hits the pegs until they fit the holes. It's a splendid system if you don't weaken. . . . How far to the river, did you say?"

"Four or five miles. We come off a ridge of some sort, and then there's a flood plain . . . and then a flood embankment of some sort."

Audley nodded. "Yes, that's the Loire right enough. . . . Did you know, Butler, that there are two rivers hereabouts with the same name, almost? . . . There's *Le* Loir, which is masculine and not very big, and *La* Loire, which is feminine and can be a perfect bitch in flood—never mind the Germans. Which only goes to show that the female of the species can be more dangerous than the male, eh?"

It was funny that he wasn't stuttering at all, thought Butler. "It isn't in flood now, sir. And there aren't any Germans behind it, so I've been told."

Audley braked sharply as the jeep ahead loomed up close. They were beginning to drop off the ridge, Butler sensed.

"No Germans?" Audley twisted the wheel. "I'll believe that when I'm the other side of the river. . . . And what makes you think there are no Germans, Butler? Who told you that?"

"A Yank, sir. One of their motorbike MPs."

"He did? And what did you tell him in exchange?"

The question floored Butler. "I beg your pardon, sir?"

"Did he ask you any questions? Like where you were going?"

Butler blinked. "Yes, he did. But I don't know where we're going."

"Ah-hah!" The noise of the plane was so loud Audley almost shouted the sound.

"He said they'd reconnoitred the other side, sir," shouted Butler. "They've patrolled about five miles, and there weren't any Germans. He said we'd have an easy crossing."

The light was growing. He could make out fields and even occasional buildings, dead and shuttered as though they were derelict for all that the fields had a carefully tended look about them. And there were tall trees with strange black balls in them which reminded him of the swarm of bees which had once settled on one of the general's apple trees . . . except that they couldn't all be bee swarms, and they were too big anyway.

"So they've reconnoitred the crossing for us . . . Let's hope they know their business," shouted Audley.

Tanks ahead, canted on the side of the road. And beyond them American half-tracks . . . and American soldiers, groups of them, some smoking, some squatting—one of them even waved a jaunty thumbs-up sign at Butler. This must be part of the 921st the MP had spoken of. He was sorry for them, that they just had numbers instead of proper names like the British Army; surely they'd much rather go into battle with the pride

of a known locality to support them instead of a number ...
Texans and New Yorkers, say. And then the thought of his
own regiment, somewhere back on the river Orne a million
miles away, twisted inside him—the Lancashire Rifles, which
was the best regiment in the Army, with battle honours to
prove it from Busaco and Ciudad Rodrigo and Waterloo to
Mons and the Somme and Ypres—and Normandy. Except
that once upon a time the Rifles had only had a number too,
which was there on their cap badge still, and maybe these
Yanks didn't all come from the same country—and when he
thought about it there were Riflemen who came from Scotland
and even Ireland, and didn't know Blackburn from Bolton—

The jeep tilted up steeply and he could see the line of a
great embankment sweeping away to disappear among the
trees on his left. Then came a wide road snaking along the top
of the embankment, which they left immediately for another
slip road, narrower and unmetalled, on the river side. But
there was no river to be made out in the half-light, only a
tangle of undergrowth mostly made up of tall willows which
rose out of a lattice of their own fallen branches. The night
was making its last stand in the undergrowth, but a pale mist
was already replacing the darkness up the track ahead.

River mist, thought Butler gratefully—that must be what
the major was relying on to cover the crossing. Noise up
above and mist below as a double precaution in spite of the
American patrol's report.

Suddenly the jeep ahead braked to a halt, and the tyres of
their own vehicle slithered on the loose sand under them as
Audley jammed his foot down. Someone came striding back
down the track, pausing at each jeep. It was Sergeant Purvis.

The sergeant halted beside Audley. "Fifty yards ahead, sir
—sharp left and you're down on the river bed. Bank's a bit
tricky, so you better take it easy there, but the going's good
after that. Follow the jeep in front to the next lot of trees and
then switch off the engine—there'll be someone to direct
you."

"What's happening, Sergeant?" said Audley.

Sergeant Purvis looked at the subaltern irresolutely for a
moment, then up and down the line of jeeps as though he was
weighing the delay to his orders against the possible conse-

quence of telling a second lieutenant what to do with his curiosity.

"Sergeant?" Audley prompted Purvis with a sharpness which suggested to Butler that he had met the same problem in the dragoons and didn't intend to let it spread to Chandos Force.

"Sir . . ." Purvis just managed to prevent himself shrugging. "The major put three recce patrols from the advance party across the river about an hour ago."

"I thought the Americans were patrolling the other side."

Purvis shuffled his feet. "They have been, sir. But the major wanted to look-see for himself, like we always do."

"When are they due back?"

This time Purvis did shrug. "I dunno, sir—pretty soon, I'd say. But you'll have to ask the major."

Audley accepted that with a nod. "Righty-ho, Sergeant. Carry on."

Purvis swung away and Audley turned to Butler. "So he doesn't trust our American friends, then. And come to that, he probably doesn't trust anyone else much either . . . a downy bird, as I said, Corporal." There was just enough light now for Butler to see that he was grinning. "'Downy' meaning 'crafty'—you don't remember your Kipling, then?"

"Only *Kim* and *The Jungle Book*, sir—and some of the poetry, like *If* . . . and the *Barrack-Room Ballads*, sir." This time Butler was determined not to be thought an illiterate, even at the risk of seeming to show off.

"Good man! But this is from *Stalky*"—Audley reached towards the gear lever as the jeep in front started to move—"you should read that. There's a touch of Stalky about the major, I'd like to think."

The sergeant's fifty yards seemed more like two hundred, but at length the vehicles in front turned sharply before a wall of tangled branches. As Audley followed, Butler saw a wide expanse of open ground walled in by mist in which he could make out the vague outlines of men and vehicles.

"Hold tight," said Audley.

The front wheels of the jeep fell away into nothing and they half-drove and half-slithered down a steep, sandy bank already deeply rutted by other wheels. For a moment or two the tyres spun sand, lost their grip, found it again, lost it, and finally pulled forward onto a firmer track between two brackish lakes of green-scummed water. As they moved out into the open, Butler saw a line of jeeps drawn up nose to tail, and behind them tree tops growing out of the mist. They must now be in one of the dry channels of the river, behind one of the islands the American MP had spoken of.

Audley followed the jeep ahead into the line and switched off the engine. Behind them the last two jeeps pulled into position. Chandos Force was on its start-line at last, thought Butler. Now the worst time would begin, the waiting time.

A figure materialised out of the mist ahead of them, tall, thin, and unmistakable.

It paused at the jeep in front. "Morning, Bassett—morning, Mason . . . stretch your legs, have a bite to eat. We've a few minutes in hand, so make the most of them."

"Morning, sir."

"Yes, sir."

Major O'Conor advanced toward them, grinning broadly. "Ah, the modern languages section! *Bonjour, David—guten Morgen, Oberjäger Butler.*" He raised his ashplant stick in salute.

"Bonjour, mon commandant," said Audley.

Butler couldn't bring himself to play silly games. "Sir," he said. "Good morning, sir."

The major nodded. "Well, so far it does look like a good morning, I'm happy to say. We've had three patrols on the other side, and so far two have reported a clear run, so we shall probably go in about fifteen minutes." He looked up into the lightening sky, from which the noise of engines had now diminished to a distant hum. "When we shall summon back our RAF friend, don't you worry."

"Do we have any air support today, sir?" asked Audley.

"Oh yes. If we get into real trouble—which we won't—but if we do, we've access to a limejuice strike of our very own, David."

Audley took a deep breath. "Well, that's a relief, sir—limejuice saved our bacon several times back in Normandy."

"Oh, we shall be all right, don't you fret," the major reassured him. "The Hun's thin on the ground, where we're going—plenty of back roads, thick, wooded country. We've operated in far worse than this . . . Anyway, stretch your legs while you can, both of you. Just don't stray too far. Wouldn't want to lose you just when the fun's beginning, eh?"

They watched him move on down the line, silent for a moment. Then Audley took another deep breath. "Phew! Looks as if we're playing for the First Fifteen after all, with a limejuice of our own, by God!"

"'Limejuice,' sir?"

"Rocket-firing Typhoons—ground-strafing experts. When we ran into anything we couldn't handle—which was anything bigger than a German with a pea-shooter in a biscuit tin, if the FOOs couldn't get their guns on it they'd give us a limejuice." Audley's face clouded suddenly, and he seemed to be staring at something in the mist beyond Butler's right shoulder. "Last time they did it, it went wrong. The Germans shot down our spotter plane, and the Tiffies couldn't find the target . . . and then the Germans made mincemeat of us." He swallowed, shook his head, and focussed on Butler again. "That's water under the b-b-b-bridge now, anyway. So let's stretch our legs like the man said, Butler."

"Yes, sir." Butler stepped out of the jeep and was reminded immediately by his left foot of just how he ought to be making the most of these last precious minutes. This was not only the last opportunity he might get but also the last time he might have anything like privacy for what had to be done. "If you'll excuse me for a minute or two, sir—"

"Okay, Corporal." Audley had produced a dog-eared paperback book from inside his battle dress and a pair of steel-rimmed spectacles from his breast pocket. He looped the spectacles over his ears and settled them far down his nose—presumably he was farsighted—and then started to walk up and down, oblivious of everything and everyone around him.

Butler strolled down the line of jeeps. The bandits seemed to have taken the major's advice in a variety of different ways: several of them were brewing up on a small primus stove; one was pumping up the tyres of one of the bicycles which were among the unit's stranger items of equipment, while another loaded a big .50 Browning machine gun. At the end of the line a man was shaving.

Rubbing his hand over his own chin, Butler felt a fine sandpaper of stubble. It wouldn't show yet, that was one small advantage of his red hair. But even if it had been black as night he wouldn't have wasted any of his precious water on it—that was reserved for his treacherous foot. It was a pity there was no acceptable water close to hand, but the river (which he supposed lay on the other side of the island) was hardly safe, and he didn't fancy the slimy green pools he had passed a few minutes earlier.

What he needed now was a little cover, and there ahead of him now lay just the place.

The spring floods had gouged a miniature cliff in the side of the island, and in so doing had undermined the roots of a tall willow and brought it down into the channel. Later floods hadn't been quite powerful enough to wrench it out altogether but had festooned it with drifted branches and feathery debris. Behind that he would be snug as a bug in a rug.

He stepped carefully over the outflung branches and settled himself down on a little beach of fine sand which had gathered under the overhang behind the broad trunk of the willow. It was a relief to loosen his equipment, and an even greater relief to take his boot off and trickle water over his foot.

He examined his toes with familiar distaste. Beneath the faded purple the skin was crinkled and unwholesome, and the gentian violet stung as he dabbed it into the raw slits which the fungus had opened between them.

As always, he thought of Sammy Murch again as the purple stain spread over his skin, and the thought was more painful than the sting of the gentian violet. He would never be able to make it up with Sammy now: Sammy would be only another name chiselled on the town war memorial, which already had the names of two of his uncles from the previous war. One of them had been killed in the very last week of the war, he remembered, after three years in the trenches; which everyone agreed was rotten bad luck.

Then a colder thought struck him. If what the major had said was true they were getting near the end of this war too, but there was still time for more names to be added to Sammy's. So with the same bad luck he might meet Sammy again after all. He might meet him this very day, even this very hour.

But that was a contemptible and unsoldierly thought, he told himself savagely. It was no good worrying about a thing like that—the general had warned him against it specifically: people who worried too much about themselves soon got themselves killed, the general had said, and what was worse they got other people killed with them.

So he would think of something else—

He would think of . . . of *food*.

The second oatcake he had taken out to eat in the truck was there waiting for him still, and it would be prudent to eat it now. So he would let his toes enjoy the fresh air while he ate it, at least until the RAF noise-maker returned.

He corked up the gentian violet bottle carefully and packed it back into his ammunition pouch. Then he set his back comfortably against the cliff and unpacked the oatcake. He would savour each separate mouthful, and he would take one small swallow of water to every two mouthfuls. And as a bonus he would also eat a slab of ration chocolate.

It was a pity he hadn't got a book to read, like Second Lieutenant Audley. It would be interesting to know what Audley was reading—it would be something strange and scholarly probably, because Audley was strange and scholarly—

As he lifted the oatcake towards his mouth a cascade of sand and small stones tumbled from the cliff overhang above him, pattering onto his feet.

"This will do, Sergeant-major."

Butler went stiff with horror. It was happening again—it wasn't possible, but it was happening again.

"Sir!"

"Keep your voice down, man, damn it!"

Butler stared at one purple foot and one booted foot. Very slowly he began to draw them in—

"Yes, sir—sorry, sir."

—until his knees were raised tightly against his ammunition pouches. If he kept very quiet . . . if neither of them stepped any closer to the edge of the overhang . . . maybe—

Butler frowned at his knees. When the sergeant-major wasn't shouting his voice became deeper and harsher, as though his throat was full of gravel. And he had heard that voice before.

"All right. So what do we do with young Butler?"

The sergeant-major coughed. *"I'm afraid he's got to go, sir."*

Butler's heart shrivelled. He was going to be returned to his unit in disgrace, with the indelible black mark of drunkenness against his name.

"Pity. He seemed a pleasant enough lad—quite innocent, I would have thought."

Butler's hand closed on the oatcake in a spasm of shame. He had betrayed the major—and the general. And himself.

"That's as may be, sir. But he asked a question about Sergeant Scott and Mr. Wilson all the same."

"He did, did he?"

"Yes, sir. And near choked the life out of Taffy to get an answer, too."

"Hmm . . . very well then, Sergeant-major." The major's voice was suddenly hard and flat. *"Kill him with the others."*

9. How Chandos Force crossed the river of no return

"Kill him with the others."

It was bitterly cold—sharp enough to see his teeth chattering. This far south in August it shouldn't be freezing cold like this.

But of course it wasn't cold at all.

He was cold.

"Kill him with the others—yes."

"Very good, sir. You think they were both briefed then?"

"No, Sergeant-major—frankly, I don't see how they could have been. For a start I don't see how Military Intelligence could have known where I was going for replacements before they even knew the replacements were necessary."

"Aye, you're right there, sir. The colonel wasn't main

pleased when we turned up with them last night when it was too late to do anything about them."

"In the circumstances that's hardly surprising, Sergeant-major. He didn't know about Scott and Wilson—and we weren't meant to know that they were his men. But there was nothing he could do about Audley and Butler without admitting that he'd planted Scott and Wilson in our midst—the two youngsters are perfectly adequate interpreters, after all."

"Just so, sir. And yet we've struck unluckily the second time too, so it seems . . ."

"Are you criticising me, Sergeant-major?"

"No, sir. I was just thinking to myself that we've been a bit unlucky, that's all, not getting a pair of villains."

"My dear man—I could hardly go looking for villains publicly. The whole object of the operation was to leave the record nice and clean behind us: we lost a couple of interpreters and we replaced them. I deliberately went to a couple of entirely different units which happened to be commanded by old friends of mine, so there's no way these two can have been nobbled by Intelligence. It's bad luck that neither of them appears corruptible, because they would have been useful. That's all."

"Then, begging your pardon, sir—why kill them?"

"Why? Because I prefer certainties to odds, that's why. Because Audley's too damn quick-witted and Butler doesn't know when to mind his own business—that's why. And because Colonel Clinton is a man who obviously likes to take double precautions, and once we get over the river we'll have enough on our plate without risking his getting at those two, *that's why!* Right?"

"Right, sir. Point taken. And the colonel's driver?"

"Ah—now he's the man who has to be kept intact at all costs, Sergeant-major. He's the key to the treasure house."

"You don't mean he's Intelligence, like the colonel, sir?"

"On the contrary, Sergeant-major. He's pure bone-headed Royal Army Service Corps of the pre-war regular variety. But he's also the man who drove the loot out of Paris in '40, so he knows where it is even better than Clinton does."

"Christ Almighty!"

"Ah, you can say that again, man. Driver Hewett is our ace

in the hole—our walking map, Sergeant-major. He doesn't know what it was he took out, apparently, because they had some elaborate cover plan to put the French off the scent even back then. But he knows exactly where they planted it—"

Cold.

He sat hugging himself, trying to get the blood circulating again, staring at the thinning mist on the far side of the sandy channel.

He had started to feel cold while they were talking, and he had felt colder as they walked away. And now that he was alone he was freezing cold—

"Right you are, sir. All three of them."

"And the sooner the better, I think. Just one ... comprehensive accident, eh?"

"Won't be an accident this time, sir."

Freezing cold.

But there was something else now: the far distant drone of engines was louder—or was he imagining it?

He raised himself on one knee and cocked his head to catch the sound. Whatever happened he had to get back to Mr. Audley as quickly as possible—

The sound was louder. But there was also another sound: the sharp crack of a broken twig right behind him.

"Hullo, Jackie boyo," said Corporal Jones.

Butler swivelled on his knee and started to rise.

"No—don't get up for me—I like you better kneeling, boyo." Jones gestured meaningfully with the stubby Beretta which he held pistol-fashion in his left hand. "That's right ... now put your hands up—"

Hände hoch—

"—and turn round—"

Dreh dich um—

It was all happening again. Only it was all different.

"Not towards me—away from me, boyo, away from me."

Butler stared at Jones. There was something odd about the way the little man was standing—something odd about the way he was holding the submachine gun left-handed. He hadn't been left-handed the night before when he'd pulled the corks and poured the wine, or when he'd stroked that gun of his, the best little gun ever made.

The gun moved again. "Nasty habit—eavesdropping," said Jones softly. "So turn round, like I'm telling you."

His right hand was held out of sight, that was the other thing that was strange about him.

And then, just as suddenly, it wasn't strange at all. Until the noise of the plane was much louder the threat of the gun might be an empty one, but that right hand wasn't empty—it was no more empty than the sound he had heard had been the crack of a dead twig snapping underfoot. There weren't any twigs where Jones was standing, there was only soft sand.

He started to dig the toe of his right boot into the sand behind him.

It all depended which way the flick-knife was held, for the upwards or the downwards blow. The instructors always recommended the upwards one, which came in under the overlapping ribs. But Taffy Jones was planning a stab from behind and above, which surely meant a downward thrust.

His toe was firm now. But he dare not watch that right hand, that would give the game away. Instead, he had to choose in advance whether to reach high or low for an arm which might swing either upwards or downwards, with no chance of changing his mind after he had chosen.

Downwards, then. His own raised left hand was in a better position for that, anyway . . . and his right one was still full of crushed oatcake.

But first he must play innocent—innocent and beaten—to give himself the extra fraction of time he needed to cover the two yards between them, before Jones could swing that right arm up and back for the killing stab.

He let his shoulders droop submissively. "For Christ's sake, Taf—what . . . what am I supposed to have done? If it's last night . . . I don't know what came over me . . . I didn't know what I was doing, Taf—I lost my rag—I was bloody sick—"

He threw himself at Jones.

* * *

Two thoughts—
His webbing belt was undone and his ammunition pouches were swinging—
It was too far, and he wasn't going to reach that wrist—

Third thought—
Oh, God! It was coming upwards—he had chosen wrong—

As he hit Jones with the force of a battering ram he felt a tremendous blow on his chest, over his heart—
The death blow—
Jones was falling backwards, his feet swept from under him.
No pain—
Jones's arms seemed imprisoned under him. With his left hand Butler scrabbled frantically for the knife arm—it was moving out, moving out—
He rammed the oatcake into Jones's face, grinding it into the man's eyes. Jones let out an incoherent sound and wrenched his knife arm free. As it came round Butler caught the wrist and deflected the swing so that the knife plunged into the sand alongside them. While he held it there he pressed down on the smaller man with all his weight to keep the left hand imprisoned against the submachine gun, reaching at the same time with his own free hand for his bayonet in the tangle of equipment on his back. His fingers found the scabbard, then lost it again as Jones heaved under him, straining to lift the knife out of the sand. The equipment moved and the scabbard came into his hand again . . . he ran his fingers up to the barrel-locking device—
Stupid little spike bayonet, eight inches of steel with no handle . . . why couldn't he have had a proper sword-bayonet with a proper grip, like his father had had—
He couldn't get it out—the angle was wrong and the frog was twisted and his arm wasn't long enough—and he couldn't hold Jones's wrist much longer—couldn't get it out and hold down Jones at the same time—
No more time!
He rolled to his left. Jones's imprisoned left hand broke

free and the clutching fingers caught his hair. In the same instant he pulled out the bayonet and stabbed upwards, under Jones's belt, with every last shred of strength that he had.

The little man's fingers gouged into Butler's scalp and the body arched under him convulsively, throwing him sideways. There seemed to be noise all round him: a ghastly rattling throaty cry of agony and the roar of aircraft engines above him.

He flung himself off the body and rolled away from it in an equal convulsion of panic, landing on all fours two yards away, the breath catching in his own chest like a death rattle.

The engines drummed in his head as though they were inside his brain.

Jones lay spread-eagled in the middle of a circle of churned-up sand, his hands clenched like talons.

Butler stared at him for a moment, and then down at himself. It didn't seem surprising to him that Jones was dead—he had felt the bayonet sink in, like a garden fork into damp clay soil, and knew now that however useless that eight-inch spike might be for chopping wood and opening tins, it was more than sufficient for its designed purpose. But that blow above his heart—he had felt that . . . he had even heard it grate on the breastbone.

He ran his hand curiously over his left breast and then stared stupidly at it. There was no pain . . . and no blood.

He was alive.

And Jones was dead.

Kill him with the others!

Oh, God!

And the sound of those engines wasn't in his head.

Automatic reflexes took over. His hands buckled his belt, straightened his equipment. His feet carried him limping across the sand to where Jones lay . . . one boot off, one boot on.

His bayonet was a black plug in Jones's side: his hand plucked it out, eight bright shiny red inches to be wiped in the sand and slid back into the scabbard. Then there was Jones's gun, the best little gun, and the knife, four razor-sharp un-blooded inches of it . . .

Jones was no weight at all; such a little man to cause such a lot of trouble. But no trouble in the end when dragged feet first to the overhang, just a scuffed trail in the sand.

He threw the best little gun and the knife onto the body and picked up his sock and his gaiter and his boot, and last of all his Sten. Then he reached up and sank his fingers into the soft earth. He felt the lip of the overhanging bank tremble as he rocked his hands back and forward.

"Corporal Butler!"

The voice was pitched high and urgent, somewhere away to his left. He heaved desperately at the overhang.

"Corporal Butler!"

A wide section of the overhang tore away, falling sound-lessly onto the body, spreading over a face on which in the last instant before it was covered he saw that there were still flakes of crushed oatmeal.

It wasn't enough—there was still a clenched hand protrud-ing from the debris—but there was no time for anything more.

He prised his foot into his boot, picked up the sock and the gaiter and the Sten, and ran towards the voice.

Audley loomed out of the mist ahead of him. "For Christ's sake, man—do you want to miss the boat?"

"I'm sorry, sir." Butler adjusted his cap-comforter from the rakish angle Jones had pushed it in his last spasm of life.

"Didn't you hear me calling?" snapped Audley.

Butler swallowed. "Yes, sir—sorry, sir. But you . . . you caught me at a disadvantage, sir."

"What d'you mean—at a disadvantage?"

"Well, sir . . ." The truth flared up impossibly in front of Butler: *I was just hiding Corporal Jones's body, Mr. Audley, sir.*

How could he possibly say that?

"Yes?" said Audley irritably.

He tried to kill me because I overheard the major talking to the sergeant-major, sir. They're planning to kill us both, sir —you and me . . . and Colonel Clinton, sir.

It was hopeless: there was no way he could say that without

Audley taking him for a raving madman—no possible way. At least, not now and not yet and not here.

"Yes, sir . . . well, with my trousers down, like, sir." The lie blossomed on his tongue effortlessly. That must be how murderers lied, with the blood still wet on their hands.

He looked at his hands involuntarily. There was a vivid purple stain on the left thumb and forefinger, and on the palm too, but no spot of blood anywhere to be seen. It was a proper murderer's weapon, that eight-inch spike, and no mistake.

"Oh," said Audley.

A solitary jeep loomed up ahead. It was their jeep, but now it was surrounded by a group of American soldiers who were examining a Bren gun which lay on the top of its load of equipment.

"You don't get a goddamn move on"—an American with no visible badges of rank addressed Audley familiarly—"you're gonna be late for your own goddamn funeral, buddy."

"Oh . . . righty-ho," said Audley. He grinned encouragingly at Butler across the jeep. "We mustn't miss that, must we, Corporal? It just wouldn't be the same without us."

The jeep lurched forward, its wheels spinning furiously as Audley put his foot down. Butler hung on, his mind spinning just as furiously as the wheels. He had tried many times to imagine what this moment would be like, the crossing of the last line into enemy country. But never in his darkest dreams had he conceived it would be like this—that he would be riding into it with death at his back more certain than any danger ahead, and the only incentive for going forward that horrible thing he had left behind him half covered with sand.

"Funny thing . . ." Audley spun the steering wheel as the jeep skidded out of the deep ruts he was following ". . . back in medieval times the French used to call the English soldiers 'goddamns'"—he spun the wheel in the opposite direction—"because that was their favourite swear word—"

There were more Americans ahead of them, and more American vehicles too—jeeps, half-tracks, and a couple of strange-looking lorries. A heavily built soldier in a soft field cap pointed decisively to the left and signalled them urgently in the same direction with his other hand, like a traffic policeman.

"—but now that's an Americanism, and our favourite word is quite different."

They were swinging round the end of the island.

"And it's a good thing the French don't call us by *that* word," concluded Audley. "It wouldn't be at all polite."

Also he'd never expected to go into battle discussing medieval swear words, thought Butler with a touch of hysteria. Nothing was as he had imagined it.

The river!

It looked grey and placid, almost oily, what he could see of it, with the shapes on the far side still mist-shrouded. Moored broadside about ten yards out in it was a curious contraption which looked like a pair of small pontoons lashed together and covered with steel strips that reminded him of his old Meccano set back home. More ingenious American improvisation, obviously.

"Come on, Audley," called an English voice out of the small group of men standing on the contraption.

Another of the soft-capped Americans appeared alongside them, a stocky man with an armful of NCO's chevrons.

"Okay, let's go—follow the tracks, Lieutenant—just keep to the tracks," said the American quietly.

Audley guided the jeep down towards the water's edge. Suddenly there was a metallic sound beneath them and the vehicle was running as smoothly as on a proper road: the Americans must have laid more of that Meccano under the sand here, right down to the river, where the going would be treacherous . . . and into it too, by God! thought Butler as the jeep moved just as smoothly through the water.

"That's great"—the American was wading beside them—"now there's a ramp just ahead—you're doing fine."

The jeep lifted miraculously in the water, and then up onto the pontoon, fetching up against chocks on the far side with a bump.

"Chocks under—okay, take her away!" The stocky NCO grinned at Butler as he pulled himself aboard. "No sweat, eh?"

The man's quiet confidence and efficiency was infectious: Butler found himself grinning back.

"No sweat," he said.

Two Americans with wooden poles were pushing the makeshift ferry out into the river. Behind them an outboard motor buzzed into life like an angry bee.

"We just go downstream a piece," said the American. "Then you're on your own, soldier."

Butler stared around him. Obviously they weren't crossing by the shortest route, but that was hardly surprising since the best—or the safest—landing point need not coincide with the perfect cover provided by the dry channel behind the island. Behind him the far end of the island was already indistinct, and he was relieved to see it go. He was still in the middle of a nightmare, but nothing worse could happen in it than had already happened back there. Half his mind was already struggling to erase Corporal Jones from the other half before the reality became indelible.

But it had happened. He stared down at the purple stain on his hand again, wanting it not to be there.

It had happened: he had heard the major—

He had killed Corporal Jones.

"I'm not going to ask you what the hell you were doing back there, Audley," said Colonel Clinton. "But just don't do it again."

Butler looked across the jeep.

"No, sir," said Audley.

Butler stared for a moment at Colonel Clinton, then stared around wildly. The trees on the far side of the river were more distinct now, they were drifting diagonally towards them down the river. Away ahead the bank curved in a great arc as it bent northwards—

"All three of them."

"And the sooner the better, I think. Just one comprehensive accident."

The hair on his neck seemed to be moving. All three of them. The sooner the better. All three of them—

"It won't be an accident this time, sir."

Thump—

Butler seized the Bren gun and slammed back the cocking handle.

"What the hell—?" said Colonel Clinton.

Thump—

"Christ—a mortar!" exclaimed Audley. "Christ—"

As Butler fought to lift the Bren to bear on the riverbank downstream the water ahead of them burst into spray and there was a sharp, cloth-tearing burst of noise. The American alongside Butler was slammed into the side of the jeep and then bounced off outwards into the river. The sound of an explosion echoed out of the mist behind them, then another—

The cloth-tearing noise chattered out again, cutting through the sound of the engines above them. The American steering the outboard motor was plucked off the back of the pontoon —one minute he was there in front of Butler's eyes, then he was gone. The craft slewed round stern away from the current, out of control, but the movement brought the Bren to bear on the bank ahead.

Butler loosed off a long burst, then another, hosing down the undergrowth. Something clanged loudly in his ear.

"Get the tiller!" shouted Audley. "We're drifting towards them!"

Butler fired again—the longest burst he had ever fired from a Bren. The water exploded again, three feet to his left, throwing water over him. The Bren stopped abruptly.

"Magazine!" he heard himself shouting. Out of nowhere Audley's hand appeared, snatching off the empty magazine and snapping another one in its place. The colonel's head lifted into view, almost in line with the muzzle of the Bren, and then bobbed down again in the instant that Audley slapped his shoulder. As he pressed the trigger again he felt the craft begin to change direction under him—the colonel was in the suicide spot, steering them back towards the shore. In the last seconds before the bank swung out of his sights he loosed off the whole magazine in an almost continuous roar, the gun bucking and hammering against his shoulder.

Audley was no longer with him—he felt the jeep's engine spring to life and there was a jarring *crunch* as they collided with the bank.

"Leave it! Leave it!" someone shouted, and Butler threw

himself out of his seat into the water. The muzzle of his Sten
raked his chin and the river closed over his head. Then a helping
hand grabbed his arm and hauled him forward—he felt himself
twisted in the water and rose gasping to catch a last glimpse of the
jeep drifting away on the pontoon. Someone was swearing—
swearing strange words—in his ear. Then the water closed in
again, filling his eyes and his mouth—

He was spewing up water and being pulled forward and
upwards bodily. He could hear the sound of explosions in the
distance.

"Are you hit, Corporal?" said Audley.

Butler blinked the water out of his eyes. They were already
halfway up a steep bank, bushes all around them. "No, sir."

"Just drowned—fine . . . Colonel, you're bleeding like a
stuck pig, but we've got to get out of here—"

A machine gun chattered loudly a few yards away, but with an
unnatural clarity Butler could distinguish its slower beat from the
cloth-tearing sound of the gun which had caught them.

"Anyone alive down there?"

There was a crackling of undergrowth just below them on the
slope. Audley fumbled with his holstered revolver, but before he
could draw it the stocky American NCO who had directed them
onto the pontoon emerged from the foliage, still swearing the
strange oaths Butler had heard moments before. He took one
look at them and then sank exhausted onto his face.

"Anyone alive down there?" the voice above them called again
cautiously.

"No bloody thanks to you," said Audley. "But yes."

"Then for fuck's sake come on out of there! We're pulling out
any minute."

"Then give us a hand, for fuck's sake," snarled Audley.
"Colonel Clinton's hit—"

"I'm all right," said the colonel. "We're coming!"

Butler looked back at the American. "Yank!"

"Okay." The American raised himself suddenly. "Let's go."

Butler undid one of his ammunition pouches and extracted a
Sten magazine. With it there came out a bright purple fragment of
cotton waste, sopping wet—oh, God! he'd broken his bottle of
gentian violet, he realised despairingly. Bloody hell!

"Butler—come on, man!" Audley called back to him.

The machine gun fired again, away to his right, and all of a sudden *Epidermophyton inguinale* ceased to be important. He checked the position of the top round under the lips of the magazine, cocked the Sten back to the safety slot, and pushed the magazine home. With friends like Major bloody O'Conor around, never mind the bloody Germans, it wouldn't do to leave anything to chance.

"Come on, Butler!"

Butler blundered in the direction of the voice, his feet squelching inside his boots. The side of the bank was high and steep—much higher and steeper than the island on the other side—so that he found himself sliding and slithering along its length, grabbing at branches and young trees to keep himself upright.

"Up here, lad," commanded a familiar voice.

Butler scrambled up the last few yards of sandy soil and burst out onto a roadway. Directly in front of him a soldier was wrapping a bloodstained bandage round the colonel's arm.

"You the last?" said Sergeant Purvis.

"Yes, Sergeant," Butler managed to pant. "I think so."

"Right." Purvis turned up the road. "Last one, sir."

"Very good, Sergeant Purvis." Major O'Conor's voice was calm, almost lazy. "We'll be on our way, then. . . . You pick up Smith and Fowler and catch us up."

Butler stared at the major. It didn't seem right that he should look the same and sound the same: treachery and murder ought to show.

"All right, sir? Jolly good!" The major addressed the wounded and ashen-faced Colonel Clinton briskly. "If you'd be so good as to join me down the road there—" He pointed, then swung towards Audley. "Now then, young David, we must get you remounted"—he looked up and down the line of jeeps, finally settling his eye on the last but one—"Basset! You and Mason double up with the sergeant-major, and tell Corporal Jones to report to me on the double."

Butler caught his breath. It hadn't even occurred to him that Jones would be missed, he hadn't thought about it.

Audley wiped his hand across his face. "What happened, sir?" he said politely.

"A bit of bad luck, that's all," said the major.

"Horseshit," said the American NCO. "You had a goddamn patrol out—you had *three* goddamn patrols out."

The major ignored the American. "German patrol," he said. "We're dealing with it. But now we must get a bit of a move on before they start checking up on it."

"Then they'll be after us, sir—" Audley began.

The major cut him off with a raised hand. "Don't fret, my dear boy! In five minutes from now I'll put a limejuice down on this spot to cover our tracks. By the time they sort things out—if they ever do—we shall be long gone." He looked down his nose at the American. "Now as for you, Sergeant . . . you can stay here or swim back to your friends on the other side or come with us—which would you rather do now?"

Butler felt the blood rise to his cheeks with shame.

"Come with us, Sergeant," said Audley quickly. "You'll be m-most welcome to ride with us."

The American glanced at Audley doubtfully, then down the line of jeeps, as though he had no very great confidence in the value of a British welcome.

"Corporal Butler here can smell Germans before anyone else can even see them," said Audley, reacting to the doubtful glance.

The major's good eye flicked disconcertingly onto Butler for a second, then returned to the American. "Make your mind up, Sergeant—stay, swim, or come."

The machine gun fired again.

The American drew a deep breath. "Okay, Lieutenant, you've got yourself another passenger."

Bassett came pounding down the road towards them. "Major, sir!" He skidded to a halt in front of the major. "Corporal Jones is missing, sir—the s'arnt-major says for me to tell you, sir."

"Missing?"

"Yes, sir. He didn't come across with the point section, and he hasn't reported since, sir, S'arnt-major Swayne says."

"Damnation!" exclaimed the major. He frowned, then turned suddenly to Audley. "He didn't come with you by any chance, David?"

"Who, sir?"

"Jones—the man who drove you last night."

"Oh, the Welshman! I don't think so—if he was I certainly didn't see him. Did you, Butler?"

There was a rustle in the bushes further down the road, beyond the last jeep, and Sergeant Purvis stepped out onto the grass verge. He carried a German light machine gun on his shoulder.

Butler shied away from the outright lie which had been on the tip of his tongue. A lie might be disproved later—the American sergeant could even contradict it here and now. But he could at least sow a seed of doubt—

"There was somebody in the front, sir—I thought . . . maybe it was Jones, I don't know—but when the Germans opened up on us—I can't say for sure, sir, to be honest."

Another soldier appeared out of the hedge behind Purvis, who was frowning at them in surprise as though he hadn't expected them to be still there. Which, if limejuice was already on its way, was hardly to be wondered at.

"Have you seen Jones, Purvis?" said the major.

"Jones? No, sir. He's with the point section." Purvis paused. "We lost Lance-corporal Fowler, sir."

"You *what*?"

"Shot through the head, sir. Machine gun."

Major O'Conor stared at the sergeant speechlessly for a moment. Butler noticed one of his bony hands opening and closing spasmodically as though he was releasing emotion through it.

"Right!" The hand became a fist. "Let's get out of here. *Mount up!*"

"Can you drive, Sergeant?" Audley asked the American.

"Lieutenant?" The question seemed to throw the American.

"Silly question." Audley smiled. "Will you drive this thing?" He pointed to the jeep.

"Sure, Lieutenant—be pleased to." The American looked doubtfully at Butler nevertheless, as though unwilling to usurp another NCO's job.

Audley intercepted the look. "That'll free the corporal's nose for Germans," he said lightly. "And his trigger finger."

Butler climbed into the back gratefully, making himself comfortable as best he could on the top of a bazooka, carrying satchels of its projectiles and several cartons of C rations.

Audley climbed into the passenger's seat and at once offered his hand to the American. "David Audley, late Royal
South Wessex D-D-D . . . Dragoons," he said.

That was very strange, thought Butler. Audley had hardly
stuttered at all during the last few hours. But now he was back
on form.

The American took the hand. "Frank Winston . . . late
Combat Engineers, I guess."

"Ah—so you're the river-crossing expert!"

"Some crossing!" Sergeant Winston grimaced. "I'm a demolition specialist actually . . ." He pointed to Audley's cap
badge, with its prancing horses. "So you're a horse soldier?"

"I w-wish I w-was," said Audley, reminding Butler of the
fisherman on the bridge in Norman Switzerland. "But up to
n-now I've been more of a d-demolition specialist." He
paused. "And this is Corporal Butler, late of the Lancashire
Rifles."

Sergeant Winston looked at Butler curiously. "With a nose
for Germans, huh?"

The jeeps ahead were starting to move, and not before
bloody time, thought Butler.

"Ye-ess . . ." Audley was also regarding him thoughtfully.
"You were *remarkably* quick off the mark back there in the
river, Corporal."

"I heard the mortar, sir." The lie came out automatically;
lying was a reflex like any other, once the right stimulus was
applied.

The jeep moved forward smoothly.

But Audley was still watching him. "You did? I could have
sworn you were reaching for that Bren even before I heard it, you
know . . . and I also could have sworn Corporal Jones wasn't on
that boat-thing of the sergeant's—there were just the three
Americans and Colonel Clinton when I drove onto it."

Sergeant Winston nodded. "That's the way it was."

Suddenly Butler knew how tired and wet and frightened he
was. And he was aware also that the weight of fear and
knowledge—knowledge that he didn't understand and which
made no sense to him—was greater than he could bear.

"No, sir—he wasn't," he said. "And those weren't Germans who machine-gunned us, either."

10. How Master Sergeant Winston joined the British Army

They travelled half a mile along the road before Butler realised that they weren't on the proper bank of the Loire at all, but on another flood embankment matching the one they'd crossed on the friendly northern shore.

Which wasn't friendly any more, with what he'd left behind him half-buried in the sand for the next passer-by to see . . .

He thrust the foul memory into the back of his mind before it could panic him and concentrated on his new surroundings: this was enemy country at last, in which every piece of cover might conceal a German, and he must keep his wits about him.

The jeeps were turning sharply, one after another, onto a narrow track which twisted off the embankment road down its landward side. Sergeant Winston swung their vehicle after the jeep ahead of them, spinning the wheel with a skill Butler envied. At the bottom of the track they passed a small farmhouse shuttered like the ones on the far bank, its ancient paint flaking from the woodwork. Whatever the French were like, they weren't house-proud like back home, where a scrubbed step and a well-polished door-knob mattered more than a threadbare coat and a patched elbow.

It didn't surprise him that there was no sign of life to be seen: the rattle of those machine guns and the thump of the mortar bombs would have sent sensible civilians into their cellars, to pray that they hadn't drawn the card in the lottery that decreed which house should be smashed to rubble and matchwood and which should be left without a scratch.

The jeep turned again sharply, manoeuvred between two more blankly shuttered houses, and set off down a long, straight road in a dead flat countryside of small fields and lines of poplar trees. It was like the landscape he had glimpsed in the misty half-light ont he nightmare side, only now he could see that the strange dark balls in the trees weren't bee swarms at all, but some sort of parasitic vegetation . . . and the fields—vines and vegetables and orchards—were as well tended as gardens: it was funny that the houses should be so unkempt but the land so cherished.

Audley swivelled in his seat. "All right, Corporal," he said conversationally, *"talk."*

"Yes, sir . . ."

But when it came to the ultimate point, he found he didn't know what to say, or even how to start.

I've got this trouble with my foot, sir—

"Come on, Corporal—they weren't Germans? Well, who the hell were they, for God's sake?"

That was the end of the story, not the beginning of it. But where was the beginning?

"I don't know how to start, sir," he said.

"Just tell it like it was, man," said Sergeant Winston.

Butler gritted his teeth. "I've got this trouble with my foot, sir—it's called 'athlete's foot,' sir—"

"What?" said Audley incredulously.

"Let him tell it his way," said Sergeant Winston.

He started to tell it like it was.

The jeep in front slowed down again and finally pulled in alongside others parked on the edge of a small copse.

Sergeant-major Swayne came down the road towards them, accompanied by a soldier Butler didn't recognise.

The sergeant-major stopped beside Audley. "Main road ahead, sir. When we're sure it's still clear we'll be going across." He looked across at the American. "You keep your foot down when we start moving—understand?" he said.

Sergeant Winston studied him for a second or two. "Okay."

The soldier had continued on past them. Butler heard the crunch of boots on the road behind them and Sergeant Purvis appeared.

"You wanted me, Sergeant-major?" Purvis found time to give Butler a friendly nod.

"You take over point section, Sergeant," said the sergeant-major. "Hobbes and Macpherson are out ahead of you."

"Taffy not turned up then?" Purvis shook his head in disbelief. "I'd never have thought it of him—I always thought he was born to be bloody hanged."

"Harrumph!" grunted the sergeant-major disapprovingly.

"What happens after the main road, Sergeant-major?" asked Audley.

"Two miles of open country, sir. We take that at the double if the road doesn't throw up the dust. . . . Then there's good wooded country, sir." The sergeant-major straightened. "Now, if you'll excuse me, sir—"

"Carry on, Sergeant-major." Audley smiled at the American as Swayne marched away, carrying Sergeant Purvis in his wake. "You've just heard my favorite command, Sergeant Winston. It's the only one I can rely on not to get me into trouble. At least until now."

"Is that a fact?" Winston turned towards Butler. "But I think I'd like to hear you say 'Carry on, Corporal' right now."

Butler looked over his shoulder, then back at Audley. Of all the bandits, Sergeant Purvis was the only one he would have been inclined to half-trust. But the villainous-looking replacement in Purvis's jeep was another matter.

"I think we'll just wait a minute," said Audley, evidently coming to the same conclusion. "When we get on the road again . . ."

Far away behind them there came a whining snarl of distant engines; not the steady beat of the aircraft which had circled above them at the river, but a sharper and more malevolent sound.

"Limejuice," whispered Audley, staring back into the pale bluish morning sky. "Limejuice!"

"Huh?" said Winston.

"Typhoons." Audley searched the sky. "If there are any Germans left back at the river, then God help the poor devils."

"Jee-sus!" murmured Winston, looking in the same direction. "The stubby bastards with the rockets—Typhoons?"

Audley's mouth twisted one-sidedly, as though the sergeant had touched his bruised shoulder. "That's right."

Winston whistled softly. "Man—I saw some of their handiwork at Mortain. But how'd they get here so quickly?"

"Standing patrol in the air. The major must have put them up before dawn, just in case."

The American looked around him. "Just for . . . you guys? A standing fighter-bomber strike on call?" His eyes came back to Audley. "You're not joking?"

Audley shook his head. "No joke."

Engines burst into life ahead of them, drowning the sound of those other more powerful engines away to the north just as their note changed.

"No joke," muttered Sergeant Winston. "Then let's get to hell out of here, like the man said."

They'd just reached the road junction when the sound behind overtook them. The jeep ahead bounced into the air as it roared up the incline of the minor road onto the major one, warning Butler to hold on for dear life. He felt the bazooka and the C rations lift under him as the distant crash of the exploding rockets and the rattle of cannon fire passed over his head. He wondered how the little shuttered homes beside the embankment had fared.

He glimpsed a long, straight road, and a fairy-tale house with round towers topped by conical roofs of smooth blue-black slate. Then they were over the junction and racing down another narrow tree-shadowed road like the one they'd just left, the jeep lifting in another stomach-sickening bounce as they did so. Something flicked past them away over the fields to his left, a mere blur of movement flashing on and off between the trees so fast that it mocked their own furious pace. Then, with a tremendous surge of power, an RAF Typhoon rose across the funnel of sky ahead of them in an almost vertical climb. The sun glinted for a fraction of a second on its cockpit hood before it curved out of Butler's sight, turning it into a thing of beauty in the instant of its disappearance.

"He's going to make another pass," shouted Audley.

"Don't mind me if I don't stay to watch," Winston shouted back at him.

The land started to rise gently under them. They passed another shuttered farmstead with no sign of life around it except a goat tethered to a pear tree in a parched orchard. The goat had huge udders—Butler had never seen a goat with such big udders. Come to that, he thought, he had only once before seen a goat.

Then the trees thickened on each side of them and their speed came down to a more comfortable level.

"Go on, Corporal," said Audley. "What did the major say then?"

Kill him with the others—

They listened in silence right to the end—or at least to the edited end Butler found himself fabricating, with that one unendurable fact omitted.

And then for what seemed an age they continued in silence, until he began to feel a different fear spreading within him over the hard lump of panic that already constricted his chest.

They didn't believe him . . .

Finally Audley turned towards him again.

"Jones tried to stab you . . . you were kneeling, and he told you to turn round. But you jumped him, and you knocked him cold—that's right?"

Butler nodded wordlessly. Put like that—and put like that after his report of the conversation between the major and the sergeant-major—he hardly believed himself.

"And you had a fight with Jones the night before—that's last night?" said Sergeant Winston.

"Yes . . . but—" Butler saw with horror how those two separate but connected events could be rearranged to make a very different story. "But that was why they wanted to—to kill me," he said desperately.

"Uh-huh." Winston nodded at the road ahead. "And just how cold did you knock this guy Jones? Very cold, maybe?"

Butler looked wildly at Audley. "Sir—he tried to stab me—he *did* stab me—I *felt* him stab me—"

"Well, you sure as hell don't sound stabbed to me, man," said Winston.

Butler looked down at himself disbelievingly, his hands open.

Audley stared at his left hand. "No blood . . . not unless you've got purple—" He stopped suddenly, the stare becoming fixed on Butler's midriff. "Just a moment though . . . let's have a closer look at you, Corporal."

He reached down and lifted one of Butler's ammunition pouches up so that he could see the bottom of it. "Well, well!"

"What is it?" asked Winston quickly.

Audley dropped the pouch back into place. Butler seized it and tried to twist it, but the Sten magazines inside prevented him from seeing what Audley had stared at. All he could make out was the beginning of a dark purple stain on the edge.

"He's got a one-inch slit on the bottom of the pouch," said Audley. "And . . ."

"And . . . ?"

"This webbing of ours is extremely tough, Sergeant. It takes quite a lot of force to go through it."

"Like a knife, huh?"

"Like a knife. And then a couple of Sten mags and a bottle of what's-it . . ." Audley looked into Butler's eyes. "Well, well!"

Winston glanced quickly at Audley. "You're thinking maybe . . . ?"

"I'm thinking a lot of things, Sergeant."

"Like what?"

Audley didn't reply. Instead he rubbed his hand over his face as though he was wiping cobwebs from it. As he reached his mouth his hand stopped.

"Like what?" Winston repeated.

"Like . . . like limejuice *was* pretty quick off the mark this morning just now. . . . We used to reckon on ten minutes at the least, and that was one hell of a lot closer to their forward landing strips than we are here."

"But they got a standing patrol, you said."

"So I did. But *he* said he wasn't expecting any trouble at the crossing—it was going to be a piece of cake."

"He could be just careful?"

"That's exactly what I'm thinking—he could be just very careful indeed. As the corporal said, he could prefer certainties to odds, Sergeant."

This time Sergeant Winston didn't reply.

"And there was something damn queer about the way he acted back there..." Audley's hand rubbed his stubbly chin. "When we were jumped on the river...by a German patrol —when you made that memorable observation of yours. 'Horseshit' was it?"

Winston grunted. "He had his goddamn patrols out, for Christ's sake."

"That's right. And if there's one thing about this crew of desperadoes it's that they're highly professional at smelling out Germans. Because they've been keeping one jump ahead of them for months in Jugoslavia."

"So they fouled this one up, you mean?"

"Or maybe they didn't foul it up—also as Corporal Butler says.... Or maybe they did foul it up, at that!"

"I don't get you now, Lieutenant. They didn't—and they did?"

"That's right. They were laying it on for us, the colonel, the corporal, and me—three birds with one stone—the birds who weren't wanted any more *en voyage*. And then the corporal messes things up with his quick reflexes and his Bren gun: they were expecting sitting ducks, and they got thirty rounds rapid just where it hurt." Audley's thin lips twisted. "Naughty Corporal Butler!"

Winston rocked in his seat uneasily. "Hell—but how d'you know they weren't Germans? That guy had an MG 42—and that was an MG 42 firing at us, I'd know that goddamn noise anywhere!" He shook his head. "I heard that first time on Omaha Beach and I'm not ever going to shake that out of my head, Lieutenant, you can believe that for sure."

"They've got all sorts of guns with them," said Butler.

"That's right." Audley nodded at him. "These people are weapon specialists. The job they had in Jugoslavia was instructing the partisans in weapon training. The major's second in command—Captain Crawford—was explaining to me last night...half the men Marshal Tito has don't know one end of a gun from the other, they're shepherds and schoolboys, and they have to fight with what they can get—not just our weapons, but German and Italian...and Russian too, now. And the marshal asked our people for a squad to train his chaps, and these are one lot of them. They're a sort of mobile musketry school."

They stopped again.

This time the woods were all around them, thick and silent. Friendly woods, Butler told himself: friendly and concealing woods where no enemies were, and the feeling of unease and watching eyes all around him was just the town-bred boy's unfamiliarity with anywhere away from bricks and mortar and stone and slate, and straight ordered lines and sharp angles of houses and walls and roofs.

But he knew he was deceiving himself now, and that the enemy was all around him, much closer than what might lie hidden behind the green tangles.

Major O'Conor was striding towards them again, the ash-plant swinging nonchalantly for all the world as though he was a country gentleman walking his acres.

"Ah, David!" The major waved the stick. "Limejuice to your liking, eh?"

"Yes, sir. B-b-b..."—Audley fought the word—"better them than us, sir."

The major laughed a quick, mirthless laugh. "I couldn't agree with you more. I had a bit of that in 1940—and another bit in Crete in '41. So I'm quite content to see them on the receiving end, I can tell you, by jiminy." His eye swept over Butler. "No Germans to smell here, Corporal..." The eye came to the American sergeant. "Bit short with you back there by the river, Sergeant, but not much time, you understand—Germans and all that... But welcome to Chandos Force, any-way."

"Major, sir"—Winston gripped the wheel with both hands—"I'm sure we'll get along just fine."

"That's the spirit!" The eye roved over the jeep. "Sergeant-major! Get this bazooka out of this jeep—and the projectiles too. I want that up front in Cranston's jeep. He knows how to use the damn thing." The major's golden smile showed. "They can carry some more petrol instead."

"Sir!" shouted the sergeant-major in the distance.

The major tapped the bonnet of the jeep. "Another main

road two or three miles ahead, David," he said conversationally. "All being well, we'll hop that in the next stride. Then
we should be right as rain for quite a way . . . my chaps know
the drill backwards. Just follow instructions and you'll have
no trouble."

Audley nodded. "Righty-ho, sir . . . how's the colonel, sir?"

"Hah! Lost a bit of blood, but nothing serious. Fleshy part
of the arm, that's all—orderly's got him nicely wrapped up.
Good night's rest and he'll be as right as rain too."

Butler surrendered the bazooka and its ammunition to a
couple of bandits in exchange for jerrycans of petrol. It was
hard to equate this major, all friendliness and businesslike
confidence, with the cold-blooded bugger he'd overheard
under the bank of the island beside the Loire. He glanced at
Audley to reassure himself that he wasn't dreaming: the subaltern was watching the major with a strangely blank look on
his face, as though he too found the adjustment beyond him.

"Jolly good!" The major lifted the ashplant in farewell, and
strode back up the road.

The American sergeant watched him go for a few seconds,
and then turned towards Audley. For another two or three
seconds the Englishman and the American stared at each
other.

"Horseshit?" said Audley.

Winston nodded. "Horseshit." He paused. "But that's how
it feels . . . how it really is—well, you better know better than
I do, because that isn't quite the brand of horseshit I'm used
to, Lieutenant."

They moved on again, but more slowly this time.

"Back at the river—'Germans and all that' . . ." said Audley.

"Yeah?"

"A patrol, he said. And 'we're dealing with it,' he said
too."

"That's right. And he sure as hell wasn't very worried by it
either," Winston agreed. "Which seems kind of surprising to
me in the circumstances."

"Right! And particularly in the circumstances that he'd sent only two men to deal with it."

"Smith and Fowler," said Butler. "And he lost Fowler. And he was angry."

"He wasn't just angry." Audley stared from one to the other quickly. "*He was surprised.*"

"Man—you're dead right." Winston nodded so quickly that the jeep swerved slightly. "He *was* surprised."

"Which in the circumstances is surprising," concluded Audley.

"Huh! Which in the circumstances means—no Germans," said Winston. Suddenly he half-turned in the driving seat. "How hard did you say you hit that guy—who was it?—Jones?"

Butler swallowed. "Pretty hard, I suppose."

"Uh-huh . . ." Winston grunted knowingly. "Like maybe so he won't wake up this side of never, don't tell me. So now with the ambush that makes your score two-nil . . . and if we meet any Germans we can stop and ask them if they'll give you an Iron Cross—"

"Lay off, Sergeant," said Audley sharply. "If it wasn't for Corporal Butler we'd all be food for the crayfish in the river now."

The subaltern was looking at him, Butler realised. "Sir—"

"Never mind. Forget it."

"Never mind?" The American's voice rose. "Holy God, Lieutenant! if it wasn't for you British fighting among your-selves I'd be back the other side of the river now fighting the war I was drafted for—and you want me to forget that like it hadn't happened?"

"No. But—"

"No—hell, no! And if I had any sense I ought to take the next turning and get the hell out of here—limejuice, for God's sake—and *loot*!" The American's foot went down on the accelerator as the jeep in front started to pull away from them. "What loot—do I get to know that before one side or the other blows my head off?"

"We don't know," said Audley promptly, as though he had seen the question coming. "All we know is that it's very valu-able."

The woods were thinning ahead of them: Butler could see light between the trees on both sides of the road.

"That's great—here we go again, hold on—I always wanted to die rich—"

This time there was no bump. And this time the main road was even wider and straighter, with a wide verge of rough grass on each side of it. Looking quickly to each side of him, Butler saw it stretching away into the far distance, to his left towards a gap on the skyline and to his right away into infinity. Where were all the people in France—not just the Germans, that quarter of a million of them, but the millions of Frenchmen and Frenchwomen? They couldn't all be huddled in cellars waiting for the liberation.

Then they were across into the forest again, the trees as thick as ever. Before he had landed in Normandy he had thought of France as a land of pretty girls and the Eiffel Tower. After three days in Normandy it had become a land of ruined villages and shapeless old people and foul smells. Now it was a place of misty sand and endless woodland.

"Uh-*huh* . . ." It almost seemed that the American sergeant was beginning to enjoy his unhappiness. "And where is this very valuable loot, that has a limejuice all of its very own? . . . Don't tell me—you don't know that either?"

"Not far from here," said Audley stiffly. "The major said we could reach it tomorrow if we were lucky."

"But you don't know where it is? I guess the major wouldn't have told you that?"- Winston looked quickly sideways at Audley.

"It's in Touraine," said Butler. "I know that."

"Which is like saying 'It's in South Dakota, or Illinois, or Florida,'" said Winston. "And we're in Touraine now, Corporal—and if you don't know where you're going, I sure as hell don't either."

"But we can find that out from Colonel Clinton just as soon as we harbour for the night," said Audley. "And we can tell him what's happening."

Winston shook his head. "You can—I'm not. The moment you go anywhere near that colonel of yours—you and the corporal—that's the moment you won't find me around. Because the place where you three are together isn't going to be a very healthy place to be . . . I've been there once, and I still don't know how I got out of it in one piece."

There was sense in that, thought Butler. The only comfort in their present position was that Colonel Clinton was somewhere else up front.

"Our best bet is to duck out of this tonight, first chance we get," said Winston. "That way we live to fight another day, Lieutenant."

Audley was silent for a moment. "We can't do that."

"Why not, for heck's sake?"

Audley looked at Butler. "Because we're the real Chandos Force—and we've got a job to do," he said flatly.

The American was silent in his turn, driving steadily. Then he leaned back towards Butler. "Are you . . . the real Chandos Force too, Corporal?"

"Corporal Butler goes with me," said Audley.

"I see." The sergeant sat forward again. "Well, don't mind me if I wave a different flag—"

"That's fair enough." Audley's voice sharpened.

"I haven't quite finished, Lieutenant." Winston's voice sharpened to match. "I don't know whether you can take your major or whether you can't. But I'm pretty sure if he suspects you're on to him, you're gonna cramp his style if you disappear from under him—that'll make him think twice, whatever he's planning, not knowing what you're up to, huh?"

There was even more sense in that, thought Butler—the addition of the American sergeant to their strength was beginning to look like a greater blessing merely than his jeep-driving expertise.

He glanced hopefully at Audley. In his experience second lieutenants could not be relied on for anything but the simplest reaction to events, since that was all that was expected of them. But one day he hoped to do better than that himself, and now he prayed that Audley might live up to his CO's estimation.

"Looks like another halt ahead," said Winston. "So think it over, Lieutenant."

The jeeps slowed down as before, pulling into the side of the road under the shadow of the trees with a gentle rise stretching ahead of them to the crest of the next ridge.

But this time, to Butler's relief, it was Sergeant Purvis who came back towards them.

"Sir"—Purvis sounded breathless, but cheerful—"the major's compliments, and we shall be going through a village very soon. Nothing to worry about—I've had a look-see myself and I've put two men over the top of the hill beyond the village. The major's in there now, asking around if there's any suspicious persons been seen in the vicinity— won't take my word for it yet, like he used to for poor old Taf..." He grinned suddenly at Butler, with the ghost of a wink. "Now if you were to lend me the corporal there—I hear tell he's got a bit of a nose, like Taf had—Corporal Jones, that is..."

"I'll think about it, Sergeant," said Audley. "Are we halting in the village?"

"Lord—no, sir! Never stop inside a place, we don't. Too many prying eyes, there are ... not unless it's been okayed by the partisans, and we don't know any of them here." Purvis shook his head. "No, sir, we'll go straight through, and in four separate groups—that way if there is anyone watching that shouldn't be he'll likely get the wrong idea about our strength. You two"—he waved his hand to include the jeep behind—"are the rear guard, with me as tail-end Charlie." He grinned again. "Just go straight across the village square and there's a sign to St. Laurent-les-Caves. Then up the hill till you meet up with the rest."

"All right, Sergeant." Audley nodded. "We'll manage."

"Of course you will, sir. Just take it nice and steady—not too fast and not too slow. But don't stop for anyone, no matter who... and do keep an eye out for the kiddies, sir—if you catch them on the wrong side of the road from their mothers they'll like as not run across in front of you in a flash."

There was something infinitely comforting about Sergeant Purvis, decided Butler. And not the least element in that comfort was his capacity for worrying about other people, even about small French children in a village in the middle of nowhere. If there was anyone they could risk trusting in Chandos Force, Purvis was the one.

Also, he was beginning to get the hang of Major O'Conor's

operating rules, which seemed to be a variation on the hallowed principle of fire-and-movement. Very skilful reconnaissance—what Sergeant Purvis would no doubt describe as "look-see"—and movement had obviously kept them alive and operational for months in the far more hazardous conditions of occupied Jugoslavia.

It was a pity—indeed, it was also almost beyond his understanding—that the major had somehow gone to the bad.

And it was a pity also that the very blindest chance had made Audley and himself—and the colonel and Sergeant Winston—the innocent victims of his villainy.

He frowned at the back of Sergeant Winston's neck. The American's bad luck was enough to rattle even a man of such evident common sense and efficiency, which all senior NCOs in the engineers appeared to share: to be cut off from his unit among foreigners, was bad enough. But to be cut off among villainous foreigners in enemy territory. . .

He realised that all three of them were wrapped in thought, but that the thoughts must be very different. And the heaviest burden lay on the broad but utterly inexperienced shoulders of the young dragoon subaltern, with his stutter and his bruises and his Cambridge scholarship which was of as little use to him now as a packet of fish and chips.

Indeed, a packet of fish and chips would be a lot more use, he thought, feeling hungrily in his haversack. His fingers closed on the familiar oatmeal block.

And then he knew that he could never face a mouthful of oatmeal again, not even if he was starving, not even if it was the last edible thing in the whole world. There had been oatmeal in Jones's eyes and in his eyebrows and in his nostrils.

He munched a bar of ration chocolate and tried to think of something else.

Loot . . . the colonel had called it "valuable property," but the major had called it *loot*—

Oatmeal.

So the major must know what it was—obviously he knew what it was, or he wouldn't be planning to do . . . but what was he planning to do? And, come to that, what had the colonel himself been planning to do?

Oatmeal.

He reached inside his battle-dress blouse for his pocket watch. It was still incredibly early; everything seemed to have happened this morning on a time scale of its own, outside ordinary time. Back home at this hour his father would be having his breakfast, or maybe getting a proper shine on his boots before setting out for work. And the general . . .

He opened the watch case a little more—JAMES BUTLER 15-5-42 FROM H.G.C. 6.9.91—if anyone came into possession of this watch they would take those two dates for birthdays, he thought wryly, and not the days on which the British Army had acquired two of its recruits. His own "42" date might stump them a bit, but they'd probably take the fifty-one-year gap as separating grandson from grandfather.

Which in a matter of thinking wasn't completely wide of the truth, he understood quite suddenly and for the first time: in a way the general had become the grandfather he'd never had, and he had become the grandson the general lacked. The odds had been hugely against its happening, not just because of the difference between the little terrace houses of Jubilee Street and the stately homes of Lynwood Road but also because of the greater gulf between his father's position and politics and those of the general.

But it had happened.

And it had begun happening during one lunchbreak, when he'd been curled up with his book on the edge of the rhododendrons, out of sight, so he had thought—

"What are you reading, boy?"

"*The River War,* sir. It's by Mr. Winston Churchill." (If he asks you a question always answer loud and clear, Sands had told him. And truthfully too—he can see clear through you like a sheet of glass.)

"Not studying?"

"It's history, sir." (Was that a lie? "Isn't it?")

"Hmm . . . well, perhaps it is. Mr. Churchill would be pleased to hear you say so, anyway. . . . And which bit do you like best—the battle of Omdurman?"

"Yes, sir."

"Of course. And in the battle the charge of the 21st Lancers, I suppose, eh?"

"No, sir. The bit about MacDonald's brigade—the Soudanese and the Egyptians, sir—how they and the Lincolns fought off the Green Flag dervishes."

"Indeed? Then read it to me, boy."

"Yes, sir—it comes after the Black Flags had been beaten. Then the Green Flags suddenly came down from the hills . . ." (His fingers ran through the pages, but the book knew the place better than he did, opening itself ready for him.) "'*Had the Khalifa's attack been simultaneous with that which now developed, the position of MacDonald's brigade must have been almost hopeless—*'"

(This was the great passage, the one he knew so well that he could close his eyes on it.)

"'*All depended on MacDonald, and that officer, who by valour and conduct in war had won his way from the rank of a private soldier to the command of a brigade, was equal to the emergency—*'"

(The words flowed on. Not even E. M. Wilmot Buxton could equal Winston Churchill in describing a battle.)

"'*Thus ended the Battle of Omdurman—the most signal triumph ever gained by the arms of science over barbarians.*'"

"Most signal massacre, more like, my boy. They didn't have a chance, the poor barbarians."

"Against MacDonald they did, sir." (He couldn't have MacDonald slandered, not even by the general.) "Were you there, sir?"

"Hah . . . no. The Lancashire Rifles did not have that honour . . . Well, maybe against MacDonald the barbarians did." (The general's blue eyes were looking at him: he was a sheet of clear glass.) "But you don't want to be a soldier, surely?"

"Yes, sir. Like MacDonald."

"Like MacDonald? And what does your father say about that?"

"My father?" (He was still clear glass: they both knew what his father would say to that.)

"Yes—your father."

"I don't know. But I'm going to be a soldier all the same."

* * *

Ambition, thought Butler. That was the bridge between Jubilee Street and Lynwood Road.

"Move out!" Sergeant Purvis shouted from ahead of them.

The rise ahead was empty now except for the sergeant's jeep, with its massive .50 Browning mounted in front. The sergeant himself was standing up in it, one hand on the gun and the other waving them forward.

Over the crest the road curved away through the trees, past a fork with a gaudily painted calvary, its hanging Christ bright with blood, and a signpost bearing the legend 1K. 7 SERMIGNY 6K 4 ST. LAURENT. At least they were on the right road.

"About a mile," said Winston. "Have you decided, Lieutenant?"

"We can't break off here," said Audley. "Not with two jeeps behind us."

Butler looked back. The jeep behind them was closing up, but Sergeant Purvis's was only just topping the crest. The sergeant was taking his tail-end Charlie role as seriously as he would have expected.

Now there were houses ahead of them, the first outlines of Sermigny, and behind them a jumble of roofs surmounted by a stubby little church spire. With any luck he was about to see his first Frenchman since joining Chandos Force.

Not that they were going to make an exactly triumphant entrance into the village; the forest road was hardly more than an overgrown farm track and the houses he had seen along it were more like broken-down barns than homes. Between them he could just glimpse orderly rows of vines.

And there at last was a real live Frenchman, a little fat man in worn blue dungarees. He stared pop-eyed at Butler across the narrow street, and then started to wave wildly.

The poor sod thought he was being liberated, thought Butler guiltily—that possibility was something which hadn't occurred to him until this very moment.

He heard the man shouting unintelligibly behind them, then Winston swung the jeep out of the shadow of the street into the light of the village square.

It was black with Germans.

11. How they visited the village of Sermigny

A German soldier skipped out of the way of the jeep to the safety of the pavement.

"Drive on!" said Audley out of the side of his mouth. "Not too fast—*don't move, Corporal*—drive on, man, *drive on!*"

There were two more Germans crossing directly ahead of them. Audley signalled them out of the way with an urgent gesture.

"*Achtung!*" he barked.

The Germans increased their pace smartly.

Butler sat like a stuffed dummy, one hand gripping the body mechanism of his Sten convulsively, the other clutching thin air.

They were driving down one side of a tree-lined square, between a line of grey lorries under the trees on one side— lorries so heavily camouflaged with branches that the trees seemed to be growing out of them—and a wall of drag shops and houses. The intervals between the lorries were crammed with German troops in full marching order, some in steel helmets but most in soft field caps, with their helmets hanging from their packs.

"Turning ahead—" Audley lifted his hand in a vague half-salute. "Smile, *Oberjäger*—what's 'clear the road' in German, for Christ's sake? Something *die Strasse*—?"

"*Bahnen Sie die Strasse,*" hazarded Butler.

"*Bahnen Sie die Strasse,*" repeated Audley to himself.

Winston started to turn the wheel, then straightened it instantly. A second later Butler saw why: the side road was jammed with horse-drawn transport—and with more Germans. And, what was worse, at the head was a group of jack-booted officers pouring over a wide-spread map held between them. In the second that it took to pass the turning one of them looked up to stare directly into Butler's smiling face. At least, it was the nearest he could get to obeying Audley's command—he could feel his cheek muscles drawn back.

They were past the turning. A shop door opened just ahead and two soldiers stepped blindly into the road, their arms filled with long French loaves.

Audley half rose from his seat. "*Bahnen Sie die Strasse!*" he shouted. "*Achtung! Achtung!*"

There was a shout behind them, and the sound of another motor engine.

"The other jeeps," said Audley. "Let's go, Sergeant."

"Yes, *sir!*" Winston stood on the accelerator.

As the engine roared there came a single shot from the rear, then a burst of firing. One of the loaf-carrying Germans dropped his load and threw himself backwards, upsetting his comrade. The jeep's tyres screamed and skidded on the cobbled road surface. Butler had a fleeting, confused impression of men scattering in the last lorry interval to his left; dead ahead of them there were more men scattering—men who had been sitting on the steps of the church. Winston swung the steering wheel to the right, then to the left, flinging Butler from one side of the jeep to the other.

They were into a narrow passage—so narrow that the jeep barely fitted between its walls and the sound of its engine filled his senses.

"Shoot, Butler!" screamed Audley.

For a moment Butler didn't understand the order—there was nothing he could see ahead of them to shoot at. Then he realised that anyone firing down the passage at them from behind could hardly miss.

As he twisted in his seat there was another burst of gunfire behind them, followed by a grinding crash of metal on metal which ended in an explosive crash.

The passage was empty—

"Shoot!" Audley shouted again.

Butler loosed off the Sten at nothing—he couldn't have hit anything if it had been there, with the jeep bucking under him.

"More!"

He put another burst down the empty passage and saw dust and chips of stone fly from the walls of a house as the bullets ricocheted from one side to another.

"On the right—there!" shouted Audley.

"I can see it—hold tight!" Winston shouted back.

The jeep braked hard. Just as the Sten magazine emptied there came a single shot from the far end of the lane and in the same instant a bullet cracked over Butler's head. The jeep swung sharply to the right, unsighting him.

"Holy God!" said Winston. "It's a dead end!"

Butler turned. They had travelled no more than two or three yards down a passage almost as narrow as the alleyway they'd left behind. But now directly in front of them was a pair of heavy wooden doors.

Audley sprang out of the jeep and ran to the doors. For a second he rattled the iron handle on one of them, then he hammered desperately on them with his fists.

"Open up, open up! *Ouvrez,* for God's sake—*ouvrez les portes!*" He turned back towards them. "It's no good—they're locked . . . We've got to ram the bloody thing . . . Butler— hold off the Germans."

Butler ran back up the passage, fumbling in his ammunition pouch for a fresh magazine. There was no time to take a preliminary look-out, he could already hear the hammering of iron-shod boots.

One thing at least, he thought as he snapped the magazine home: a left-facing corner gave better cover than a right-facing one—he could fire round it without showing the whole of his body.

The jeep's engine roared again, and an instant later there was a loud crash from behind him.

He stepped half into the open, swinging the Sten into the firing position.

The enemy—

They were there in plain sight, thirty yards down the alley, but even before he could fire they seemed to vanish into convenient doorways—he marvelled that human beings could move so quickly as he opened fire on the emptiness.

Another crash behind him.

"It's no good," shouted Audley. "They're too strong!"

Something sailed through the air from down the alley to bounce off the wall of a house two yards below him. He shrank back round his corner, pressing himself flat against the wall behind him. The house shook with a sudden deafening concussion.

They were all going to die here—

He sprang out into the alley again and emptied the Sten into a cloud of dust.

"Come on, Butler," Audley shouted at him. "We're making a run for it—"

The jeep was jammed up close to the wooden doors. Sergeant Winston was nowhere to be seen—Butler looked around stupidly.

There was a strong smell of petrol—

"Over the gates—on the jeep and over the gates," Audley urged him.

Butler leapt onto the bonnet of the jeep and threw himself over the top of the wooden doors. As he did so he had a vision of a great white angel with high folded wings stretching out its arms to welcome him. Then he landed with a bone-jarring thud beside Sergeant Winston, who was crouched beside the gates slopping petrol out of a jerrycan.

Audley dropped beside them.

Another grenade exploded behind them somewhere.

Sergeant Winston clicked his cigarette lighter in the puddle of petrol, which ignited with an explosive *whumppp*.

"Let's get the hell out of here," said Winston.

WHUMPPP!

The wooden doors shook and a great tongue of orange flame rose above them.

"Holy God! Come on, Corporal!" said Winston, dragging at Butler's arm.

"Steady on." Audley took Butler's other arm. "That first grenade almost got him, I think—come on, Butler . . . it's time to be moving, old lad."

Butler had been staring at the beautiful white angel, whose arms were still raised in welcome. He felt himself being lifted and swivelled—now there was a great white cross in front of him.

Something stung his cheek.

He was in a monumental mason's yard, just like the one in Inkerman Street, which he'd passed a thousand times on his way to school.

"Sorry." He shook his head. "I'm all right, sir."

"Well, you won't be for long," said Winston. "If we don't get out of here soon we're gonna have to find a real good excuse for disturbing the peace—"

They were running.

White blocks of marble . . . a door in a wall—Sergeant Winston kicked it open . . . a vegetable garden—rows of French beans—Butler giggled at the sight of them, because if there was anywhere in the world where there ought to be rows of French beans it was in a French vegetable patch . . . and beetroot, with red-veined leaves, and fine big savoys, better even than in the general's garden.

The garden ended in a trim little hedge: Audley went through it as though he still had a tank around him. Butler followed him and found himself in a dusty little lane, with an open vineyard on the far side of it. The sky above him was blue and cloudless and for the first time he felt the warmth of the sun on his face.

"Come on, man!"

He blinked at the sun. Audley and Winston were already pounding down the lane ahead of him.

"Come on!" Audley was shouting at him.

He started to run again. His head seemed to be spinning, but his legs worked independently—it was like running downhill when the hill was so steep that the only way to keep upright was to run faster and faster.

There were trees now along the roadside, and he followed the other two off the lane into their shadow on the field's edge. The going was harder on the crumbly soil and he felt enraged with them that they should thus slow him down unnecessarily when he'd been running so well—

Audley pulled him down into the field between the vines.

"Crawl." Audley pointed at the American's backside, which was disappearing down the leafy avenue of the row. *"Crawl!"*

Butler crawled as best he could, with the Sten banging backwards and forwards and sideways on its strap round his neck.

"Faster!" urged Audley from behind. "Go on, go on, *go on!*"

Butler's heart was pounding on his chest by now, but he drew reserves of strength from the anger within him—he wasn't quite sure who or what he was angry with, but he certainly didn't intend to let any bloody tank officer, or any bloody American, outcrawl him. Marching, running, or crawling, no one could beat a rifleman—

Suddenly his legs were jerked from under him and Audley was pressing him down into the dirt.

"Quiet!" Audley hissed into his ear.

All he could see was endless vine bushes, the stems of which were gnarled and knotted as though the vines had grown slowly and painfully out of the soil over many years.

He was also aware that his head ached—there was a hammer inside it which grew louder and louder . . . and then faded.

"We'll crawl some more now . . . can you crawl some more, Corporal?" Audley's voice in his ear was solicitous.

Butler raised himself on one elbow. "Yes, sir."

"I'll take the Sten," said Audley.

"That's all right, sir—"

"I'll take it," Audley insisted.

"Yes, sir . . . I'd better put a fresh mag in then." He fumbled for another magazine and rearmed the gun. "There we are then, sir."

Audley was looking at him strangely. "You sure you feel okay?"

"Sir?" Butler frowned. "Why shouldn't I feel okay?"

The strange expression changed to one of surprise. "Don't you know you've been hit?"

"What?"

"Corporal . . ." Audley reached forward and touched the side of Butler's head. "Let's just have a look—"

"Ouch!" The subaltern's fingers stung like fire. He brushed them away and touched the same spot. "Ouch!"

His own fingers were covered with blood.

"Phew!" Audley breathed a sigh of relief. "It's only a flesh wound, I think—but you look as if half the side of your head has been blown off . . . yes . . . I can see where it creased the side of your skull and clipped your ear: it just dazed you a bit, that's all." He grinned at Butler. "It's only blood, that's all—that's a relief."

Butler looked down at his hand in horror. It was *his blood*.

There was a rustle among the vines ahead of them.

Sergeant Winston crawled into view. "We better shift our asses out of here before those motorcyclists come back," he said.

Motorcyclists?

"You okay, Corporal?" Winston addressed Butler. He sounded remarkably casual in the circumstances, thought Butler.

"Yes," he said sharply.

"Great." Winston nodded encouragingly at him. "That's head wounds for you—you can walk, you're alive. You can't walk, you're dead. So let's crawl instead, huh?"

They crawled.

The field went on and on forever, and Butler felt sicker and sicker, and angrier and angrier.

Then the hammering returned which had seemed before to be inside his skull, but which now came from the lane they had left. Only now it was also a long way away.

They hugged the earth until it had faded.

"They got better things to do than look for us," said Winston hopefully. "Come to that, the way the jeep went up, maybe they think we're still riding in it, with a bit of luck."

"True. But they could be looking to see whether there are any more of us," murmured Audley. "Which there won't be."

Butler stared at him. He was beginning to remember the confused events of their passage through Sermigny in greater detail.

"The other jeeps didn't get through," he said.

"Correction," snapped Audley. "The other jeep—singular."

Butler stared at him for a moment. Then he knew suddenly why he had been so angry—why he was still angry—and why he was going to remain angry until the score was evened.

"That treacherous bugger Purvis!" he whispered.

"And O'Conor," agreed Audley. "In fact—O'Conor first and last. Purvis merely set us up. He merely directed us."

"Holy God!" said Sergeant Winston.

"Yes," said Audley. " 'I've had a look-see myself—take it nice and easy, and don't run over any kiddies'—we let ourselves be taken, and he took us. Two little birds with one stone, and he even got someone else to throw it."

"But . . . the other jeep?" Butler raised his hand to scratch his scalp, which was itching, and then thought better of it. The bleeding seemed to have stopped of its own accord; he didn't know why it had stopped, only that was no more surprising than the fact that he couldn't remember when or how it had started. But it was better left alone, anyway.

"His own men, you mean?" Audley nodded thoughtfully. "Yes, that was pretty average cold-blooded—even by O'Conor's standards. . . . But then there's no reason why the whole of Chandos Force should be privy to the major's little scheme for liberating His Majesty's property on his own account . . . in fact, when you think about it—the more you think about it, the less likely it is that anyone except his inner circle knows what he's planning."

"Why not? Butler had a feeling that Audley was right, but after Sergeant Purvis's appalling treachery nothing was certain any more, and he felt that everyone was guilty until proven innocent.

"Why not? Well . . . because loot has to be divided, for one thing, so the fewer there are, the bigger the shares. And the fewer there are, the safer the secret is—and I don't think even Major O'Conor could have assembled an entire platoon of gangsters like himself." Audley turned towards the American. "What d'you think, Sergeant?"

Winston grunted. "Well, those two guys in the jeep behind us certainly weren't in on the deal, that's for sure." He raised himself cautiously above the vines. "But if you want to know what I think—I think we ought to put some more distance between us and those krauts while we can."

"Can you see anything?"

Winston lowered his head. "Nope. There's a column of smoke back there—looks like we started quite a fire, so maybe that'll keep them occupied some."

"There is, is there?" Audley lifted himself to peer over the leaves. "So there is, by jiminy! Now that's very promising . . ."

"Promising?"

"Yeah—how?"

Audley sank down again. "If those chaps weren't 'in on the deal' . . . I was just wondering how the esteemed sergeant—what was his name?" He looked at Butler.

"Purvis," spat Butler.

"Purvis, yes—how Sergeant Purvis will have reported our disappearance to the rest of them—including Colonel Clinton."

Winston frowned at him. "Hell, Lieutenant . . . that's no problem. I can just see that smiling sonofabitch explaining how we took the wrong turning and ran into the village before he could stop us."

"Exactly. They may even have heard the firing in the distance."

"So what?"

"So what will the major do, then?"

Winston frowned more deeply, his forehead creasing. "He'll shift his ass—?" He stared at Audley. "He'll . . . ?"

"Limejuice," said Butler.

"That's right." Audley gave Butler a twisted non-smile. "He'll do what he'd do if it was a genuine accident—he'll cover his tracks and spread alarm and confusion among the enemy with an air strike. He'll have to do it to keep up the pretence—and I rather think he would have done it anyway. Because it makes good sense."

This time Butler frowned—and discovered in doing so that it hurt to frown now. "Good sense . . . sir?"

"Ye-ess . . . a downy bird . . . Because even if there weren't any Germans at the Loire crossing when we came over they'll be wondering what the hell happened there by now, with that limejuice strike. So now he's given them the answer—which was us blundering into Sermigny." Audley paused, staring up at the blue sky above them and listening to the stillness for a moment. "And *now* . . . if he's the downy bird I take him to be . . . he'll ram the answer home with another drop of limejuice."

They all listened, but there was only an empty silence.

"What d'you think, Sergeant?" said Audley finally.

"Lieutenant"—Winston gave the silence another five seconds—"I think the sooner we crawl our asses out of here the better."

They crawled again.

But this time they crawled more steadily, and without the hampering Sten, Butler was able to fall into the rhythm of it, timing the movement of his left hand to his right knee, and that of his right hand to his left knee until they became automatic.

Ahead of him the American sergeant moved just rhythmically down the narrow avenue of vines, with their clusters of small green grapes and odd-shaped leaves. He had never imagined grapes growing on small bushes like these, but rather on high trellises like in the Kentish hop fields; nor did the grapes look anything like as juicy as the ones he remembered from Christmas before the war, when they had been one of the extra-special treats—though a treat not in the same class as the orange in the toe of his stocking.

More strange than the grapes were the American's boots, which were queer, high-laced things that reminded him of pictures of Edwardian ladies' boots; and they had no metal studs on their soles—that was why the American Army marched so unnaturally silently, of course—

The boots slid sideways suddenly.

"There's a wood just up ahead," said Winston.

Audley crawled up alongside them, breathing heavily—that was the difference from being encumbered by the machine-carbine, which outweighed its lightness with its awkwardness, thought Butler charitably.

"Okay. Let's get into it," said Audley.

"And then where?" asked Winston.

That was the question which had been looming in the back of Butler's mind all the time as he crawled, beyond the immediate problem of surviving.

What were they going to do?

Audley looked up into the sky, as though gauging his position. "Well . . . so far as I can make out, we're southeast of the village—maybe south-southeast—which means this is the wood we came out of, probably."

Winston squinted towards the sun. "Yeah—could be."

"Right . . . so if we head due east through the wood we should hit that other road—the one *they* took?" Audley looked at Winston questioningly.

Winston nodded slowly. "Could be, yeah."

"Then we head south."

Butler looked from one to the other of them as they stared at each other.

"I get you," said Winston. "And then the first Frenchman you meet, you ask if your buddies have passed that way, huh?"

"That's right, Sergeant."

The American smiled. "You know, Lieutenant, I kind of thought you were going to say that—I really did."

"You did?" said Audley stiffly. "That was clever of you, Sergeant."

"Sure. You're still the real Chandos Force. All two of you."

Audley took a deep breath. "I was . . . very much hoping it would be all three of us, Sergeant. I was hoping that very much." He took another breath. "We could use some help."

The sergeant chewed his lip. "Yeah, I can see that." He looked at Butler. "What d'you think, Corporal?"

Butler's mouth opened. "Who—me?"

Winston gazed at him for a second, shook his head, and then turned back to Audley.

"Okay, Lieutenant," he said. "Let's get the real Chandos Force on the road."

12. How they met strangers in the forest

The drawback of the wood was that it was impossible to move quietly in it.

Once they had put the first belt of trees and bushes between themselves and the vineyard they were able to walk free and upright, and that was a marvellous relief. But the ground was thick with twigs and small fallen branches which crunched

and crackled and snapped underfoot until Butler felt that the
whole German army, or at least that part of it which was south
of the Loire and hadn't yet heard that the war was almost
over, must hear them.

That was a childish imagining, he knew, but it also seemed
to affect the others, because they both trod as delicately as
they could, and indicated to him that he should do the same.
The problem was that it was difficult to keep his eyes on his
feet and at the same time avoid the foliage that brushed
against his face, something that would normally not have
worried him at all but which now became extremely painful.
Try as he would, he could not stop the branches whipping the
wounds on the side of his head and his ear: they seemed ma-
levolently determined to draw blood again, so that finally he
found himself stumbling along with one hand clamped over
the injuries and the other stretched out ahead of him like that
of a blind man feeling his way in the dark.

At the same time he experienced a growing irritation with
Audley for holding on to his precious Sten gun. He recognised
the emotion as being no less childish than his fear of the noise
they were making and his preoccupation with the pain of su-
perficial scratches; and that the young officer had only taken
the Sten in the first place as an act of kindness. But without it
he felt naked and defenceless in the knowledge that if they did
meet up with any Germans the lack of it left him no choice
other than to surrender or to run like a rabbit. Which was not
only unfair, but doubly unfair, because Audley still had his
holstered pistol—which was the only other weapon they possessed between them.

For the first time he began to think of the impossibility of
what Audley was proposing to do.

It wasn't just impossible—it was ridiculous.

They didn't know where they were—

They didn't know where they were going—

They didn't know where the major was going—

And even if they were able by some miracle to find out the
answer to that last question they had no prospect of catching
up with the major before he did whatever it was that he intended to do, whatever that was exactly, which they didn't
know—

Apart from which, there were still the sodding Germans to think about, because however experienced the major and his bloody bandits were at keeping out of harm's way, Second Lieutenant Audley's knowledge of war was limited to the destruction of tanks, and mostly British tanks, and Sergeant Winston was of all things, for Christ's sake, a demolition expert who probably didn't know one end of a rifle from the other—

Not that they'd even *got* a rifle—all they'd got was a Sten and a bloody revolver, and Mr. Audley was now carrying both of those—

"Are you all right, Butler?" asked Audley.

"Sir?" Butler looked at his right hand.

"You were mumbling and"—Audley stared at him—"and you've started bleeding again, man."

Butler could see that from the bright wet blood on his hand. Looking at it made him feel dizzy.

"Sit down," ordered Audley.

"I'm okay."

"I know you're okay. I'm just going to patch you up a bit, that's all. So sit down like a good fellow."

Butler sat down. There was a crashing in the bushes and Sergeant Winston appeared. Audley must have sent him up ahead to scout the route, he decided. Look-see and movement, in the best Chandos Force manner, that would be.

There was a glugging sound and then Audley handed him a large red silk handkerchief, soaking wet.

"Wipe your face with that, Corporal—freshen up." Audley's voice changed. "What's it like up ahead?"

"Like this for about half a mile. But then there's a track goes more or less in the right direction." Winston paused. "And I guess you were right."

"Right? . . . That's fine, Corporal. Now hold this dressing on the side of your head." Audley took the silk handkerchief in exchange. "How was I right?"

Butler applied the field dressing cautiously to the side of his head. He could well understand why Audley was so concerned about his well-being, since he constituted one third of the available manpower. But the subaltern needn't have worried, he thought grimly: if there was one thing worse than the madness of going on it was the prospect of being abandoned as unfit.

"How bad is he?" asked the American.

"I'm perfectly all right," said Butler.

"Huh?" Winston addressed the sound to Audley.

"The corporal?" Audley bent over him. "Oh, he's okay . . . I'm going to tie the dressing down with this handkerchief, Corporal. When I tighten it—that's when it'll hurt. . . . Yes, he's okay. That second grenade went off right in his face and all he's got is a couple of scratches and mild shock—"

What second grenade? There had been a second grenade which had gone off somewhere behind them, on the other side of the wooden gates, but—*ouch!*

What second grenade?

"—so he was obviously born to be hanged, like Corporal Jones. . . . But how was I right, Sergeant?" Audley surveyed his handiwork. "Well, it doesn't improve your appearance much, I must say. As the Iron Duke said, I don't know what effect you'll have on the enemy, but by God you frighten me. . . . But I think it'll hold for the time being. How was I right, did you say, Sergeant?"

Winston lifted his hand, one finger raised to silence them. In the far distance there was an angry, buzzing drone—no, it was not so much far off as high up. He had been listening to it for a minute or two—it had been growing inside his mind while they had been talking, Butler realised. And he had heard it before.

"Yes . . ." Audley looked at Butler. "Well, at least we won't have to be worrying about the Germans following us, not for the time being anyway . . . all right, Corporal?"

They pushed on at a steady dogtrot, careless of the noise they made.

Butler was aware, with a curious sense of detachment, that he felt very much better. He couldn't quite work out what had happened back in the village: there seemed to be a gap in his memory now, although there hadn't been any loss of consciousness at the time. But after that there had been some bad moments—he could see now that they had been bad moments by comparing the clarity of his present thoughts with the hazi-

ness of his recollection of their escape from the village into
the woods.

He was also aware that the drone of limejuice was building
up into a roar. The first time he had heard it the sound had
been overlaid by the acceleration of the jeep's engine at the
road crossing near the big house with the fairy-tale towers;
now the trees surrounding them and the makeshift bandage
which covered his damaged ear did nothing to mute it, but
only seemed to spread it until it echoed all around them until
it changed abruptly to a high-pitched shriek directly over their
heads.

Suddenly they weren't dogtrotting any more, they were
running as though their lives depended on their legs again.

With his new-found detachment, Butler realised as he ran
that they were running away from nothing. The Typhoons
were attacking the village, drawn irresistibly by that column
of smoke like wasps to a jam pot. What they were experienc-
ing—and he could feel the same fear pounding in his own
chest—was what the old sweats in the battalion, the survivors
of Dunkirk, had warned him against: the panic which made
men believe that every dive-bomber was lining itself up on
them alone.

Not even the distant sound of explosions far behind them
slowed down their speed. Rather, the explosions seemed to
urge them on—Butler could feel another logic taking over,
whispering to him that he couldn't be too far away from what
was happening behind him. The farther away the better, *the
farther away the better, the farther away the better*.

Not until they finally burst out of the last of the thick undergrowth into a plantation of tall pine trees did they start to
slow down.

"Which way?" said Audley breathlessly, skidding at last to
a halt.

"Hell, Lieutenant"—Winston panted, looking around
him—"I didn't come this way first time"—he pointed towards a great tangle of what looked like blackberry bushes on
the far side of the plantation—"that way, I guess."

Audley stared at the bushes for a moment, then sank onto
one knee behind a pine tree. "What was it like? Did it look as
if it's used much?" he said.

Butler was suddenly aware that the noise behind them had stopped and the drone of the Typhoon engines was dying away. The loudest sound now was the thudding of his own heart.

"The track?" Winston frowned from behind his tree towards Audley. "It looked kind of overgrown to me, what I could see of it. You want me to take another look, Lieutenant?"

"No." Audley was still staring at the bushes ahead, moving his head from one side to the other to scan the green wall more closely, as though there was something he had glimpsed momentarily and then lost.

"You seen something?" Winston stared intently in the same direction.

"No." Audley's voice had dropped to an urgent whisper. "But I can smell something, by God!"

"Smell—?" Winston cut the question off.

Butler started to draw in a deep breath through his nose and then stopped as quickly as Winston had stopped speaking.

It was a sweet-rotten smell, not the dead-cow smell, which was foul enough, but something different and fouler which caught in the back of his throat. He breathed out carefully through his mouth, grateful that there was nothing in his stomach; it wasn't that he hadn't encountered this particular death-smell before—it was very much a Normandy-smell—but rather that here, beyond the killing ground, it had caught him by surprise.

"Yeah . . ." Winston sniffed again, crouching down behind a tree as he did so. "Which way, d'you reckon?"

"Must be somewhere ahead," said Audley.

"Yeah . . ." Winston peered to the left and right, and then moved silently across the pine needles to sink down beside Audley. "Gimme the gun, Lieutenant, and I'll go take a look."

Audley surrendered the Sten before Butler could think of protesting, but then caught the American by the arm. "Not you, Sergeant—I'll go."

"Aw—come on, Lieutenant!" Winston tried to shake off the hand. "You're the brains of the outfit."

Butler came to a lightning decision: they were both equally unsuited to scouting, the heavily built engineer sergeant and the large dragoon subaltern, and it was high time he justified his own existence as something more than the useless walking wounded.

He ran lightly across the plantation to a tree near Audley's.

"Sir"—the trick was not to give them time to argue, so he started to move again as they turned towards him—"cover me—"

The thick carpet of pine needles deadened his footfalls as he zigzagged from tree to tree, heading for the only gap he could see in the thicket ahead. Beyond the gap and in the chinks in the thicket he could see the bright sunlight unfiltered by over-hanging greenery: it was like looking from a cool, shadowy room into the open, where nothing was hidden from sight.

There was a thin scatter of brambles, weak and straggling for lack of direct light, among the last trees of the plantation. Their trailing ends plucked at his battle dress, but without the encumbrance of the Sten he had both hands free to part them without making any sound. As he did so the stink of dead flesh thickened horribly around him, filling his nose and his mouth and his lungs. It seemed to grow worse with every step he took, until suddenly he knew with absolute certainty that all his care in making a silent approach to the track was un-necessary: whatever there was out there, it was long past lis-tening to anything—nothing alive and breathing could endure to hang around within range of this smell, which begged only for the mercy of a burial detail. He would stake his stripes on that.

The sunlight lay three steps ahead of him. Only as he was in the act of taking the third, when it was really too late to draw back, did it occur to him that he was staking more than his stripes on his sense of smell.

Twenty yards down the track, half hidden in the under-growth on the other side into which it had been driven, was a German lorry.

Behind it, farther down, was another vehicle—a decrepit-looking truck—surrounded by several smashed-open ammu-nition boxes, and beyond that what looked like a civilian car with its touring hood half raised, its doors hanging open. Like the lorry, they had both been driven off the narrow track into the overgrown verge. The track itself stretched away beyond them, open and deserted, and so silent that he could hear the buzz of insects.

"Butler"—Audley was crouching in the shadow at the edge of the plantation—"can you see anything?"

A big dragonfly flew across the bonnet of the lorry, hovered for an instant in a flash of iridescent blue, and then set off fearlessly down the line of vehicles. Butler watched it settle on one of the splintered boxes. His eye came back to the lorry again: its windscreen was bullet-scarred.

He beckoned to Audley. "It's all clear," he said.

Audley stepped out through the thicket into the sunlight, stared for one long moment at the abandoned vehicles, and then pushed his pistol back into its webbing holster.

Sergeant Wilson appeared at his shoulder, wrinkling his nose against the smell. "Jesus! Looks like someone's been picking off the stragglers, eh?"

Audley looked at him quickly. "The stragglers? Yes—I see . . . you mean the French Resistance?"

"Can't be anyone else this far south of the river. Our patrols didn't tangle with anyone." Winston walked towards the lorry, pointing to its pock-marked side. "That's sure as hell not nice, and it's not point-fives either, so it's not an air strike—those babies punch bigger holes than that. This is small-arms stuff did this."

"Uh-huh?" Audley had circled warily round to the back of the truck as the American was speaking. He raised his hand towards the bullet-torn canvas flap.

"Hey, hold on, Lieutenant," Winston cautioned him, grimacing. "The way it stinks here, maybe what's in there's better left alone, huh?"

"Oh . . . yes." Audley stared at the flap for a moment, then dropped his hand, wiping the palm against his trousers as though the nearness to the lorry had contaminated it.

They moved on to the truck which had carried the ammunition boxes. It was a bit like a box itself, with an old-fashioned, home-made look about it which reminded Butler of the ancient vehicle which the scouts had hired to transport the troop and its equipment to the Lake District for that last camp before the war.

Winston ran a professional eye over it, shaking his head in

wonderment. "Man—they sure are scraping the bottom of the barrel," he murmured.

Audley stepped up onto the runningboard and peered into the high, open cab. There was a sudden buzzing sound and a cloud of flies rose into the air—great bloated obscene things the size of young wasps. Audley shied away from them, jumping back onto the grass with an exclamation of disgust.

"What's the matter?" said Winston quickly.

"Nothing." Audley blinked and shook his head. "Just blood."

"Blood?"

"Dried blood . . . four, five days old." Audley went on shaking his head. "Just . . . it just reminded me of s-s-something, that's all."

Beyond the truck and the shattered boxes lay a big BMW motorcycle. Winston pounced on it eagerly.

"Now this is more like it"—he heaved the machine upright —"aw, shit—the goddamn thing's smashed to hell!" He let it fall back into the grass. "Front fork's snapped, handlebars twisted—like it ran smack into something."

"Indeed?" Audley bent over the motorcycle. "Yes, I think you're right. . . ." He straightened up, staring back the way they had come and then forward at the last vehicle, the civilian car. "You know there's something funny about this little lot—something decidedly queer . . ."

"Funny?" Winston stared at him.

"Yes. Funny peculiar, not funny ha-ha." Audley nodded, studying the line again. "I thought it was a straightforward ambush when I first saw it—took it for granted. But you know . . . it isn't an ambush at all." He shook his head emphatically. "These things were all shot up somewhere else, I think—and then they were brought here and dumped."

Winston frowned, first at Audley, then at the vehicles, then back at Audley again. "How d'you figure that, Lieutenant?"

Audley pointed at the ground behind the ancient truck. "See the tyre tracks in the earth there?"

Butler followed the pointing finger. Weighed down by its load, the truck had pressed deeply into the verge where it had left the hard-compacted surface of the track.

"Sure, but—"

"The ground was damp when they ran it off the road." Audley pointed back towards the lorry. "But that didn't dig into the ground, and it's a lot bigger and heavier than this one. And that isn't the only thing—" He gestured at the tyre-ruts again. "See how the grass has sprung up. That's what I first noticed about the lorry: the way the grass and the weeds had recovered. Which means they've both been here for several days, maybe a week or more, as well as being parked at different times."

Butler shifted his attention to the motorcycle. That, after all, had been what had started Audley's detective process. So the decisive clue must be somehow connected with it, and the best way of proving his own powers of observation was to spot it before Audley had time to reveal it first.

To his joy the clue was obvious.

"But the motorbike's only just been ditched here," he said eagerly, pointing to the clear line of crushed grass which marked the machine's route from the track to its last resting place. "And there's no sign that it crashed here, either."

Audley grinned at him. "That's exactly it, Corporal—spot on! In fact it can't have been here for more than a day, I'd guess."

"Aye, sir..." Butler stared down the track. The young officer's pleasure at his own cleverness was a bit comical—he could imagine how it might annoy his superiors and make him a figure of fun among his NCOs and troopers. The very fact that he would often be right and one step ahead of the field— as he had been in the barn the night before—would make matters worse, not better. That was what Colonel Sykes had meant when he had observed that Mr. Audley was perhaps too clever for his own good: the function of second lieutenants was not to be clever but to obey orders and lead their men and be killed. At least, that was their function in the Lancashire Rifles, as laid down by the adjutant. Those who were capable of more than that were expected to hide their light under a bushel, and that was obviously a lesson Mr. Audley hadn't learnt.

And yet, and yet... and yet even though under the young officer's innocent self-esteem there was also a suggestion of typical bloody-minded public-school arrogance—he hadn't

learnt that lesson because such lessons didn't apply to him—
there was a challenge. Rank meant nothing to David Audley:
only the man who could outthink him was his superior officer.

"Aye." He looked Audley in the eye. "And we're close to
the road, that means."

The confirmation was there in Audley's face: the recognition that Corporal Butler was something more than cannon
fodder.

"What d'you mean?"

Winston started towards the civilian car. "He means nobody
rode that goddamn bike here—not with a broken front fork.
They pushed it." The last sentence was delivered over his
shoulder as he reached for the clips on one side of the car's
bonnet. "Which means . . . we're close to the goddamn road."

"Oh . . ." Audley looked chagrined. "You're right—and I
should have thought of that."

"Hell, no! What you should have thought"—Winston threw
back one half of the bonnet with a clang—"is whether I can
get this thing going. Because if we're going to catch up with
those sons-of-bitches we've got to have wheels under us." He
glanced quickly at Butler. "Check the gas, Corporal—the
tank'll be round the back somewheres."

On second thought maybe the American's practical common sense was going to be of more use than Audley's powers
of deduction, decided Butler.

"Do you think you can?" said Audley excitedly. "By
God—d'you think you can, Sergeant?"

"I dunno, but I'm sure as hell going to try." Winston
frowned at the engine. "It shouldn't be too difficult . . . if the
battery's okay . . . and if there's—now what the fuck is that,
for God's sake? Oh, I get it . . . yeah, I get it—the last time I
tried this, Lieutenant, my pa kicked my ass so hard I couldn't
sit down for a week."

"Indeed? And why did he do that?"

"It was his car. . . . But whether it works with a kraut
car . . ."

"It's a French car actually, I rather think."

"Yeah? Now if there's gas—"

Butler skipped guiltily to the rear of the car. There was the filler cap, sure enough—but how was he expected to discover whether there was any petrol in the tank?

Winston lifted his head out of the engine. "Any luck?"

There was a strong smell of petrol, in as far as any other smell could be called strong in the presence of the one from the back of the lorry.

"There's petrol in the tank," he said hopefully. "I can smell it."

"Yeah . . . there's petrol this end. But whether there's more than a smell . . ." Winston looked at Audley. "So we give it a try, Lieutenant?"

Audley shrugged. "What have we got to lose?"

Winston smiled, his ugly face suddenly transformed, even though it was a rueful smile. "Well, I guess if you don't know then it's too late to tell you. But . . . okay—here we go!"

Butler crossed his fingers. He didn't know what Winston meant, but he knew that Americans were wizards with machines.

The engine whirred—coughed—whirred again, coughed again, fell silent. Hope faded.

"It's no good?" said Audley.

"Hell no! One more try and I think we're there—"

"*No!*" said a new voice behind them.

For a fraction of a second Butler was aware that all three of them had frozen, Winston with the wires he had loosened in his hands, Audley and himself foolishly gawping into the engine at the magic the American was about to perform. It flashed through his mind that they had been behaving as though they were the last three people in the world, with all thoughts of caution blotted out by the prospect of pursuing the major. They had been caught as defenceless as babes-in-arms—babes without arms.

He turned round slowly.

Dreh dich langsam un—?

"*Nous sommes des amis,*" said Audley. "*Je suis un officier anglais.*"

There was not one, but three men facing them—and now a fourth stepped out of the bushes farther down the track, to cover them with a machine pistol.

"That I can see—fortunately for you." The speaker was a

slightly built man wearing a pale grey double-breasted suit which looked too big for him. He carried no weapon, but in the circumstances he didn't need to: the men standing on either side of him were armed to the teeth, cross-bandoleered complete with German stick grenades in their belts. And somehow the cloth caps which they wore made them even more dangerous-looking: Butler had the strange feeling that they were his enemies no less than the Germans—that they were primed and ready to shoot down anything in uniform, grey or khaki or olive drab. All it needed was one word from the little man in the double-breasted suit.

The Frenchman's eyes flicked over them, lingering momentarily on Audley's black beret and on Sergeant Winston. Finally he came back to Audley.

"You are SAS—you have a mission here?" he snapped.

Audley's chin lifted. "Not locally. We were reinforcing an operation to the southwest. But we ran into some Germans—"

"What operation?"

Audley shrugged. "Does it matter? What matters is—we need some transport to catch up with our main party." He slapped the car's mudguard. "If it's all the same to you, m'sieur, we'll be on our way."

The Frenchman compressed his lips. "For the moment that is not possible."

"Indeed?" Audley managed to sound arrogant. "And may one ask why it isn't possible?"

"One may, yes." The Frenchman gave as good as he'd received. "One may also come and see for oneself."

"See what?"

"Why you must delay your departure." The Frenchman looked at his wristwatch. "Perhaps it would even be to your advantage."

"Oh yes?"

"Oh yes." The compressed lips twisted. "You wish for transport. . . . Well, we may perhaps be able to get you something better"—he pointed to the car—"than that."

"Like what?" asked Winston. "Like a Sherman, maybe?"

"Not a tank, no." The Frenchman raised an eyebrow at the sergeant. "But a German staff car—would that suit you?"

13.   How Second Lieutenant Audley took a prisoner

Butler snuggled himself comfortably on the thick bed of leaves behind the beech tree, munched the last two squares of his bar of ration chocolate, and decided that things had taken another distinct turn for the better.

For one thing, and a most comforting thing too, he'd got the Sten back—*his* Sten. And this had been accomplished without recrimination simply by picking it up from where Sergeant Winston had laid it down, and not returning it to him. Winston had given him an old-fashioned look, true; but then he'd shrugged his acceptance of the repossession—and now one of the French Resistance men had obligingly furnished him with a Luger pistol, so that he couldn't argue that he was unarmed even though the Luger looked well worn and would probably jam after the first shot.

And for another thing, and an equally comforting one for all that the condition was a temporary one, they were no longer alone in a sea of Germans. There were at least ten Frenchmen on this side of the road, and as many more on the other side; and if they were irregulars who could hardly be expected to stand up to real fighting like trained soldiers at least they were well armed—he'd seen two LMGs as well as a variety of submachine guns—and if they did run away it was their country, so they would know where to run.

And, possibly best of all, this was an ideal spot for an ambush.

He peered round the trunk of the beech tree down to the narrow roadway below, running his eye back along it from the culvert on his left to where it disappeared round the curve of the hillside fifty or sixty yards to his right.

It was a perfect killing ground. By the time anyone driving round that curve saw the ten-foot gap which had been blown in the culvert they would be smack in the middle of two converging fields of fire. They couldn't go on, and with the narrowness of the road—the hill slope on one side and an eight-foot drop on the other—they couldn't turn round. Their only chance was to back up, and to do that they'd have to stop dead first. And when they stopped dead they'd *be* dead.

It would be as easy as cowboys and Indians—

He frowned suddenly at the image as it occurred to him that somehow he'd become one of the Indians. And although he tried to reverse the thought—for God's sake, the men in the staff car would be *Germans*—it wouldn't change.

Somewhere along the line of the past twenty-four hours everything had become mixed up, where before it had been so clear. On this, his first day of war, nothing had been as he had imagined it would be. Everything he had trained for, everything he knew, everyone he knew—the real world and the real war—it was all far away, back in Normandy.

Even the enemy was different.

In the last couple of hours—or however many hours it was —he had killed two men, two human beings, and both of them had been British soldiers like himself.

And yet both of those British soldiers had been his enemies. In fact, they had been his enemies more certainly than any of the Germans he had seen in the village square at Sermigny— more certainly even than the German soldier who had hurled the grenade at him in the alley. Because that German had only been trying to kill the British soldier who had been trying to kill him. Whereas Corporal Jones and the machine-gunner beside the Loire had been set on killing *him*—944 Butler J, Jack Butler, little Jackie Butler—*him*. And for no better reason than because the major preferred certainties to odds.

Which made it not war, but plain murder—

"Hey, mac—"

Butler blinked, and found that he'd turned away from the road and was staring fixedly at the dead leaves six inches from his nose.

"Hey, mac—you okay?"

Sergeant Winston had crawled from his position behind the neighbouring tree right up beside him.

He stared at the American. "It's Jack, not mac," he said automatically, wondering as he did so why the sergeant should take him for a Scotsman.

"Jack then. Are you okay?"

Butler frowned again. "Yes . . . of course I'm okay. I was

just thinking—I was wondering whether we're the cowboys or the Indians, that's all."

"Wondering *what*?" Winston's face creased up in sudden bewilderment. "I don't get you."

Butler poked the leaves savagely with his finger, wishing he hadn't spoken. "I don't get myself."

"What d'you mean—cowboys and Indians?" Winston pressed him. "You kidding me or something?"

"No . . . I don't know." Butler concentrated on the miniature trench he was digging in the leaves. For no reason he thought of the German who had been carrying the armful of loaves. "I suppose . . . I don't know . . . it doesn't seem right, killing Germans like this—I didn't think I'd ever feel like this. I thought it'd be the easiest thing in the world." He looked at Winston. "I was looking forward to it."

Winston appeared thunderstruck. "You never killed a German before?"

No, just two Englishmen, thought Butler miserably.

"No," he said.

"What about back in the village?"

Butler swallowed. "I don't think I hit anybody."

"Well—Jee-sus Christ!" Winston rocked on his heels. "Jee-*sus!*" Then he started to chuckle. "Jee-*sus!*"

Butler flushed angrily.

Winston shook his head helplessly for a moment. "Man—Jack—don't get me wrong! I'm not laughing at you—I tell you, I never *seen* a German until today, except prisoners. Not even on Omaha . . . But *you*—I had you figured for a hard-nosed bastard, a real fire-eater."

"Me?"

"Sure. Like—shoot first and to hell with the questions, and a bayonet in the guts if you haven't got a gun handy—" He stopped abruptly and stared hard at Butler. "You're really not kidding me?"

A sound from the road drew Butler's attention momentarily. Audley and the Frenchman in the suit were crossing it just beyond the culvert, followed by a party of Resistance men.

He turned back to Winston. "I wish I was."

"Okay." Winston nodded. "Then you just think how much

the krauts would be worrying about you if they were up here waiting. Because my guess is—not one hell of a lot."

Butler was still struggling with the idea of himself as one of Major O'Conor's hardened veterans. "I suppose you're right."

"I know I'm right. They're the Indians, Jack—and the only good Injun is a dead one, you can take that from me."

The memory of the major had concentrated Butler's mind. When he thought about it, it wasn't the Germans who had confused the issue—it was the major.

He nodded. "I think it's just that if there's anyone I'd like to kill at this minute, it'd be Major O'Conor."

"And that sonofabitch sergeant—now you're talking!" Winston jabbed a finger towards him. "In fact, talking of cowboys and Indians, you ever seen a movie called *Stagecoach*?"

"No."

"You should have—it's a great movie. Got Claire Trevor in it, and I really go for her in a big way . . . but, see, there's this young cowboy on the stagecoach wants to get to town to kill the three men who gunned down his brother. And they get chased by Indians on the way—yeah, the young guy lost his horse, just like us, which is why he has to take the stage. And they're right down to their last bullet—"

"When the cavalry arrives." Audley appeared round the side of the tree. "That's *Stagecoach*—made by John Ford, who also made *The Grapes of Wrath*—I saw it on my last leave. Right?"

Winston looked up at the officer, a trace of irritation in his expression. "That's right, Lieutenant. Except it came out in the States about two years before the war," he said coolly.

"Two years before your war, not ours," said Audley. "But that's beside the point just now. Because our joint war starts in about eight minutes. There'll be two vehicles—a *Kübelwagen* with three men in it and the staff car with four. The *Kübel* is the escort—it has a machine gun mounted. Of the men in the staff car, at least two are in civvies—the French think they're Gestapo. But there's also a Wehrmacht officer, possibly a high-ranking one—could be Waffen SS. They want him alive if possible, or at least not too badly damaged. Make a useful hostage, apparently."

"Okay, Lieutenant." Winston nodded. "For him, we'll aim low."

"No." Audley shook his head quickly. "We don't shoot at all, unless we absolutely have to. The French have got it all worked out, they've done it before on this very spot. The only difference is that this time they're going to try to keep the vehicles unmarked so we can use them afterwards."

"You mean . . . we just sit and watch?"

"Not quite. They do the shooting. But in return for the staff car—or the *Kübel* if we prefer it—we take the prisoner for them."

"Oh, just great! They sit behind their trees and pick the bastards off, and we take the risks!" Winston grunted scornfully. "You sure drive a hard bargain, Lieutenant—or they do."

"They'll be taking risks too, don't you worry, Sergeant," snapped Audley. "And if you thought for a moment instead of bellyaching you'd realise it makes sense, our trying for the general or whoever he is. These Frenchmen aren't choosy about taking prisoners—I think this lot are all Communists and they're settling old scores. And if the general knows that, which he certainly will know, then he'll fight like the rest of them. But if he sees our uniforms then there's a good chance he'll surrender—that's the whole bloody point."

"Huh!" Winston subsided. "Okay, Lieutenant."

Audley looked at Butler. "Any questions, Corporal?"

Butler thought for a moment. "How do the French know so much about the Germans, sir—how do they know they're coming this way, even?"

The corner of Audley's mouth twisted. "They've got it all organised, as I said. They come from a village down the road, and they wait until one or two German vehicles come through on their own—they let the bigger convoys through. But when something like this lot comes along they put up a sign on the main road—a sign in German, a proper Wehrmacht diversion sign—saying the bridge farther along is down. And they've got one of their own chaps in Milice uniform who offers to take the Germans round a back road which is safe. . . . You just wait and see, anyway."

"Seems a lot of trouble. Why don't they deal with them

there and then?" murmured Winston, staring down at the road.

"Because they're scared stiff of reprisals. It seems the SS wiped out a village down south where one of their divisions was held up . . ."

"Wiped out?"

"That's what they say. So the stragglers they cut off have to disappear completely—that's what we found back there"—Audley nodded in the direction they'd come—"the evidence, you might say."

"The smell is what I remember," said Winston.

Audley stood up, and incredibly he was grinning. "Yes, the smell . . ." He looked at his watch. "Three minutes . . . Yes, they killed the poor devils. But they did bury them."

Winston frowned, first at Butler, then at Audley. "Huh?"

Audley looked from one to the other. "The first time they were after weapons and ammunition—in the lorry. But they were unlucky."

"Unlucky?"

Audley started to move. "Yes. They captured a ton of over-ripe cheese," he said over his shoulder.

Butler watched him move to a nearby tree.

"Cheese," whispered Winston. He stared past Butler towards Audley. "Now . . . there goes a genuine one-hundred-per-cent hard-nosed sonofabitch." He looked at Butler. "We've got to watch ourselves, you and me, Jack—like the young guy in *Stagecoach* had to watch the sheriff."

"What d'you mean?" asked Butler.

The American continued to look at him. "Yeah . . . I didn't finish, did I? They were down to their last bullet when the cavalry arrived and killed off the Indians. And then when they got to town the sheriff let the young guy go and settle up with the bad guys—he even offered him some more ammunition. So he was okay—the sheriff was."

"Yes?"

Winston looked again towards Audley. "I just don't know about the lieutenant . . ." He turned towards Butler. "But then the young guy took off his hat—and you know what there was in it?"

"No?"

"Three bullets. And you know . . . I think we'd better keep a couple of bullets too, just in case."

Cheese.

Butler lowered his head until his chin was touching the leaves. There was a one-inch gap between them and the fallen tree trunk behind which he'd settled in preference to his original position. As a firing position he was too low and narrow to be any use, but it was a perfect observation slit, giving him a clear view of the road, and if he wasn't going to be able to take part in the ambush, he was determined to watch.

Well, it hadn't smelt like any cheese he'd ever smelt; at least, not like the soapy mousetrap Cheddar favoured by the Army, which sweated and grew grey-green hairy mould in its old age but didn't smell much. But then he'd never been close to a ton of it; and French cheese was obviously very different from English—that smell had been a fearful, liquid-putrescent one.

Now he could hear the distant sound of engines—

So dead horses smelt worse than dead men, and dead mules smelt worse than dead horses, but dead cheese smelt worse even than dead mules. That was one thing his dad hadn't discovered in the trenches. . . .

A small, grey, jeeplike car came into view—it was at once more carlike than the jeep, with its high body, but less carlike with its little sloping bonnet carrying its spare wheel and its feeble, whining engine.

Four Germans—no, three Germans and a fourth man in a dark blue uniform and an oversized floppy beret—

The small car—Audley's Kübel it had to be—braking sharply as the driver saw the wrecked culvert, rocking and skidding almost broadside. The soldier in the passenger's seat half rose to his feet, then ducked as the machine-gunner started to traverse his weapon behind him.

Now there was a second vehicle in view—it was the staff car, a heavy, powerful-looking vehicle with a closed canvas hood and sidescreens. Even before it had quite pulled up the front passenger's door had swung open and a civilian wearing a dark felt hat raised himself above the level of the hood without getting out. He stared round suspiciously at the silent woods all around him.

The machine-gunner traversed his weapon left and right, up and down, left and right again. Butler could feel the tension and the fear spreading out from the men in the vehicles, like ripples in a pond lapping over him, making his heart beat faster.

Nothing happened.

Suddenly the blue-uniformed man moved—if that was the French Resistance man in the Milice uniform, then, by God, he was a brave one, thought Butler admiringly. He sprang out of the Kübel and took half a dozen cautious steps to peer over the edge of the gap in the culvert. Then he turned and called to the civilian in the staff car, pointing down into the gap.

The civilian stepped down onto the road and started towards the culvert, swinging to the left and right as he advanced to keep his eye on the woods. When he reached the gap the blue-uniformed man spoke quickly to him, gesticulating into the hole at their feet.

The civilian nodded finally, then swung back towards the Kübel and barked an order. As the Kübel's driver and the man beside him jumped obediently onto the roadway the Milice man eased himself over the edge of the gap into the crater.

A moment later the end of a stout plank appeared out of the crater.

So that was it, thought Butler: there were planks in there, the material of a temporary bridge which had spanned the gap. And the false Milice man was tempting the Germans into replacing them—tempting them away from the vehicles.

One of the rear doors of the staff car opened and another felt-hatted civilian raised cautiously, just as the first one had done.

The scene had fragmented into three separate areas of activity, which Butler found he could no longer observe simultaneously.

Above the staff car's canvas hood the second civilian was scanning the trees intently, just as his predecessor had done; on the Kübel the machine-gunner continued to traverse the gun, searching for a target; and beside the crater the two soldiers were hauling at the plank, under the direction of the first civilian.

Butler's senses all seemed to be stretched to breaking point: he could see every detail below him, he could smell the exhaust gases of the idling engines mixed very faintly with the stronger odour of the leaf mould and forest duff right under his nose; he could hear the sound of the individual engines, and beyond them the very absence of sound, and beneath both the thud of his own heart.

Now!

He was staring at his own chosen objective, the shadowy figure in the back seat of the staff car, when the first shot rang out.

The sound of the shot was overtaken by that of a second shot in the same instant that he saw the machine-gunner start to fall. And then all single sounds were lost in the crashing burst of fire from all around him.

"Come on!" shouted Audley.

Butler hurled himself down the slope. The firing had stopped as though by magic—he could still hear it ringing and echoing—but now everyone was shouting and he was shouting too.

And above the shouting was the continuous blaring of a car horn.

"Hände hoch! Hände hoch!" roared Audley as he sprang onto the road two yards ahead.

Butler saw him leap at the car like a tiger and wrench the driver's door open.

"Ich bin Offizier englischer!" he shouted ungrammatically.

The driver slumped out onto the road and the car horn stopped.

Butler tore at the rear door.

The only remaining occupant of the car was cowering down between the seats on the floor of the car.

"Ich bin Engländer," said Butler to the field-grey back.

Audley thrust himself and his revolver into the front of the car. *"Ich bin Offizier englischer,"* he repeated hoarsely. *"Hände hoch."*

The field-grey back began to move.

"Gott sei Dank! Gott sei Dank!"

They had taken their prisoner, and he was undamaged.

The German raised himself from the floor and turned towards them. He took in both of them carefully for a moment before settling on Audley.

"Lieutenant," he said in English that was only slightly accented, "I surrender myself to you."

Then, as they stared at him in surprise, he raised his hands in what Butler thought for a second was supplication.

They had taken their prisoner right enough—and he was a German officer too.

And he was also all of twenty years old.

And he was handcuffed.

14.   How Hauptmann Grafenberg fell out of the frying pan

"Oh my God!" said Sergeant Winston hoarsely.

Butler pulled back from the staff car and swung towards the American in alarm.

"My God." The suet-pudding colour of Winston's face under its tan went with the horror and disgust in his voice.

For a moment Butler thought the sergeant had been hit; then, even before the evidence of his own eyes cancelled the thought, he realised that wasn't possible. The enemy hadn't had time to fire a shot, and from the moment Audley had jumped up from cover the French hadn't fired another one. The ambush had been over ten seconds after it had started.

And besides, Sergeant Winston was obviously not wounded: he was standing stock-still on the edge of the road behind the staff car, his Luger pointing at the ground beside him. He was simply staring towards the crater.

Butler followed the stare. The man in the Milice uniform was rolling the body of a soldier over onto its back—the jack-booted legs seemed unwilling at first to follow the torso, but finally twisted with it, splaying out stiffly and horribly like a dummy's.

He looked back at Winston. Somehow there must be more

to it than that. Winston might not be a battle-hardened veteran, but he hadn't behaved until now like a man who'd be scared sick at the sight of death. He might not have seen any fighting Germans until today, but he must have seen enough of that on Omaha Beach, by God!

"What's the matter?" he said sharply, the disquiet he felt edging out concern from his own voice.

"The matter?" Winston repeated the words under his breath before turning to him. "The matter is—you were goddamn right, mac—we are the fucking Indians."

"What's this?" Audley straightened up beside them. He took in Winston's stricken expression, and then the scene at the edge of the crater, where the Milice man was methodically stripping the Germans. His bruised cheek twitched slightly as he turned back towards the American. "He's dead, for God's sake."

Winston watched the Milice man. "Yeah . . . he's dead"—he paused—*"now."*

"Now?" Audley stared at the American, then back at the Milice man, and then finally at Butler. "Did you see, Corporal?"

"I saw," Winston snapped. "I saw."

Audley bit his lip. Suddenly he looked around him nervously.

"That's right, Lieutenant," said Winston. "You take a good look."

There were Resistance men coming down the road behind them, and others advancing through the trees across the road. Up the hillside Butler could see more of them.

He caught Winston's eye and knew that now he was frightened too.

Winston nodded. "You got there, mac—Jack, huh? You play with Indians . . . and they play rough."

"But—" Butler could see the little man in the suit picking his way round the crater. He was trying to keep his shoes clean.

"So we've got them their general, like they wanted," said Winston.

Their general? Oh, God! thought Butler, remembering the

white-faced boy in the staff car—the boy in the handcuffs who had just a moment ago thanked the same God.

"So now we're maybe surplus to requirements," said Winston.

"Cock your Sten, Corporal," said Audley.

"What?"

"Cock the bloody thing!" Audley hissed at him. "Cock it and smile!"

Butler looked down at the machine carbine and saw to his horror that it wasn't cocked. He'd charged down the hillside shouting like—like an Indian. But he hadn't remembered to cock his gun.

The little man in the suit came towards them.

Audley ostentatiously replaced his pistol in its holster. Then he took four quick paces towards the Frenchman and threw his arms round him.

"*Bravo, mon camarade! Bien joué!*" he cried loudly, kissing the little man first on one cheek, and then on the other. "Jolly good show!" He released the little man and grabbed the hand of the man next to him, pumping it vigorously. "*Je vous remercie—je vous remercie beaucoup. Au nom des armées anglaises et americaines je vous remercie—vive la Résistance! Vive la Libération! Vive la France!*"

"*Monsieur—*" The man in the suit raised his hand to silence him, but Audley took not a blind bit of notice. Instead he gestured to include everyone in earshot.

"*Mes amis—j'ai de bonnes nouvelles pour vous—de très bonnes nouvelles. Aujourd'hui des chars americains font le passage de la Loire. Le débarquement des puissances alliées au sud de la France a commencé. Les allemands sont finis. C'est la victoire!*" Audley raised his arms to suit his words, his fingers giving the V-sign.

The Resistance men stared at him as though he was mad.

Winston stepped forward to Audley's side, stuffing his pistol into his waistband as he did so. "That's dead right—this is a big day. And I can tell you—General Patton's sure going to be glad to hear how you boys helped us. Yes, *sir!*"

Butler looked around despairingly. Audley could hardly have got less reaction from his listeners if he'd been speaking

in ancient Greek—or if he'd been telling them that the war
was not won, but lost.

There came a scraping sound from behind him, followed by
a quick half-suppressed grunt of pain.

The young German officer stumbled forward, prodded from
behind. The man in the suit looked at him in astonishment.

"Yes . . ." Audley smiled ruefully. "Well, we don't seem to
have got ourselves a general after all. And it does rather look
as if we've actually released a prisoner, not captured one,
eh?"

The Frenchman ignored him. *"Sprechen Sie franzosisch?"*

"Nein." The prisoner brushed at a lock of straw-coloured
hair which had fallen across his face.

Audley gave a grunt. "But he speaks good English." He
half-turned towards the German. "Name and rank?"

The German stiffened, abandoning the attempt to shift the
hair. "Grafenberg, Hauptmann—captain," he said.

There were only two pips on the boy's shoulder strap—but
that was right for a captain, Butler remembered. What was
more to the point was that there was no other telltale badge,
which meant he was straight Wehrmacht. It didn't surprise
him that there were now captains just out of nappies in the
German army: back in 1940 there'd been plenty of flight-
lieutenants like that in the RAF.

"Unit?" said Audley quickly. "What unit, stationed where?"

Captain Grafenberg looked at him helplessly, rocking
slightly on his heels as though the question hurt him. "Grafenberg, Hauptmann," he whispered.

Audley grinned. "Of course! Just name, rank, and number
—and I'm not going to bother about that. I accept your surrender, Captain."

"No—" began the Frenchman.

"Yes. And in the circumstances I also require your *parole—*
your word of honour"—Audley fired the words in a machine-
gun burst—*"immediately."*

"No!" snapped the Frenchman.

"Yes!" said Captain Grafenberg. "Yes—my word of honour—I give my word of honour—"

"Good. I accept your word of honour, under the rules of
war. It will hold good until I hand you over to the first Allied

unit we meet, which will probably be one from the American army—is that clearly understood, Captain?"

"Yes, Lieutenant." Captain Grafenberg brushed the hair out of his face with his manacled hands. "I understand."

"Very good." Audley nodded. "Corporal Butler!"

"Sir!"

"You will take charge of the prisoner, Corporal." Audley turned back to the Frenchman. "Now, m'sieur . . . you wanted a senior officer, but all we've caught is a junior one, who can't possibly be of any use to you—he'll just be an embarrassment—an encumbrance . . . *un embarras, n'est-ce pas?*"

The Frenchman gave Audley a very old-fashioned look, and then flicked a quick glance at Butler just in time to catch him lowering his Sten.

He watched Butler for a moment before speaking. "You are . . . a rash young man, Lieutenant, I think."

"Maybe."

"Not maybe. *Morte la bête, mort le venin*—if they have no use they are better dead."

"You can't kill them all."

"But we can kill as many as we catch." The Frenchman's lips drooped at one corner. "You have not had four years of them."

"No?" Audley's chin lifted in that characteristically arrogant way of his. "You know, I could have sworn we'd been fighting them too."

Winston coughed. "Lieutenant," he said out of the side of his mouth, "we got some distance to make, remember?"

"I hadn't forgotten." Audley shook his head stiffly.

"And a job to do," Winston persisted. "A job, huh?"

Audley took the warning at last. "Of course . . ." The arrogance was gone from his voice. "Look, m'sieur—if they have no use, you said. Give us one of the cars and we'll take him with us. Because where we're going we may find a use for him. I'll be responsible for him—personally."

This time the Frenchman's lips twisted in the other direction. "Oh yes? And when you are a prisoner—a prisoner under your rules of war—and he is free again . . . and I am dead—and we are dead . . . and our little town is like

Oradour-sur-Glane, where the women and children are also dead—you will still be responsible? Personally?"

"What d'you mean, 'when he's free again'?" Audley grabbed the German's handcuffed hands and lifted them up. "What the hell are these—charm bracelets?"

The Frenchman stared at the handcuffs for a moment. Then he shrugged. "So he has committed some crime. But he is still a German officer."

"Very true. But if they're taking the trouble to pull him out of the battle"—Audley dropped the German's hands and pointed to the staff car—"then he's in big trouble himself. And that makes him practically one of us."

Audley's voice was no longer arrogant—it was vehement.

"Lieutenant—" Winston started to interrupt again.

"Shut up, Sergeant!" snapped Audley.

Winston raised his eyebrows at Butler hopelessly.

"So you say *'morte la bête, mort le venin'—vous voulez qu'il tombe de Charybde en Scylla*," went on Audley. "But I say that's the very reason why he can be of use to us."

Butler saw, out of the corner of his eye, that the Resistance men were clearing up around them: one of them was lugging a body up the hillside while another scuffed leaves and dirt into the pool of blood which the dead soldier had left. And as they did so one piece of his mind was obstinately attempting to translate Audley's French—"dead the beast, dead the"... what on earth was *le venin*?—while his finger lay on the trigger of the cocked Sten.

Madness!

"No, Lieutenant—"

Why did everybody else pronounce that rank differently? thought Butler irritably. To the American it was *loo*-tenant and to the Frenchman it was *lyuhtenon*—

"—because if his friends get him back—"

"Why should they get him back?" cut in Audley.

"Why?" The Frenchman sniffed. "Because the American tanks have not crossed the river. They are heading north and east past Orléans . . . so if his friends get him back—and when he feels the muzzle kiss the back of his neck—then he will remember that he is a German officer. And then he will trade us in exchange for his life—"

"No!" said the German.

The Frenchman looked at the German, at first impassively and then with a trace of pity. "Oh yes—there is your word of honour, I know—"

"No." The boy's shoulders sagged.

"What then?"

The lock of hair had fallen across the white face again, and the German's other eye had closed. The ring under it was so dark as to look almost like a bruise: it was not just the face of defeat, but of disintegration.

"Ich bin ein Kind des Todes . . . aus dem Regen in die Traufe." The eye opened, almost defiantly. "There are not enough Frenchmen in France to trade for me. There is in the car . . . a case . . ." He frowned. "A briefcase."

The Frenchman stiffened, looked quickly at the staff car, and then at Audley. *"Un moment, Lieutenant . . ."*

They watched him dive into the staff car and retrieve the briefcase. But when he'd ripped it open he showed no inclination to share its contents with them.

Winston leaned forward towards the German. "Captain . . . this had better be good."

Captain Grafenberg looked at him questioningly. "Please?"

"I mean"—Winston heaved a sigh—"I hope you've done something real bad—like surrendered half the German army maybe. Or put arsenic in Rommel's coffee. Or given Himmler the V-sign."

"Please?" The captain looked as though he was ready to burst into tears.

"Because if you haven't, then I think you and the lieutenant there have got us into one hell of a mess." Winston turned suddenly towards Audley, and Butler saw to his surprise that he was grinning. "Not that I don't go along with you, Lieutenant, *sir*. It's just that I never thought I was going to die in the defence of the German army, that's all. The British army —I've just about gotten used to that. But the German army . . . I'd really like a little more time to adjust to that. What d'you think, Corporal Jack?" He tilted his head towards Butler.

The question caught Butler by surprise.

"That's what I thought," said Winston. "Like *The Charge*

of the Light Brigade, starring Errol Flynn, you *don't* think—
not until the lieutenant has passed on the thought to you—"

"Balls!" snapped Butler. "There isn't anything to think
about. We just don't kill prisoners."

"You don't?" Winston raised his voice in scorn. "Well, I
think you've got a lot to learn, Jack old buddy. In fact—"

"Bloody shut up—both of you!" said Audley angrily.
"Hauptmann Grafenberg . . . would you please tell us what it
is you've done?"

Grafenberg straightened himself but didn't answer.

Audley waited patiently.

"I am sorry," said Grafenberg finally.

"*You're* sorry," Winston exclaimed.

"Hush!" Audley paused. Then he pointed at Winston, without taking his eyes off the German's face. "Sergeant . . . Frank
Winston, United States Army." With the other hand he
pointed at Butler. "Corporal . . . Corporal Jack Butler, Lancashire Rifles." He tapped his own chest. "Audley, David . . .
second lieutenant, Queen Charlotte's Own Royal South
Wessex Dragoons."

Chandos Force, thought Butler irrelevantly—the real
Chandos Force, even though it had lost its way en route to its
unknown target. But then Hauptmann Grafenberg could
hardly be expected to know that.

But also he knew why Audley had made the introduction so
formally: *if we're going to fight for you, Hauptmann Grafenberg, at least we're going to know why!*

"I am sorry." Grafenberg looked at each of them in turn,
lastly at Audley. "Second Lieutenant—"

Second *Left*enant—

"—I have not done . . . anything at all."

"What?" said Audley. "Nothing?"

Grafenberg shook his head.

"Well"—Audley's voice cracked—"what's in the briefcase,
for God's sake, man?"

Winston nodded meaningfully to his right, past Butler's
shoulder. "I think we're just about to find that out, Lieutenant."

Butler twisted round in the direction of the American's nod,
to find the Frenchman coming towards them again. He was

aware of the Sten in his hands, still cocked and dangerous. But now it felt curiously heavy—heavy with the memory of the German machine-gunner who had been picked off with that first sniper's shot before he could squeeze his trigger.

The Frenchman faced Hauptmann Grafenberg. "Erwin Grafenberg, Hauptmann, 924th Anti-tank Battalion?"

"*Jawohl.*"

"So!" The Frenchman turned on his heel towards Audley. "Where do you wish to go?" he asked.

"Where—?" Audley swallowed. "Yes... well, if you'd just give us one of these vehicles... then we'll follow our noses."

"What is the name of your Operation?"

"Our Operation?"

"Yes. Your Operation." The Frenchman's tone was polite but firm. "It has a code name, naturally."

"Oh yes—naturally. Of course, that is..." Audley nodded. "Yes, it has."

"Which is?"

"Which is none of your business, m'sieur, I think," said Audley firmly.

"Oh Jesus Christ!" murmured Winston. "Here we go again!"

"You want a vehicle, Lieutenant," said the Frenchman.

"No, I was *promised* a vehicle—by you."

"In exchange for a prisoner."

They stared at each other obstinately.

Suddenly Sergeant Winston stirred restlessly, looking first to the right, then to the left, then behind him.

"Hell now... I've been thinking"—he looked seriously at Audley, then at the Frenchman—"do the krauts ever come this way normally?"

"*M'sieur?*"

"I mean—do they come this way if you don't steer 'em this way? Like, it seems a kind of quiet back road, I mean."

The Frenchman frowned. "No, they do not come this way. It is not the main road."

"Great! So you and the lieutenant—and the kraut—can sit here and argue, and no one's gonna disturb you... and me and the corporal can take the car... and when the war's over we can come back and tell you who won it." Winston spread his hands in the manner of one modestly offering his answer to a difficult problem. "Or, if you like, we'll just tell you when it's over—then you can go on arguing . . . about which of you won it, huh?"

Audley and the Frenchman both stared at him for a second or two, and then again at each other.

Suddenly the Frenchman raised his hands apologetically. "M'sieur—Lieutenant—you will understand that we have learnt to be cautious . . . to ask questions. Perhaps too many questions. But it is how we have stayed alive, you see."

Audley nodded slowly. "Yes," he agreed.

"So . . . you shall have your vehicle—and your prisoner . . . and we will also help you find your way—I shall give you a driver to guide you . . . *Pierrot!*"

One of the Resistance men who had been working on the restoration of the plank bridge over the crater straightened up and turned towards them obediently.

Audley relaxed. "Well . . . I suppose there are times when we're a bit too jolly careful for our own good, at that!" He glanced for a moment towards Butler. "Eh, Corporal?"

"Sir?" Butler had the distinct impression that the look Audley had given him had been for one fraction of a second much less friendly than his tone of voice. "Yes, sir."

Audley grinned at the Frenchman. "Bulldog—Operation Bulldog, that's us."

The Frenchman frowned. "Bull . . . dog?"

Audley struck his forehead. "I'm an idiot! I mean Bullsblood, of course. Just got the wrong word-association—Bullsblood it is."

"Ah—Bullsblood."

"That's right. It's a road interdiction mission." Audley grinned again. "But if you don't mind, I'll spare you the details."

"A very proper precaution." The Frenchman nodded. "And now . . . *Pierrot, mon vieux*—"

"Hey, m'sieur, just hold it a sec!" Sergeant Winston pointed towards the German. "You never did get round to telling us what he did—was it real bad?"

"Bad?" The Frenchman gave Grafenberg a curious glance.

"No, it was not bad. It was what he did not do that was bad . . . and that—that was very bad."

"And what was it he didn't do, then?"

"He failed to kill Adolf Hitler, m'sieur."

15.   How they encountered the Jabos

It was true what Dad had said, thought Butler: Germans smelt differently from Englishmen.

But then, to be fair, Captain Grafenberg was probably thinking much the same thing. And whenever the captain had last washed, he knew for a fact that he himself hadn't had anything like a decent wash for a week, so he must be ripening up a treat on his own account. In addition to which, since the captain was wedged between him and Sergeant Winston in the back of the staff car, he would have both American and British smells to contend with.

The car completed its backward passage up the road and swung sharply into the entrance to the track along which the other ambushed vehicles were hidden.

Butler caught a strong whiff of garlic on Pierrot's breath: that made, altogether, a pretty formidable Allied presence, he decided.

They backed up the track for ten yards. Then the Kübel backed in ahead of them.

"We gonna have an escort?" asked Winston.

Audley watched the Kübel set off ahead of them. "For the first ten kilometres, according to the schoolmaster," he said.

"The schoolmaster?"

"Yes. It seems that he's a schoolmaster when he's not killing Germans," said Audley. "Or that's what they call him, anyway."

"Like Bullsblood?" said Butler.

"Or Bullshit?" said Winston.

Audley turned towards them from the front seat. "Now just hold it," he said warningly.

Pierrot put the car in gear and pulled onto the road a hundred yards behind the Kübel.

"We get to know where we're going, though?" said Winston.

Audley stared ahead of him. "To their headquarters. Then they're going to see if there's any information about the main party." He turned towards them again. "I said . . . hold it."

Winston frowned across the German at Butler.

Audley smiled at Pierrot. "Do you have the key to the handcuffs, m'sieur?" he enquired politely.

"Huh?" Pierrot looked at him quickly.

"Do—you—have—the—key—to—the—handcuffs?" repeated Audley slowly.

Butler lifted up the German's handcuffs. *"La clef?"* he said.

"Oh, *la clef!*" Pierrot nodded. *"C'est dans ma poche."*

Audley gave Butler an exasperated look, then turned back to Pierrot. "Do—you—speak—English?"

"M'sieur?"

Audley smiled. "Is it a fact that your sister sleeps with your father?" he said amiably.

Pierrot shrugged. *"Je ne comprends pas, m'sieur."*

Winston leaned forward suddenly. "Okay, Lieutenant"—he held up a finger behind Pierrot's back—"when we slow down at the next intersection, I'll stick this knife of mine into his back—right?"

"Exactly right, Sergeant." Audley nodded. "And I'll grab the steering wheel. Just make sure you stick that knife of yours in the right spot, eh?"

Winston waggled his finger. "You betcha."

Audley stared ahead again. "Here we go, then."

The Kübel slowed in front of them as the road forked. Butler watched fascinated as Winston placed the tip of his finger gently below Pierrot's shoulderblade.

"Now, Sergeant," said Audley conversationally, tapping the dashboard with his left hand.

Winston jabbed his finger.

Pierrot wriggled slightly. *"Qu'est-ce que c'est?"*

"Sorry, mac"—Winston leaned forward apologetically—"I was just stabbing you by accident. *Pardonnez*, huh?"

Pierrot shrugged.

"Okay, Lieutenant," said Winston. "You can take it from my finger that he's not with us. So now what?"

"So now we're in trouble again," said Audley.

"You don't say!" Winston gave a grunt. "And what sort of trouble this time?"

"We're being double-crossed." Audley nodded at Butler. "D'you remember the colonel gave us the cover if we got picked up—no matter who we were picked up by?"

"Yes, sir."

"Yes ... well, I thought it smelt to high heaven then, and now I'm bloody sure of it." Audley gave Pierrot another friendly grin. "These people know there's something in the wind."

"How d'you figure that?" asked Winston.

"The wrong code name," said Butler suddenly. "You gave him the wrong code name—and he knew it was the wrong one. He was waiting for you to give the cover—the right cover." Then he frowned at Audley. "But how did you come to suspect him, sir?"

"I didn't exactly suspect him. But when he was showing me the ambush setup he kept asking questions in between—he wanted to know where the main party was, and where they were going."

Winston nodded. "Yeah, I get you ... and when you wouldn't play ball he gave us lover-boy here, to make sure you didn't run out on him." He patted Pierrot's shoulder. "You're doing a great job, man."

Butler stared blindly at the road ahead. If Audley was right they were in all kinds of trouble now—trouble multiplied by ten. What they had run into had been practically a reception committee lying in wait for them. The German at his side had fallen into the trap almost incidentally—the Frenchman had picked him up almost as a man hunting a fox might bag a rabbit or two on the side for the pot while he searched for the killer of his chickens.

And, what was more, it meant that the major himself had slipped through the net.

"Wow-ee ..." Winston breathed out noisily. "You really got yourself into the shit right up to your chin, Lieutenant!"

"What d'you mean?"

"Man—I mean when that schoolteacher gets you home he's going to take you apart piece by piece to find out where the major's heading for." Winston shook his head. "And the joke is—you don't know . . . and he's not going to believe you one little bit."

Audley scowled at the American. "But that goes for you too, Sergeant," he said nastily.

"Me? Hell no!" Winston sat back. "I'm just a poor Yankee who's got caught up in a private fight." He gestured with his head towards the German. "Me and the kraut—we're just a couple of innocent bystanders . . . Say, Captain—did you really try and kill the Führer? I heard tell someone tried to blow him up just recently—was that you?"

Captain Grafenberg looked around him a little wildly, from the American to Audley and back. As well he might, thought Butler bitterly: if ever there was a case of *aus dem Regen in die Traufe* it was now.

"No—*nein*," he said hoarsely.

"Well, Captain, I wouldn't deny it if I were you. Right now, in this company, I'd say I did it and I was just sorry it hadn't worked out. Because that's going to be almost as good as saying that you voted for FDR in the last election—if you say it loud enough and often enough they'll probably make you a general after the war, if you live so long." Winston winked at Butler. "If any of us live so long, that is."

The German captain looked at Audley. "Lieutenant . . . if you please . . ." He trailed off miserably.

"Okay!" Winston lifted his hand. "So he didn't try to kill the Führer. But I still think I've given him good advice."

Butler was suddenly aware that his foot hurt again, and that there was a dull pulse of pain centred on his ear. But he was also conscious that his physical problems were now minor ones.

"I bloody wish you'd give us some good advice," he said before he could stop himself.

"Shit, man! You've already got my advice," said Winston conversationally, lifting up his finger. "Next time this old car slows down you take your bayonet and you stick it in lover-boy—and then you run like hell."

Butler stared at Pierrot's back.

"That's right!" Winston nodded round the German. "Only don't include me when you do it. Because as of now you two are on your own—you and the French can double-cross each other until you're blue in the face. The man didn't draft me to get mixed up in private fights."

Butler was no longer listening to him, but was staring at the countryside round him for the first time.

They were coming out of the woodland at last, into a more open terrain of fields and copses, well cultivated but un-English as usual in its lack of hedges and proper ditches, and distinctively French with its line of spindly trees marking the straight road that climbed the ridge ahead of them.

Butler met Audley's eyes and read the same conclusion in them: if they were going to make a break for it they needed better cover than this; a forest for choice, but woodland of some sort for sure if they were to outrun the machine gun on the Kübel.

But without the sergeant . . .

He looked at the American.

"No sir!" Winston said quickly. "I mean it. I don't mind running away from Germans—that's part of the deal . . . but running away from Germans *and* Frenchmen—"

"*Sssh—*" The German sat bolt upright between them, his manacled hands raised.

"What the hell—" said Winston.

"*Jabo!*"

"What?"

The German was listening intently. "*Jabo!*" he repeated.

"Year-bo?"

Grafenberg turned on him. "*Jabo—Jabo!*" He switched to Audley. "Lieutenant—*Achtung, Jagdbomberen*—fighters!"

Butler heard the snarl of aircraft.

"Oh, sure!" Winston ducked his head to peer through the side-screen. "I've got them . . . Mustangs, two of them . . . no sweat, Captain—they're ours, man."

The engine note changed.

"No—no—*no!*" Grafenberg's voice cracked. "We are the enemy—*du lieber Gott!*—don't you understand?"

"Oh my God!" whispered Audley. "He's right. We're the enemy!"

"Oh, Jee-*sus!*" exclaimed Winston, ducking down to peer out of the side-screen again. "Now I've lost them—"

"Down the road—they'll be coming down the road—" Grafenberg hunched himself down to get a view ahead.

"So we better get off it." Winston shook Pierrot's shoulder. "Fighter-bombers, man—we gotta get off the road."

The car swerved. "*Qu'y a-t-il?*" protested Pierrot angrily.

"*Des*—bloody hell!—*des chasseurs* . . . no, *des chasseurs-bombardiers*—*ils vont nous attaquer,*" shouted Audley desperately. "*Quittez la route, pour l'amour de Dieu—quittez la route!*"

Pierrot rocked away from him. "*Que voulez-vous dire—?*" He did a double-take of Audley, as though the lieutenant's newly found fluency surprised him more than what he'd actually said. "Hey?"

"Here he comes!" cried Grafenberg.

Butler saw a black dot framed between the trees on the skyline—a dot which grew and sprouted wings as he watched it.

Winston and Audley both simultaneously grabbed at the steering wheel, the American from behind and Audley from the right. The car lurched to the right, tyres screaming. A tree flashed in front of them and then the car left the road with a tremendous grinding crash. Butler was thrown upwards and sideways—he bounced off the canvas roof and came down partly on top of the German, who cried out in pain. The car crashed down again. The door beside Butler burst open and the side-screen fell away just as he was bracing himself for the next neck-breaking bounce—this time he hit the canvas less hard but descended agonisingly onto his Sten. Sound and pain were indistinguishable for a second, and then both were overtaken by a terrifying vision of corn-stubble rushing up and past his face. But just as it was about to hit him his webbing straps tightened against his shoulders and he was jerked backwards into the car again. The door bounced back and hammered him into the car, filling his head with exploding stars and deafening noise.

Suddenly he was conscious that the sound had been outside him—it was receding.

He clawed himself upright.

Winston and Audley and the Frenchman Pierrot were still
fighting for the wheel, all shouting at each other at the same
time.

They were in the cornfield alongside the road, bright sunlight all around them. And they were also still moving, although there was now something desperately wrong with the
car—a juddering, grinding underneath them.

"Back under the trees!" shouted Grafenberg gutturally, his
English accent breaking down. "Under zerr trrees!"

This time there seemed to be a measure of agreement
among the contestants, and the car swung back towards the
line of trees beside the road. But the flash of comfort this
brought to Butler's confused mind was instantly blotted out by
the sound of the reason for it—the same sound he had heard
as the German had screamed *Jagdbomberen*.

Hunting-bombers, he thought foolishly.

He saw the RSM's face: *There is a requirement for a German-speaking non-commissioned officer.*

The hornet sound of the approaching Mustang dissolved the
RSM's face. It wasn't fair, he decided angrily. It wasn't fair
that it should have been him. And it wasn't fair that they
should be here. And it wasn't fair that their own planes should
attack them.

There was a bright orange flash ahead of them—

The car was moving so slowly—

The flash blossomed, and to his horror he saw the Kübel
lying on its side in the road, burning fiercely.

"Turn the goddamn wheel!" shouted Winston. "She won't
take the ditch again—"

The staff car swung sharply to the right again, parallel to
the road, but still in the field and just under the canopy of
branches. As it did so there was a sharp, hammering noise and
the road burst into dust and sparks alongside them. The
Frenchman wrenched the wheel instinctively away from the
road.

"Stop the car!" commanded Grafenberg.

"There's a copse up ahead." Audley pointed.

"We would not get to it in time," snapped Grafenberg. "If
we stop he may think he has hit us—if we go on then he
knows we are still alive. So we go behind the trees on the

other side of the road, then there is a chance. Believe me— *I know!*"

"Right—everyone out—on the double!" said Audley.

Butler threw himself out of the car. He was halfway across the road before he realised he had left his Sten behind and that he didn't give a damn. Anything—any humiliation—was better than being a helpless target.

"Do not move—and do not look up," Grafenberg shouted. "Whatever you do—do not look up!"

Butler hugged the ground in the shadow under his tree, listening to the high drone of engines above him. The earth was dry and powdery between the patches of dead grass below his face; as he stared at it a droplet of moisture fell from him into the powder. He didn't know whether it was blood or sweat, or maybe even a tear of fright. His eyes felt wet, so it probably was a tear, he decided. He couldn't remember when he'd last cried, but it had been a long time ago, and it would certainly have been with pain, not fear as it was now. He hadn't cried with fear since he'd had nightmares as a kid.

He lowered his face slowly down until he was able to wipe it on his battle-dress cuff. The cuff was greasy with sweat at the edge, and there was a darker stain on it which was probably blood from his ear. Now it had tears as well, then—but that was no more than Mr. Churchill had promised everyone years ago: blood, sweat, and tears. And that was rather clever, remembering those words, even though he'd never be able to bring himself to tell anyone how he'd remembered them just after his own side had tried to kill him.

And that was the third time in one day—

Was it really only one day?

"Okay, Butler?" said Audley.

Butler rose to his feet quickly to prove to Audley that he wasn't in the least frightened. "Sir!"

Audley was standing in the middle of the road with his hands on his hips. Butler had the very distinct impression that the second lieutenant was also doing his best to prove how second lieutenants ought to behave.

"Jee-*sus!*" Winston came out from behind his tree, dusting down his combat jacket. "Jee-*sus!*"

"Sssh!" Grafenberg held up his hands again, listening.

Butler's stomach turned over.

"Oh—no—" began Winston.

They all listened. Finally Grafenberg relaxed. "No . . . there were only two. Sometimes . . ." He shrugged. "Sometimes there are four—or twenty-four. But we are lucky."

"Well, you could have fooled me. But I guess you know better, mac."

"Yes, I do know better. *Sie haben Wichtigeres zu tun*—so we are lucky." Grafenberg looked at Audley. "And now?"

As Butler turned towards Audley there was a sharp double *crack* behind him. Audley jumped as though he'd been shot.

"The Frenchman!" exclaimed Winston.

They all looked down the road towards the burning Kübel, from which the sound had come. Pierrot was bending over a body at the side of the road, fifty yards away, and as they looked at him he turned. For a moment he stared at them, straightening up slowly, then he started to run back down the road away from them.

Audley took a step forwards, fumbling at his holster, and then stopped as Pierrot left the road to zigzag among the trees.

"Yeah . . . that's right, Lieutenant," murmured Winston. "You can maybe run after him, but you sure aren't going to hit him with that thing."

Audley watched the departing figure dwindle in the distance.

"So now we'd better stir our asses to get someplace else, huh?" Winston's voice was suddenly gentler and more encouraging—so much so that Butler looked at him with surprise. "It'll take him an hour or two to find his buddies. We could still get lucky."

For the first time Butler saw Winston not just as an American and a foreigner, but as a senior NCO who—no matter what army he belonged to—had the job of jollying along young men like Audley when they no longer knew what to do. And it was his own plain duty no less to support the sergeant.

"The car, sir—" he said quickly.

"—Isn't going anywhere," snapped Winston. "It's a goddamn miracle it got us where it did."

Audley straightened up. "And you're back with us, Sergeant?"

Winston grinned horribly. "Seems I got no choice, Lieutenant, sir . . . so—which way?" He pointed up the road.

Audley looked round, squinting up at the sun. "South—then southeast," he said.

"Yes . . ." Winston nodded patiently. "But where to, Lieutenant?"

Audley stared southwards without answering, as though he hadn't heard the question.

Winston waited for a moment or two, and then moved round to block the subaltern's view. "Lieutenant, we have to have some kind of plan, for God's sake. We have to know where we're going—or at least we have to know whether we're still chasing the major or just running away from the frogs. So you tell us, huh?"

"Yes—" Audley roused himself. "Yes, of course."

"Okay." The American paused. "So?"

Audley drew a deep breath. "About fifteen kilometres south of here—or it may be southeast . . . and it may be more than fifteen kilometres, but we should be able to pick up the signposts if we keep going . . ." He frowned.

"Yes?"

"There's a village called La Roche Tourtenay—it's off the road to Loches somewhere. And the Château Le Chais d'Auray is a mile to the west of it."

"The château—? Is that where the major's heading?"

"No." Audley shook his head. "But that's where we're going, Sergeant."

"Why there?"

"Wait and see." Audley turned decisively to Butler. "Get your Sten, Corporal . . . Hauptmann—I'm sorry about the handcuffs. But we'll deal with them when we get to Le Chais d'Auray."

Sergeant Winston stood unmoving in front of Audley.

"You know this place—the Château Shay-dough-ray?"

"Yes, Sergeant."

"You've known it all along?"

"Yes."

"And we've been heading for it from the start—but you just forgot to tell us. Is that it?"

"No. That isn't it at all, Sergeant."

"So why are we heading for it now, then?"

"Why?" Audley closed his eyes for a second. "If you were on the run back in Texas—"

"Chicago, Illinois. And Jesus!—I wish I was there now!"

"Chicago, Illinois. If you were on the run in Chicago, Illinois—on the run from the gangsters, Sergeant . . . would you go home to your parents?"

"Hell no! Not unless—" Winston stopped.

"Not unless you were desperate. Not unless you'd tried everything else." Audley regarded the American stonily. "So I am desperate now—and I can't think of anything else. So I'm going home."

16. How Second Lieutenant Audley came home again

Butler lay exhausted among the vines on the edge of the track to the Château Le Chais d'Auray, watching the moonlight polish the dark slates on the little conical tower nearest to him.

The important thing was not to go to sleep, he decided.

They had marched the day into the afternoon, and the afternoon into the evening, and the evening into the night.

First they had force-marched out of necessity, simply to put distance between themselves and the scene of the air strike.

Then they had settled into the rhythm of a route march, by side roads and country tracks, and over fields to skirt round villages, and through hedges and thickets to avoid prying eyes.

But a route march was no problem: it was what a soldier's legs were for, and the farmlands of Touraine were nothing to a soldier who had trained on the high moors of Lancashire and Yorkshire and the mountains of Wales.

Yet each five-minute halt was a little more welcome than the last one. And after each halt it took a little longer to get back into the rhythm. And so, by slow degrees, the route march became an endurance test.

But at least they were going somewhere at last, because Second Lieutenant Audley studied each signpost and changed direction accordingly.

And once, when they surprised a small boy beside a fish-pond, Audley exchanged their last slab of ration chocolate for a pointing finger.

Loches?

That way, the finger pointed.

La Roche?

That way.

Channay-les Pins?

That way.

The urchin never said a word from first to last, and scuttled away smartly as they set out for Channay. After which they retraced their steps and headed for La Roche.

Audley didn't trust anyone any more, not even small boys.

Or German captains.

"Hauptmann . . ." Audley seemed embarrassed. The great bruise on his cheek was less black now, more like a dark stain half camouflaged by dust and sweat.

The German stirred nervously where he lay, brushing at his hair with his chained hands. "Lieutenant?"

"There are . . . some things we have to get quite clear."

"Some things?" The German swallowed nervously. "What things, please?"

"The Frenchman said you were in the plot against Hitler. But you've said that you weren't." Audley paused, then pointed to the handcuffs. "So why are you wearing those?"

"Yeah." Winston rolled sideways from where he'd flopped down exhausted a moment before. He held up his head with one hand and started to massage his thigh with the other. "I'd like to get the answer to that too, Captain."

The German looked from one to the other. "I have given you my *parole*—my word of honour."

"That's right—so you did." The American nodded. "But I

heard tell that all you boys swear an oath to the Führer. Like a word of honour, huh?" He nodded again. "And that makes you a kind of a problem to us."

"How . . . a kind of problem, please?"

"Well now . . . it wouldn't be a problem if you had tried to give the Führer the business, like the Frenchman said you had. Because then you'd be on our side, because that 'ud be the only side you'd got left. But that's where the problem starts."

"Please?" The German turned towards Audley. "I will keep my word—as a German officer."

"That's exactly what's worrying me." Winston rubbed his thigh harder. "Because that Frenchman wasn't kidding us. He looked at those papers, and he went off the boil about you and he was ready to get back to the main business of shitting *us* up. But now you say that's all baloney, you never touched the Führer . . . so if those cuffs aren't for that—if they're just for screwing the general's daughter, or stealing the PX blind, or something —then like the Frenchman said, which word of honour are you going to stick to if we meet up with any of your buddies? The Führer's word—or our word, hey?" He stopped rubbing his thigh and pointed his finger at Audley. "Right, Lieutenant?"

"Yes . . . well, broadly speaking . . ." Audley watched the German, ". . . right."

For a moment the young German said nothing. Then he squared his shoulders defiantly. "If that is what you think, Lieutenant—" he began reproachfully.

"No." Audley cut him off. "It isn't as simple as that. I was quite prepared—damn it, perfectly prepared—to take your word for *us*. But if we go on now to . . . where we're going . . . then other people could be involved. And I don't have the right to risk them—not on your word, or my word, or anyone's word."

Château Le Chais d'Auray, thought Butler quickly. Audley had let slip that name when the sergeant had pressed him for their destination. And he had let it slip in the German's presence, that was what had been distracting him.

So now they couldn't leave him, they had to either shoot him or take him with them. And if they took him with them they needed to trust him.

Butler stared at the young German with a curious sense of

detachment. This, he told himself, was a genuine, one-hundred-per-cent German soldier, one of the species he'd been trained and primed to kill on sight without a second thought. The boy even *looked* like a German—even in his rumpled, sweat-stained uniform and without his officer's hat he still looked a lot more like a German than the fat soldier with the loaves in Sermigny.

So now, although *we just don't kill prisoners* and a few hours ago they would have fought for that principle, what would he do if Audley was to say *shoot him*?

He would do it, of course.

The German was staring at him.

"I was on the Eastern Front, with my battalion . . . in the 4th Army, near Vitebsk. An anti-tank battalion . . . in April I was promoted and sent on a special course at home, at—at home—on the use of the new Jagdpanzers . . . I saw my father, who was on the staff of Admiral Canaris. And my brother, my elder brother, who worked for General Olbricht, also in Berlin . . .

"Halfway through the course I was posted to the staff of General von Stulpnagel in Paris . . . which I did not understand —killing tanks I understand, not paper-work. So I asked for a combat posting—if not to the Jagdpanzers, at least to one of the 8.8-centimetre gun battalions on the West Wall. They sent me to Nantes, to report on the state of the landward defences—the landward defences! 'Landward defences—none.' Then I am in command of . . . of transport despatch. I count horses into trains —the Amis bomb the trains, the French steal the horses. I am trained to destroy Josef Stalins, and I count horses—"

("Tough shit," murmurs Sergeant Winston. "I'm trained to blow up blockhouses.")

"Then there is the *attentat* of the second July—we heard the Führer's voice on the radio that night—I am in Nantes, counting horses . . ."

("Safest place to be," murmurs Sergeant Winston.)

("Shut up," says Second Lieutenant Audley.)

"Then General Olbricht is executed . . . and I am afraid for my brother, that he will be unjustly suspected. And also Admiral Canaris is arrested . . . I am afraid for my father too.

Even more afraid, for I have heard him speak criticisms, even before the war.

"Then General von Stulpnagel is executed. And he has been a friend of my father, also from before the war."

("Wow-ee," murmurs Sergeant Winston. "Now it's really getting close to home . . . except that you're just still counting horses' legs and dividing by four, huh?")

"And . . . at last I get a letter from my father. It was delivered to me by a man I do not know, but he is an *Abwehr* officer I think . . . This is . . . maybe two weeks ago. But it is written, the letter, on nineteenth July—"

(Hauptmann Grafenberg is speaking so softly now, almost whispering, that Butler has to move closer to hear his words. The German does not notice this at first, he is speaking to the ground in front of him now; when he finally does he clears his throat and speaks up; but not for long, and soon he is whispering again.)

"He says that if I receive this letter—when I receive it—he will be dead. And my brother too.

"But to tell me that is not the reason for which he writes, it is to tell me that I must go north to Normandy with the next convoy—that I can do that easily because I am the transportation officer, and I have the necessary documentation. And when I am in Normandy I must pass through the lines and surrender myself to the first American I meet—"

And after that they had gone, with Audley setting the pace as though he was determined to outmarch them all.

And then the endurance test became a nightmare.

The side of Butler's head had started to ache again and his toes began to itch inside his boot. He could also feel with every other step the impression which his Sten had punched into his buttock, where he had fallen on it in the staff car.

All of which was compounded by the confusion of his feelings over the German—

(Bayonet practice: *What the fucking hell are you doing, son—poking that sandbag like you were sorry for it? That's not a sandbag, son—that only looks like a sandbag. THAT'S A BLOODY GERMAN, THAT IS! He'll rape your mother,*

*he'll rape your sister, AND BY GOD IF YOU DON'T WATCH
OUT HE'LL RAPE YOU! So you're here to stick your bayonet
in his guts and your butt plate in his teeth and your boot in his
balls, and I want to hear you yell with joy when you do it—
AND DON'T YOU DARE BE SORRY FOR HIM OR I'LL
GIVE YOU SOMETHING TO BE SORRY ABOUT!)*

"But why didn't you get out while you could, then?" Audley
had asked. "Why did you wait for the Gestapo to come for you?"

"You heard what the man said," Sergeant Winston had answered for the German. "Because he hadn't done anything—
he'd counted his horses, like a good little boy—"

Not true, Butler thought. Or not the whole truth.

The whole truth was that when the utterly unbelievable
happened ordinary blokes didn't believe it, not until it was too
late. The only thing they could think of doing was nothing at
all—they just stood around like bullocks waiting their turn
outside the municipal slaughterhouse.

He'd stood in the mist that way, back on the riverbed, even
after he'd heard the major sentence him to death—heard him
with his own ears. Because if it had been Sergeant Purvis who
had come out of the mist behind him, and not Corporal Jones,
whom he already hated and distrusted in his heart . . . if it had
been Sergeant Purvis, not Corporal Jones—then he would
have been one of the bullocks.

There came a time when all he wanted to do was to stop
and lie down. But while he was deciding how many steps he
would take before he would do that—fifty, or a hundred, or
five hundred?—the effort involved in making the decision became greater than the effort required in *not* making it.

And then the nightmare became a dream.

He was inside E. Wilmot Buxton's blue and gold *Story of
the Crusades,* marching between the general and his father,
because that way they couldn't argue with each other about
whether Winston Churchill had really ordered the troops to
fire on the miners during the General Strike—

*The exhausted remnant of the crusading host, now much
reduced, took the road to the Holy City, the end of all their
endeavours—*

He was half aware that the Château Le Chais d'Auray was not the Holy City, and that it was certainly not the end of all their endeavours.

But for the time being it would do, it would do.

There was a scrunch of boots on gravel in the shadows thrown by the trees in the moonlight on the road.

"Psst!" Winston hissed from the next row of vines. "Here, Lieutenant!"

Audley tiptoed out of the shadow across the pale line of the road and threw himself down on the earth beside them.

"Anybody at home?"

Audley breathed out. "There isn't a sound, and not a light either—I've been right round the house and the building. Not a sound . . . but they're there."

"How d'you know?"

Audley picked up a handful of the dry earth and squeezed it out. "Not a weed to be seen. Another month, then they'll be harvesting these grapes." He reached out towards a bunch of grapes on the vine near him. "I wonder what the vintage of '44 will be like. . . . It would be nice if it was a really great one, to remember us by, wouldn't it!"

"Shit! The hell with the grapes! How d'you know they're there?"

The subaltern's face was white in the moonlight. "Because the grapes are here, Sergeant. As they've been for a thousand years, since they learnt the art of pruning—you know that, Sergeant? They learnt the art of pruning here. The donkeys of the Abbey of Marmoutier got into the vines, and ate them. And when the vines grew again the ones they'd eaten gave the finest grapes—that's the one miracle of St. Martin of Tours that they remember here. So you can drink a full pitcher of Loire wine and not hurt yourself, that's what they say—"

Not true, thought Butler.

Or perhaps it was *true*. If he hadn't drunk a full pitcher, and been sick as a dog—maybe that was another miracle of St. Martin of Tours—

"So what do we do?" grated the American. "Drink a pitcher of Loire wine, and not hurt ourselves?"

"That would be nice. But no . . ." Audley peered around him. "Corporal Butler, are you there?"

"Sir!" said Butler. He had known one fraction of a second before Audley had spoken that the subaltern would say "Corporal Butler," because that was what he would have said.

Because not being a bullock was what life was all about, even right outside the slaughterhouse. And especially right outside the towers of the Holy City.

Obedience was duty. But duty was free will—the soldier's free will, which was the last and best free will of all. The general had tried to teach him that, but he'd never understood until now what the general had meant. But now he knew.

"Sir."

Audley looked into the shadow where he lay. "We'll go in and find out. You'll cover me." He turned to the sergeant's patch of shadow. "You wait with Hauptmann Grafenberg. If there's trouble, then you're on your own. Just get to blazes out of here—"

"Hell, no—"

"Hell, yes! This is our show. So if it's a balls-up then it's our balls-up." Audley's voice softened. "Don't worry, Sergeant. My thumbs tell me we're okay. If my thumbs are wrong, there'll be nothing you can do about it. But then somebody's got to survive, otherwise we've done all this for nothing, don't you see?"

Done all what? Butler asked himself. He really didn't know any more what it was they were doing. They were chasing the major, of course. But what he was doing, and what they would do if they ever caught up with him, that had somehow ceased to be of any real importance. It was the doing, not the objective, that mattered.

"Okay, Lieutenant." Winston conceded the point doubtfully. "But then I do what I want—right?"

"Okay. Just so long as the château isn't full of Panzer Grenadiers—" Audley caught the words. "Hauptmann . . ."

The vines stirred. "Lieutenant?"

"We're going to have a look at the château, the corporal and I—you understand?"

"I understand. You have my word."

"But I want you to understand something else, Hauptmann. We are not fighting your chaps now."

"I understand. You are escaping."

"No. For Christ's sake—" Audley stopped short, suddenly at a loss. "Oh, damn it, Sergeant, you tell him . . . if you can. I'm past caring almost . . . come on, Corporal—"

The muscles in Butler's legs were double-knotted, he could feel them twist with each step.

"I'm absolutely buggered, you know, Jack," said Audley conversationally. "It is Jack—isn't it?"

"Yes, sir."

"Yes . . ." Audley nodded to himself. "I thought that was it. Is that short for John or James, I never have worked out which?"

"John, sir." Butler wanted to say more, but couldn't think of anything to say.

"John, is that it?" Audley nodded again. "You know, the first time I walked down this road—or whatever you'd call it—I was nine years old. And there are forty-eight trees in this road, from the main road to the château—twenty-four each side."

"Yes, sir?"

"Twenty-four each side. The first time I made it forty-nine, and the second time forty-seven. But there are actually forty-eight. Would you have guessed as many as that?"

"I don't rightly know, sir."

"Well, of course, you can't really see in the dark." Audley pointed towards the house. "I had a room up there, near the tower. I had a feather bolster instead of a pillow—I never could get used to it. That, and not having porridge for breakfast."

They came off the compacted surface of the roadway onto a side square of loose gravel in front of the house—gravel which crunched noisily under their boots, much more loudly than the scatters of small stones on the roadway.

There was the rattle of a chain, faint but sharp in the dark ahead of them, and a dog began to bark inside the house, each bark echoing and re-echoing as the animal roared against itself furiously.

Butler cocked his Sten automatically and set his back on one side of the doorway as Audley reached up to bang on the door with the side of his fist. The dull thump—*thump-thump-thump*

—drove the dog inside frantic with rage: Butler could hear its paws scrape and skid on the floor as it strained against its chain.

Audley banged on the door again.

Suddenly the barking subsided into a continuous growl.

"*Qui est là?*"

Audley pressed his face to the edge of the door. "M'sieur Boucard?"

"*Qui est là?*"

"*M'sieur Boucard, c'est David Audley . . . David Audley, le fils de Walter Audley, de Steeple Horley, en Angleterre.*"

The growling continued.

"*C'est David Audley, M'sieur Boucard—tu ne me remets pas?*"

There were other sounds behind the door now; someone even hushed the watchdog into silence.

A man's voice and a woman's voice . . . but Butler couldn't catch any of the words.

Audley placed both hands against the door and leant forward on them. "M'sieur Boucard—"

"*C'est toi, David?*"

"*Oui, maman, c'est moi*—what's left of me," said Audley wearily.

17. How Corporal Butler made a promise to a lady

The lamp on the hall table was turned down so low that Butler couldn't make out the woman's features even after she had stopped hugging Audley, but more particularly because most of his attention was on the shotgun which the man of the house was pointing at him.

"Oh . . . my little David—but you have grown so much! You are so big!" The woman held Audley at arm's length.

"And so smelly, Maman . . . I'm afraid I didn't wash behind the ears this morning, as you always taught me to," said Audley carefully, as though he was pronouncing a password.

The shotgun stopped pointing at Butler: perhaps it really was a password at that, thought Butler—an old shared memory which Audley had deliberately produced to prove that he was indeed that long-lost "little David."

"My dear boy!" Monsieur Boucard's English was not merely perfect, it was decidedly upper-class. "My dear boy!"

"It's good to see you again, sir . . . Maman, allow me to present my friend Corporal Jack Butler—Corporal, Madame Boucard, my godmother, and M'sieur Boucard, one of my father's oldest friends."

Butler just had time to wipe his sweaty hand before accepting Madame Boucard's.

"Corporal Jack, I am so pleased to meet you—" Madame Boucard peered up at him. "Turn up the lamp, if you please, Georges."

The lamp flared into brightness, shooting great shadows all around. For a moment Butler registered only the substantial remains of what must once have been marvellous beauty, but then her expression changed to one of alarm and concern.

"Oh—*mon Dieu!*" Madame Boucard raised a hand towards him. "You are hurt, Corporal Jack—you are wounded." She swung round quickly. "Madeleine! Madeleine! *Le caporal est blessé—vite, vite!*"

There came a scuffling from the back of the hallway, from the darkness on the far side of the great bare staircase which rose up ahead of them.

Butler blinked stupidly from the darkness back to Madame Boucard. "It's quite all right, madame. It's only a"—he shied away from the word "scratch," which was the sort of thing Audley would have said, but which didn't sound right on his own lips—"a graze . . . and it happened hours ago. I'm okay now, really I am."

"So . . ." Boucard frowned at him for a couple of seconds, then turned towards Audley. "You have been prisoners, David? And you have escaped from the Germans?"

It was a sensible conclusion, thought Butler. Whatever they looked like, they could hardly be mistaken for the spearhead of a victorious army pursuing a defeated enemy. And in any case the French in these parts would be expecting the Americans, not the British.

"No, sir. At least, not exactly, that is," Audley floundered.

"What do you mean 'not exactly'?" Boucard's voice was businesslike.

"Well, sir—we're not exactly escaping from . . . the Germans. We haven't seen a German for hours—" Audley trailed off, obviously remembering suddenly the German he'd left beside the road a couple of hundred yards away. "I mean, the Germans aren't following us. But . . . we aren't alone, sir."

"You have comrades outside?"

"Just nearby, yes," Audley admitted reluctantly.

"How many?"

"Just two, sir. One of them's an American and . . ." Audley broke off nervously. "We won't stay, sir—that wouldn't be right. What I really want is food and drink—and some information. I think you may be able to give me a line on a place . . . a place we must rendezvous with someone. But we won't stay here." He shook his head. "I was thinking—maybe we could hide for the night in the old mill, down by the stream—"

Butler felt a half-hysterical urge to laugh. This was a new Audley far removed from the obstinate dragoon subaltern; this was "little David" in a soldier's battle dress many sizes too big for him.

Boucard chuckled. "My dear David, kindly don't be ridiculous. Do you really think you are the first escaper to come through Le Chais? My dear boy, the only difference between you and all the others is that you have come on your own initiative, because you knew us. Which is why we weren't expecting you . . . whereas all the others—they have come down the line—British, American, French, Polish . . . they were expected. But no one is more welcome than you and your friends, believe me!"

There was another scuffle in the shadows.

"Maman—"

Madame Boucard took Butler's arm gently. "Come, Corporal Jack. If you will be so good as to accompany me to the kitchen, my daughter is trained in first aid."

Butler looked questioningly at Audley.

"Go on, man—do what you're told." Audley nodded almost eagerly, as though the task of explaining to Boucard that he was about to add a new nationality to the list of escapers was one he preferred to tackle in private.

Butler followed Madame Boucard past the staircase and down a stone-flagged passage on which his iron-shod boots rang sharply. The sound and the feel of the hard surface under his feet reminded him of something he didn't wish to recall, but couldn't help remembering now—something which the lamplight itself had already stirred in his memory: the friendly kitchen in which he had met the NCOs of Chandos Force just twenty-four hours before, at the beginning of the nightmare.

It didn't seem possible that it was only twenty-four hours since then. Half his life had been lived in those hours—half his life and on four separate times nearly his death also. Perhaps being touched on the shoulder by death so very personally transformed the nature of time, spreading it out unnaturally at each touch and using it up, swallowing it up. . . .

There was more warm light behind a glass-panelled door; and when the door opened there was also a warm smell, the heavenly smell of thick, nourishing soup. Until the moment he smelt it Butler knew he would have set exhaustion above hunger, but now he could only think that he couldn't remember when he had last eaten anything which smelt like that soup.

There was a steaming bowl on the table, but the bandages beside it told their own tale: the soup must be in the pan on the great black kitchen range.

"Corporal Jack, this is my daughter, Madeleine," Madame Boucard said graciously. "*Ma chérie,* Corporal Jack is a friend and comrade of our David, our own David."

It required a prodigious effort to look away from the soup to the daughter, but the effort had to be made.

"Mademoiselle," said Butler.

Madeleine Boucard was almost as beautiful as the pan of soup, with her little, pale, heart-shaped face framed in hair turned to red-gold by the lamplight.

And Madeleine Boucard was also looking at him with the same mixture of alarm and concern her mother had shown.

Butler passed his hand across his stubbly chin, uncertain as to how to react to that look, which made him feel a fraud, because of his red silk bandage.

"Mademoiselle . . . I'm really quite okay," he managed to stammer. "But . . . if you've got anything to eat. Like a little soup, maybe?"

Mother and daughter exchanged looks, then Madame Boucard stepped towards the dresser. For a moment Butler hoped she was going to get him a soup-plate, but to his disappointment she offered him only a small tray.

He accepted the tray automatically. "Madame?"

"*Regardez,* Corporal Jack—look, please."

Butler glanced down at the tray. He saw that it was not a tray at all, but a mirror.

"Look, please," repeated Madame Boucard.

Butler raised the mirror and then almost dropped it with shock.

The face under the commando cap and the red silk handkerchief was a mask of dried blood and grime from which two white eyes goggled at him. In some places the blood and the dirt had mingled, and runnels of sweat had scoured the mixture; in others the blood had already blackened and cracked where the skin had creased. The mask was the more frightening and unrecognisable for being his own.

"Sit down, if you please," said Madeleine briskly.

Butler sat down.

"There now . . ." She removed the cap and began to untie the handkerchief. "You know, I did not recognise him—David—it is so dark and he is so big, so grown upwards as Maman says. But then it is six years past since he was living with us . . . it is very tight—*le noeud*—how do you say in English?"

"The knot?"

"The knot—yes, the knot—knot," the girl repeated the word to herself. "I remember it now."

"You speak very good English—and your mother and father too, mademoiselle. I mean really perfect English," said Butler shyly.

"Myself . . . not perfect, though it is kind of you to say so . . . *eh bien!* It is untied at last . . . my mother and my father, yes. But then so they should. My mother is half English by birth, and my father, he was educated at an English school . . . now, I am going to wash these wounds of yours with the warm water . . . at a most famous and expensive school, where he learnt to play rugby football. Do you play rugby football?"

Butler held his head very still. She was talking to him to take his mind off what she was doing, that was an old nursing

trick. And no matter what, it was the least he could do to
pretend that she'd succeeded.

"No, mademoiselle. I played soccer, but not very well. My
game was cricket."

It wasn't difficult really: her hands were as soft as thistle-
down—*ouch!* That was the dressing coming off.

"There now—that's done. Now, if you will move your
head a little towards the light . . . so! That's good. . . . Was this
a bullet?"

"I don't honestly know, mademoiselle. It may have been a
grenade fragment."

"Mmm . . . ?" She was finding it difficult now to concentrate on her work and make conversation in a foreign language. "Cricket . . . a little more to the side, please . . ."

Butler found himself gazing directly down the front of her
dress at two small but perfect breasts six inches from his face.

"Am I hurting you?" She drew back suddenly.

Butler closed his eyes. "No, mademoiselle," he said.

The soft hands continued cleaning him up again. Cautiously
he opened his eyes and discovered to his great joy that the
breasts were still in view.

"My father played at cricket when he was in England, but it
is not played in France . . ."

Butler held his breath, trying to imprint the vision on his
memory. He had never seen anything like this before, except in
pictures and photographs. Other men, even other boys at
school, had managed to see it all and do it all; but he had
somehow never had the opportunity . . . or the inclination or the
time or the courage—or whatever it was . . . and now he regret-
ted it bitterly. He had passed his exams and learnt German
instead, but now those didn't seem such clever things to have
done.

"But for the war I would have gone to school in England
too—to a school in Chelt-en-ham. Do you know Chelt-en-
ham?"

"No, mademoiselle," Butler croaked. "But . . . you speak
English so well no one would . . . know that you hadn't been
educated there."

"Oh, that is because Maman has this rule—nothing but
English at meals." She drew back to survey her handiwork, and

he lifted his eyes just in time to meet hers. She smiled at him. "In fact, the only times I have spoken French at meals was when David lived with us. Then it was only French—poor David, I was sorry for him . . . well, a little sorry. He was very clever. His accent was not good, but he learnt everything so quickly."

She sounded almost as though she hadn't much liked Audley, Butler thought. But then at twelve and thirteen boys and girls generally didn't much like each other, even when they spoke the same language, so far as he could remember.

All the same he felt himself envying Audley desperately all the advantages he had had. He, Butler, had a lot of ground to make up, and very little time.

Perhaps no time at all.

Here and now especially no time at all.

"You have known David long?"

"David?" Butler stared at her stupidly, then looked quickly round the kitchen. The mother had gone—from the moment he had sat down he had forgotten about her. But she had gone, anyway.

"You have known him long?" She repeated the question.

"No." He swallowed. "You are the most beautiful girl I've ever seen," he heard himself say.

"Oh . . ." She looked at him in surprise, only half-smiling. "My father once said . . . that is what the soldiers will say . . . but you are the first, the very first."

"You are the very first girl I've said it to." It was like hearing someone else speaking, but somehow that made it easier.

"Perhaps you have not seen many girls. You have been too busy fighting, perhaps," she said lightly. "But you will see other girls. Then you will say it to them also."

"I'll never see any other girls, I shall only see you."

She looked at him seriously, no longer even half-smiling. *"Vous ne perdez pas de temps."*

Butler struggled with the French words, although their meaning was plain enough. He had been thinking the very same thing only half a minute before, after all.

"I have not *lost* any time, mademoiselle. I don't have any time to lose. In an hour or so from now, we shall have gone

—David . . . and I. We have a job to finish. Then we will return to our regiments—somehow."

"But—"

Butler raised his hand. "No. I don't want you to say anything, or promise anything. I will make the promise."

"But Corporal Jack—"

Corporal Jack . . .

Well, that was just part of the promise, he decided. Half his brain had been telling him that he was crazy—that she was beautiful and he was lightheaded with hunger and tiredness, and that anything which happened so quickly had to be shallow-rooted in those facts.

But the other half had already promised him that nothing he wanted badly enough was out of his reach.

Not Corporal Butler, but Second Lieutenant Butler.

Captain Butler.

Colonel Butler.

Colonel and Mrs. Butler.

Mrs. Madeleine Butler.

With his red hair and her red hair—red-gold hair—they would have red-headed sons and daughters for sure.

"I will come back to this house after the war," said Butler. "And I won't be just a corporal either—I shall be an officer. And . . ." Suddenly he felt himself run out of steam. "And . . ."

She regarded him gravely.

He had to say something, but now for the life of him he couldn't think of anything to say. All his new-found eloquence had deserted him without warning.

"And then we shall see," said Madeleine Boucard gently. "Very well, C—. . . very well, Jack. When you come back to me we shall see—you have promised that, then."

Butler nodded.

"Good. And now I will bandage your head, if you will permit me." She smiled at him, and touched his cheek lightly with her hand. "And you know what?"

He shook his head dumbly.

"I think I will hold you to that promise," she said.

18. How Madame Boucard guessed right—and wrong

"Another glass of wine—allow me to fill your glass, Jack," said Monsieur Boucard politely.

"No, sir—thanking you kindly, sir." Butler stopped his hand just in time from covering his wineglass. Such vulgar actions were obviously out of place in this company, and he was as desperately keen not to be caught out by them as he was determined not to be trapped again by the deceptively gentle wine of Touraine.

But there too was a dilemma, for this was not just any old wine, but the produce of Le Chais d'Auray itself, as Audley had carefully explained. So it was essential to qualify his refusal in some way.

"Not that it isn't a beautiful wine—" He caught his tongue before he could add "sir"; there had been one "sir" too many in the previous sentence as it was, and that was another thing to watch.

In fact, there were altogether too many things to watch—even though the food had driven back his fatigue and put fresh heart into him—when all he wanted to do was to watch the lamplight on Madeleine Boucard's hair.

But that also was forbidden—and forbidden not only by the "don't stare" rule Dad had clouted into him long ago, but also by another of Rifleman Callaghan's sovereign remedies which sprang to mind now as gratuitously as when Callaghan had once offered it to the whole barrack room, flushed with beer and conquest: *Happen you fancy t' daughter, lads—then just smile sweet at t' mother first!*

He had always despised Callaghan, and now he despised himself and felt ashamed to think of the bugger in the same breath as Madeleine Boucard—Callaghan, whose endless seductions of local girls were the shame and the pride of the platoon.

He thrust the coarse memory out of his mind. Jack Butler

was not Pat Callaghan, any more than Madeleine Boucard was
any hapless local girl—or the Château Le Chais d'Auray was
a Lancashire Rifles barrack room.

And yet, for all that, he found himself smiling now at Madame Boucard, and seeing in her features the source and ori-
gin of Madeleine's beauty.

And she smiled back at him, and the smile caught his
breath in his throat.

The mother, the daughter, the wine, and the food, the spar-
kle of flame reflected on glass and silver and polished mahog-
any—it was all as unreal as the calm which the books said lay
in the centre of a hurricane. It was even more impossible than
the other things that had happened to him.

He touched the bandage on his head and let his glance
touch the girl, and knew that both of them were real. And he
knew that by the same token the promise he had made her was
real too, even though he had been out of his depth and out of
his class and more than half out of his head when he'd made
it—real even though she'd probably only been humouring
him, as any nice girl in an awkward spot might do: he
couldn't blame her for that, with a crazy foreign soldier on her
hands, a soldier who'd just come out of the dark from nowhere, and who was going back into the dark to nowhere soon
enough—

No, not real for her maybe. But real for him, and so bind-
ing on him that it would make him indestructible until he'd
discharged it—

Suddenly he was aware that she had said something to him,
only he'd been too busy dreaming as he looked at her, and had
missed the words.

"Are you all right, Jack?" Her eyes were dark with concern.

Butler shook off the dream. Ever since the fight in Sermigny everyone had been asking him if he was all right; it
was time to set the record straight once and for all.

"Aye—never better." He grinned at her and nodded. Then
he swung towards Audley, switching off the grin as he turned.
"Fit for duty."

It somehow didn't sound the way he'd intended it to sound—
it came out not so much as a statement, but more something
halfway between a question and a challenge. And yet when he

thought about it in the silence which followed he wondered if he hadn't meant it to be just that: half a question and half a challenge. Because all they'd had since he'd sat down at the table was the small talk of polite conversation between Audley and the Boucards: small talk in which he couldn't have joined even if it hadn't been layered below his concern for his own behaviour, so that he only half-heard it anyway...

—The excellence of Maman's supper—

Monsieur Boucard's expressive shrug: *Those living on their own land, with their own produce, they have been the fortunate ones, these four years* ...

—And with the wine of Le Chais to drive away gloom—

Alas, not such good years. Except perhaps the '43 ...

—Not the '44?—

Shrug. *The prospects were not promising. Old Jean-Pierre*—

—Old Jean-Pierre! As crusty as ever? And Dominique and Marcel? And Dr. de Courcy?—

Ah! Now it is Dr. de Courcy who—

(Boucard had cut off there suddenly, as though an alarm bell had sounded inside his head, and had flicked the merest suggestion of a covert glance at Hauptmann Grafenberg.)

(Hauptmann Grafenberg sat there between Madeleine Boucard and Sergeant Winston, very stiff and formal, swallowing his soup nervously for all the world as though he was as worried about his manners as was Butler himself.)

(Hauptmann Grafenberg hadn't noticed Boucard's quick glance, he had been staring down at his plate; and when he did finally look up into the silence his eyes had the blank, withdrawn expression of a man who could only see the pictures that were running inside his own head; and, for a bet, those would be desolate pictures, thought Butler sympathetically; because if here at this table the young German was no longer altogether an enemy he was certainly very far from being among friends; his former friends were now his enemies, and his former enemies were not his friends—he had no family and no country and no cause; and none of it was his own fault and his own doing, God help him!)

—Dr. de Courcy who—?

Will be glad to see you, my boy ...

Small talk. Polite phrases as far removed from the world
outside as light was from darkness, and the soft curve of Madeleine Boucard's breasts from the aching muscles of his own
body.

"Fit for duty." Boucard repeated the words thoughtfully.
"But what duty is this, with which I can help you? That is, if
you are not escaping, as you say you are not?"

As he spoke he glanced again in Hauptmann Grafenberg's
direction, and this time the young German picked up the signal.

"You will wish me to . . . withdraw, I think." He pushed
back his chair and stood up.

"No. On the contrary, Hauptmann—I want you to stay,"
said Audley. "Do please sit down."

Hauptmann Grafenberg remained standing. "I think it is
better that I do not hear what you are to do. I would prefer not
to, please."

Sergeant Winston stirred. "He means you got his word of
honour, Lieutenant, but he'd rather keep his peace of mind—
what he's got left of it. Right, Captain?"

The German looked at the American sergeant, brushing as
ineffectively as ever at the hair which fell across his face, but
before he could say anything, Audley held up his hand.

"No. I understand that, but it can't be like that. First because we can't leave you here—"

"David—" Boucard interrupted.

"No, sir. We can't and we won't. I wouldn't have come
here otherwise . . . but there's another reason too—for *my*
peace of mind, you might say. Because I need a witness."

Madame Boucard leaned forward. "A witness, David? A
witness for what?"

"For what we may have to do, Maman." Audley blinked at
her uncertainly, as though still unable to reconcile his twin
roles of small godson and large dragoon lieutenant.

"What you *may* have to do?" Madame had no such difficulty:
for her the years and inches and the King's Commission had
clearly changed nothing. "And what is it that you *may* have to do
which requires the attendance of a German officer?"

"It doesn't exactly . . . require a German," said Audley hastily. "It just happens he'll make a damn good witness, is what I mean."

"There's no need to swear."

"No, Maman—I beg your pardon." The unbruised cheek reddened in the lamplight. Audley swayed from side to side for a moment, and then suddenly seemed to notice the German again. "Oh, do sit down, for God's sake, there's a g-g-good chap."

Hauptmann Grafenberg brushed at his hair again, but remained standing. "Herr Leutnant—"

Madame Boucard gave a small cough. "Please be so good as to sit, Captain."

Hauptmann Grafenberg sat down.

"Now, David—?" She turned back to Audley.

But all Audley's courage seemed to have deserted him, together with his wits and the power of speech. Instead he began to straighten the place mat in front of him, and then the plate on the place mat, and after that the knife on the plate.

The trouble was that silence didn't make matters better, it made them worse by answering the question in Butler's mind with a terrifying certainty.

What we may have to do.

"Hell!" said Sergeant Winston. "I beg your pardon, ma'am —but hell all the same. Because we got ourselves into one hell of a mess, so hell is right. But it isn't the lieutenant's fault, he's just doing his duty the way he sees it." He paused defiantly. "And the way I see it too, come to that, so I guess you can freeze me too."

Butler felt ashamed that he had left it to a foreigner to defend his officer, which was what he should have done without a second thought.

"And me too, madame," he said.

Madame Boucard smiled at him, and then at the sergeant. "I never doubted that for one moment."

"No, ma'am?" Sergeant Winston tested the statement to destruction. "That's good, ma'am."

"I agree, Sergeant." She took the verdict like a lady—and an equal. "Very well, then, David—so you are going to assassinate someone."

Audley's mouth opened, then closed again.

She nodded at him. "Very well—kill, if you prefer the word."

Audley swallowed. "Yes—I prefer the word."

"Of course. Killing is what soldiers do."

"We're soldiers, Maman."

Madame Boucard inclined her head fractionally, as though to concede what could hardly be denied but not one jot more.

Sergeant Winston stirred restlessly. "Seems to me, ma'am, you know a lot more than you're telling." He gave Audley a thoughtful glance. "But then you're not the first person we met today like that."

"No." Audley shook his head. "My godmother's just a very good guesser. She always was."

"Uh-huh? So she still is." Sergeant Winston regarded Madame Boucard speculatively. "But I'd still be obliged to know how you guess so good, godmother."

The expressive eyebrow lifted again. "Is it of so much importance to you, Sergeant—to know how an old woman guesses?"

Winston shook his head. "Normally, ma'am—no. I had a grandma could see clear through me and a brick wall both, so it's no surprise you can figure us. But then it was just my . . . backside was at risk. This time it's my skin. And the way things have been happening to us today—I guess I'm more suspicious than I was yesterday, even of godmothers."

Both eyebrows came down into a frown. "The way things have been happening to you?"

"Uh-uh." The American grinned and shook his head. "I got my question in first, ma'am. So I get my answer first."

For an instant she looked at him severely, but then the corner of her mouth lifted. "*Vraiment* . . . I can see why your grandmother kept her eye on you, Sergeant. But—very well. When a man says there is something he may have to do, then it is usually something he doesn't want to do. And when the man wears a uniform and protests that he is also only doing his duty, then that is even more certainly the case—for then he is about to do something either very brave or very wicked. Or perhaps both . . . or perhaps he doesn't know which, even."

She paused to look for a moment at Audley. "Now . . . my godson there—your lieutenant—if he was here to blow up a bridge or destroy a railway line . . . if there are still such things left in France that have not already been destroyed . . . he would not need to explain that it was his duty. It would not even occur to him to explain it . . . nor would he need a witness to it.

"Nor, I think, if he was merely engaged in killing Germans"—she gave Hauptmann Grafenberg a grave little bow—"would he need to justify such an action, any more than our guest would need to explain why he was forced by his duty to kill Englishmen and Americans. . . .

"And also my godson is not so insensitive that he would invite a German officer to witness such . . . duty. Which really leaves us with only one possibility." She looked for the first time towards her husband. "Which we have already foreseen, my husband and I—a sad but necessary duty, which we will not hinder."

Butler frowned at Audley, suddenly mystified.

Audley's face was a picture—a mirror image of his own mystification. And then suddenly it was transformed by understanding and relief.

"My God, Maman! Is that what you think we're here for?"

Boucard shook his head. "Not the British, my boy—or not the British by themselves. But we realise that Général de Gaulle and the Allies are not going to let the Communists take over, and ever since they have started to move Popular Front units into this area we've been expecting a countermove of some sort from the Free French and the Allies—particularly after today's news from the south."

"You know about the landing?" Audley said quickly.

Boucard smiled. "The Americans captured St. Tropez this afternoon, and their paras are already closing in on Draguignan . . . yes, we know. But what matters to us now is what happens here."

"Jee-sus Christ!" Winston exploded.

"Sergeant!"

"I'm sorry, ma'am—but"—Winston appealed to Audley—"what the hell are they on about? *Communists?*"

Audley grinned wryly at him. "Welcome to Europe, Sergeant. They think we're here to kill Frenchmen—and French Communists for choice."

Butler found himself staring at Hauptmann Grafenberg—

he didn't know why, but perhaps it was because of all the faces at the table the young German officer's was the most completely bewildered.

Except that the German was also staring at *him*.

A few minutes before he had felt sorry for his enemy, because he had seen in his painful confusion the bitter truth that there was more to losing a war than just being beaten in fair fight by the stronger side.

But now he himself was discovering that winning a war was more complicated than beating the enemy—that when one enemy was beaten there were suddenly more enemies and new enemies. Enemies stretching away into infinity—

Germans killing Germans.

Frenchmen killing Frenchmen.

"Hell, ma'am—for once you really guessed wrong," said the American. "We're not here to kill Frenchmen. We're here to kill the goddamn British."

It was perfectly logical, thought Butler.

Or, if not perfectly logical, it had five years' blessing, all but a couple of weeks, behind it. And that was how Dad would have argued it, first with the other union officials round the kitchen table, then with the bosses—

Custom and practice.

"We have the custom and practice of the shop floor behind us. There's no getting away from that, lads."

And the only difference was that then it was peacetime, and you struck—or they locked you out—and the one that broke first was the loser.

But since September 3, 1939, it had been war, and the custom and practice of war was killing, and the one that dies first was the loser.

"Traitors, you mean," said Boucard.

"Not . . . traitors, exactly." Audley shook his head. "More like criminals, sir—thieves, certainly."

"And murderers," cut in Winston, looking at Audley. "What happened in that village—to those other guys—that was murder, by God. Even though they got the krauts to pull the trigger."

And Mr. Wilson and Sergeant Scott, the dead interpreters whose shoes they were wearing, thought Butler fiercely. That had been murder plain and simple.

"Aye—murderers," he echoed the American, the anger within him edging the words. When he thought about it, the trail of death Major O'Conor had left behind him had all been plain murder, not war at all: not just the two interpreters and the men in the jeep behind them at Sermigny, but the dead men at the river ambush, and those who must have died in the limejuice strike on Sermigny—Germans and French civilians alike, and even the Resistance men strafed by the Mustangs. They had all been the victims of the major's greed.

Even Corporal Jones—it had been the major's hand on the bayonet in Taffy's guts, not his own.

None of that had been war, just murder.

"I see." Boucard stared at each of them in turn. "So you have been sent to . . . execute them, is that it?"

Audley blinked. "It isn't quite as simple as that. We have to stop their doing . . . what they're planning to do."

"And killing them is the only way?" Madame Boucard paused. "Is that it, David?"

Audley blinked again, shifting nervously in his chair.

"Is it, David?" she repeated softly.

"It's the only way I can think of." Audley looked directly at her. "Maman—if I was a general or a colonel . . . if we had a squadron of Cromwells parked in your drive, ready to go . . . maybe I could come up with something clever." He shook his head. "But I'm not, and there aren't. There are just three of us, and we have to do the job somehow."

"Huh!" Sergeant Winston grunted. "Always supposing we can even find the bastards."

Audley glanced at him sidelong. "Oh, we can find them now, I think," he said.

"So you *do* know where they're heading?" Winston made the question sound like an accusation.

"No." Audley looked at Winston for a second, then turned to Boucard. "But I think you'll know, sir. In fact I'm betting on it."

"Me?" Boucard frowned. "Then I'm afraid you have lost

your bet, my boy. Because I know of only two Englishmen in Touraine at this moment, and both of them are guests under my roof—they are sitting at this table."

"Yes, sir. But you'll know where the men we're after are heading all the same, I think."

Boucard shook his head. "No, David. We are an escape route, not a resistance group. Unless they are escaping—"

"They're sure as hell not doing that," said Winston.

"Then I simply do not have the sort of information you need." Boucard shrugged. "I might try to get it for you, it is true . . . there are ways, there are people . . . but it would take time. And I would guess that it is time that you lack?"

"Yes, sir . . ." Audley turned suddenly towards Madame. "Maman, you remember we once went on a picnic to that château built right across a river—you had a special place just downstream on the south bank, on the towpath, where we had a terrific view of it?"

"Madame looked at him in surprise.

"Just north of here, Maman?"

"Yes . . . I remember. Chenonceaux." She nodded. "You made the occasion memorable by falling in the river."

"So I did . . . though actually Madeleine pushed me." Audley's lips twitched. "The river Cher?"

"The Cher—yes." She nodded again. "Is that the place you are seeking?"

"No, I don't think so. We've come too far south already for that, unless"—Audley looked to Boucard—"have the Germans occupied the château there?"

"No." Boucard shook his head. "On the contrary, we've used the place to get people across the river—in the days when the demarcation line between the zones was there."

"What demarcation line?" asked Winston.

"Between German-occupied France and Vichy France," said Audley triumphantly. "I *thought* it was there—I read it was there years ago—and I wondered what would happen to the château. I remember wondering"—he took in both Winston and Butler with a sweeping glance—"you see, the château's built over the river, from one side to the other, like a bridge. Like old London Bridge was, and Ponte Vecchio in Florence—"

"So what?" snapped Winston. "If that isn't where the major's heading, what the hell does it matter?"

"It's the whole point." Audley pounded his fist into his open palm. "As soon as the major told us we were going south of the river—and with what little he told us about what we were doing—I knew exactly the sort of place we were heading for. Not the place itself, but the *sort* of place."

"I don't get you," said Winston.

"Because it was in the unoccupied zone—in Vichy France, not in the German territory," said Audley.

"But—hell, Lieutenant, the krauts are everywhere."

"But they weren't in 1940."

"In 1940?" Boucard sat up straight. "What has 1940 to do with all this?"

"Everything, sir." Audley's voice had the same mixture of arrogance and eagerness that Butler remembered from his collision with Colonel Clinton back in the barn: this was exactly what his own CO had meant by "having too many brains for his own good" and not the wit to hide them.

"Look, sir—Maman"—only the eagerness to prove how clever he was made the subaltern's arrogance endurable— "there's a story to this. I can't tell it all to you, but I can tell some of it."

"You were always very kind, David," said Madeleine. "So do tell us."

Butler did a double-take on her, suddenly aware that the future Mrs. Butler had sharp claws.

"Eh?" Audley looked at the girl vaguely, and Butler decided to be grateful that he had no problem of childhood sweethearts to overcome; that push into the river Cher all those years ago had been deliberate, not accidental.

"Madeleine!" Madame said sharply. "Go on, David."

"Yes . . ." Audley grimaced at Madeleine. "Yes—well, in 1940 we took something out of Paris—"

"We?" interrupted Madame.

"The British, Maman. When everything was cracking up, we got this thing out—"

"This thing?"

"I don't know what it was—honestly. But it was very valuable—and we got it out in an ambulance. . . . It was some-

thing worth stealing, it has to be—otherwise the major
wouldn't"—Audley spread his hands—"honestly, I don't
know, Maman. But it was British, and it was valuable—"

"You've been told it was British, and it was valuable—?"

"Hush!" snapped Boucard. "Let the boy tell his story, *au
nom de Dieu*!"

Audley gave Boucard a grateful glance. "They got this far,
somewhere. And then the ambulance broke down—"

"Ran out of gas," murmured Winston.

"Maybe. But this far, anyway. And they hid it in a château
somewhere."

"In the country of châteaux?" said Boucard incredulously.
"David—in all France—here of all places . . . Chambord and
Chenonceaux, Blois and Amboise—Villandry and Azay—
Usse and Loches . . . there are fifty châteaux within a morn-
ing's drive of here where I could hide anything you wish. Big
châteaux and little châteaux—Cinq-Mars-la-Pile, perhaps. Or
Montpouçon, down in the wash-house by the stream there.
You have to be joking, my dear boy."

"No, sir."

"No? Well, if you are not joking, then what are you saying?"

Audley leaned forward. "Sir—I'm saying—if you hid
something in—say Montpouçon . . . or Varenne, in 1940 . . .
could you get it out again in 1941—or '42, or '43? With half
a dozen good men on a dark night? Could you get it out?
Christ! Of course you could! But what I'm looking for, don't
you see, is a château you *couldn't* get it out of—until now."

He looked around the table. "All along—ever since the major
ditched us—half of me has been telling me that we didn't stand
a chance of getting him unless we could either catch up with him
or at least pick up his trail. But the other half of me kept telling
me that we didn't need to do either of those things, not if we
could get to where he was going ahead of him.

"But then the first half of me reminded me that we didn't
damn well know where he was going.

"But the second half wouldn't take that for an answer—"

The American tapped the table. "But you don't know—you
said so yourself, Lieutenant."

"I don't know the *name*, Sergeant. But I know the—the

specification. A château south of the Loire—available in
1940—"

The light dawned on Butler. "Occupied by the Germans,
sir. The major said so when we were in the jeep together."

"Exactly. That's the whole point—occupied by the Germans, although it was in the Vichy zone of unoccupied
France. Or if it wasn't occupied by the Germans straight off it
must have still been closed up tight as the Bank of England by
1941, otherwise we could have lifted the stuff out of there
before now. But occupied by the Germans now, anyway—"

Madame Boucard sat bolt upright. "Pont-Civray."

"Pont-...." Audley swung towards her.

"Civray." Madame Boucard nodded. "Le Château de Pont-
Civray. About fifteen kilometres from here. You may even
have heard us speak of it, David—in the old days."

"No, Maman—I don't think so."

"Then it was our...delicacy. It was—acquired, shall we
say?—acquired by an Englishman from an old family here,
the De Lissacs. They said that Etienne de Lissac couldn't see
the cards he had in his hand, and the Englishman could see
both sides of the cards in both hands...but that may have
been mere scandal-mongering." She inclined her head very
slightly. "*En tout cas*...the Englishman moved in—that was
in 1938—and had the house gutted. The builders were still
there in 1940 when the Germans came."

"The Germans!"

"Oh, yes...almost directly after the Armistice, they took
over the château—some in uniform, and some out of uniform." She caught her husband's eye. "What was it they
called themselves?"

"*L'Association de l'Amitié Franco-Allemande*—there was
at least someone who had a sense of humour of a sort," said
Boucard grimly. "To take over an Englishman's castle for
what they had in mind—their brand of Franco-German
friendship."

"Which was?"

"It was the liaison centre for the Gestapo and the Service
d'Ordre Legionnaire—which is now the Milice—the scum of
the scum." Boucard's eyes flashed. "Even the Englishman
was preferable to that alliance."

Audley nodded. "So security would have been tight?"

"At Pont-Civray? My dear boy—Pont-Civray has not been a healthy place these last four years. Not since . . ." Boucard trailed off.

"Not since 1940," said Audley.

19.   How Second Lieutenant Audley got the truth off his chest

Dad was right about hay, Butler decided: it wasn't nearly as good as straw for sleeping in.

The night before he had been so dog-weary that it hadn't really mattered, he had been too tired to analyse its defects even though he had been the last one to go to sleep. But now, with what must be the first hint of dawn in the open doorway, he was conscious that it was dustier and mustier and pricklier, and above all colder, than straw ricks of happy memory.

He rubbed his sleep-crusted eyes and was surprised at the clarity of his mind. His body had been warm and relaxed when he had let it sink at last into the hay, but his brain had been a football crowd of unruly thoughts; now his body was cold and stiff, but a few hours of oblivion seemed to have shaken his thoughts into order. He could even remember how he had approved Mr. Audley's obstinate refusal of beds in the château in preference to the hayloft in the old barn by the stream; and how he had wondered later, as he listened to the subaltern mumble and groan in his sleep, whether that refusal had been due to knowledge of his sleeping habits rather than to military prudence.

Not that it mattered now, for young Mr. Audley was quiet at last and in a very few minutes it would be dawn.

And the dawn of a very special day, too.

He straightened his legs cautiously, so as not to wake the others. This was, for a guess, the same hour when he had parted the canvas flaps on the truck yesterday morning and had looked out over the darkened vineyards of Touraine across the river. He had seen the rows of vines in the flare of the

American military policeman's lighter, and had not known
they were vines because he had never seen a vineyard before;
and also because he hadn't known where he was any more
than where he was going.

But since then the world had changed, and he had changed
with it.

He had killed his first man.

He had been betrayed by men he had trusted.

He had fought his first Germans.

(He had fought his first Germans, but not very efficiently;
and then he had run away from them in terror.)

He had been wounded.

(But not very badly, and his wound had covered a multitude
of weaknesses thereafter, so he had been lucky there.)

He had spoken to his first German, his first prisoner.

(Why was it so astonishing that Germans were so *ordinary*?
The soldier with the loaves . . . and then Hauptmann Grafenberg, who really wasn't so very different from Second Lieutenant Audley—)

(No. Say, not so different from his own company officers in
the Rifles. Mr. Audley was something else and something very
different from both. He didn't even know whether he liked and
admired Mr. Audley, or whether he disliked and mistrusted him.
But it was the general who always said that brains alone didn't
make an officer, there had to be a heart somewhere—)

A heart!

Somehow, he didn't know how, on the day that all this had
happened to him, he had lost his heart to a girl he hardly
knew, and a foreigner too. And God only knew what Dad
would make of that, apart from his other ambition—

French girls—a wink and a nod, man to man—*are a bit of
all right. So just you watch your step, Jack boy!*

Contradictory advice that had been. And even the general
had been less than helpful there—

Women—generals do not wink—*are the very devil. But
fortunately you will be otherwise engaged, I fancy.*

Well, there was nothing that Dad or the general—or he
himself, for that matter—could do about last night. He could

no more remove the name from his heart than he could avoid
the bullet which had his name on it.

It was dead quiet with that peculiar before-dawn stillness
which he recognised now, but to which as a town-bred boy he
knew he would never grow accustomed. Beyond the breathing
of the other men in the loft he could even hear the soft *swish*
of the stream below, reminding him that before it had been
downgraded to a barn the old building had been a water mill.

He ran his hand across his face at the thought of water,
feeling the stubble under his fingers ends. Shaving didn't
really matter much in the circumstances, particularly with his
colouring, but the chances of washing his feet was not to be
missed: it was the least he could do for them, and also the
most since the destruction of his bottle of gentian violet.

He eased himself sideways across the mounds of hay until
he was able to slide down almost noiselessly into the open
space by the doorway. Nobody stirred in the darkness behind
him; the one and only advantage hay had over straw was that
it didn't crunch and crackle so much.

But then, as he took his first cautious step towards the
opening, a darker nucleus moved on the stone platform outside.

"Who's that?" whispered Audley.

Butler stopped. "Me, sir—Butler."

"Come on out then. No need to wake the others yet."

Butler tiptoed onto the platform. The air was surprisingly
more chilly than in the loft, so much so that he shivered as he
drew it into his lungs, and wished that he had stayed inside.
Now he would have to talk to the officer, when he didn't feel
like talking to anyone, least of all to Audley, who had no heart
to grow cold in the morning chill.

But Audley didn't say anything; he merely sank down again
with his back against the stone and stared into the black noth-
ingness of the woods ahead of him.

His very silence unnerved Butler. It was too dark to go
blundering down the steps to the stream—much darker than he
had expected from the patch of sky he had seen from inside the

loft. If he went he would probably fall in, or drop his boots into the water, or do something just as silly. But if he stayed . . .

"I thought I'd just . . . stretch my legs, sir," he said.

"Good idea—so long as you don't break one of them," Audley murmured. "But be my guest, Jack."

Jack?

Butler took another look at the darkness and decided against it. But then decided also that he couldn't just go back into the loft.

"Did you sleep okay, sir?" he asked politely.

Audley didn't reply, and the silence lengthened until Butler began to think he hadn't actually asked the question, it had been something he had said inside his head.

Then Audley shifted his position. "No, I didn't sleep okay," he said, still staring ahead of him. "I dreamt my usual dream. And then I dreamt it again. And then I came out here. Though I suppose I did sleep in between the two main features—I must have done."

"Your usual dream, sir?" The statement demanded the question. "A nightmare, you mean?"

Audley appeared to consider the question as though it hadn't occurred to him before. "I suppose it must be," he said finally. "But it just doesn't seem like one, that's all."

Butler began to feel embarrassed. "No, sir?"

"No, sir." Audley turned towards him, his face a vague blur in the darkness. "You looking forward to going back to your battalion, Jack?"

No doubt about that answer! "Yes, sir."

Back in the battalion a man knew who his enemies were— and in which direction they were likely to be.

"No taste for cloak-and-dagger?"

"Not trained for it, sir."

"No? Well, you've done damn well so far. We wouldn't be here now if you hadn't had your wits about you."

Butler's spirits rose, then fell as the truth grinned foolishly at him from behind appearances. "More like luck than wits."

"I doubt that. Don't sell yourself short."

"No, sir." Butler decided to change the subject. "I bet you'll be glad to get back to your regiment, sir."

"Me?" Audley made a sound that wasn't a laugh. "I tell you, Jack—if I never see a tank again, that'll be too soon. And it'ud be to the British Army's advantage if I didn't, too: I was one damn bad tank commander, and that's the truth."

Butler wished he hadn't changed the subject. "Your CO didn't seem to think so, sir."

"He didn't?" This time the sound was a laugh—of a sort, anyway. "Well, now . . . he probably wouldn't at that . . . which just goes to show how deceptive appearances can be, you know."

Amen to that, thought Butler. But surely that couldn't be true about everyone?

"In fact I know just why he thought that." Audley turned towards him again. "And I'll tell you why—it makes a rather nice cautionary tale in its way."

Butler stared at him.

The white blur shook up and down. "Yes . . . I think I must have just the merest touch of claustrophobia—or cold feet as they call it in the Mess—but I couldn't bear to batten down inside my tank. I liked to have as much of me outside the steel coffin as possible, no matter what. Much easier to bail out if you get brewed up too . . ." He fell silent for a few seconds. "Besides, the last tank I had, the previous commander had his head blown off—his body slipped down inside . . . whole thing was swimming in blood, and you wouldn't believe how difficult it is to clean out a tank. In fact you can't clean it out—and you know what happens then, eh?"

Butler couldn't think of anything to say.

"Flies," said Audley. "Bloody thing was full of flies—great big fat things. Couldn't get rid of them. Which was another reason I never battened down—I can't bear flies. Especially flies full of blood belonging to a friend of mine. That's what I dream about—flies." He paused again. "When I get home I'm going to buy myself the biggest fly-swatter you ever saw, and ten dozen flypapers, and I'm going to declare total war on the blighters. . . ."

He seemed to have lost the thread, but Butler was loath to recall him to it, whatever it was.

"Yes . . ." Audley's voice strengthened. "So there was me, with my head and shoulders always sticking out of the top, because otherwise I'd get the screaming ab-dabs—and that's how all the really brave chaps like to ride, and damn the snipers. 'Proper cavalry spirit'—that's what the CO called it—'standing up in the stirrups to look.' Except I was so scared into a blue funk, I was more frightened of the flies than the snipers . . . and that last time, when the Tiger jumped three of us—we were the last one he got—I was out of the turret two seconds before he pressed the tit, not blown out but bailed out, and knocked myself out cold in the process. Which is what they found when they came to pick up the pieces: three brewed-up Cromwells and one heroically concussed cornet of dragoons." His voice cracked. "And the Tiger knocked out by a Firefly posting an AP up his back-passage . . . so don't let anyone ever tell you about the victors and the vanquished, Jack. In war there are only the dead and the survivors, and the dead don't win anything. But if they think they're going to get me back inside a tank again, they're going to have to carry me kicking and screaming—and stuttering too. Because that's where I got that bloody stutter of mine . . . and the farther away from the regiment I got, the farther away from my stutter—isn't that a funny thing, now?"

Butler stared and stared into the darkness, and was glad of it because it hid whatever expression he was wearing on his face—whatever it was, it felt hot as though he was blushing, though whether that was for himself or for Audley he couldn't make out.

"Phew!" Audley breathed out. "They say confession is good for the soul, and I feel better for that already. But it must be somewhat less reassuring for the recipient, I should think, eh?"

Butler swallowed. "No, sir." He reached feverishly into his imagination. "I think—I think you're no different from me—when I said it was luck, not wits, that counts. What people see, that's the truth for them."

"Uh-huh? 'Beauty is only skin-deep, but it's only the skin you see'? But I don't think that's really a very sound basis for action, I'm afraid."

Butler reached out again, and Rifleman Callaghan came to his rescue. "I dunno about that, sir. But there's a man in my platoon who always says it's better to be lucky than beautiful . . . I reckon we're both lucky, it looks like."

There was no point in adding that Rifleman Callaghan was

referring to his conquests in the ATS quarters, not to matters of life and death in France; and that in his victories it was not survival but a clean pair of heels that mattered.

"You may be right—I hope you are," Audley mused. "On the other hand . . ."

Butler reached out for one last time, despairingly. Things had gone quite far enough, and he didn't want to go into the fight today with any more of Audley's burdens on his back. Also, if there was such a thing as good luck, and they still had it, he didn't fancy listening to Audley try to take it to pieces to see how it worked, as though it was a cheap watch. It was one thing to take a watch to pieces, but a very different thing to make it work again afterwards.

"There's one thing I'd like to know, sir," he said.

It took Audley a moment to shake himself free from his own thoughts. "Yes . . . ? Well, what's that?"

What was there that he'd like to know? Butler asked himself desperately. He'd exchanged one problem for another.

He'd like to know what had been carried out of Paris in that ambulance four years before, to the Château de Pont-Civray. But Audley didn't know the answer to that, so he could only ask such a silly question as a last resort.

What would Rifleman Callaghan have done in such a fix?

"I don't really know how to ask it," he temporised.

"You don't?" Audley gave a short laugh. "Then I bet I know what it is."

Well, that was one for Callaghan's book, thought Butler: by a pure fluke he'd reversed the question, and what he was going to get now was what Audley himself would like to know.

"The major," said Audley.

The major?

"Yes, sir." Butler controlled his voice with an effort. "The major."

It was growing lighter; he could just begin to make out Audley's features, though not yet his expression. Which was a blessing, because it meant that Audley couldn't see him either.

"I know . . ." Audley nodded. "Because I've been thinking about him too. Ever since Maman spelt it out last night I've been thinking about him off and on."

Butler decided to say nothing.

Audley looked at him for a moment, and then turned away again to stare at the wood, in which the trees nearest them were just beginning to emerge as individual shapes.

"It's funny . . . I knew from the second we decided to go after him that if we did catch up with him we'd have to kill him. Not only because it's the only thing *we* can do, but because if we don't he'll certainly kill us—it'll be the only thing *he* can do."

Butler frowned. He hadn't thought of it that way.

Audley shook his head at the trees. "I've never killed a man before . . . I mean, I've never killed a man I knew—in cold-blood like this. Maman was quite right, as usual: the word is 'assassinate'—God knows how she guessed, but that's what it is. Just one step up from murder, really."

Butler cleared his throat. "I don't see that, sir. Not so as to worry about it anyway. Not after what we've been through."

"Oh—it doesn't worry me, not at all. Quite the opposite actually. As I say, it's funny . . . but the last twenty-four hours or so I've been really almost happy for the first time since I landed in Normandy."

"Happy?" Butler repeated the word incredulously.

"I said it was funny, didn't I!" Audley rocked forwards. "I suppose being away from . . . from the regiment has something to do with it. Away anywhere. Even here."

There came a sudden sound of flapping wings from the wood, making Butler sit up sharply in alarm.

"It's all right," Audley reassured him. "He's just gone on his morning patrol. If it'ud been anything else he'd have sounded his danger call."

Butler stared at the young officer curiously, wondering suddenly how much guilty truth and how much honest battle fatigue there had been in the story of the fight with the Tiger. What was certain was that too much brains and too much imagination could be an extra burden in the front line: Audley was like a racehorse down a coal mine, desperately pretending to be a pit pony.

The wood was quiet again.

"I didn't think much about the major, anyway." Audley took up the thread once more. "The best part of yesterday . . . I suppose the problem of catching him seemed more important than doing what we had to do when we did catch him—if we ever did. But now . . ." He trailed off.

Butler felt strangely protective. "We'll just do what we have to. Duty isn't a problem, sir."

Audley turned towards him. "Yes—but now I want to know *why*, don't you see?"

"Why what, sir?"

"Why Major O'Conor's gone rotten on us, man—wasn't that what you wanted to ask in the first place?"

Butler blinked. "Oh . . . yes, sir—it was. But I didn't think you'd know the answer to that, of course."

"But maybe I do."

"You do?" Butler's surprise was genuine.

"I said 'maybe.' The trouble is I know so little about him, really—just what they said . . . and what he said too . . . in the Mess last night." Audley paused. "No, I mean the night before last. It seems only last night . . . and yet it also seems a hell of a long time ago."

So Audley was having trouble with time too, thought Butler. "Yes, sir?"

Audley nodded. "He wasn't just in the show from 1940 onwards. He was in the first lot, in 1918—did you know that?"

Butler nodded back. "Yes, sir. I recognised the ribbons."

"Yes, of course—I hadn't thought of that. . . . Well, he was a second lieutenant. Won the MC up beyond Ypres somewhere, right at the end of things. And he wanted to stay on afterwards and make a career of it, but they wouldn't have him—that's what he said. I can't imagine why anyone in his right mind should want to do that, but I think he did—very much."

Butler opened his mouth to say something, but the words wouldn't come out.

"It's pretty remarkable that he got back in at the sharp end in 1939. He'd been a schoolmaster or something like that—maybe he was a Territorial officer, I suppose. That might be it. But it's still remarkable."

There was a lump in Butler's throat. "If a man wants something enough, sir . . ."

"But he wanted it enough in 1918—or 1919. Anyway he did get back in—France in '40, then the Middle East—Greece and Crete. North Africa and then Italy. And finally

Jugoslavia as a weapons adviser to a big Partisan outfit—a DSO for that, so he must have been damn good. It seems incredible, doesn't it?"

"That he should go wrong on us?" Butler found himself staring at the trees. It did seem incredible. It even required an effort of will to recall the voice and the words he had heard spoken just above him on the island in the Loire, even though both were etched deep into his memory. "Yes, it does, sir."

"And yet it was there, the night before last."

It was there?

"What was there, sir?"

"Something wrong. He kept asking me what I was going to do after the war. Like, did I really want to go up to Cambridge."

"They asked me that too, sir. What I wanted to do after the war. The . . . Corporal Jones did. And Sergeant Purvis."

Somehow Sergeant Purvis's treachery seemed the blackest of all. The major was an Olympian figure, a being from another world, to be admired or hated rather than understood—and it was difficult to hate what he didn't understand. But Sergeant Purvis—and the sergeant-major too—had been men he knew and trusted as the backbone of the British Army. The major was like the general, his idol. But *they* were no different from Dad, and that made their treachery worse and killing too good for them, the buggers.

"They did?" Audley gave him a knowing look: he could see that now and he'd have to watch his own face. "Yes . . . well, I suppose they were checking us both for the same thing. The other two chaps were from Intelligence—Colonel Clinton's men. That's why the major got rid of them. Maybe he hoped to recruit us into the plot—at least for the time being, anyway . . . I don't know. But that's the key to it, I think." His mouth twisted. "In fact, when I think about it, he as good as said as much, by golly! Do you know that, Jack?"

Jack.

Equals.

"No. What did he say?"

They were equals. Mr. Audley and Corporal Butler were just for the time being. He would learn and he would catch up because he had learnt. And he would be a better officer than Audley because of that.

"He said things would be rough after the war."

"They said that too." He couldn't quite bring himself to say *David*. That would only come with friendship, if not equality.

"Huh! He said the war was won, but we hadn't won it—we'd just fought it. He said the Yanks and the Russians had won, we'd lost. At least, *the British* had lost. But there was still a chance for individual chaps to grab what was going and get something out of it—did they say that to you, Jack?"

The lump was there again. "More or less."

Audley nodded. "I gave him the wrong answer too. I said everything I wanted was at Cambridge, waiting for me—"

He was only one breath away from asking what was waiting for Corporal Butler to keep him on the straight and narrow road, thought Butler. And he had to be headed off from that question.

"What did he say to that, sir?" he said hastily.

"Oh, he sheered off. He said he was glad I'd got myself a cushy billet. And then he said something I thought was rather clever: he said that the difference between wise countries and wise men was that wise countries prepared for war in peacetime, whereas the wise man was the one who prepared for peace in wartime." He gave Butler a twisted grin. "The laugh is—I thought he was talking about me. But actually he was referring to himself, I suppose: kill everyone who gets in the way, grab the loot, and keep going, that's his formula."

"Keep going where?"

Audley shrugged. "Switzerland, I guess. That's where I'd go if I was him."

"But what about everyone else? They'd know, I mean."

"If there is any 'they' after he's finished. With the sergeant-major and that sergeant of his, plus whoever else is in on the scheme—with the Germans retreating and the French settling their private scores, there should be enough chaos for him to remove the eyewitnesses. And even if he isn't quite as cold-blooded as that—well, maybe most of the chaps don't even know what he's up to, so he can go missing and stand a good chance of being listed as a dead hero."

Put like that the risk the major was taking wasn't really so risky as that, thought Butler. The only real hazard was the Germans, but now that they were retreating all the major had to do was to keep out of their road, and that was precisely where his special skill lay. Otherwise, a couple of jeeploads of British soldiers were more likely to be welcomed and helped on their way than questioned. France would be wide open to them.

"That doesn't answer the why, but it does spell out the how," said Audley. "And maybe the two add up to the same thing, anyway: it was his last and best opportunity of getting rich—he simply couldn't resist the opportunity."

There was more to it than that, Butler's instinct told him. Audley might be right about the temptation—he probably was. But there was also the long bitterness of those civilian years which the major had endured. Audley would never understand that, even though he had half suspected it, because it didn't make sense to him.

But he, Jack Butler, could understand it very well indeed.

He could almost sympathise with it.

He could even guess at how it might rust a man's soul, the thought of the might-have-been, the lost comradeship and wasted youth, the thwarted skills and ambitions. Not even the opportunities of this war would have made up for all that; they might even have made it worse when the major saw the luckier subalterns of 1918 now commanding brigades and divisions all around him, while he was only a superannuated major teaching guerrillas how to shoot, somewhere in the back-of-beyond of the Jugoslav mountains.

And he knew he was right because he could still feel the ache in his own guts where his stomach had turned over with fear at the news that the war was ending quickly—too quickly, just as it had once done for the major. Indeed, the fear was still there, twisting inside him.

Except that it wasn't going to happen to him, the same thing. He wasn't going to let it happen, one way or another.

But he couldn't tell Audley any of *that*.

"You're probably right, sir," he began coolly. "He must—"

"Sssh!" Audley held up his hand to cut him off, turning an ear towards the wood as he did so.

Butler couldn't hear a sound other than the swish of the stream.

"Someone's coming," whispered Audley.

The only noise Butler could hear was still that of the water, but the conviction in that whisper was enough for him. He twisted sideways and reached inside the doorway for his Sten.

"On the path, down by the stream—*there!*" Audley hissed, pointing towards the fringe of trees to the left of them.

"I've got him," Butler whispered back, his eyes fixed on the flicker of movement in the stillness while his fingers closed on the cocking handle. There was something wonderfully comforting about the feel of the weapon and the oily, metallic smell of it in his nostrils. He remembered having read somewhere, years back, how savage warriors caressed their spears and talked to them before battle—

"It looks like just one," murmured Audley. "I can't see anyone else. Which means—keep your fingers crossed, Jack!"

All Butler's fingers were otherwise engaged, particularly one of them. But there was still a corner of his mind that wasn't concentrating on the movement between the trees.

"Sir?"

Audley watched the trees intently. "If it's Boucard, then they're not going to help us. But if it's Dr. de Courcy . . ."

That was the big "if," of course, Butler remembered belatedly. M'sieur Boucard ran the safe house of the escape route on which they'd stumbled with such incredible beginner's luck. But it was the local doctor who controlled the escapers' transfer from one place to the next along that route—the doctor whose own journeys could always be explained by the requirements of his job.

Suddenly he was aware of his own heart thumping within his chest. Another dozen yards or so, and they would be able to see who it was—

Boucard or the doctor.

Failure or success?

Except that reaching Pont-Civray was itself no guarantee of success, only of somebody's death.

Maybe Jack Butler's death even?

Audley relaxed beside him.

"Over here, Doctor!" he called out.

Dr. de Courcy halted in the middle of the car-track just below them, took off his black Homburg hat, and methodically set about wiping the sweat-band with a clean handkerchief from his

breast pocket. Only when he'd completed this task to his satisfaction and had returned the handkerchief to his pocket and the
hat to his head, did he at last look up at them.

*"Eh bien, David Audley! Tu as éventé la mèche comme
toujours. Mais cette fois tu as dépassé les bornes,"* he said
harshly.

A rustle in the hayloft behind them distracted Butler's attempt to disentangle the meaning from the French words.

"So what's that meant to mean?" Sergeant Winston stepped
onto the platform, wiping the sleep from his eyes. "And
who's the funeral director?"

"Dr. de Courcy"—Audley's voice faltered—"Sergeant
Winston, of the United States Army."

"Oh—yeah . . ." Winston nodded apologetically. "Sorry,
Doc! Early morning—big mouth." He looked at Audley
questioningly. "Are we in trouble again, Lieutenant?"

Audley stared at Dr. de Courcy uncertainly. "He says . . .
we've let the cat out of the bag, somehow—?"

The doctor shook his head. "Not the cat. Another animal,
perhaps . . ."

"Another animal?"

"A tiger this time, David Audley. A man-eating tiger. And
he has your scent in his nose, I fear."

20. How Dr. de Courcy made a bargain

"The guys in the wood, Lieutenant," Sergeant Winston
prompted Audley. He nodded thoughtfully at Butler, and
Butler knew he was remembering the cold-blooded way
they'd killed the wounded German soldiers in the Kübel.

"Yes," said Audley, still staring at Dr. de Courcy. "But
there has to be more to it than that, I'm thinking."

"Sure there is: we got away from them, and they don't like it."

Audley shook his head. "More than that . . . What are we
supposed to have done, Doctor?"

De Courcy looked at him curiously. "You ask me that?"

"That's right, Doc." Winston leaned forward. "We're asking. So you tell us."

De Courcy frowned, glancing at each of them in turn.

"Well . . there are fifty dead in Sermigny, to the north of here . . . not counting the Germans. But that might be counted an accident of war, and not your fault. . . . But the four men you ambushed on the road—Communists, I admit, but men of the Resistance also. And the German prisoner you released" —he shrugged—"no doubt you had your reasons. But innocence is not the game to play."

"Innocence?" Winston exploded. *"Innocence!"*

"Hold it, Sergeant!" Audley held up his hand. "We haven't killed anyone, Doctor. Not Frenchmen, anyway. I give you my word of honour on that."

"Yeah. And my word too," snapped Winston. "Not that I haven't been goddamn tempted."

De Courcy's eyes clouded. "And I, Sergeant—I have seen the bodies of the men you killed. And also . . . M'sieur Boucard tells me you have a German officer with you. So where does that leave your word of honour, Sergeant?"

The American drew a deep breath, but then turned abruptly to Audley. "Lieutenant—are you thinking what I'm thinking?" he said slowly.

Audley nodded. "I shouldn't be at all surprised. I think you people have a word for it, too, don't you?"

"We do—several words. 'Framed' is one—and 'suckers' is another. And I guess that both apply to us, by God!" Winston swung back towards the Frenchman. "You saw the bodies, Doc—you actually saw them?"

"Yes."

"Did you examine them?" said Audley.

De Courcy frowned. "Why should I examine them? They were dead."

"Yeah, I'll bet they were," said Winston. "The way they died they'd be *very* dead."

"The way they died?" For the first time there was doubt in de Courcy's voice.

"That's right. They were hit by six point-five Brownings belonging to one trigger-happy P-51 pilot. And we didn't have a thing to do with it, except to get the hell out of the way of the same thing."

Audley nodded. "That's exactly the way it happened, Doctor. We were strafed on the road—we were in two captured

German vehicles, and the Mustangs took us for the real thing. But we got off the road in time, and they didn't." He turned to Butler. "Would you ask Hauptmann Grafenberg to join us, Corporal, please."

Butler peered into the darkness of the hayloft, but before he could speak, he saw a movement in the aisle between the banks of hay on each side of the opening.

"Sir—"

"I have heard, Corporal." The German stepped forward towards the doormat, pulling at his crumpled uniform with one hand in a hopeless attempt to straighten it and brushing with the other at the hay which festooned it.

"Good morning, Hauptmann," said Audley politely. "Doctor, I'd like you to meet Hauptmann Grafenberg of the German army."

The young German blinked at the light and stiffened to attention. If anything he looked even worse than the day before, thought Butler, as though he had spent the night with things even nastier than the blood-bloated flies which plagued Audley's dreams.

"Hauptmann, I'd be very grateful if . . . you'd be so good as to tell the doctor what happened to us on the road yesterday afternoon," said Audley.

The German looked down at the Frenchman. "It is not necessary—I have heard what has been said . . . and it is the truth." He swallowed awkwardly, as though the words were painful. "Except—it is not correct that I . . . that the Herr Lieutenant released me. It was to him that I surrendered."

Winston leaned forward again, stabbing a finger at de Courcy. "Which means that someone has been lying through his teeth about us, Doc—because the driver who was with us when the P-51s hit us, he ran like a jack rabbit. So they know what happened as well as we do."

Dr. de Courcy's eyes narrowed. "But . . . why should they lie about you, Sergeant—if they knew so much?"

"Hell, Doc—that doesn't take much figuring. They knew we were coming and they were waiting for us. So they scooped us up, but then we gave them the slip. So now they want whoever's got us to turn us in." Winston straightened up. "Like two plus two equals four—right, Lieutenant?"

Butler followed the sergeant's look to Audley, and was surprised to see how pale the subaltern's face was; it was paler than it ought to be after the German's testimony and the sergeant's triumphant mathematical assertion—paler even than thirty-six hours of strain and danger had already made it when *I've been really almost happy for the first time since I landed in Normandy.*

So there was something the sergeant had missed... something that made two plus two equals four the wrong answer.

And then it hit him like a gut-punch: *from the moment that the major had shouted "Hände hoch, Tommy" out of the hedge at him two plus two had never equalled four.*

He studied the Frenchman's face critically for the first time. Apart from that narrow look about the eyes it was entirely without expression—as empty as the woods had seemed where the French had ambushed the German vehicles. No fear, no anger, no belief, no disbelief, no surprise.

Two plus two equals *five.*

"Permission to speak to the doctor, sir," he said.

"What the hell?" Winston regarded him curiously. But the American army had no discipline, of course.

"Corporal?" Audley's glance was hardly less curious. "All right—go ahead."

"Thank you, sir." Butler dismissed them both from his mind and concentrated on the Frenchman. "M'sieur Boucard has explained the situation to you, sir, I expect?"

Now the Frenchman was studying him for the first time also, and seeing him as a soldier with a gun in his hands—a dirty, dishevelled British Tommy with a bandaged head, a person of no account, Butler thought gleefully.

But then, of course, he couldn't know what Butler knew—

All depended on MacDonald, and that officer, who by valour and conduct in war had won his way from the rank of a private soldier to the command of a brigade, was equal to the emergency—

The Frenchman hadn't answered yet, and that was a good sign.

"Sir?" he enquired politely.

"Yes." The answer was accompanied by a frown.

"So you do know our objective, sir?"

The doctor's lips tightened. "I know what I have been told," he said curtly. "Yes."

"That's fine, sir. Then you know our objective." Butler nodded, listening in his inner ear to the sweet sound of the bugles at Omdurman. "So the only question is—how quickly can you get us to Pont-Civray? Because the way things are, we probably don't have much time."

Now there was an emotion in de Courcy's face: he looked at Butler incredulously. "You think it is easy to get to Pont-Civray?"

"Hey, Jack—" Winston began.

"No!" snapped Butler, without looking at the American. "We've been buggered around enough—now there's going to be no more buggering around . . . and the answer to that is— *yes*, sir. You've been running an escape route in these parts for three or four years. If you can move men around under the noses of the Germans and the French police, then you can move us to Pont-Civray, which is only just down the road from here, somewhere. So the answer is yes, sir—for you it is easy. *All you have to do is to state your terms.*"

"My—terms?"

"Yes, sir. You said yourself that innocence isn't the game to play. So—with respect—I suggest you practise what you preach."

"My terms . . ." De Courcy left the question mark off the words this time. "What makes you think I have . . . terms?"

Butler turned to Audley. "Do you want to take over, sir?"

Audley was smiling at him, really smiling, as he shook his head. "You've got the ball, Jack—you make the touchdown."

"Very good, sir." Butler tightened his grip on the Sten as he turned back to the Frenchman. Like MacDonald wheeling his battalions and batteries, he knew that it could only be done if it was done right. And it wasn't a small thing that Audley was doing himself, trusting him to do it.

He looked down over the stubby barrel at the Frenchman.

"You didn't never believe"—he stumbled over the grammar —"you never did believe we killed those men, sir. If you had believed it then you wouldn't be here—you'd have turned us in, as the sergeant said. Or if you didn't want to turn Mr. Audley in, for old times' sake, then you still wouldn't have wanted to help us—and you certainly wouldn't have come down here by yourself to tell us to our faces that we were murderers, and we could stew in our own juice. You'd have sent M'sieur Boucard maybe, but you wouldn't have come yourself."

"What makes you so sure of that?"

Butler lifted the Sten. "This does, sir. Because if I'd killed four Frenchmen then a fifth one wouldn't worry me—because if Mr. Audley says 'shoot' then I shoot." He shook his head. "But you came—sir—"

"That at least is true."

Butler felt a small knot of anger tie itself inside him. "Aye, and there's not much bloody truth round here, either."

"Steady, Jack," said Audley.

"Yes, sir." Butler stepped back from his anger. "But instead of being straight with us you've been playing your own little game."

"And what game is that?" asked de Courcy.

The question sounded casual—almost insultingly casual, and certainly condescending. A day or two back a question like that would have thrown him, thought Butler. Even a few minutes ago it might have put him off his stroke, because he hadn't understood the rules of the game. But now it was different.

"Why—sir—you've told us that yourself." He gave the Frenchman back a common corporal's surprise in return for the condescension. It wasn't a game, of course, and they both knew it. But the trick was to behave as though it was—it was as simple and easy as that. He had taken a long time to learn that rule, but he had learnt it in the end.

"Pardon?" De Courcy's English accent slipped. "I told you?"

"Oh yes, sir." It wasn't difficult to insult a man if you knew how. "Your man-eating tigers—the men who are after us— they didn't really want to know why we were here, and what we were doing. So happens they knew that." He grinned innocently. "What they wanted to know is where we were going—that was what they didn't know."

"Bravo!" encouraged Audley softly.

"But you, sir—you know where we're going, because M'sieur Boucard's told you. And you know what we're going to do as well—because he'll have told you that too. What you don't know is the why—and that's your game, sir."

"Man—but Boucard will have told him that too," said Winston.

"No, Sergeant," said Audley quickly. "Not the real why. Not—well, not the tiger's why. They couldn't possibly know what we are planning to do, and it wouldn't worry them if they did know—Englishmen hunting Englishmen—what do they care about that? What they're after is what the major is after, don't you see!" He swung towards Butler. "Right, Corporal?"

Butler swelled with pride. "That's it, sir—right bang on the nose." He nodded to the American. "We're the pig in the middle, Sarge. But there's more than one on each side of us, that's what we haven't realised." Suddenly the pride dipped as it occurred to him that he wasn't sure what sides there were among the French.

"The Communists versus the Free French—General de Gaulle's people," Audley supplied the answer. "Good for you, Corporal!"

"Yes, sir." Butler adjusted his expression to one of knowing approval. One thing his own general had been dead wrong about was that a soldier didn't need to know much about politics.

Winston stared from one to the other of them. "But . . . but we don't—" He bit the end of the sentence off. "*Shit!*" he said feelingly.

Audley laughed—a little too shrilly for Butler's peace of mind. "That's exactly right, Sergeant: *we don't*—and *shit* is the appropriate reaction." The laugh caught in his throat and he stifled a cough. "I'm sorry—but it would be really rather funny if it wasn't happening to us, of all people!" He shook his head helplessly.

"Funny?" The American growled, looking to Butler for support. "You think it's *rah-ther* funny, Jack—*re-ally rah-ther* funny?" He stared at Butler menacingly. "Does it seem funny to you?"

Butler didn't think it was in the least funny. The remembrance of what had happened on the banks of the Loire was still a raw wound in his mind, and the murderously efficient Frenchmen in the wood—the men who were hunting for him now—were all frightening, not funny. He didn't wish to be disloyal to Audley, but there was certainly nothing there which could conceivably be regarded as even faintly amusing. Even the game he'd just learnt to play was no joke, for all that the winning of it was intensely satisfying.

But Audley was still giggling—

And now, what was worse—much worse, was that the American sergeant's face was breaking up too: even as he stared at Butler he was losing control of it—he was smiling foolishly—he was beginning to laugh.

He was laughing, now.

"Shit!" The American suddenly draped his arm on Audley's shoulder familiarly. "We don't know—but they think we do! But we don't—"

He broke down feebly, shaking his head.

Butler looked around desperately, catching first the blank look on Hauptmann Grafenberg's face, and then the equally questioning expression on the doctor's.

"I'm sorry—I really am—" Audley began.

"Re-ally," echoed Sergeant Winston. "Doc—it's just that you're a horse trader—"

"A horse trader?" De Courcy frowned. "What is—a horse trader?"

"Aw—they come in all shapes and sizes. But mostly crooked."

Winston finally managed to control himself. "You want me to tell him, Lieutenant?"

"Be my guest." Audley gestured towards the doctor.

"Okay." Winston bowed to Audley, then to the doctor. "It's just . . . we don't have anything to trade. No horses, no mules —not even a goddamn donkey! All we've got is our boots— and Corporal Butler's gun."

De Courcy stared at them. "What do you mean?"

"He means"—Audley's voice was at last serious—"that we haven't the faintest idea what the loot is. If the Communists got us—or the Gestapo got us—even if the Spanish Inquisition got us—it wouldn't do them one damn bit of good. Because we don't know."

De Courcy continued to stare at them, though now there was a hint of something else in his face; perhaps the beginning of either puzzlement or disbelief, Butler couldn't decide which.

Winston shook his head at Audley. "I don't think we're getting through . . . and maybe that's not surprising when you think about it, Lieutenant. Because we have to be crazy to want to go to Pont-Civray, seems to me. Which means . . . unless he's crazy too there's no way we're going to convince him we're on the level. No way at all."

It hadn't been real laughter, Butler realised belatedly as Audley's eyes shifted from the American to him: it had been something much closer to hysteria. However much the subaltern pretended that all this was more to his taste than tank warfare in the *bocage*—he might even believe that it was—he was near to the end of his resources.

And, what was more, the American was right: it *was* crazy, what he had been leading and driving them to do, this mad compulsion to catch up with the major. What would they do if they did catch up with him, the three of them? The odds would still be hugely against them.

But then perhaps that was what he wanted.

Perhaps it wasn't so much a case of *But now I want to know why, don't you see?* as *If they think they're going to get me back inside a tank, they're going to have to carry me kicking and screaming.*

It wasn't fair—to be caught up in something like this.

It never had been fair—to be taken away from his battalion and his company, and from his platoon and his section—just because he spoke a few words of German.

With a Lancashire-Polish accent.

It wasn't bloody well fair.

Audley was looking at him as though he expected a clever answer to a question which had no answer at all. And although he was sorry for Audley . . . although he was sorry for Audley in the same way that he was sorry for Hauptmann Grafenberg . . . he knew that he wouldn't have given him an answer even if he could think of one.

And then Audley wasn't looking at him any more; or, rather, not at *him,* as much as at his battle-dress sleeve, with its corporal's stripes.

He looked down at the stripes himself. The stout thread he

had used to sew them on had come loose, so that one end was
lifting away from the sleeve. He must have snagged them on
something, probably a tree branch during their panic flight
through the wood near Sermigny—

"Two reasons," said Audley, turning suddenly back towards
Dr. de Courcy. "There are two reasons why you should believe us."

"Two reasons?"

"Or six, if you like." Audley glanced quickly at the American sergeant, then back once again to de Courcy. And he was
smiling now. "Or a dozen, even—take your pick, Doctor."

"One would be enough, David." Curiously, the doctor
sounded almost relieved.

"One then." The smile was gone from Audley's face as he
reached across his chest to touch the pip on his left epaulette
with his index finger. "This one will do well enough."

De Courcy frowned. "That is—a reason?"

"Oh yes, it's a reason. It's a good reason—in fact it's the best
damn reason in the world!" Audley's voice was bitter. "I said we
didn't know what the major was after, but that's not strictly true.
We know the damn thing's valuable—we know it's top secret.
And you know what we are?" The finger tapped the pip. "Second lieutenant." The finger left the single pip and pointed
towards Butler's stripes. "And a corporal"—and then at Winston—"and a sergeant." He paused just long enough to take a
fresh breath. "And you know what that makes us, Doctor? I'll
tell you: it makes us the lowest form of animal life." The
bitterness was almost passionate. "Second lieutenants don't
have to think, Doctor—so they don't have to know. Who's
going to tell us top secrets? Not the Colonel Clintons of this
world, that's for sure. And as for the major—he didn't intend us
to get this far, we were jut a bit of window dressing to keep the
colonel happy, that's all. So telling us *why* wasn't necessary. We
weren't damn well going anywhere!"

The subaltern's vehemence took Butler aback, coupled as it
was with the extraordinary reason for it. Anger at being betrayed by one's own comrades was one thing—he had felt
that himself. But to get angry because one's superior officers
didn't explain all the whys and wherefores of their orders, that

was ridiculous. A bullock might just as well expect the slaughterman to explain why he was turning it into beef!

"Colonel—Clinton?" De Courcy's mouth opened and closed.

"Of Intelligence, so-called," said Audley scornfully. "He was supposed to be running this show—he could give you the answer to your question. Or he could have. But *we* can't."

It really was not knowing *why* that enraged Audley, thought Butler. In one breath he admitted being the lowest form of animal life, but in the next was objecting to it, and the objection marked him for what he truly was: a mere civilian in uniform.

But the rage also gave his words sincerity—the proof of that was plain on Dr. de Courcy's face.

"Could have?" said de Courcy. "What do you mean—could have?"

"Hell, Doc—the major had the same plans for the colonel as he had for us." Sergeant Winston drew his finger across his throat. "The colonel was strictly surplus to requirements."

De Courcy stared at them all, then gestured abruptly as though gathering them to him. "Come!" he commanded.

"To Pont-Civray?" Audley snapped the words out.

"To Pont-Civray." De Courcy repeated the gesture more urgently. "Those four men weren't the only . . . casualties I saw yesterday, apart from those of Sermigny. There was also a British officer my people brought in—a colonel. From near a village not far from here, seven or eight kilometres. But there was no identification on him."

"Dead?" said Audley.

"Not dead. But left for dead. He had a bullet in his back, David."

Winston looked at Audley. "Sounds like the major's style."

"Hmm . . . yes." Audley rubbed his chin. "And it also sounds as though we may be too late, I'm thinking. If the major was as close to Pont-Civray yesterday as we are now . . ."

"No." De Courcy shook his head. "We are not too late"—he drew a gold watch from his fob pocket—"perhaps not quite too late. But we must hurry now."

"How d'you know we're not too late?" said Audley.

"Because the Gestapo are not due to leave the château until midday today, that is how I know."

"But the major won't know that. Or even if he does he may

not choose to wait—he's got some tough men with him, Doctor, and he won't like hanging around."

"Perhaps not. But they also have some tough men with them, the Gestapo: they have a Waffen-SS motorised company to escort them. Also they have made it very plain that they are leaving, and that if there is the least attempt to hinder them they will turn Civray St. Michel into another Oradour-sur-Glane." De Courcy gave Audley a hard look. "You know what happened at Oradour, David?"

"There was a massacre of some sort there, wasn't there?"

"A massacre of some sort?" De Courcy's voice harshened. "The SS herded all the men into a barn, and the women and children into the church, and then they burnt the barn and the church and the whole village . . . yes, David—there was a massacre of some sort at Oradour-sur-Glane. And that is why you can depend on the people of Civray St. Michel to make very sure that your major knows that the Gestapo are leaving the château. And that if he wants to attack the Germans he will have to fight Frenchmen first."

Sergeant Winston looked at the doctor suspiciously. "Seems to me you know one hell of a lot, what's going on round here, Doc—for a simple country doctor. Like even what the krauts are doing."

De Courcy shrugged. "I told you—they have made no secret of it." Then suddenly he straightened up. "You do not believe me, Sergeant?"

"You're damn right, I don't believe you!" Winston traded one hard look for another. "Like Jack here said, we're the goddamn pig in the middle. But that was when you were playing hard to get, and now you're saying 'Come on down, boys—Pont-Civray here we come!' So now I'm saying . . . you know so much, you just prove we're not the pig that's being taken to market, huh?"

Butler looked at de Courcy and thought on that instant that the sergeant was right: he didn't look like a country doctor any more. On him the neat black suit and the Homburg hat and the gold watch and chain seemed as much a disguise as Second Lieutenant Audley's battle dress and pistol.

"Very well, Sergeant—if you wish for frankness, then I

will be frank." The corner of de Courcy's mouth lifted. "I will be *français* too."

"That's okay by me. Like the lieutenant said—be my guest."

"No. You are my guest—all of you." De Courcy swept a hand to include them all. "You are here in France with your guns and your tanks—American, British, *and* German. But you are here *en tourists*. You are merely passing through France . . . I know so much, Sergeant, because it is my business to know—because it is my country, not yours." He stared proudly at Audley. "And this thing you British want so badly—it is better that it stays hidden until we can decide to whom it belongs, I think."

"But—" Audley began, "but it belongs to us."

"No, David. You say it belongs to you. But you do not even know what it is. And the Communists—they intend that it shall belong to them. And your major . . . he plans that it shall belong to him. But I say *it came out of Paris in 1940, and I do not trust any of you.*"

Sergeant Winston chuckled suddenly. "Yeah—well, I go along with you there, Doc." He grinned at Audley. "Don't get me wrong, Lieutenant—I think you're on the level. And Jack here . . . But your top brass could be as crooked as a three-dollar bill." He nodded encouragingly at de Courcy. "You can count me in so far, Doc—we give the loot to its owner, that's dealing from the top of the deck. But just how do you plan on doing that?"

"Very simply, Sergeant. I have established that you do not know where it is hidden—you have said as much, and I believe you. Your colonel . . . Clinton knows, but he is in no condition to tell anyone, even if he lives—not for the time being *en tout cas*. Which only leaves your major—yes?" De Courcy lifted an eyebrow at Audley. "Whom you intend to . . . execute as a traitor?"

"You're damn right!" exclaimed Sergeant Winston.

Except that he was damn wrong, thought Butler. Because there was also the colonel's driver—had Winston forgotten him?

Or had he mentioned the driver?

He couldn't remember. They had been driving down off the

embankment—he had been telling them what had happened.
. . . He must have told them about the driver—

*He's the key to the treasure house, Sergeant-major. He's
our walking map!*

He must have told them!

But he couldn't remember—and Audley's face was as innocent as a baby's—

Too innocent?

Then Audley nodded abruptly. "All right, sir. If those are
your terms, then we accept them. You want Major O'Conor
dead—"

Too innocent!

"You'll take us to Pont-Civray." Audley's jaw tightened.
"We'll kill him."

"How are you going to get us there, Doc?" asked Winston.

De Courcy smiled. "How should a doctor move his patients
in an emergency?"

They followed him down the path.

Once again, it wasn't how he had ever imagined going to
war: a Frenchman taking two Englishmen and an American
and a German . . . to kill an Englishman.

Winston grinned at him. "You did okay back there, Jack.
But how the hell did you know he'd crack—the doc?"

How the hell had he known?

He lifted the Sten. "I had the gun, Sergeant. He didn't."

That was what Rifleman Callaghan always said: The man
with the gun always wins the argument.

21. How the Germans spoilt a good plan

"When you think about it, it's rather appropriate," said Audley reflectively, to no one in particular.

Butler had been thinking about it, but that hadn't been his
conclusion. He had thought, more simply, that it was a pity they
couldn't see where they were being taken; but also that with the

way his toes were already acting up it was a bloody sight better than foot-slogging. If the pigs really were being transported to market, at least their last journey was being made in comfort.

Sergeant Winston surfaced from out of his own thoughts. "What is?" he inquired.

"This." Audley waved his hand around vaguely.

Winston looked towards the doctor. "Yeah, I guess it is at that." He grinned suddenly. "We should be glad you aren't a garbage collector, Doc——"

"No." Audley shook his head. "I mean . . . this is how it all started—in an ambulance. This is how they brought the loot out of Paris in 1940—in an ambulance. And now us."

"Uh-huh?" Winston shrugged. "Well, just so we get there in one piece is all I care about first. But it's what the hell we do when we get there that worries me, Lieutenant. You planning to gun the major down just like that—just wait for him to show up and let him have it? Is that it?"

Audley ran his finger nervously between his neck and his collar. The light coming through the frosted window beside him caught the sheen of sweat on his forehead. Happen he didn't like being cooped up blind in the enclosed space of the ambulance, thought Butler, and that sweat was a memory of old terrors. But much more likely it was fear of what was to come, which had been all airy-fairy talk until now, with the odds against it ever being put to the test of reality.

Trouble was, he could never see through the skin for sure, not until it was too late. All he knew was that Second Lieutenant Audley was a great talker, and clever with it—no doubt about that. But what he was when the words were all said and there was no more room for cleverness, that still remained to be seen.

"Is that it?" Winston repeated the question brutally, as though he sensed the same uncertainty in the subaltern.

And yet for all that maybe they weren't being fair, thought Butler. Because it was one thing to follow and obey, and another and quite different thing to decide and to lead, knowing that the burden of responsibility was on one's own shoulders, no matter whose finger was on the trigger.

He cleared his throat. "We could call on him to surrender first, sir," he said.

Winston gave an angry grunt. "Oh sure—we do that and we throw away the only chance we've got, which is catching the bastard by surprise."

Audley's jaw tightened. "We can still do that—if we can get into the château first." He turned towards Dr. de Courcy questioningly.

De Courcy nodded slowly. "Yes," he said.

"Uh-huh?" Winston paused. "And just how are you planning to do that, Doc?"

"It need not worry you, Sergeant. It can be done."

"So it can be done—so it still worries me." Winston paused again. "So you tell me how, huh?"

De Courcy shrugged. "Very well . . . the Germans will not leave until midday. In the meantime they will be on the alert—it is a time of danger for them, the moment of withdrawal—"

Winston raised his hand. "I don't want to care about the Germans, Doc. They don't worry me. It's the major—he worries me. Because by midday he'll be sitting on the goddamn doorstep just waiting for the krauts to move out. That is, if he isn't there already—which he probably is. And the moment they do move . . . he's not the sort of guy to wait until the dust settles, Doc. They move out—he'll move in."

The Frenchman half-smiled. "And that is what I am relying on, Sergeant."

Winston frowned. "I don't get you."

"That is because you do not know the Château of Pont-Civray."

"You mean—there's a secret way in?"

"No, not a secret way." De Courcy shook his head. "But *another* way, simply."

"Then the major may be watching it—simply."

"But there is no reason why he should." De Courcy leant forward to emphasise his point. "To the west of the château, in the woods beside the river, there is a path. Once it was a carriageway to the West Lodge, but it had not been used for many years even before the Germans came. It is . . . how do you say?—*couvert*—grown over."

"Overgrown—I get you. But if you're banking on the major not having cased the château—" Winston shook his head back at the Frenchman. "What sort of perimeter defences has it got?"

"Barbed wire, two fences. With mines in between."

"That won't stop him. It didn't stop us on Easy Red at Omaha, Doc—and the krauts were throwing all kinds of shit at us. So it sure as hell won't stop him breaking in."

"But he has no need to. He waits only for the Germans to leave, Sergeant. You worry about him, but he does not worry about *you*—he thinks you are dead, is that not so?"

"Okay. So we're dead—?"

"Therefore he waits for the Germans to leave, and they can only leave by the main entrance—it is the only way open to vehicles. So it is there that he will be watching, to see them go, so that he may bring his own vehicles in at the same point." De Courcy nodded in agreement with himself. "But we—we will be watching at the West Lodge. Because the Germans have a guard-post there—it is from there that they watch the river and patrol the perimeter wire through the wood. That will be our point of entry."

The frown was becoming a fixture on the American's face. "Now you're really losing me, Doc. If the krauts weren't on the alert I might just get us through the wire and the mines—I got enough practice for that on Omaha. But if there's a guard-post there how's that going to get us to the château ahead of the major?"

"But very simply, Sergeant!" De Courcy sat back on the bunk. "The last thing the Germans will do before they leave—the very last thing—will be to withdraw their guards from the perimeter. That will be our signal to enter." He lifted his hand expressively. "Then as they leave by the front entrance, we will move in behind them before the major enters."

There was still doubt in Winston's eyes as he shifted their attention to Audley. "What d'you think, Lieutenant?"

"It sounds . . . logical," said Audley. "If they really are evacuating the château completely."

"There is no doubt about that," cut in de Courcy confidently. "It is not simply that they have said as much. For two days now they have been burning their documents—that is the surest sign of all."

"Just so long as they don't leave a rear guard," said Winston, looking round the ambulance. "We don't have the muscle to fight the real war."

De Courcy shook his head. "They will use all their men for the escort—with things as they are, they are too nervous to do anything else, believe me. They are not looking for trouble any more."

That was an echo from the past, Butler recalled bitterly—an echo of what the major himself had said on the evening he had joined Chandos Force. And in that at least the major had spoken the complete truth: it had never been the Germans who had threatened the success of the operation; they had made all their own trouble, one way or another.

"Okay. So what then?" Sergeant Winston conceded the point grudgingly. "We get to the château maybe a couple of minutes ahead of the major—like firstest with the fewest. So what then?"

De Courcy looked at Audley quickly. "Then . . . it is the major you want. One clear shot *tout simplement.*"

Audley swallowed *tout simplement* like a spoonful of liquid paraffin. "Yes."

"Then this way you will have your best chance of it. He will come up the driveway from the main gate—an avenue of trees of perhaps six hundred metres . . . then there is the old *donjon*—how d'you say?" De Courcy searched for the translation.

"The keep," said Audley. "You mean a tower, like at Chenonceaux?"

"A tower—yes. It was the original fortification beside the bridge over the river. But now it is a ruin, an emptiness. Merely the walls stand."

"It was all a ruin in the old days, pretty much, wasn't it?" said Audley.

"Until the Englishman came, yes. He rebuilt the château, and they were working on the bridge—they completed that just in time for the Germans. But the donjon is still unrepaired . . . But no matter! Beside it is the bridge, and beyond the bridge on the other side of the river lies the château." De Courcy lifted a finger. "So . . . the major must cross the bridge—and the open space in front of the château too. And on the bridge there is no cover." He paused. *"And all you want is one clear shot."*

For a second no one spoke, then Winston turned to Audley. "Lieutenant—?"

Tout simplement, thought Butler. It seemed too good—and too simple—to be true. It even had the priceless advantage of giving them a chance of escape afterwards, since one man with a gun could cover the bridge after the shot had been fired, discouraging pursuit.

"He'll send in a patrol first to check out the place," said Winston. "To make sure all the krauts have gone."

Audley nodded. "So he will. But we can lie low ... or rather, we can lie high, up in the château ..." He frowned with concentration. "He'll send in a patrol. But if they report it's all clear, then he'll come in alone ... with just the ones who are in on the plan."

"That smiling sonofabitch sergeant, you mean?" Winston growled.

It would be two clear shots if the American was holding the gun. And maybe not just if he was, thought Butler vengefully.

"And the sergeant-major," said Audley. "I suppose there could be others too, but I can't think he's planning to split the loot too many ways."

"Yeah. And the fewer there are in on the deal, the less chance there is of anyone ever realising what he's done, I guess," Winston agreed. He grinned at Butler suddenly. "What d'you think, Jack? You reckon you're good enough with that thing?" He pointed to the Sten on Butler's lap.

Butler drew a sharp breath. It hadn't occurred to him that he would be given the assassin's job, but he realised instantly that it made sense, however unwelcome the task. Whatever the defects of the Sten for the role, its rate of fire made it better than Audley's revolver and the Luger the American had picked up from the road after the ambush. Only experts could hit anything with handguns at more than point-blank range.

All the same he looked at Audley doubtfully. "A Lee-Enfield would be better, sir. Over fifty yards you can't be dead sure with a Sten, sir. We'll just have to let them get right up close, that's all."

Dr. de Courcy smiled suddenly, and bent forward to reach under the bunk. "Then perhaps I can help you there, too. Not with a Lee-Enfield"—with an effort he slid a battered tin box out from beneath him—"but with something just as good."

The lid of the box carried a large red cross, and the box itself was full of bandages and rags. De Courcy plunged his hand into them and lifted a rifle into view.

"With the compliments of the French army, Corporal—a Lebel from the '14–'18. It will shoot Englishmen just as accurately as Germans, I think."

Butler reached down towards the rifle, but Audley's hand snaked past his to grasp it first.

"Sir?" Butler looked at him questioningly.

"Mine, I think, Corporal," said the subaltern. "You'll need the Sten to cover the bridge afterwards."

Butler frowned. "But, sir—"

"My job, too." Audley sounded almost relieved. "Don't worry, Corporal. Even second lieutenants can fire rifles—they do teach us some useful skills." He turned to the American. "All right with you, Sergeant?"

Winston looked at the subaltern curiously. It wasn't exactly an expression of approval, Butler decided, but it was as close to that sentiment as he had come since he had first climbed into the driving seat of the jeep on the road beside the Loire. "Hell, Lieutenant—I wouldn't dream of cramping your style. If you British got a rule that only officers can shoot officers, that's okay by me. Just so you hold it nice and steady when the time comes . . ." He shrugged, and then grinned. "Maybe we're due for a good break at that, I guess."

The American's good humour reassured Butler's own doubts. If it was suddenly too easy—too good to be true—then perhaps that was only what they deserved after so much bad luck. Not so much the bad luck that had enabled them to get so far against all the odds; that might qualify as good luck. But the bad luck which had taken all three of them away from the safety of the real war, where a man knew what he was supposed to be doing.

He stared at Hauptmann Grafenberg, sitting quiet and withdrawn on the floor in the corner, almost unnoticed. Never in his wildest dreams had he imagined he would travel across France with a German prisoner in his baggage. And yet, when he thought about it, it was only the German who had derived the good luck from their misfortunes: without them he might have been dead by now, or on his way to death.

Winston followed his gaze. "Yeah . . . So what do we do with him, eh?" He threw the question at Audley.

As he spoke the ambulance slowed suddenly, with a squeak of ancient brakes, and then lurched to a halt. De Courcy twisted on his bunk and slid back a panel in the partition which divided them from the driver's compartment.

"Qu'est-ce qui se passe, Gaston?" he hissed urgently.

The mutter of French was lost to Butler in the sound of a bicycle wheel skidding on gravel and a breathless treble voice, not one word of which he could catch through the narrow gap in the partition.

At length de Courcy turned back to them. "There are German vehicles on the main road ahead of us—the Civray road. We must wait until they have passed."

"Are we far from the château?" asked Audley.

"Very close." De Courcy shook his head. "We cross over here, onto the Marigny road. There is a bridge over the river, two kilometres perhaps, then the turning to the West Lodge is just over the bridge. Do not worry—Jean-Pierre will tell us when the way is clear."

"That's . . . the kid that we heard just now?" Winston's nose wrinkled at the idea of depending on a child's judgment. "A kid?"

The doctor regarded him equably. "Jean-Pierre is small for his age, but he would not thank you for the description. This morning he is a Frenchman, Sergeant."

"How old a Frenchman?"

"Eleven years. And before you decide eleven years are too few I should tell you that his younger brother Louis-Marie is watching the main gate of the château just up the road."

"Jee-sus!" The American's eyes widened. "Haven't you got any *men*, Doc? I thought your side was going to take over here after the krauts lit out—you going to use the kindergarten to keep the Commies in line?"

The doctor's expression hardened. "In two weeks from now General de Lattre de Tassigny's army will be here, Sergeant —the French army which is landing in southern France at this moment."

Sergeant Winston scratched the end of his nose. "Great. Except so far as we're concerned that's going to be just about two weeks too late, don't you think, Doc?"

Before the Frenchman could react to the jibe, Second Lieutenant Audley intervened. "I can see that children do make good road-watchers, Doctor. In fact, I remember my father and the other chaps in the Home Guard in 1940 planning to use them if the Germans landed . . . but . . . but where *are* your people? I mean, not the escape-route people, like old M'sieur Boucard—but the proper Maquis types? If we had a few of them we wouldn't need—*this*." He lifted the old Lebel rifle.

The hard look on the Frenchman's face creased up like a celluloid mask on the Guy's face writhing in the flames of a November Fifth bonfire. He spread his hands in a gesture of despair—Frenchmen could say more with their hands than some Englishmen could say with their mouths, thought Butler.

But the gesture was lost on Sergeant Winston. "I guess it suits them better if we take the risks, Lieutenant," he murmured.

The hard mask returned instantly. "It does not suit me at all—it suits me very badly," de Courcy snapped. "A week ago we had men in this area, both sabotage teams working with British and American officers, and our own combat units. But since then we have been moving them every night to the southwest, to the German supply routes, to support the invasion of the south. When Boucard's messenger reached me during the night . . ." The hands rose again. "You are not far from the truth, Sergeant. Children and greybeards—they are the best men I have at short notice. Children and greybeards!"

"And the Communists?" Audley made the question sound oddly polite.

"They are not . . . amenable to orders. But there were not many of them here—until two days ago." De Courcy looked at Audley candidly "A week ago we could have prevented the arrival of the larger group. And when they did arrive . . . we thought they were moving in support of our own units—to the south."

"Huh!" Sergeant Winston crammed a world of bitterness into a small sound. "A week ago you could keep them out—and in two weeks' time you expect the French army. Looks like they hit the motherlode first time, the only chance they got!"

De Courcy stared at Audley. "I do not think it was luck: they were here before you arrived. I fear they have an agent in your Intelligence operation, David."

Audley closed his eyes. "And I fear—I fear it's worse than that, sir. Or at least more humiliating." He sat back, opening his eyes and staring into space. "Much more humiliating."

"What d'you mean?" Winston turned towards him. "Humiliating for who?"

"For our Intelligence. They've been fooled right down the line—that's my guess."

"What's new about that? Jesus, Lieutenant—half the guys that buy it out here, it's because some clever sonofabitch back in headquarters wasn't clever enough. They got a man in your outfit somewhere and they knew you were coming. Surprise, surprise."

"No, I don't mean that—and I don't think that was quite how it was." Audley shook his head. "I think these French Communists—or whoever's running their show—I think they boxed smarter than that."

"In what way—smarter?"

Audley sat forward. "It's the timing of the thing. It never did seem quite right, even at the beginning." He glanced at Butler. "You remember when Colonel Clinton briefed us in the barn—'speed and surprise, and no truck with the French'?"

Butler nodded.

Audley nodded back. "It started to smell then, but I smelt the wrong answer. I thought the French knew where the loot was, and we were simply making sure we got in first to take it."

"Yeah—but they don't know where it is," said Winston.

"Quite right. Or at least they don't know exactly. . . . It wouldn't surprise me one bit if they knew it was somewhere in the Pont-Civray château—"

"Uh-uh." Winston shook his head. "You're forgetting the reception committee in the wood. They didn't know where we were going."

"So they *said*. But they could just as easily have been there to make sure we got through—to keep the Germans off our backs and to help us on our way. While keeping a discreet eye on us, of course." Audley paused. "But all that's beside the point . . . which is the whole timing of the Chandos Operation."

Winston frowned at the subaltern. "What's with the timing?"

"It's all wrong, Sergeant. If this loot is so damn well hidden that the Germans didn't find it in four years of occupation, sitting right on top of it, and the French Communists don't know exactly where it is themselves, then what the blue blazes are we doing trying to unearth it now, when so many things could go wrong? We're like the chap who insisted on trying to make love to his host's daughter standing up in a hammock in broad daylight, when all he had to do was to wait until night came and he could crawl into her bed in comfort. We could have waited a fortnight—or a month—or a year, and it would have been perfectly safe. But we had to go and try it now!"

In the moment of silence which followed Audley's bitter complaint Butler heard the swish of bicycle tyres skidding on gravel once more. Jean-Pierre had returned.

Winston shrugged. "So you timed it wrong. But the jails are full of guys who did that—and the morgues."

Audley shook his head. "I don't think we timed it at all, Sergeant. I think the Communists timed it for us—I think they just simply fed our Intelligence with the false information that they already knew where the loot was, and they were getting all set to pick it up themselves as soon as the Germans had moved out. Then all they had to do was to sit back and wait for us to turn up—"

There came a crunch of footsteps on the road outside, followed by a heavy blow on the rear doors of the ambulance.

"*Patron!*"

"*Attends un moment,*" commanded de Courcy. "Go on, David."

"*Patron!*" the voice insisted.

"*Je te dis d'attendre!*" shouted de Courcy. "Go on."

"That's really all there is to it. Our job may have been to lead them to it, I don't know. But what they're waiting for is for us to find it—to actually find it. All they've done is to make sure we do that at exactly the right moment for them, when they have the muscle to take it off us."

"*Patron!*" The fist banged on the door again, and this time the urgency in the voice overrode any possibility of refusal.

"Which makes it all the more important that your major

dies before he can betray his secret," said de Courcy harshly. "In the meanwhile—*Excusez-moi.*"

He rose from his seat and pushed past them to the doors. *"Qu-est-ce que c'est,* Gaston—Jean-Pierre—*Louis-Marie, que' est-ce que tu peux bien faire ici?"* He unbarred the door and stepped out of the ambulance, closing the door behind him.

Winston stared for a moment at the closed door. "You don't think maybe you were taking a risk, talking in front of that guy, Lieutenant?"

"Dr. de Courcy?" Audley shook his head. "No, Sergeant. The doctor's a good republican, not a Communist. And besides, if he had switched, then he wouldn't have bothered with us once he knew we couldn't find the loot for him. All we can do is stop anyone else finding it—and he knows that." He shook his head again. "Our problems will start when we've dealt with the major . . . You know what we've got ourselves into?"

"One hell of a mess, Lieutenant—that's for sure."

Audley stared into space. "An understatement. When I think about all the trouble they've been to—the Communists planting false information on us . . . our side setting up a special operation at short notice—with a hand-picked bunch of professional thugs—hand-picked because they had no connection with the French, too . . . then I begin to wonder just what it is that we're trying so hard not to find." He switched back to Winston, and then suddenly to Hauptmann Grafenberg. "I owe you an apology, Captain."

The German straightened up in surprise. *"Bitte?"*

"I should have left you with the Boucards. But I had a plan to use you to get into the château. It would have been as dangerous for you as for us"—he shrugged apologetically, almost like a Frenchman—"but it was all I could think of. Fortunately it isn't necessary now."

The young German stared at him blankly. "I am at your service, Herr Leutnant." Then an odd flash of recognition animated his face. "I understand that you have . . . a difficult duty to perform. And I understand also that I am in your debt for the risk you took on my behalf."

"Yeah. And I guess you understand also that we've stopped fighting Germans too, huh?" murmured Winston.

"Yes." The German gave a quick nod. "That too, I understand."

The American gave a short laugh. "That's right, mein Herr —welcome to World War Three."

Audley sat up sharply. "My God, Sergeant! You're exactly right: World War Three is what it is—the first skirmish of World War Three! What a perfectly *bloody* prospect!"

Butler felt strangely comforted. General Sir Henry Chesney had been right all along. And he, Corporal Butler, might live to be Second Lieutenant Butler yet if he survived the next few hours.

The ambulance doors swung open.

"Trouble," said Winston instantly.

He was right, thought Butler: trouble was written all over de Courcy's face.

"They are in the château." His voice cracked.

"Who?" said Audley.

"Your comrades—your major!"

"But—how can they be?"

De Courcy pointed. "The German vehicles—the ones which have been passing on the road—they were from the château. They left four hours ahead of time. Louis-Marie saw the first of your men go in—men in khaki with blackened faces, from the woods opposite the main gate."

Butler looked at Audley.

Everyone was looking at Audley.

"And also . . ." For once words failed Dr. de Courcy.

"Also?" echoed Audley.

"There are strangers on the road, Louis-Marie says. Frenchmen who are not from Civray."

"Surprise, surprise," said Winston.

Audley looked at him. "We should have reckoned on the Germans doing that, Sergeant," he said mildly. "It was the obvious thing to do, when you think about it."

"It was? So now what's the obvious thing for us to do, Lieutenant?"

The obvious thing was to run away as fast and as far as possible, thought Butler. But that was the one thing they couldn't do, nevertheless: they had a date with World War Three which couldn't be broken.

"The obvious thing"—Audley blinked—"is to blacken our faces and harden our hearts—and go and see what's happening."

22. How they passed the gate of Château Pont-Civray

Butler jabbed the barrel of the Sten into Hauptmann Grafenberg's back, propelling him forward into the open.

Forty yards.

"*Hände hoch*, Fritz," he ordered loudly, pitching his voice towards the gates. "Keep 'em up high, you bugger—that's it!"

One thing was for sure, he thought: the Anglo-Franco-American assault on the West Gate of Château Pont-Civray was in the best Chandos Force tradition.

It was bold as brass, ruthless, deceitful, and treacherous.

Thirty yards.

Another thing was for sure, too: if the man on the gate was one of the major's gang, then the moment he recognised the features of the dead Corporal Butler beneath their disguise of burnt cork, then the dead Corporal Butler would be dead. Sergeant Winston, snugged down in the undergrowth behind him with the Lebel, might avenge him. But at fifty yards' range he could hardly be expected to read the enemy's mind quickly enough to save him.

Funny to think so easily now of another British soldier as the enemy.

Twenty yards.

The man was gaping at them now—he could see the blacker hole of the open mouth in the soldier's blackened face.

But would realisation follow surprise at the sight of the

strange group which was approaching him—the German officer at British gunpoint, and behind them Audley bent almost double under the weight of Dr. de Courcy's body?

He heard Audley grunt realistically behind him. The little Frenchman was a featherweight to the big subaltern, but Audley was much more concerned to keep his comical black-and-white minstrel face to the ground; it was odd that Audley still looked so very much like himself despite the burnt cork and the removal of his pips.

Ten yards.

The man's mouth was still open, and the machine pistol was still held across his body.

Bold as brass, Audley had said. *If he's not in on it he'll think twice before shooting you if you've got a prisoner—and I'm carrying a wounded man!*

They were up to the gateway.

Big iron gates, old and rusty and heavily wired.

Smaller iron gate, with a heavy iron chain and padlock. But the padlock was oiled—

Bold as brass! Everything depended on him now—

Brigadier MacDonald, who by valour and conduct—

"Up against the gates, Fritz—move."

Hauptmann Grafenberg moved obediently up to the gates, facing the soldier on the other side. The soldier's mouth closed, and his eyes flicked uncertainly from Butler to the German, then back again to Butler. At least he wasn't an NCO, thought Butler gratefully; the blackened features were unrecognisable, and he could only pray that his own were equally so.

But he mustn't think of that—and above all he mustn't give the man himself time to think of it either.

But I'm no play-actor, sir.

Then don't play-act, Corporal. Just do what you'd do and say what you'd say if you had to get a prisoner to the major.

"Don't just stand there, for Christ's sake!" he snarled. "Open the bloody gate!"

The man licked his lips. "But, Corporal—"

"Don't you bloody argue with me." Butler bit off the protest furiously. "If you don't get this gate open double quick the major'll have your guts for garters—and when he's finished with them I'll use them for bootlaces, by God!" He counted a three-second pause. "Don't argue—*move!*"

The machine pistol moved, not the man, and Butler's own guts turned to mush.

"But, Corporal—it's locked." The soldier pointed the gun at the lock.

Butler was taken flat aback for a moment. Then common sense reasserted itself. The man was an idiot, but that was no reason why he should be an idiot too. He had guarded gates not unlike this in his time, and had been Corporal of the Guard on them too. There was an ugly little concrete pillbox just to the right of them: that had to be the guardhouse, and guardhouses the world over must be the same, British, German, or Chinese.

He nodded towards the pillbox. "Don't talk daft—get the bloody key out of there," he snapped.

The soldier looked from Butler to the pillbox, then back at the padlock, then back to Butler again. An idiot indeed, thought Butler; and it was surprising, almost disappointing, that Chandos Force had such boneheads in its ranks. But then perhaps he had a natural-born skill in weapons training which had endeared him to the major originally, and his deficiency in general intelligence and curiosity would now commend itself to the major for the simple job of covering the flank of the theft against intruders, with no questions asked.

But that didn't matter now, except insofar as it was a bonus for the intruders. Or intruders prepared to cloak subtlety with the bluster of an angry corporal, anyway—

"Don't just *fucking* stand there"—Butler glowered through the gate—"get moving, man!"

The soldier's reflexes took over, in obedience to confident authority. "Right, Corporal."

Butler watched him disappear into the pillbox, his brief sense of triumph quickly overlayed by doubt. In the first place, depending on what sort of routine the Germans had for checking the outer wire here, there might not be a key in there at all. And in the second place even an idiot might have second thoughts once he was out of range of the strange corporal's blistering tongue—or he might even have time to remember more precise orders which the major might have given him about admitting strangers.

The same disquieting thoughts had evidently passed through Audley's head. "Watch him when he comes out, for God's sake," he hissed urgently out of the corner of his mouth, shuffling up to Butler's shoulder.

If he comes out, thought Butler, adjusting the angle of the Sten to the observation slit in the pillbox. From the moment the snout of the man's machine pistol showed in the gap he'd have maybe a tenth of a second if he was lucky. And no time at all if he wasn't.

"Let me go——" Audley cut off the sentence abruptly at the first glimpse of movement in the entrance to the pillbox.

Butler felt his chest swell with indrawn breath; then he saw the soldier hold up a loop of wire, jingling the key and grinning foolishly as he did so.

"Got it, Corporal," he called out happily.

"I can see that," snapped Butler ungraciously. "Get stuck into it, then——I can't stand here all bloody day."

As the man fumbled awkwardly, one-handed, to insert the key into the lock, Audley moved up to the small gate.

Let me go first——the movement answered the question which had been boiling up inside Butler. So Audley had plans for what he was going to do once he was inside, and it was his plain duty to attract the guard's attention to give those plans their best chance.

The chain rattled loose, freed from the padlock.

"Watch it, Fritz!" Butler barked warningly to Hauptmann Grafenberg.

The German hadn't in fact moved a muscle since reaching his assigned position: he had done his job simply by being there and being so obviously the genuine article. But now he stiffened automatically at Butler's meaningless command, taking the soldier's attention from the smaller gate at precisely the moment when Audley shuffled forwards towards it.

"Keep those arms up——high!" Butler reinforced the warning as Audley turned his unencumbered shoulder to push open the gate, an action which also very sensibly turned his face away from the man on the other side.

"Right, Fritz——*jildi*, you bugger," Butler addressed the

German again just as Audley went through the gate. He didn't know what *jildi* meant, but it was his old CSM's standard word for rousing sluggards to their duty and it came to his tongue naturally.

Hauptmann Grafenberg didn't understand it either, but he swayed uncertainly at the sound of it, and the movement was just enough to distract the soldier's eye from Audley as the subaltern began to lower Dr. de Courcy's body to the ground two yards inside the gate and slightly behind him. Given the choice of watching either a comrade with a wounded civilian or a German prisoner he was instinctively drawn to the known enemy.

"Here, you!" said Audley.

"What—?"

The soldier had no time for a second word before Audley leapt at him. Butler had a blurred impression of the subaltern's large fist coming up from ground level and overtaking his body to connect with the man's jaw with his full weight behind it: it was as though Audley had packed into one blow every ounce of the accumulated anger and frustration he felt at being cannon fodder.

The soldier's legs shot from under him and his body cannoned off the fist into the gates with a force that shook them and made Butler himself wince. The padlock and the machine pistol flew off in different directions, clattering against the wrought ironwork; the man himself bounced off the gates to receive Audley's other fist in the guts.

Butler levelled the Sten through the bars at the two men as they rolled on the ground, but he knew it was no longer necessary: not even Joe Louis could have taken a punch like that and still come up fighting.

The struggle ended before it started, with Audley astride a body which had obviously been unconscious even before he had grappled with it, but which he still hammered at unmercifully.

"Stop it, for Christ's sake—he's finished, can't you see!" Butler cried out. "Stop it!"

Audley checked his raised fist, and sat motionless for a moment as the dust settled around him, his chest and shoulders heaving.

"Let him be, sir," said Butler.

Audley lowered his fist slowly—there was blood on it, and he stared at the blood uncomprehendingly.

Butler could hear footsteps behind him. Beyond the gates Dr. de Courcy was on his knees, staring at Audley. Then he got up and put his hand on the subaltern's shoulder.

"That was one hell of a Sunday punch," said Winston. "Better him than me!"

Audley stood up quickly. He shook his head, and then stared around him. "Yes," he said huskily to no one in particular.

"We got to get moving, Lieutenant," said Winston.

"Yes—right—" Audley started to wipe his face with his bloodstained hand, and then stopped abruptly. He looked at Butler, then at Winston. "Get . . . his gun, Sergeant. Take off his battle-dress blouse and put it on"—he pointed down at the body without looking at it—" and give the rifle to Dr. de Courcy . . . don't bother about the trousers, no one'll notice—and they're all wearing different bits of uniform, anyway." His cheek twitched nervously under its minstrel disguise, but Butler no longer felt like laughing at him. "The blouse'll be enough—and the beret."

Winston bent over the body and Audley stared across him to Hauptmann Grafenberg.

"This is as far as you go, Captain. We're quits now—one all. I give you back your parole." He blinked furiously. "You can wait for us to come back if you like—or you can take your chance from here. Just . . . thanks for helping us, anyway."

Grafenberg frowned. "But I have not done anything."

Audley shook his head. "From where I'm standing you've done quite a lot."

"Then perhaps I can do more." The German gave a tiny shrug.

"Yeah. And perhaps you can get yourself killed." Winston didn't even bother to look up.

"Perhaps." Grafenberg didn't bother to look down.

Audley swallowed. "It really isn't your war, you know, Captain."

"Huh!" Winston rolled the unconscious body over. "You can say that again for me."

Grafenberg moved sideways until he stood in the open gateway. "True. But then I do not have a war any more."

"Then you ought to quit while you're ahead." Winston peeled off the blouse.

"And since you have given back to me my parole—my word of honour—then I am at liberty to volunteer, I think?" Grafenberg ignored the American. "And also . . . with me you may do again what you have done here—I think that also."

Winston stood up between them, ripping open his own combat jacket as he did so. "And I think you're right—and I *also* think you're nuts." He nodded to Butler as he stripped off the jacket. "Give us the gun then, Jack. And the—whatever it is—"

Butler handed him the machine pistol and the greasy beret.

"Okay"—Winston adjusted the beret with a savage tug—okay, Lieutenant. Let's go, then."

"Wait—" Audley began desperately, still staring at the German.

"Wait, hell!" Winston pointed the machine pistol at the German. "He wants to get himself killed, that's his business. One war's as good as another, so he gets what he wants, it makes no difference one way or the other. Just so we get it over quickly, that's all. *Let's go, Captain!*"

23.   How Chandos Force fought its last fight

They heard the sound of the sledge hammer before the château came into view through the trees.

BANG-tap.

BANG-tap—the diminished echo followed each blow.

BANG-tap.

"Over there!" Dr. de Courcy pointed to the left just as Butler caught sight of the familiar creamy stone and blue-black slate pinnacles ahead between the trees.

"But that's on the other side of the river—not in the château." Audley's words came a fraction of a second before Butler identified the angle of difference between the sight of the château and the sound of the hammer.

They plunged through the screen of undergrowth separating the track from the river, suddenly heedless of the discipline which had marched them from the gate.

"Down, for God's sake!" Audley's command caught Butler just in time as the undergrowth thinned at the river's edge. He caught sight of the dark olive-green water, and a high stone-walled bank opposite which surprised him as he threw himself flat: somehow he had expected the broad sandy channel of the Loire, but here the river—whatever river it was—had been caught between man-made banks.

BANG-tap.

"The tower?" Audley threw himself down beside him.

"The bridge," hissed Winston on his other side. "The god-damn bridge!"

BANG-tap.

The words and the sound both drew Butler's eye upstream, to a graceful, two-arched bridge. On the far bank it was domi-nated by a great round tower which was connected to it by a wall of stone filling the gap between the drop of the bank and the abutment from which the first arch rose—

BANG-tap.

There were three British soldiers standing at the foot of the wall—

BANG-tap.

—and one of them was attacking the wall with a sledge hammer.

It was Sergeant Purvis.

"What the hell . . . ?" The American left the rest of the ques-tion unasked.

"The fourth arch," said Dr. de Courcy from behind them.

"What d'you mean—the fourth arch?" Audley turned back to him.

"There used to be four arches"—de Courcy pointed—"two large ones, which you can see . . . and a small arch on each side. The smaller arches were—how do you say?—flood arches for when the river is high, between February and March every year, and sometimes in the late spring."

BANG-tap. The heavy sledge hammer rebounded off the wall again. Sergeant Purvis stepped back from the wall, spat on each palm in turn like a navvy, and wiped his brow with his arm.

Audley stared at the bridge. "You mean—they've filled in the little arch, someone has?"

Butler looked at the doctor suddenly. "Didn't you say they

repaired the bridge in 1940, sir—when they were working on the château?"

"Christ! Of course they did!" Audley hammered the ground with his fist. "That's what they must have been doing—shoring up the little arch with a wall on each side, probably to strengthen the abutments. The way the river curves, that's the side that must take the full force of the floods—" He stopped suddenly.

"So what?" said Winston.

Audley looked at him. "So—there's a space under the bridge between the two walls, man! And no one's ever going to knock down those walls just for fun—they're possibly what's supposed to be holding the bridge up. Nobody knocks down repair work—"

BANG-tap—BANG-tap.

"Nobody . . ." Winston twisted towards the bridge again. "Jee-sus, Lieutenant—you're damn right—"

Now Butler knew what to look for he could see the line of the original arch in the wall, and once he could see it the newer stonework which filled it became obvious, for all that it had been carefully matched with the older work.

"Give me the rifle, Doc," growled Winston. "I can hit that bastard from here easy—no trouble at all."

But as he reached for the rifle Audley caught his arm. "That won't do any good. We hit one of them and there are still plenty more."

Winston looked quickly at the group beside the wall, then back to Audley. "I can maybe get two before they get under cover—"

"No. That isn't the major there with them—or the sergeant-major either." Audley shook his head.

"Then we can wait for them to show up. Because if that's where the stuff's cached, the second that sonofabitch gets through the wall then they're gonna show, Lieutenant. You can bet on that."

"And then it'll be too bloody late." Audley began to crawl backwards. "Apart from which I doubt you can wing more than one at this range—with that old rifle. And then they'll flush us out of here in no time flat. They've got LMGs and mortars and bazookas, and they know how to use the damn things too. . . . Come on, let's get moving."

Winston crawled after the subaltern, protesting. "Jee-sus,

Lieutenant—if it'll be too late then it's already too late *now*, for God's sake! There's no way we're gonna stop them—no way."

Once he had reached the safety of the path Audley stood up.

"Very well—there's no way." He lifted his chin obstinately. "So we change the plan, Sergeant, that's all. Come on—and that's an order."

"Like hell it is!" Winston faced him.

"Sergeant"—Butler touched the American's arm lightly— "there isn't time to argue."

"Yeah. But time to get killed." Winston shrugged off the touch. "You got another plan, Lieutenant—just like that?"

"No, Sergeant—not just like that. I've got the other plan we always had. The Army's solution to all problems. The one thing we're both real experts in." Audley's voice was suddenly weary. "It's just a damn shame someone didn't remember the rules back here in 1940, that's all." He paused. "Instead of trying to be clever."

"What rules?"

"What rules?" Audley laughed shrilly, as though on the edge of hysteria. "God Almighty, Sergeant—back in '40 we destroyed a whole army's equipment rather than let the Germans get it! *'Equipment and stores likely to fall into enemy hands must be denied them by demolition.'*" He stabbed a finger in the direction of the bridge. "There's a muddy river out there, and a sledge hammer—and you've got a lighter in your pocket. . . . And, by God, there's precious little in this dirty, stinking world that can't be drowned or smashed or burnt so that it's no use to anyone." Audley's finger balled into his fist and the fist hammered his own chest. "You want to know who I am, Sergeant? I'm the Open Scholar of Queen's who knocked down the medieval church at Tilly-le-Bocage with half a dozen well-placed shots! When it comes to destroying things, I'm a professional—and we are going to destroy what's under that bridge, believe me." He looked quickly at Butler. "Right, Corporal Butler?"

"Right, sir," said Butler.

They hit their second Chandos Force soldier at the edge of the wood, with the château plain to see.

And *hit* was again the operative word.

* * *

"Wot the 'ell's this, then?"

Butler swung his back to the man instantly, thanking God for the rival attraction of Hauptmann Grafenberg, who had the stupid bugger staring pop-eyed: it was the bandit with the Uncle Joe Stalin moustache who had stood right next to him in the barn.

"Where's t' major?" The best chance of safety lay in the Lancashire accent he had been trying to lose for two years and more. "Happen we've got summut for 'im, eh?"

"Back at the gate, sorting out the frogs—" The bandit cut off the automatic answer. "But 'oo the 'ell—*ooof!*"

The question was cut off abruptly and finally by the barrel of Sergeant Winston's machine pistol swung viciously on the back of the man's neck.

There was a garden—or it had once been a garden, but now the trim little hedges and the espalier fruit trees had run riot, and the flower beds were choked with weeds.

"Frogs at the gate," said Audley. "Could be that the major's having trouble with your friends, Doctor—could it?"

"Not my friends, David," said de Courcy.

Overgrown garden giving place to gravel square at the side of the château—

Broken boxes and the remains of a giant bonfire, the fitful wind stirring thousands of charred fragments of paper, black against the pale brown of the gravel.

They have been burning their files—

More debris: all the wreck of a hurriedly abandoned military outpost and the litter of defeat—

And just ahead a broader stretch of gravel, with the welcoming parapet of the bridge to the left—

"Smartly now," snapped Audley. "March as though you own the place."

"What the devil!"

An officer's voice. Butler tried desperately to catch Audley's eye, but the subaltern was out of view behind his left shoulder, leaving him closest to the voice.

He turned towards the château.

It was one of the officers who had joined them in the barn —or it must be, though again he couldn't recognise the blackened face.

"Prisoner, sir. Caught 'im by t' gate in t' wood back there." Butler jerked his head in the direction from which they'd come.

"A prisoner?" The officer took three more steps towards Butler, frowning at him. "What d'you mean? And who the devil—"

"Herr Oberleutnant!" Hauptmann Grafenberg interrupted him sharply. "I must protest in the strongest possible terms at my treatment! My rights under the Geneva Convention have been flagrantly violated—"

"What—?" The officer swung towards him.

It was then that Butler understood, in the last hundredth of a second before he hit the officer, exactly why Second Lieutenant Audley had put so much force into that punch of his.

Striking a private soldier in the British Army—and striking him unawares too—must have been on about the same level of impossibility for Second Lieutenant Audley as what he was about to do was for him. And that added the force of absolute desperation to the action: when a corporal hit a captain there was no possible room for half-measure.

And he knew also why Audley had said *Here, you* too—

"Sir—" he said sharply.

The officer turned to receive his fist.

As they marched onto the bridge he was most strangely aware of the different pieces of him that objected to what was happening to them.

He could feel his toes itch—

His ear ached with a dull pulse of pain—

And now his skinned knuckles burned.

Everything was unnaturally sharp and clear in the sunlight: the weathered parapet of the bridge, the gravel under his feet, the great windowless tower rising up into the blue sky.

And now there was a gap between the end of the parapet

and the curve of the tower—a gap in which he could see the beginning of a stone stair spreading to the left and right beneath them. And away beyond it the river rippling and flashing, olive-green and silver.

Audley went through the gap without missing a step.

Journey's end, thought Butler stupidly.

But not in lovers meeting.

"That'll do very nicely, Sergeant Purvis," said Audley, holding out his revolver stiffly, two-handed. "You can put it down now—just let it go—and back up, both of you."

"Or don't let it go—I'd like that," supplemented Sergeant Winston. "Then I can shoot you with a clear conscience, you sonofabitch."

Purvis looked at them for a second without recognition. As he had turned towards them, before Audley had spoken, Butler had caught the ghost of that familiar smile which he'd last seen at the road junction to Sermigny. But now the ghost was gone, and almost as quickly the uncomprehending look became one of frozen surprise at being faced by other ghosts: the dead of Sermigny risen from their graves.

The sledge hammer dropped with a clatter among the jumble of stones and the scatter of mortar fragments which lay on the pavement around the sergeant's feet. In the few minutes since they'd last glimpsed him he had completed his job: clear from waist height to the curve of the original arch there was a gaping hole in the stonework, and Butler realised that he hadn't heard that regular *bang-tap* on the hammer striking solid masonry since they had met up with the guard on the edge of the wood.

"And who might you be, then?" inquired Audley of the soldier beside Sergeant Purvis.

"Me?" The soldier looked around desperately.

"Me—sir," snapped Audley.

"Sir?" The little man did a double take on Audley, saw no badges of rank, but surrendered to the voice of authority. "Yes, sir—Driver Hewett, sir . . . Colonel Clinton's driver that was, sir—I mean, Colonel Clinton that was, sir."

"Ah yes—the walking map!" Audley relaxed slightly. "And what happened to the colonel, then—he walked off the map, did he?"

"The map, sir?" Driver Hewett's face screwed up in misery. "I dunno about that, sir. But a sniper got the colonel last evening, that's what. Walking with the major, 'e was"—he looked nervously at Sergeant Purvis—"so they say, that is—sir."

"I'll bet," murmured Winston. "So you just showed the major where you'd stashed the loot, huh?"

The American accent threw Driver Hewett momentarily. "Yes, sir. Those were my orders—from the colonel himself. 'If anything happens to me, 'e says . . .'" He licked his lips. "But I didn't . . . stash the loot, like you say, sir—" His eyes widened suddenly as he caught sight of Hauptmann Grafenberg and Dr. de Courcy. "Christ!"

"What the hell did you do, then?" The American lifted the machine pistol threateningly. "You led that bastard here, for a start, huh?"

Years of gangster films had clearly left their mark on Driver Hewett. He pointed to the hole. "I—I only finished the wall, sir. The officers unloaded the ambulance all by themselves. Wouldn't let me touch a thing—not even watch them at it, they wouldn't—same as when they'd loaded it. The brigadier in 'is red dabs, an' all."

"What brigadier? What officers?" Audley stared at the hole.

"Dunno their names, sir—except Captain Spicer wot brought me up from the 'ospital to the place in Paris. Just officers—except they weren't real officers, of course—" Hewett gave Audley a meaningful look, half confiding and half doubting that Audley himself qualified for the courtesy.

"What d'you mean—not real officers?"

"Well . . . doctors, of course—like Captain Spicer. I mean, 'e was an officer, but 'e didn't know one end of a gun from the other. 'E was a doctor—RAMC—'Rob All My Comrades.' Not *real* officers."

"Oh my God!" whispered Audley.

"Doctors?" said Sergeant Winston. *"Doctors?"*

Audley looked at him. "It was an ambulance, Sergeant. That's what doctors use—ambulances. Give me your cigarette lighter—and keep an eye on that man." He pointed at Sergeant Purvis.

Butler watched him climb into the hole, to drop with a

crunch into the darkness. The lighter flared, went out, then flared again.

"I only built the wall, sir," said Driver Hewett plaintively. "It was half built when we got here—the builders had all scarpered. 'Fact, everyone had scarpered—cleared orf. It was a wonder we got away, come to that . . . after the bleeding ambulance packed up. Got out of Bordeaux we did, the last boat. Took us ten days to get there . . . But I only built the wall, that's all I did."

"And a very good wall too." Dr. de Courcy spoke soothingly from just beside Butler. "A most professional wall."

"Well, it ought to be," said Hewett, becoming talkative with fright. "Bricklayer I was, before I joined up in '38. An' it was all 'ere ready—the sand and the cement, and the stone too, ready dressed. T'other wall was up and they'd part done this 'un—up beyond drainage channels." He pointed to the small gratings at the foot of the wall. "It weren't but a two- or three-hour job, really."

"But still a good wall," said de Courcy encouragingly. "And the . . . the place in Paris—where was that?"

"Bloody 'ell, I dunno, mister. Captain Spicer, 'e knew where to go . . . turn left, turn right—an' when we get there, 'Stay in the cab, Hewett, ready to drive off quick' 'e says. Which wasn't surprising seeing as 'ow the jerries were already in Paris when we drove out—I know that for a fact, because the brigadier said so to Captain Spicer, an' everyone else 'ad already scarpered except 'im and me—we'd been ordered to stay be'ind. An' I didn't reckon we'd 'ave got out neither, except the captain 'e knew Paris like the back of 'is 'and, 'aving studied there before the war an' spoke the lingo." He shook his head. "But where it was—there you've got me."

"But you remembered what it was like," de Courcy persisted.

Hewett shrugged. "Well . . . it wasn't a hospital—leastways there weren't no patients I seen . . . though there was a young chap in a white coat went by. . . . But it was a big place, with a brass plate on the front, an' double doors. You drive through into a courtyard—I 'ad to back up against another pair of doors—that's when the captain tells me to stay in the cab an' mind my own business." He thought for a moment, his wrin-

kled monkey face screwed up with the effort. "I remember as
we drove out there was this little bit of a park right opposite,
with a green statue looking at you."

"A green statue?"

"Well, not green exactly—sort of greeny-blue, an' streaky
like someone 'ad tipped a tin of paint over it. Yes—an' I
remember thinking it looked funny too because 'e was holding
'is 'and up and reading from a book—the statue—but 'e
wasn't a parson because 'e 'ad a French army hat on, like
their officers wear, an' medals on 'is chest."

De Courcy stiffened, and Butler heard him draw in his breath.

"Zeller," whispered the doctor.

"Who, sir?" asked Butler.

"Zeller," said the doctor aloud, staring right through Butler.
"Henri Auguste Zeller. The Saviour of Hanoi."

There was an expression on his face that suddenly frightened Butler. "A general, sir?"

De Courcy focussed on him. "A general? Yes—a general."
He glanced at Driver Hewett. "But not a *real* general."

"Then what—" The words were dried up in Butler's mouth
by the wild thoughts which were beginning to come together
in his mind.

De Courcy's eyes turned back to him. "It was the Zeller
Institute, Corporal," he said. "That's where they went—L'Institut Zeller."

There came a sharp, crunching sound from the hole in the
wall. "That's right, sir," said Audley. "L'Institut Zeller, rue
des Carmes—and let's get to hell out of here on the double!"
He began to scramble out through the hole.

De Courcy pushed past Butler and seized the subaltern's
arm. "David—in God's name—what is in there?"

Audley faced him. "What do they do in the Institut Zeller,
Doctor—you tell me!" He paused. "Medical research, eh?"

De Courcy clenched his teeth. "It is one of the main centres
in France for microparasitical studies, David—"

"Micro—what the hell is that?" snapped Sergeant Winston.

"Germs," said Audley shortly. "Germs, Sergeant."

"Bacteriology and virology," said de Courcy. "Yellow fever
and cholera—I know they were working on influenza vac-
cines and—and *la poliomyelite*. It was Zeller himself who

pioneered the treatment of plague in Hanoi—he was a pupil of Pasteur—David, *what is in there?*"

"Plague!" Audley's lip twisted. "Chandos Force, by God! Someone's got a very pretty sense of humour, I'll say that for them—let's get out of here, then. Come on!"

Butler looked uncertainly from Audley to the American, who was still watching Sergeant Purvis like a hawk.

"Tell the man, Lieutenant—and tell me too, for Christ's sake," growled Winston out the corner of his mouth.

"In there?" Audley pointed into the hole, his voice rising. "In there? You really want to know what's in there—you really want to know?" His voice cracked insanely.

Butler heard the sound behind him a thousand years too late.

"Right then—don't let me hear one of you breathe!"

A thousand years too late. And if he lived another thousand years he would never forget that voice.

Butler held his breath as Audley stared past him.

"That's good. Now—put down your weapons *slowly*."

The subaltern's chin lifted in that characteristically obstinate movement Butler knew so well. "Nobody moves," he said hoarsely. "Nobody moves."

The Sten was sweaty in Butler's hands and his back crawled.

There was a scrape of boots behind him.

"Well, bless my soul!"

The other voice—the voice which had frozen him once before, under the bank of that sandy island by the Loire.

Kill him with the others!

"Bless my soul!" repeated Major O'Conor. "Now . . . let that be a lesson to you, Sergeant-major—"

How could they have been so careless, thought Butler brokenly: to stand here gabbing as though they had all the time in the world, so wrapped up in the hole and its contents that they hadn't even bothered to set someone on watch—how could they have been so careless?

"—Never underrate a friend when you ask him for a favour!"

"Sir?" The same neutral sound he had first heard by the stream in the bocage of Normandy.

Oh God, how could they have been so careless? Butler's finger tightened on the trigger.

"Yes . . . I asked Chris Sykes for a good man, and he gave me one, don't you see?" The major's tone was curiously sad. "And a German prisoner into the bargain too. You've done well, young Audley—I'll say that for you. And it took some doing, I shouldn't wonder, eh?"

Butler stared at Audley's blackened face and felt the subaltern's will weaken.

"Sir—" His own voice came from far away.

"It's all right." Audley swallowed painfully. "We still outnumber you, sir," he addressed the major.

"Tck! Tck! Don't be silly, boy." The major injected a world of regret into the words. "Your men are facing the wrong direction, and you've no idea how competent Sergeant-major Swayne is at close quarters—eh, Sergeant-major?"

"Sir!" the sergeant-major agreed.

"But you'll still lose, sir," said Audley.

For a moment Major O'Conor didn't reply, and Butler had a vision of that dead eye staring fishlike at Audley beside him. Then the real world came into focus: the broad back of the American just ahead of him to his left, and beyond that Sergeant Purvis and Driver Hewett frozen like waxwork figures on the very edge of the pavement with the river behind them.

Somewhere behind him and to the left were the Frenchman and the German, but they didn't come into it. Because before he could swing halfway through the full circle the sergeant-major would cut him down, and the American—aye, and probably Purvis and Hewett too, which was a fear already stamped on their faces. And if Second Lieutenant Audley thought that would slow the sergeant-major down he was backing a bloody loser, he decided bitterly.

"Because of your French friends beyond the gate, do you mean?" the major said. "You've never seen my lads in action, young man—they'll go through the rabble like a dose of salts, believe me. If you're relying on them then I'm afraid you're going to be awfully disappointed."

Judging by the performance of the Communist partisans in the ambush it would be the major who was disappointed, thought Butler. But that would be too late for them. If they moved they were dead and if they surrendered they were dead, he had no doubt about that: the major had gone too far to leave any of them alive behind him. The only surprising thing was that they were still alive.

Audley shook his head. "I don't mean that, sir"—he pointed to the hole in the wall—"I mean that," he said thickly.

Again there was a slight pause.

"The payroll, you mean?" There was something different in the major's voice: it was hard to interpret the nuances of meaning in a man's voice when one couldn't see his face.

The payroll—?

"The *what?*" Audley's mouth opened.

"You haven't had time to look, then?" The major chuckled, and Butler knew what he had missed: the smile of triumph— the winner's smirk.

"But then of course the late lamented Colonel Clinton was rather security-conscious, I must admit—strictly classified to field rank and above, his little secret." Major O'Conor savoured the thought like a sugarplum. "But don't tell me you weren't curious, young Audley—didn't you lie awake wondering about it? Of course you did, eh!"

"The payroll?" Audley still gaped at him.

"The sinews of war, my dear boy—and of peace too, by God! The last big payroll of the old British Expeditionary Force, no less . . . and as poor Clinton really doesn't need it any more, the sergeant-major and I—and the good Purvis there—we are going to draw it in lieu of back pay and allowances and demobilisation gratuities. Five years' devoted service in conditions of extreme discomfort and danger—you can look on it as payment in full for a job well done, or you can look at it as a winner-takes-all lottery." The major's tone sharpened. "Last time I was a loser. This time I'm a winner, that's the sum of it, boy."

"No—" Audley began. "No—"

"Yes. What did you think it was, eh? *Objets d'art* of some sort? Or a secret weapon? I'm sorry, my boy . . . just filthy lucre, that's all. Not worth missing Cambridge for—and certainly not worth dying for. So do be a sensible young fellow and tell your heroes to put down their weapons quietly. We don't want any shooting—once it starts it's apt to become infectious—"

That was why, Butler realised suddenly: gunfire from within the château might spark off the confrontation at the main gate! The major's kindly concern for their survival was as false as his glass eye.

"—but if the sergeant-major has to shoot, believe me, young Audley—he will shoot." The threat at the last was as naked as a Windmill girl. "And that will be just ten seconds from now, I'm sorry to say."

"Lieutenant—" Winston tensed up. "Lietuenant—"

"No, wait!" Audley's voice cracked with strain. "He lied to you, Major—Colonel Clinton lied to you"—he pointed into the hole wildly—"there's no money in there. There never was any money in there—"

"What?"

"He lied to you—it was just a cover story—as Bullsblood was a cover for Chandos." Audley's face twitched uncontrollably at the name. "Chandos!" he repeated bitterly.

"Hold it, Sergeant-major," snapped O'Conor. "What d'you mean, boy—a cover? What d'you mean?"

Audley blinked. "It wasn't—money, sir. There's no money."

"You're lying, damn you—he told me . . ." The major's voice trailed off. "He told me . . ." He choked on the words "he told me. . . ."

It was no longer the voice of triumph: it was an old man with ashes in his mouth. Ashes which dried up his words.

"How do you know it isn't money, sir?" The sergeant-major's bark cut through the silence.

Audley's glance shifted. "Because I've been in there, Sergeant-major. And I've seen what's in there."

The unasked question hung in the sunlight. Butler was aware suddenly that Audley was staring past him at a different angle, and staring with a peculiar intensity.

"You want to know what's in there, Sergeant-major? You really want to know?" said Audley. "You want me to tell you?"

That was odd, thought Butler: the meaningless repetition of the question, as though Audley had any possible doubt—

And then, just as suddenly, Butler knew exactly where the sergeant-major stood on the steps behind him . . . behind, slightly to the right—slightly to the right, above—

"You really want me to tell you, Sergeant-major?" said Audley again.

He was fighting to take the sergeant-major's attention, Butler knew. Or at least to take enough of it to give him that tiny fraction of a second's purchase for what had to be done.

Don't you ever point that gun at me again—unless you intend to shoot me with it!

"Well, I'll tell you, Sergeant-major—"

Not yet.

Because whatever Audley was going to say he must have judged that it would be enough to give Corporal Butler at least a chance.

And at the moment he had no chance.

"I hope you've got a sense of humour, Sergeant-major. Because you're going to need one—"

Butler knew he was right now: whatever it was coming, it was designed to hurt.

"He was right—money's not worth dying for. Not worth risking men's lives for either, with all the millions they've spent. It always had to be nastier than that—"

Dad had been a sergeant-major: that was a funny thing to think of at a time like this. Sergeant-major Butler!

"Not worth dying at all now, really. We've won the war—"

He would never be a sergeant-major. He would be an officer—or a dead corporal.

"But that's this war. We haven't won the next war yet, Sergeant-major. So that's still worth dying for—the Third World War—"

The sergeant-major and the major . . . rather like Sergeant-major Butler and Colonel Chesney—General Chesney. The only two people in the world he loved.

Except now there was maybe a third—

He hadn't thought of Madeleine Boucard for three whole hours—

Third?

Third World War?

"That's right, Sergeant-major: the Third World War. Do you know we even guessed at it before we got here? What we didn't realise is that they'll have new weapons for the next war—King Tigers'll be as out of date as longbows next time—"

Now?

But he couldn't move. He wanted to know what Audley was going to say next.

"And longbows are rather appropriate—you know that? Longbows are what Sir John Chandos had back in the 1350s. Killed a lot of Frenchmen with them, by golly—Agincourt, Poitiers—and Spaniards at Najera too. But he wasn't the top killer of the time, Sergeant-major—he was a real pro, *but he wasn't in the same class as the Black Death, Sergeant-major*—"

Plague.

Audley pointed into the hole. "The boxes in there have INSTITUT ZELLER stamped on them. And Institut Zeller is where they came from. And I don't know what the Zeller Institute was playing with in 1940, but I can make a damn good guess, Sergeant-major—"

Butler stared into the hole in horror. War was one thing, but disease . . . loathsome and invisible, was a nightmare from the pit—

"—because we've been playing with it too, Sergeant-major. A friend of mine in the Sappers had to wire off the beaches on a Scottish island, Sergeant-major—he said an experiment there had gone wrong. So nothing can live there for a hundred years now. It had sheep on it, but they were all dead—dead and rotting, dozens of them. The Sappers weren't allowed near them. They weren't even allowed off the beach."

Butler's flesh crawled. Dead and rotting—

"Plague?" croaked the major. *"Plague."*

"Maybe not plague. It could be a dozen things. They were working on polio at the Institute—there's no cure for polio. If they found a virulent strain *and* a vaccine of some sort . . . polio or flu or plague . . . an army that was vaccinated wouldn't need to fight if they had a weapon like that to clear the way ahead of them, by Christ!"

The hole yawned in Butler's imagination, straining to swallow him into its darkness. He wanted only to run away.

"No wonder they didn't want the Germans to get it in '40—the Zeller research files. And no wonder the Communists

wanted it so badly." Audley paused. "And no wonder Colonel
Clinton didn't tell you what we were really after—no wonder
he lied to you, Major!"

Butler came to himself again. Killing or dying wasn't even
a choice any more. He had to get away from the black hole
under the bridge.

Audley giggled insanely. "But the really funny thing is—"

Now?

*"That it doesn't bloody matter—it's all for nothing, Ser-
geant-major—"*

The orders had gone out: Butler felt like an army poised for
the last great offensive in a hundred-year war, with every
nerve and muscle stretched like a million soldiers waiting for
the second-hand on the watch to reach the twelve on the dial,
no longer conceivably stoppable—

"Because that's the flood-arch on the bridge. See the gratings *there*—every time the river floods have come up in the
last four years the water's been inside *there*—every winter,
every spring—"

It was already too late—

"—the paper has all rotted . . . the rats and mice have
crawled in and chewed it up and eaten it—or made their nests
out of it—all the files, all the records . . . all the experiments
and the knowledge—all shredded and eaten and excreted and
flushed down the river—so we're all going to die for nothing,
Sergeant-major—for nothing—"

Now—

The second-hand hit the twelve and the bugles pealed out
inside Butler.

In that same instant he knew that he could never turn in
time, even as he turned—

The barrel of the sergeant-major's submachine gun rose in
an arc as Hauptmann Grafenberg's body collided with his
legs. The sergeant-major's knee smashed into the German's
face, throwing him sideways. The Sten jerked in Butler's
hands and the sergeant-major's face dissolved in a bloody
mask. It seemed strange to him that the face should disinte-
grate when he had aimed at the chest—

Audley had been looking at the sergeant-major's face.

Butler continued to swing on his heel—his bullets splashed into the stone, throwing dust and chips into the air—
The major—

Major O'Conor was looking at him.

Major O'Conor was reaching for his webbing-holster.
Butler thought . . . *That's silly—he can't possibly do that!*

The major was fumbling with the holster with one hand—an old man's hand with the heavy veins raised on it. He still held his ashplant stick in the other, half raised. The stick somehow seemed more menacing than the revolver, half drawn from the holster.
Don't, Major—the voice was inside Butler.
The Sten jumped in his hand before the words could come out and Butler saw the good eye shut—or was it the good eye? In that last living moment one of the major's eyes contradicted the other, and Butler never knew which as the old man was thrown backwards against the wall by the force of the bullets.

"Come on, Jack—for Christ's sake!" shouted Audley.
Butler was suddenly aware that the subaltern was lifting Hauptmann Grafenberg off the pavement at the foot of the stair, where the sergeant-major's knee had tumbled him. The German seemed half stunned, and as Audley raised him blood sprayed from his nose onto the pavement.
"*Es geht mir gut,*" mumbled the German thickly. "*Es geht mir gut.*"
Butler started towards him, but Audley waved him away. "Get up the stairs—cover us," he ordered. "Cover us, damn it! Doctor—get back over the bridge."
The command unlocked Butler's brain, and he sprinted up the stair round the great curve of the tower. To his right the bridge was still open and unguarded, but there was a British soldier running up the drive towards them on his left.
Butler opened fire automatically and the soldier cartwheeled off the drive in a tangle of arms and legs just as the empty magazine cut off the burst.
He could hear firing in the distance now, out of sight down

the drive, both the stammer of automatic weapons and the crack of single shots.

He thought, with a curious clarity: *The major was right— killing is infectious.*

Another magazine for the Sten. There were men in the trees two hundred yards away, and at that range there was no chance of hitting them. But at least he could bloody well frighten them—

The clarity persisted. It was all quite mad, all utterly pointless. Chandos Force was fighting its last battle, against the French and against itself, and for nothing.

"Come on, Jack—get moving," said Sergeant Winston from just behind him.

"I'm okay." Butler fired again at the trees.

"Sure you are. But it's time to say good-bye."

Butler thought that was a funny thing to say in the circumstances. He also thought that the solid comfort of the tower was preferable to the open stretch of the bridge.

Suddenly he remembered Sergeant Purvis.

"Where's that bugger Purvis?" He fired again.

"The hell with Purvis! *Get going, Corporal.*"

It didn't seem right that Sergeant Purvis of all people should get away.

He turned towards the American. "Where's Purvis?"

The look on Sergeant Winston's face answered the question: the sergeant was grinning at him like a wolf.

Butler swung back towards the trees.

The Sten jammed.

As his hand closed on the magazine he felt himself being dragged away from the wall and propelled onto the bridge. For an instant he was angry, and then fear started his legs moving.

The bridge was longer and narrower than it had been before, and the firing behind him was louder and closer. As he ran he heard a sudden swishing-hissing sound alongside him, and the gravel spurted madly on his left and away in a writhing snake ahead of him.

Audley grabbed him as he came to the end of the parapet and pulled him down onto the cover of the stonework, half knocking the breath out of him. The château and the blue sky and the gravel spun round as he rolled sideways.

A shadow blocked out the light.

"No!" shouted Audley. "For Christ's sake, man——"

Butler found himself staring from ground level down the long funnel of the bridge parapets, back the way he had come.

Halfway down the funnel Hauptmann Grafenberg was trying to disentangle a body which was curled up against the stonework. As he tugged at one arm another long snake of spurting gravel raced up the drive and onto the bridge towards him.

The arm suddenly seemed too heavy for him. He knelt down slowly beside the American, as though the problem of lifting him was one which required special thought and he needed time to work it out. Then, just as slowly, he toppled over alongside him.

The firing was very loud now, echoing all around them.

Butler started to rise, but Audley's hand pressed him down.

"It's no good," whispered Audley. "They're done for."

It was no good, thought Butler. They were done for.

"An' we'll be done for an' all if we stay 'ere any longer," said a voice from behind them.

Butler looked over his shoulder in surprise to find Driver Hewett crouching a yard away, nodding at him with ancient wisdom.

No winners and losers, only the survivors and the dead. Driver Hewett had been born with that knowledge, he'd never needed to learn it.

Without looking back at the bridge Butler crawled away in Audley's wake towards the safety of the woods.

MORE MYSTERIOUS PLEASURES

WILLIAM MARSHALL
The Yellowthread Street mystery series

YELLOWTHREAD STREET	#619	$3.50
THE HATCHET MAN	#620	$3.50
GELIGNITE	#621	$3.50
THIN AIR	#622	$3.95
THE FAR AWAY MAN	#623	$3.50
ROADSHOW	#624	$3.95
HEAD FIRST	#625	$3.50
FROGMOUTH	#626	$3.50

THOMAS MAXWELL

KISS ME ONCE	#523	$4.95
THE SABERDENE VARIATIONS	#628	$4.95

FREDERICK NEBEL

THE ADVENTURES OF CARDIGAN	#712	$9.95

WILLIAM F. NOLAN

THE BLACK MASK BOYS: MASTERS IN THE HARD-BOILED SCHOOL OF DETECTIVE FICTION	#713	$8.95

PETER O'DONNELL
The Modesty Blaise suspense series

DEAD MAN'S HANDLE	#526	$3.95

ELIZABETH PETERS
The Amelia Peabody mystery series

CROCODILE ON THE SANDBANK	#209	$3.95
THE CURSE OF THE PHARAOHS	#210	$3.95

The Jacqueline Kirby mystery series

THE SEVENTH SINNER	#411	$3.95
THE MURDERS OF RICHARD III	#412	$3.95

ANTHONY PRICE
The Doctor David Audley espionage series

THE LABYRINTH MAKERS	#404	$3.95
THE ALAMUT AMBUSH	#405	$3.95
COLONEL BUTLER'S WOLF	#527	$3.95
OCTOBER MEN	#529	$3.95
OTHER PATHS TO GLORY	#530	$3.95
OUR MAN IN CAMELOT	#631	$3.95
WAR GAME	#632	$4.95
THE '44 VINTAGE	#633	$3.95
TOMORROW'S GHOST	#634	$3.95
SION CROSSING	#406	$3.95
HERE BE MONSTERS	#528	$3.95
FOR THE GOOD OF THE STATE	#635	$4.95

BILL PRONZINI
GUN IN CHEEK   #714 $8.95
SON OF GUN IN CHEEK   #715 $9.95

BILL PRONZINI AND JOHN LUTZ
THE EYE   #408 $3.95

ROBERT J. RANDISI, ED.
THE EYES HAVE IT: THE FIRST PRIVATE EYE
    WRITERS OF AMERICA ANTHOLOGY   #716 $8.95
MEAN STREETS: THE SECOND PRIVATE EYE
    WRITERS OF AMERICA ANTHOLOGY   #717 $8.95

PATRICK RUELL
RED CHRISTMAS   #531 $3.50
DEATH TAKES THE LOW ROAD   #532 $3.50
DEATH OF A DORMOUSE   #636 $3.95

HANK SEARLS
THE ADVENTURES OF MIKE BLAIR   #718 $8.95

DELL SHANNON
The Lt. Luis Mendoza mystery series
CASE PENDING   #211 $3.95
THE ACE OF SPADES   #212 $3.95
EXTRA KILL   #213 $3.95
KNAVE OF HEARTS   #214 $3.95
DEATH OF A BUSYBODY   #315 $3.95
DOUBLE BLUFF   #316 $3.95
MARK OF MURDER   #417 $3.95
ROOT OF ALL EVIL   #418 $3.95

RALPH B. SIPPER, ED.
ROSS MACDONALD'S INWARD JOURNEY   #719 $8.95

JULIE SMITH
The Paul McDonald mystery series
TRUE-LIFE ADVENTURE   #407 $3.95
HUCKLEBERRY FIEND   #637 $3.95
The Rebecca Schwartz mystery series
TOURIST TRAP   #533 $3.95

ROSS H. SPENCER
THE MISSING BISHOP   #416 $3.50
MONASTERY NIGHTMARE   #534 $3.50

VINCENT STARRETT
THE PRIVATE LIFE OF SHERLOCK HOLMES   #720 $8.95

REX STOUT
UNDER THE ANDES   #419 $3.50

JULIAN SYMONS
CONAN DOYLE: PORTRAIT OF AN ARTIST   #721 $9.95

ROSS THOMAS
CAST A YELLOW SHADOW   #535 $3.95
THE SINGAPORE WINK   #536 $3.95
THE FOOLS IN TOWN ARE
   ON OUR SIDE   #537 $3.95
CHINAMAN'S CHANCE   #638 $4.50
THE EIGHTH DWARF   #639 $4.50
OUT ON THE RIM   #640 $4.95

JIM THOMPSON
THE KILL-OFF   #538 $3.95
THE NOTHING MAN   #641 $3.95
BAD BOY   #642 $3.95

COLIN WATSON
SNOBBERY WITH VIOLENCE: CRIME
   STORIES AND THEIR AUDIENCES   #722 $8.95

DONALD E. WESTLAKE
THE BUSY BODY   #541 $3.95
THE SPY IN THE OINTMENT   #542 $3.95
GOD SAVE THE MARK   #543 $3.95
The Dortmunder caper series
THE HOT ROCK   #539 $3.95
BANK SHOT   #540 $3.95

TERI WHITE
TIGHTROPE   #544 $3.95
MAX TRUEBLOOD AND
   THE JERSEY DESPERADO   #644 $3.95

COLIN WILCOX
The Lt. Frank Hastings mystery series
VICTIMS   #413 $3.95
NIGHT GAMES   #545 $3.95

DAVID WILLIAMS
The Mark Treasure mystery series
UNHOLY WRIT   #112 $3.95
TREASURE BY DEGREES   #113 $3.95

CHRIS WILTZ
The Neal Rafferty mystery series
A DIAMOND BEFORE YOU DIE   #645 $3.95

CORNELL WOOLRICH/LAWRENCE BLOCK
INTO THE NIGHT   #646 $3.95

■■■■■■■■■■■■■■■■■■■■■■■■■■■■■■■■■■■■■■

AVAILABLE AT YOUR BOOKSTORE OR DIRECT FROM THE PUBLISHER

Mysterious Press Mail Order
129 West 56th Street
New York, NY 10019

Please send me the MYSTERIOUS PRESS titles I have circled below:

103 105 106 107 112 113 209 210 211 212 213 214 301 302
303 304 308 309 315 316 401 402 403 404 405 406 407 408
409 410 411 412 413 414 415 416 417 418 419 420 421 501
502 503 504 505 506 507 508 509 510 511 512 513 514 515
516 517 518 519 520 521 522 523 524 525 526 527 528 529
530 531 532 533 534 535 536 537 538 539 540 541 542 543
544 545 601 602 603 604 605 606 607 608 609 610 611 612
613 614 615 616 617 618 619 620 621 622 623 624 625 626
627 628 629 630 631 632 633 634 635 636 637 638 639 640
641 642 643 644 645 646 701 702 703 704 705 706 707 708
709 710 711 712 713 714 715 716 717 718 719 720 721 722

I am enclosing $_____ (please add $3.00 postage and handling for the first book, and 25¢ for each additional book). Send check or money order only—no cash or C.O.D.'s please. Allow at least 4 weeks for delivery.

NAME _____

ADDRESS _____

CITY _____ STATE _____ ZIP CODE _____
New York State residents please add appropriate sales tax.